IN THE SHADOW OF CROFT TOWERS

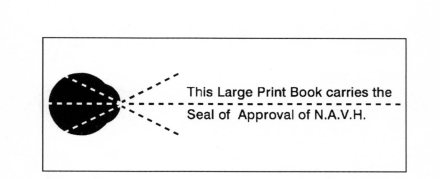

This Large Print Book carries the
Seal of Approval of N.A.V.H.

IN THE SHADOW OF CROFT TOWERS

ABIGAIL WILSON

THORNDIKE PRESS
A part of Gale, a Cengage Company

Farmington Hills, Mich • San Francisco • New York • Waterville, Maine
Meriden, Conn • Mason, Ohio • Chicago

LIBRARY OF CONGRESS CIP DATA ON FILE.
CATALOGUING IN PUBLICATION FOR THIS BOOK
IS AVAILABLE FROM THE LIBRARY OF CONGRESS

ISBN-13: 978-1-4328-6172-8 (hardcover)

Published in 2019 by arrangement with Thomas Nelson, Inc., a division of HarperCollins Christian Publishing, Inc.

Printed in Mexico
1 2 3 4 5 6 7 23 22 21 20 19

For my husband, Travis
My hero, my rock, my best friend
Without your unwavering love and
support, chasing my dreams would not
have been possible

1

1813
The English Countryside

I often wonder what my life would have been like if I had never learned the truth. I wouldn't have set off as I did for Croft Towers. I never would have met him.

It's strange what I remember about the day I left London. The mail coach was late; the weather wretched. The clock had struck midnight long before two strangers and I ducked beneath the postmaster's outstretched umbrella to board the Royal Mail and rumble across the North Downs.

That difficult journey east marked the beginning of an unseasonably cold autumn. Frigid rain pelted the coach windows. The undercarriage squealed beneath the seats as a metallic scent wound its way between the drafty boards. I gripped the windowsill, wondering if the coachman intended to hit every bump in the road.

"Far to go, miss?"

The woman's voice startled me. Dressed head to toe in red satin, she'd endured the last few darkened hours with a handful of smelling salts and a tongue hot for complaints, but she hadn't spoken to me until now. Not until the first hint of rain-soaked daylight peeked over the horizon.

I lowered my gaze and fiddled with my bonnet ribbons. "Yes, ma'am . . . Well, not too much farther, I hope."

The woman expelled a huff, her lower jaw jiggling. "Dreadful weather. I begged my Martin not to compel me to go today." She motioned to the window. "But he would have it his way."

I forced a tepid smile but found it difficult to respond. Leaving Winterridge Seminary for the last time had been harder than I'd expected.

" 'Pon my word, if this rain continues we'll have no choice but to overnight on the road."

I gripped my reticule to my chest. With the tea I purchased in Canterbury and the outrageous price of the ticket, I'd not enough money left to overnight anywhere. Why hadn't I thought of such a possibility?

The woman leaned forward, her rose scent wafting around me like a foggy curtain.

"You poor dear. All on your own, eh?" She looked at me as if she thought I'd run away from home. "Don't you worry your pretty head. My brother and I have never been ones to shirk our duty to charity."

I cringed.

"Worse comes to worst, you can always share a bedchamber with my maid."

The wiry woman seated beside her popped out of the shadows, turning her gaze on me as if I were a rabid dog.

But my self-appointed benefactor took no notice. "Yes, yes. Thompkins won't mind at all. Will you, Thompkins?"

Embarrassed, I turned to the window and bit my lip. My situation wasn't as desperate as all that. At least I hoped it wasn't. Of course, I had to admit, the gray morning had taken on a mustard-yellow glow. It was like looking through the bottom of a dirty glass. I took a deep breath. "Thank you for the kind offer, but hopefully it won't be necessary. I'm to get off at Plattsdale."

The woman raised her eyebrows. "Plattsdale? Have you family there?"

A tiny ping hit my heart, and I swallowed hard. "No, not family."

She tapped her leg with the end of her fan, then leaned forward as if she intended to share a secret. Her eyes told me otherwise. "My curiosity is piqued, my dear, piqued. Why would someone such as yourself travel there?"

I pressed my fingernails into the palm of my hand. Whatever business I had in Plattsdale was my own affair. One I certainly didn't wish to share with a nosy traveler on the common stage. But it was hardly a secret, and one I would have to grow accustomed to discussing. I forced my shoulders to relax. "I've taken the position of lady's companion to a Mrs. Chalcroft at Croft Towers."

The woman sucked in a quick breath. "Mrs. Chalcroft, is it?" She paused, then pressed her fingers to her mouth. "Faith, but I wish you well, my dear . . . I wish you well."

I didn't like the glint in the woman's eyes, as if she knew something she didn't intend to share. I waited a moment, hoping she might say more. But she had tired of me and now whispered into her maid's ear.

A rain-filled hush settled over the carriage. The gloomy sky dipped into the fog and the towering roadside oaks. As the tree branches sought to snuff out the morning light, the coach emerged from a thicket, wheels splashing through the sludge covering the road.

Amid the gusty rain a cry rang out. I bolted up straight, gripping the seat's edge. The horses lurched to a crawl. The hinges squealed in response. I scanned the windows, searching for the reason we'd slowed, when a gunshot cracked like lightning and echoed off the side of the coach. Gasping, I met the other travelers' frightened gazes.

What on earth? A heaviness hit my stomach. Every muscle told me to duck, but I couldn't help myself — I had to look.

The maid screamed, "Get down! Are you daft, miss?"

I motioned her back as I peeked out the window, pressing my forehead against the icy glass. The guard's horn sounded from the rear of the carriage.

"D-do you see anything?" The maid's voice had turned shrill.

I squinted, trying for a better view. "No . . . wait. There are riders approaching. Their faces are covered." I flung myself against the seat. "Th-they all have pistols."

I should have thought before blurting out such a thing. In a flash of lace and ribbons, the nosy woman across from me all but swooned into her maid's lap, crushing the ostrich feathers in her hat.

The maid's lips stretched thin until they

disappeared completely. "Now you done it, miss."

"I-I . . ." What could I say? I tempered my voice to sound nonchalant, even while my pulse pounded in my ears. "I hate to tell you, but I think we are being robbed."

The mail carriage surged forward before swaying to an agonizing stop, each of us frozen to our seats. For a breathless second all seemed quiet, but the unconscious woman must have recovered because she shot back up and shouted, "Not my jewels! Thompkins, hide them. Quickly." She wriggled a large emerald ring from her finger, and Thompkins slipped it down the front of her dress. I did the same with my bracelet seconds before the woman slumped back onto her maid's lap.

The coach door flew open with an awful squeak, the wind spraying us with mist.

A man appeared on the step, his face covered by a rag. "Get out." He grabbed my wrist. "All of you."

My chest tightened. I wasn't sure my legs would hold me up, but somehow I stood. I knew very well *I* didn't have any money, but the sound of the earlier shot echoed in my mind. Anything could happen. The robber was tall, his hair dark. I met his eyes as he yanked me down the steps — cold, deep gray with a hint of blue.

The icy rain slid down my shoulders as I edged beneath a nearby tree. The men shouted to one another over the rush of rain. "Be quick about it! Leave nothing untouched."

Their boots splashed in the mud as they circled the coach. "Search everything. And get that deuced lady out of the coach. I don't care if she's conscious or not."

The plump woman all but jerked back up, cowering behind her maid, then batted at the air like a wild animal. "You — you ruffians! If you think I have any intention of stepping out into the pouring — oh!"

The horses reared up at the front of the coach, their panicked neighs adding texture to the wind as it whipped through the trees.

One of the robbers raced to the front of the coach and grasped the reins. "Whoa! Easy, fellas." He was jerked forward and the entire equipage jolted a pace.

A man leaned out from the interior. "Blast you, Calvin! Keep 'em still."

The robber who wrenched me from the coach brought over the driver and the Royal Mail guard, their hands tied. He directed the barrel of his pistol at the five of us, trapping us beneath the tree.

Relentless and brutal, the downpour filled

my ears as I glanced around, the hopeless-
ness of our situation seeping further into
my soul with every cold drop. There would
be no means of escape. We were utterly and
completely at the highway-men's mercy. My
traveling companions had come to the same
conclusion, and a faint whimpering took
flight on the wind.

What must have been minutes felt like
hours as the robbers scurried in and out of
the coach, their greatcoats flinging raindrops
at will, their shouts growing louder and
more irritated. I didn't dare move, but carefully I glanced up to catch the penetrating
glare of my captor. He tilted his chin, and
by the look in his eyes, I wondered if he hid
a smile beneath that rag.

How long had the wretch been staring at
me? Considering the way my wet frock
clung to my legs, outlining my knobby
knees, I wondered if he had been looking
at . . . all of me. I jerked my attention to the
ground, warmth flooding my cheeks.

One of the men called out across the
clamber of thunder, "The devil's in it, I'm
afraid. Nothing's in the coach. Beginning to
wonder if this was all a hum. Get on with
checking the passengers. Deuced nuisance
if I'm not home for my dinner."

The robber who'd pulled me from the

coach redirected his pistol at me with a kind of lazy satisfaction. "Well? Shall we get on with this?" His voice sounded cultured with a slight musical quality to it. Educated, no doubt.

I raised my eyebrows and took a step backward. "I-I haven't any money."

He glanced once more at my dress and his voice held a hint of a laugh. "I'm well aware of that. My friends have already emptied your reticule." He lowered the pistol and stepped close, his face a few inches from my ear. "Have you a pocket?"

A prickle made its way down my spine. My frock did have a pocket, as well as something in it. A letter from Mrs. Smith to Mrs. Chalcroft. I stiffened. "Yes, but it holds nothing you would be interested in."

He lowered his voice. "Allow me to be the judge of that."

My shoulders shook, partly from the cold, but more from a surge of panic that pinned my arms to my sides.

The man shoved the pistol into his jacket. "Don't toy with me, miss. I haven't the patience or the time. Hand it over or I shall be forced to look myself."

A screech jarred me from his piercing glare. My riding companion tried to jerk away from the man clenching her arm, but it was no use. The robbers would have their bidding. My heartbeat echoed the fear in her voice. I watched in stunned silence as the woman thrust her hands into the folds of her skirt and passed her jeweled necklace to the man.

A wrinkle formed across my captor's forehead, raindrops pooling in a line. After observing the spectacle for a moment, he turned his icy blue eyes back on me. "Well?"

I thought I might be sick. I reached to tuck a wet hair behind my ear, but his iron fingers wrapped my wrist in a flash. "I'm tired of waiting."

He spun me around, jamming me against him, his head just over my shoulder. He smelled of nature, like the boys in town who'd spent the day playing in the fields. His voice came out in a whisper. "I'd rather you empty your own pocket."

"I —"

His hand pressed against my mouth. "Now."

I nodded, my arm aching from his grip. I squeezed my eyes shut for a split second. *Keep your wits about you, Sybil.* The man with the steel fingers was serious — deadly serious.

I wriggled my free hand through the slit of my damp gown, grasping the letter from

Mrs. Smith and holding it out, satisfied the man would be disappointed. But he didn't release me.

"Is this all?"

I nodded again and noticed a small triangular-shaped scar on his wrist just inside the cuff of his sleeve. Strange. The mark had an almost uniform quality to it.

He shoved me back and ripped open the letter. A few seconds later he met my gaze over the limp paper, his eyes softening. Just when I thought he was going to address me, he called out to his friends over his shoulder. "I daresay it's time to move on."

He refolded the note and slipped it into his jacket pocket. "Thank you, ladies, for a most invigorating time; however, I'm afraid we must bid you all good day." He bowed, then walked away and mounted what was more of a beast than a horse.

He motioned ahead to his friends before guiding his mount back by the group of us shivering beneath the tree. "I, uh, do apologize for any inconvenience we may have caused."

I probably imagined it, but he seemed to direct the statement to me. Heat flashed through my body. My mouth popped open, all kinds of horrid words tangled in a ball on my tongue, but none came out. Was he still smiling beneath that rag?

He met my obvious fury with a wink, then spurred his horse to a gallop, disappearing into the driving rain.

2

The mail coach lurched forward before I'd taken my seat, but the driver seemed tentative, holding the horses to a slow clip. The mood inside the carriage was dismal. I took a steady breath and tried to discover where we were, despite the fog, but time seemed lost.

The anxious morning faded to late afternoon, and my desire to reach Plattsdale grew with each irritated sigh from the other women. They stared me down as if the highway robbery were somehow my fault.

However, just as I had given up all hope of the nightmare ride ever ending, the twisting shadows parted, revealing a sign tipping in the wind — the Boar's Head Inn. Plattsdale.

The coach veered right, scattering gravel along the narrow road, then rolled to an agonizing stop. A man's call pierced the heavy silence like a bell rung a bit too loud.

There was a shuffle in the yard, but no one in the coach moved. I could read the questions on the other women's faces. Were we safe at last?

I glanced at my soggy gown and reticule, smudged by the robbers' dirty hands. What would become of me? The carriage's wooden bench squeaked beneath the sour-faced woman as she patted what was left of her coiffure. Her maid watched in silent amusement, but I looked away — chilled, hungry, and tired. Every bone in my body ached, but nothing would induce me to speak, not even to ask if I could share Thompkins's room for the night.

My cold fingers sought the bracelet on my arm, the one I received on my last birthday. Something might have to be traded for a room, but not the bracelet — not my only link to the past. If at all possible, I would travel on to Croft Towers at once, regardless of how I ached for a clean set of clothes and a soft bed.

The coach swayed as the driver swung down from the box and opened the door. The two women clawed their way from my presence, tripping over my feet, and neither looked back for me. As I feared, the offer for a room wasn't renewed.

Just as well. I didn't need their help. I

didn't need anybody's. I'd done well enough on my own so far.

One of the ostlers peeked around the side of the coach. "Still here, eh?" He took a quick glance over his shoulder to the coaching house door. "Where to now, miss?"

Startled by his gruff voice, I rose to my feet. "Is-is there a man here from Croft Towers?" I tried not to sound as desperate as I felt.

A look of relief washed across the man's face as he nodded and extended his hand to help me down. I gladly took it — clammy though it was — and followed his lead across the yard, hopeful my luck had finally turned.

The sudden thunder of horses' hooves sounded like a wind gust out of the rain, and I paused beneath the inn's narrow awning. The ostler turned as well. Three uniformed dragoons burst into the yard, their dark-blue jackets barely distinguishable from the gray drizzle. In a flash they were but a couple yards from where we stood. A few shouts and some boys rushed by me. I watched as the officers dismounted and relinquished their horses. Had they heard about the robbery somehow? I turned, hoping to ask the ostler, but he spun away in a huff. Apparently he had no intention of addressing them.

He hurried me through the door, but something about the way he hesitated as we walked into the receiving room, the way his cold eyes flitted about and landed on me, I knew he'd not meant to bring me inside. I tucked a loose hair behind my ear and tried to shake off the chill he'd caused with only a glance. He thought me a common urchin. Of course, I looked like one, which made it sting all the more.

The man wrinkled his nose, his eyes saying, Don't you dare sit on the settee as wet as you are. But he only cleared his throat. "I'll go fetch John from the taproom." With a sideways glance, he added, "Don't get too settled. I won't be but a moment."

If I had been *Lady* Sybil with an abigail and an entourage, I would have been ushered to a private parlor to rest. But as plain, boring, unchaperoned Sybil Delafield, I was left to stand and drip in the entryway.

I wandered the dimly lit room, imagining how a cup of tea would feel going down my throat. I glanced out a pair of dirty windows and stepped nearer to the fireplace. So this was Plattsdale — my new home.

There wasn't much to see outside, nor in the dingy inn. A few worn pieces of furniture, some rotten boards, the blackened fireplace. The scent of ale and musk permeated the door to the taproom. Of course, I had to admit, anything was preferable to the cramped mail coach. My knees echoed their agreement.

The front door swung open, and the dragoons from the yard sauntered inside on a gust of wind, none betraying the slightest surprise at finding me alone, dripping in the front room. I suppose even if they had been surprised, they were too well bred to acknowledge it. The tallest officer removed his shako and shook off the rain. I don't know what I expected a cavalryman to look like, but this gentleman didn't fit my romantic notions. A long nose poked out from a thin face with what I could only describe as a hard stare. He nodded. "Good day."

I expect I had been glaring, which is why he felt the need to address me. Only now I wished I hadn't called attention to myself. Granted, I had witnessed the robbery firsthand. They would probably want to speak with me. I cleared my voice. "Are you here about the highwaymen?"

"Pardon?"

"The robbery of the mail coach?"

One of the other dragoons joined him and spoke in a whisper. "The boys in the yard were just telling me about an incident on the line."

The first dragoon nodded, then turned back to face me. "I'm sorry, miss, but we're here on business from the Prince Regent. We haven't time to investigate petty theft. You'll need to take up your grievance with the local magistrate."

"I see." I tried to make my voice sound light, but I doubted I hid my irritation well. My cheeks always seemed to betray me at the worst moments. The officer was probably right to dismiss me, but the smug look on his face didn't make me feel any better.

Luckily, the ostler's return saved me from blurting out anything I might regret. Strangely enough though, he looked more irritated than I felt. He ogled my soaked gown for the second time. He spared a nervous glance for the officers, then whispered to me, "You'll have to come now, miss. The driver from the Towers is in quite a rush."

"Now?"

"Yes, right now." He thrust his stubby finger at the door, then pushed his spectacles up his nose.

So, no tea or time to dry off. I opened my mouth to protest, but he ushered me back into the dismal rain, across the yard, and onto the seat of an antiquated landau before

I could make a peep. I should have known he'd want the wet, unchaperoned girl out of sight of his guests.

I craved more than anything to remind him about the robbers with pistols, the rain and the cold, and the wretched future of a young lady with no family and no connections. But I shut my mouth and watched him seal the door without another word.

The Chalcroft landau rattled to a halt. Beyond the rain-soaked window I saw little but an eerie sky. I told myself not to panic.

The carriage door screeched open to reveal a lanky footman, who stumbled backward at the sight of me. My shaky hand sought the remains of my drenched coiffure, and I forced a measured breath before grasping my reticule.

The wide-eyed young man seemed to recover and extended an umbrella over the carriage's narrow opening. "Miss Delafield, is it?"

"Yes." I forced a tepid smile before descending the steps, my wet frock clinging to my legs, the chill wind whipping at my skirt. I'd planned such a different arrival, one meant to impress. One I'd hoped would afford me the answers I'd come for.

The footman led me across a gravel drive

and into the lurking shadow of my new home — Croft Towers. The aged structure rose up out of the misty twilight like an old king dressed in black, surveying his kingdom with a cautious eye. My chest tightened.

"This way, miss." The footman shuffled forward then stopped. "We'd planned for you to come in the front, but considering your, uh, present state, perhaps it's best —"

"Nonsense, James." A tall man with a heavy build held the front door wide, his face weathered with age, his eyes shrewd. A smile appeared for a moment, then vanished into a stern chin. "You may address me as Hodge. I am butler here at the Towers."

I nodded. "Pleased to meet you. Miss Delafield — Mrs. Chalcroft's new companion."

"I'm well aware why you are here. It was I who sent the carriage." He motioned me through the door. "Come inside, and I will figure out what is to be done with you."

I crossed the threshold into a dim marble entryway. To the side, a small candelabrum winked in the wind. The wavering light did little to compete with the overwhelming gloom of thick crossbeams and paneled walls.

Hodge frowned. "Would you be so good as to wait here?"

I nodded, wrapping my arms around my middle, a terrible empty feeling settling into my stomach. Hodge ambled off at a brisk pace, and all too quickly I found myself alone. Alone with my thoughts and doubts.

Impostor. The voice whispered from the recesses of my mind, the same one I'd heard this many weeks or more. The voice was followed by the sound of a casement clock, which ticked to life from somewhere in the darkness. Wind gusts surged against the heavy door, clambering for a way in; but the air inside the house remained motionless, heavy with dust. Unable to move or sit, the nagging chill I'd endured throughout the journey returned in full force.

A door slammed in the distance. Uneven footsteps trailed down a far-off hall. I turned, but no one entered the front room, and the steps dissolved into the pervasive darkness around me. A shiver crept up my arms. Standing as still as possible, I inspected the shadows, fighting off the unnatural feeling of being watched.

Ridiculous. I sloughed off the thought as a blur of white flickered across the alcove on the upper floor like an airy cloak or a wisp of long blond hair, moving unnaturally across the wall. My gaze darted to the landing, but I saw nothing else in the dim light.

At that moment the voices of two gentle-men wafted down the corridor on a draft from the opposite side of the room.

". . . the Royal Mail?"

"Hush. It was a blasted uncomfortable business, I'll tell you . . ."

My hand flew to my throat and I leaned forward, straining to hear more, but the sounds faded into a murmur.

"Miss Delafield?"

My nerves snapped and I spun around, my pulse racing, my hands primed to defend myself.

It was Hodge, of course, wrapped in shadows. He lifted his candle and raised a bushy eyebrow.

Letting out a slow breath, I lowered my hands and offered a smile, the way a child does when saved from an overactive imagination.

He didn't return the gesture. "Mrs. Chalcroft is in her room and is not to be disturbed this evening. She does, however, have some guests who would like a word with you in the drawing room."

Guests? I cast a quick glance up the winding staircase then back to Hodge's determined face. "I —"

He motioned ahead. "Please follow me, Miss Delafield."

My legs felt heavy, my half boots sticky on the floor, but I trailed behind him like a numb puppy, hoping deep down somehow I'd dreamed up the entire uncomfortable arrival. But I hadn't. It was all too real.

The drawing room stood in stark contrast to the rest of the house. White met my eyes from every angle — white walls, a white ceiling, white drapes, centered by a long, gilded sofa. Three shocked faces stared at me from various angles of the room. Hodge introduced me, then silently left the room.

A young man of medium build with dusky-blond hair and probing green eyes sauntered forward. "Miss Delafield, is it? I've just been told a fantastic story of your arrival by John Coachman. Highwaymen stopped the mail coach?"

I looked from one incredulous face to the next. "Yes. As you can see, I was forced to stand in the rain." My voice shook a bit more than I would have liked.

The golden-haired woman on the sofa yawned. "We were expecting you hours ago. And someone a bit older. Do you believe her, Lucius?"

"I don't know." The man tilted his chin. "Surely you've come with some sort of papers backing up your claim."

"Of course. I have —" I reached down to

my pocket just as I remembered the dreadful truth. My letter from Mrs. Smith had been stolen by the highwayman.

The subsequent silence took on a life of its own, every eye turned my direction, scrutinizing what I would say next. Well, the letter was gone. Taken by the dark-haired robber, who'd found a way to ruin my entire day.

I took a deep breath. "The note I planned to present to Mrs. Chalcroft, from my mistress" — I looked from each questioning face to the next — "was stolen in the robbery. What I need —"

The gentleman cracked a smile. "What a fantastic story."

The Grecian goddess who'd previously questioned me leaned back against the sofa, turning up her nose. "Too fantastic if you ask me."

"Well, no one did ask you." Another girl, who appeared no more than eighteen, made her way around the sofa to my side. "You must excuse my cousin. Waiting for dinner has never suited her." She grasped my elbow. "My name is Miss Eve Ellis. My great-aunt is quite glad you agreed to be her companion and traveled all this way. Come and warm yourself at once. We don't want you to catch an inflammation of the lung your first night here." She spun back to face the room. "Can't you all see she's worn to death and soaked to the bone? Please, sit here. I shall tell Mrs. Knott to prepare a bath in your room."

I looked into Miss Ellis's kind brown eyes and wanted to cry. I managed to say, "Thank you," before sliding onto the offered chair beside the fireplace as she hurried out of the room.

The blond gentleman stood with an air of authority I'd not noticed before. "Evie's right. What a cad I've been questioning you when you only just arrived — and in such a state." An appealing smile spread across his face. "I think it absurd to stand on pretenses on such a night. Do you not agree, Miss Delafield?" He ran a finger through a tuft of curly hair above his ear. "I am Mr. Cantrell. Mrs. Chalcroft is my great-aunt, and if you would, allow me to introduce my sister, Miss Cantrell. Miss Ellis is our cousin, and Mr. Roth, that gentleman asleep at the back of the room, is as well."

The beauty deigned to nod my direction but said nothing more, her eyes performing all the talking between us. As the new companion and an orphan, I was beneath her notice and unsure why her brother felt the need to introduce us at all, but I returned the gesture.

He sauntered over, leaning his shoulder against the mantel, his fingers fiddling with his quizzing glass. Then he settled his gaze on me with a kind of mocking interest as if he thought I might say something brilliant.

I should have attempted some sort of wit. I'd done so often enough for the girls at school. But in the sheltered life I led at Winterridge, I'd hardly spent two seconds in a gentleman's company, let alone an attractive one. I hadn't the foggiest idea what I was supposed to say.

Finding my mouth dry, I left the idle conversation to the others. Yet nothing could keep me from appraising Mr. Cantrell from the corner of my eye as he moved to stoke the fire. What he lacked in height, he more than made up for in poise. A sharp jaw and smooth features, handsome in a self-assured way few men can achieve without appearing arrogant.

The rising flames in the grate brought warmth to my legs in a rush, and I slid my feet beneath my chair, casting a quick glance at the door. Whatever could be taking Miss Ellis so long?

Mr. Cantrell's voice startled me. "If it is not too upsetting, Miss Delafield, I'd love to hear the whole of your story." He paused.

"While we're waiting for your room to be prepared, of course."

A thoughtful expression rounded his face as the firelight danced across his discerning eyes. I don't know why, but almost immediately I thought him a man who saw much and revealed little.

I swallowed hard. "There's not much to tell really."

"On the contrary. You have an entire room itching to know the details."

Miss Cantrell sat looking out the window, seemingly lost in thought as Mr. Roth snored from the back of the room.

Itching to know the details, indeed.

Mr. Cantrell, however, seemed earnest, so I licked my lips. "The day was quite dreary; the company intolerable."

A wide smile spread across his face, and he took a seat at my side. "Please, do continue."

"The ride had been uneventful until, well, a shot rang out and the coach stopped. Some men —"

"How many men?"

"Three, if I remember correctly."

Mr. Cantrell leaned in, his voice dropping to an intimate level. "Could you see any of their faces?"

"No. They wore rags over their noses and

mouths."

"What about their hair, could you see that?"

"One man had dark hair. Yes, very dark hair. I remember well." I didn't even have to close my eyes to bring back the vivid memory of the robber who'd held me in the rain. A shiver snaked across my shoulders. How could I ever forget?

"And the others?"

I stiffened. "I-I don't know."

Mr. Cantrell took a deep breath. "It is important that you think, Miss Delafield — think!"

Goodness. I looked away, trying to visualize the other highwaymen in my mind. But all I could see was my blue-eyed captor staring me down. Were they short or tall? The man who held my wrist was tall. Yes, very tall. But the others . . . I had no idea. Had I even looked at them? "I'm sorry. I'm just not sure I remember."

He seemed a bit irritated and stood, running his fingers through his hair. "And the mail. Did they search the mail?"

"Yes. Well, possibly." I bit my lip. "That is, I'm not certain."

"You're not certain? What the blazes did they do if they didn't search the mail?"

"I didn't say the mail was untouched.

34

Only, I didn't actually see the robbers touch it. I was held off to one side. And it was raining heavily."

Miss Cantrell leaned forward to pour herself another glass of tea from the nearby tray. "Heavens, Lucius. You're not only boring me, but poor Miss Delafield as well. It's quite obvious she took no notice of the robbery, or so she says. I am certain I would remember every sordid detail of something so odious, but we don't all possess such clarity of mind."

I gritted my teeth, certain how Miss Cantrell would react should her carriage be held at gunpoint.

"But I daresay I would never be in such an unfortunate situation — alone on the common stage." She pursed her lips as if she tasted something sour. "No. You, dear brother, always provide me the best protection whenever I travel."

Mr. Cantrell took no notice of his sister. "Can you remember anything else? Anything that might be important? I'm sure the authorities will be here in the morning to speak with you."

"I don't know." I thought back to the woman who'd sat across from me and her spiteful maid. "They did take a lady's necklace, but one of the men said they didn't find what they were looking for."

Mr. Cantrell raised his eyebrow. "Intriguing. I suppose that means the group shall strike again."

I looked up. "Again?"

"Yes. Our little band of ruffians is proving quite a nuisance."

"They have robbed before?"

Miss Cantrell wafted the back of her hand across her forehead. "Don't look so alarmed, Miss Delafield. We are quite safe here, I assure you." Then to her brother, "Heavens, you're a wretch, Lucius, to treat the poor girl so after all she has endured."

Mr. Cantrell strolled to the side table. "Elizabeth is right. I do apologize. I should be offering you something to drink, not questioning you like a Bow Street runner. Let me do so now." He held up a teapot. "Tea?" he asked, that smile winding across his face once again. "Or something else?"

I cleared my throat. "Tea would be wonderful."

A door thudded closed at the back of the room. Another man had entered and stood latching a pair of French doors. Rain was sprinkled across his coat, mud splashed on his buckskin breeches. He shook the drops from his dark hair then turned to face us.

Miss Cantrell swayed to her feet, her

slender hand settling across the white crape on her bosom. "Why, Mr. Sinclair, I had no idea you were in this part of the country. What an unexpected delight." She cast a sideways glance at her brother. "Really, what a rogue you are to keep us all in the dark."

Mr. Cantrell tilted his chin. "Yes, Sinclair. Awful late to be traveling . . . on horseback."

The man stalked across the room, pausing at the sight of me.

Miss Cantrell flitted to my side. "Come, Mr. Sinclair. You must meet our newest friend, Miss Delafield. She's to be my aunt's companion. She has been entertaining us with stories of the local highwaymen. It is all quite romantic. You would love it above all things. Please, do continue, Miss Delafield."

I froze, cowering under the room's watchful eyes.

"Highwaymen, you say?" Mr. Sinclair took a decanter from the side table and filled a glass. "In the rain?" He edged down onto a cushioned chair and held his drink to me as if in a toast. "Sounds like you've had quite the adventure."

Mr. Cantrell mumbled to himself on his way back to the sofa. "I wonder why Evie's not back yet."

I wondered the same thing.

Mr. Sinclair rubbed his forehead, seemingly uninterested in the story Miss Cantrell had declared he would *love above all things.* "Where is my godmother? I must beg my pardon for being so late."

Miss Cantrell pursed her lips. "She is . . . well . . . I suppose you will hear of it soon enough, only you mustn't be angry with us."

A muscle twitched in his jaw. "Go on."

"She was a bit agitated this afternoon, and we were forced to give her the merest drop of laudanum. Nothing too serious, mind you, but she has yet to wake."

"Laudanum? Is someone with her?"

Mr. Cantrell threw his head back and huffed. "Don't go off in the boughs, Sin. Of course someone's with her. Dawkins wouldn't leave her side." He breathed out a sigh. "I know if you'd been here you wouldn't have advised starting it again, but —"

"No, I wouldn't have."

"Listen, we did it all nice and proper. Dr. Knight prescribed the stuff." Mr. Cantrell rolled his eyes. "And you don't need to look at me like that. She's been left to my care. He said it would do her good to get some sleep. She's had quite a few of her starts of late."

"I see."

I thought this Mr. Sinclair meant to say more, but he stood, placing his hand on the back of a chair, his fingers gripped tight. His voice sounded different. "I need to dress for dinner. And Miss Delafield should be shown to her room. I don't know what she's doing in here, shivering like she is."

Miss Ellis appeared in the doorway. "I quite agree. Miss Delafield, if you would follow me?"

I let out a long breath as I stood and crossed the room, conscious of nothing but the thought of a glorious bath and a warm bed. As I passed Mr. Sinclair, I caught a glimpse of his wrist. Just beneath the edge of his York tan glove was a triangular mark — one I'd seen before.

All at once, the feel of the room shifted. My stomach lurched. I didn't want to give life to the thoughts racing in my mind, yet how could I ignore them? I met the man's icy glare and all too quickly I knew the truth. He was the highwayman who'd held me at gunpoint, who had wrenched me against his chest and now stood two feet away from me, calculating my next move.

3

Miss Ellis took my hand. "Why, Miss Delafield, you look as if you've seen a ghost."

I had, of sorts.

Mr. Sinclair didn't move. Only his eye twitched as if he dared me to tell anyone what we both knew — that he was one of the wretched thieves they had been talking about. I glanced from Miss Cantrell's haughty face to her brother's skeptical grin, and I pressed my lips together. Would anyone believe such a declaration? As Miss Cantrell had said, my story was too fantastic. And worse, such threatening words could mean the end of my position at the Towers. If I was turned away, I would learn nothing of my past.

Deep down, however, a darker thought fought for my attention, forcing my silence in a way nothing else could. What if everyone in the room already knew? I needed time to think.

I squeezed Miss Ellis's hand. "I'm simply tired and cold."

Mr. Sinclair narrowed his eyes, and for a moment I thought he might stop my leaving. He had that look about him as if he possessed the power to control everyone around him, but he smiled at me easily enough. "We must not keep you from your room."

I lifted my chin in an attempt to look confident. Did he know I'd recognized him? How close he'd come to exposure? As I passed his formidable presence on my way out the door, somehow I knew he had. I forced myself to resist the urge to look back and followed Miss Ellis into the hall, pretending my entire world hadn't flipped upside down.

The entryway loomed as quiet as before, the hush of evening taking its toll on the ancient walls, the long, leaded windows darkened for the night. Nothing seemed settled in the dim space, not the crisp air or the moving shadows. It felt as if even the furniture waited in anticipation. I couldn't help but wonder if a house such as the Towers ever slept.

Miss Ellis led me up the central staircase that curved along multiple floor-length wooden panels, which were framed by the same dark stone as the exterior. A draft from the upper floors greeted me on the landing and wound its way around my wet frock. Miss Ellis paused. "I'm ghastly sorry it took me so long to get back to you. You must be terribly uncomfortable in that gown."

I nodded, unable to stop my teeth from chattering.

"You poor dear. Your room's right ahead." She held out her candle as if she'd forgotten the way. "We would have brought you here directly, but there was some confusion about what bedchamber you were to have. Mrs. Knott had prepared the blue one on the upper floor, but Dawkins insisted that my aunt specified the room next to hers. It set off quite an argument. And, well . . ." She met my gaze as we turned down a narrow hall. "You must understand, surely."

Oh, I understood. No one wanted an orphan of uncertain birth to be housed with the rest of the family, regardless of Mrs. Chalcroft's order or where a companion was typically housed. I forced a smile and nodded.

"And with my aunt asleep and not to be wakened, we were left to sort it out on our own." She pushed open a door to our right. "Of course, Dawkins won. She always does." Miss Ellis led the way into the room using what was left of her guttering candle to light a fresh one by the door, then she crossed the room to light another.

Still shaken by the revelation in the drawing room, I inched inside. My lips parted. Never in my life had I seen such fine furnishings or such a well-laid space. By now Miss Ellis had the room aglow and stood watching me with a strange excitement.

Rose-papered walls made the perfect backdrop for the four-poster bed and matching wardrobe. Crimson curtains draped what I could only assume were three small windows at the back of an alcove, which housed a darling little escritoire. Unsure what to do or say, I found myself drawn to the scrolled fireplace, the only thing that felt familiar in such a room.

Miss Ellis unexpectedly flopped down on the bed, her cream skirt disappearing into the eiderdown's dark shadows. "Do you not like it?"

I settled onto a slat-back chair, trying to hide my exhaustion. "I-I like it very well . . . but surely Mrs. Knott was right and I should be given the other room."

"It is quite grand, isn't it? I daresay it's a good deal nicer than mine, but that is neither here nor there. They say it was once

43

my aunt's bedchamber, that at the time she wanted to be close to . . . well . . ." She pointed at the far wall. "She's been in that room there for some time."

"But surely . . ." I found I couldn't speak another word as I noticed the promised copper tub a few feet away from me on the Aubusson rug. Its cold metal sides had already been draped in white towels. Soon the servants would bring the hot water. A sigh came from somewhere deep inside as I imagined the warmth wrapping my chilled body.

I began to stand but decided not to. Perhaps it would be best to accept the room for the night and speak with Mrs. Chalcroft in the morning.

Miss Ellis seemed ahead of me. "Say no more about the accommodations, Miss Delafield. My aunt needs you near her. You'll see for yourself soon enough." Her easy smile faded as if she'd remembered something. She took a quick glance at the open doorway and lowered her voice. "I-I'm not sure what Aunt Chalcroft has planned for you or why she decided to send for a companion. I mean, I probably have no business telling you, but after what happened today, you more than anyone must know what goes on around here."

She bit her lip. "And I don't care what Lucius says; I'm old enough to have an opinion in this household. It's not as if he's my father — only my guardian." She crossed her arms. "Goodness, he acts like it's all a big secret, but he doesn't have to sit with Aunt Chalcroft day after day and listen to her ridiculous rambling . . . Well, you see . . . we all fear . . . rather, we've come to realize she's not entirely right in the head." She glanced down at her hands as if suddenly embarrassed. "She hasn't been for some time."

I can't say I was surprised by her words, only saddened. "Oh?"

Of course, Miss Ellis followed her whispered declaration with a nervous laugh, one only a young girl, spoiled for far too long, could produce. "Oh, Miss Delafield, you look positively dreadful. I-I didn't mean it to sound quite like that. Heavens, I can't exactly explain it." She cast one more peek at the doorway. "We should discuss this again later when you've had time to settle in. Don't let it worry you. In fact, forget I said anything at all. Aunt Chalcroft is not really much trouble when you have a bottle of laudanum on hand."

I thought of what Mr. Sinclair had said in the drawing room about the medication —

not that I could trust a man who'd just robbed the mail coach.

". . . and for the time being you have all of us here at the house, even Mr. Sinclair, who is wonderful with her. We all adore it when he comes to stay."

To *stay* — for how long? I tried not to show the alarm pounding in my chest. "Yes. He mentioned the medication earlier . . ."

I thought I saw a flash in Miss Ellis's eyes, but she continued talking easily enough. "Did he? Well, in general such a thing is not needed. And certainly with you here it will be so much easier."

Easier? I wished I could believe her. Nothing had gone right since I boarded the mail coach. What a position to be in. Had Mrs. Smith known about her dear friend and sent me here anyway? Surely not.

Miss Ellis jumped to her feet as if she were nothing but a bird, too self-absorbed to grasp the levity of my fears. "I'll tell Lane to send up a tray for your dinner. Portia should be here soon enough with the hot water." She pooched out her lip. "I am sorry again this seems to be taking so long. If Aunt Chalcroft had only let us know she'd hired a companion before this afternoon, we would have . . ."

I froze. Mrs. Chalcroft hadn't told anyone

of my arrival till today? No wonder the room wasn't ready. "Miss Ellis, I —"

She was pacing now with a sort of nervous hop until she eyed the tub. "I'm quite certain you have been wishing me gone for some time. Oh good, here is Portia. I will leave you to your bath, and we will talk more in the morning." She held up her hand to stave off a reply. "I'm so glad you're to stay with us, Miss Delafield."

I forced a half smile, and she knelt beside my chair in a flurry of muslin and lavender and rested her hand on mine, her brown eyes sparkling in the firelight. "You and I shall get on famously. I decided so when I first saw you in the drawing room. You see, I'm determined to find some way to be happy — even though I'm stuck here at the Towers and made to miss my London season."

As if such a statement required no answer, she rose and skipped from the room. Portia, the maid, mumbled something under her breath as she poured the bathwater before she too left me to the silence of my strange new surroundings.

I had been alone many times in my life but never more so than in that moment. Mindlessly, I crossed the room to the wardrobe, slipping the bracelet from my arm. I held it, twisting the jewels in the candlelight before depositing it in a top drawer. My head ached, and I pressed the palm of my hand to my forehead, determined not to cry.

What had I done?

I'd left the only people I knew in the world. Because of a letter and a bracelet from a complete stranger? Did I really believe I could learn the identity of my parents? After all, I'd never been able to wrestle the information from my teacher, Mrs. Smith, and she loved me far more than anyone else. More than likely, it was just as I'd supposed all these years. That I was one of many illegitimate children born out of wedlock, discarded and forgotten. Yet someone had paid for my schooling. And the bracelet.

All at once I needed to read the missive again — to be sure I'd made the prudent decision. My hands shook as I pulled the lid open on my trunk and felt along the edge. What would I have done if the highwaymen had taken that letter too?

The farther I reached, the harder my heart pounded until the tips of my fingers scraped the folded paper I'd hid in the lining. I let out a sigh of relief, pressing it to my chest. One quick glance about the room and I crossed the rug to the chair by the fire, where I slowly opened the note I'd read a hundred times before.

My dear Miss Sybil Delafield,
    Regardless of what they will think at Croft Towers or what I promised to conceal, I have sent you this bracelet as I believe it is only you who should have it.

Your Servant,
Lord Stanton

I awoke with a start. My neck felt sore and my back stiff. What had been a healthy blaze now smoldered in the grate. I blinked for a moment, trying to remember where I was. The fire's remaining embers lit the room in a sort of red haze.

I rubbed my eyes, recalling the whole frantic day quite vividly now. I had taken a bath — yes, a glorious bath — then eaten my dinner and curled up in the chair by the fireplace and fallen asleep, some time ago if the ashes in the grate were any indication. The room had grown cold around me, but the scent of woodsmoke lingered in the air. I pulled my robe tight and made my way to the bed.

An owl called from somewhere beyond the

windows. The sound of my bare feet slapping against the floorboards seemed out of place on such a still night. Just one more thing I would have to become accustomed to about living in the country. London was a world of endless noise. Here each sound demanded my full attention.

I found a small clock on the side table. Half past midnight. As I expected.

The grand poster bed welcomed me in a cold flurry of softness. I tucked my knees to my chest and snuggled into the eiderdown, hoping sleep would creep up once again and claim me before my worries had a chance to take over. I'd spent enough time thinking about my present situation.

I plumped the pillow beneath my head and tried to relax. I closed my eyes and listened to the clock on the side table. How I adored clocks. The steady beat calmed my nerves. But before long, my thoughts drifted back to Winterridge and my former life. Tears welled and for the first time in weeks I let them come, coursing down my cheeks, each one wrought by a wonderful memory now painful to think of.

My life had changed. I knew I could no more cling to the past than anyone else, but as I lay there, I wanted to feel the memories one last time before saying goodbye in my heart.

Out of the darkness I heard a crash that brought me roaring from my reflections. My eyes grew wide as I lay still and listened.

There it was again. Someone. In the hallway.

The sound of footsteps followed and I bolted into a sitting position, unconsciously grasping the covers to my chest. Who would be up at such an hour and near Mrs. Chalcroft's room? I thought back to the ghostly whiff I'd seen on the landing upon my arrival. My gaze fell to the door latch. Why hadn't I thought to lock it?

I forced the twisting feeling from my stomach. I knew very well I was being silly. It was probably just one of the men heading to his room for the night. Gradually, I allowed myself to lie back down, intending to ignore what I'd heard. But the footsteps didn't sound like a pair of pumps. The sound was more like a whishing slide as if someone crawled along the passageway.

Then silence.

I waited, counting the seconds in my mind. Then . . . nothing. Whoever or whatever was out there had stopped. Possibly right outside my room.

I didn't move, but I watched the door,

certain the person would pass on. But then I saw it. Like a flicker in the moonlight, movement of the door handle. I sucked in a breath to hold back a scream. The heavy wooden door inched open as candlelight spilled through the entryway. The hand clutching the light was unsteady, causing the room's shadows to rise and shrink in a haunting dance.

"Wh-who's there?" I hoped my voice didn't sound as shaky as I felt.

The figure didn't answer, but soon enough, the light fell on a face — a face I'd not seen before but knew instantly.

"Mrs. Chalcroft?"

It could be no other. Long wisps of gray hair lay disordered around a wrinkled face. Keen blue eyes stared me down in the darkness. What was left of her thin frame bent forward as she dragged her slippered feet into the room, pushing the door closed behind her.

I jumped up. "Is-is something wrong? Can I help you?"

She waved me away with a flick of her arthritic hand. "Sit down."

Speechless, I found myself following her command. What else could I do?

She circled my chair, her piercing gaze never leaving my face as she settled in the adjoining chair with a "humph."

I should have been frightened after all I'd heard, but I felt only pity. There was little left of the grand mistress of Croft Towers. I sat quietly, waiting for her to say something, but she seemed content merely to look at me. With anyone else, this strange treatment would have made me ill at ease, but there was something different about Mrs. Chalcroft — something I'm not sure I could explain. I relaxed against the chair, knowing she'd speak when she was ready.

The old lady rested her chin on her hand. "Hair black as night, skin pale. Freckles? You're not as I'd thought, but I believe you'll do."

I offered a slight smile.

"S-Sybil, isn't it?" Her voice shook.

She must still be feeling the effects of the laudanum.

"How old are you, child?"

I cleared my voice. "Two and twenty."

"Yes, well, I'm sorry I wasn't able to meet you properly."

My thoughts felt muddled, and I heard myself responding, "You mustn't worry. Miss Ellis took good care of me."

She grunted. "*She* would." Then she laughed. "So you met the lot of 'em?"

"I —"

"Never mind. We'll talk more of them later, when I can stomach it. I've come tonight to discuss what I'll expect from you."

I glanced at the clock. The words Miss Ellis said earlier rang in my ears — *"not right in the head."* I wondered how far Mrs. Chalcroft's eccentricity would go.

She tapped her fingernails on the arm of the chair, obviously irritated at my discomfiture. "I suppose you're wondering why I'm awake at this hour, invading your bedchamber." She watched my reaction with pleasure, then licked her lips. "I'm on to them, you know. Last time I gave it to the dog and he slept for days. This time . . . Did you happen to meet the indomitable Mr. Roth this evening?"

I widened my eyes as I remembered the person snoring in the drawing room.

"I see you did. Couldn't stay awake, could he?" She turned her attention to the fireplace and laughed. "Serves him right. It was he who brought me the medicine. As if I wouldn't know he'd put it in the tea. I, eh, switched the cups. After all I'd planned, I was afraid they might send you off."

"Send me off?" So I was an unwanted guest. Nothing could surprise me now. I supposed that was the real reason they'd

54

not prepared a room. Of course, I'd arrived far too late for them to send me anywhere in good conscience. Perhaps the highwaymen had done me a good turn after all.

"Either way, I see you're settled. Tomorrow I'll have someone show you around properly. You're here to stay whether they like it or not." She took a deep breath. "This position won't require too much of your time. You'll read to me on occasion and help me with my letters." Her face changed as she narrowed her eyes. "You ride, don't you?"

"Why, yes."

"Good. This is important, so listen closely." She leaned forward and lowered her voice. "I exchange letters and packages with a man in the village on occasion, but I'm far too old to take them myself." She reached out and patted my hand. "That's why you're here — to be my messenger, so to speak. What do you think of that?"

"Oh?" I couldn't hide the question in my voice. "I'd be happy to do anything you wish —"

"Listen. You should know straightaway I don't trust anyone in this house, not a single one. A bunch of rats, they are. They'd snoop into my personal business as if it was their right. Oh yes. They're all just here waiting around for me to die and see who I've left it all to. I have no intention of posting a single letter. They'd read every word I wrote and reseal it as if I wouldn't know what they'd been about. So I'd better not hear of you dropping a single thing I give you onto that platter of outgoing mail." Her eyes took on a grayish glow in the moonlight. "Each note I expect to be delivered within hours by your own hands, and you will tell no one of our arrangement. Do you understand?"

I whispered a sad, "Yes." But I didn't understand her, not one bit.

She raised an eyebrow. "You see why I came to you in the cover of darkness, my dear. I hope my trust is not misplaced. Mrs. Smith assured me you would do anything in your power to help me." She wrapped her fingers around my hand. "I'm not long for this world, and I've no one but you. Will you do this for an old dying woman?"

I looked her straight in the eye, unable to breathe . . . and nodded.

4

Warmth and the scent of muffins crept into the bedchamber, tempting me to open my eyes. When I did, it was almost as if the previous night's oddities had vanished into the shadows like a bad dream, one I couldn't clearly remember.

I sat up to find the maid, Portia, laying out a rose-colored gown I'd not seen before. The young girl smiled at me then turned back to the wardrobe, her auburn hair shimmering in the light. "Madam says I am to help you dress in the mornings."

I rubbed my eyes, wondering just how much sleep I'd managed to get. "Oh?" I yawned. "That is very kind of her, but I daresay it's not necessary. I've never had anyone help me before. There must be a million things you'd rather be doing. I can manage well enough on my own." I paused. "But do you think Mrs. Chalcroft might need me for anything in the mornings?"

Her pleasant smile faded. "No, she has Dawkins for that."

I was in a tenuous position as the companion — living abovestairs, but neither family nor a servant. I would have to tread carefully. "I see. I suppose that means I'll have time to awaken at my leisure most days. That will be nice." I stretched and crossed the room to look out the window, wondering just what it was people did when they had no morning responsibilities. I'd certainly never experienced such freedom.

I turned around, a bit surprised by the cold look on Portia's face. Apparently, whatever it was I found to do in the mornings, Portia meant to help me do it. The poor girl hadn't moved since I'd spoken my mind. It seemed I'd given her the worst possible insult without meaning to. I lowered my gaze. I had a lot to learn.

I tried a smile. "Of course, if you'd like to help me dress — oh, really I'd be more than pleased if you would — only . . ." I pointed at the frock in her hands. "There must be some mistake. That is a lovely gown, but it's not mine."

Portia slid her finger along the edge of the fabric as if she would like to wear it herself. She lifted her eyes. "Mrs. Chalcroft had it especially made for you." She motioned behind her. "Dawkins brought them all in this morning. She said a modiste will be by on Thursday to take them up if needed."

I blinked my eyes. *Them?*

"Oh yes." She flicked open the wardrobe.

Gowns of pale-blue, peach, green, and white hung side by side. Day gowns, evening gowns, a jaconet pelisse, even a riding habit. And smashed in the corner was the simple gray frock I'd meant to wear as a sort of uniform in my new position. I drew a deep breath. "There must be some mistake."

Portia ran her fingers along the gowns. "No mistake. Dawkins knows best and the madam, well, she does as she pleases."

I couldn't help noticing the hint of jealousy in her tone.

With a pointed huff, Portia motioned me over and guided the frock onto my shoulders and fastened it in place. I turned to the mirror, unprepared for what I would see. I had come to terms with my freckles and small mouth ages ago, but apparently — I leaned a bit closer to the mirror — the last few disquieting days had left their own marks. If possible, I'd grown thinner and a bit paler. No wonder Mrs. Chalcroft seemed repulsed the previous night. The gown, however, was nothing but beautiful.

Portia's voice at my shoulder startled me.

"The family breakfasts on the ground floor. I will show you the way."

Rolls, breads, and preserves lay across a high table at the back of the room, their scents heavy at the door. Several members of the Chalcroft family had already found their way to the breakfast room and sat in relative silence — all absorbed in their own little worlds.

Though I was dry and comfortable, I hadn't completely shaken the uneasy feelings of the previous night. I paused at the threshold, hoping to gain my bearings before entering the room, but Mr. Cantrell must have been watching the door because he rose to greet me. "Miss Delafield. I hope you've passed a pleasant night."

Something about the turn of his voice made me wonder if he knew of my late-night visitor. But how could he? "Yes. I'm feeling much better today. Thank you."

"I'm glad to hear it. You must be famished. Please, come get something to eat." He extended his arm and led me to the narrow side table with all the ease of an old friend.

I cast a quick glance about the room, searching for the dark-haired highwayman, but I'd been given a gratifying reprieve. He was nowhere to be seen.

Mr. Cantrell seemed to enjoy the sound of his own voice and prattled on about nothing in particular. I suppose he still felt sorry for me, for the treatment I'd received the previous night, but it felt good not to have to carry the conversation.

He motioned down the length of the table filled with platters and dishes of various breakfast foods. "We serve ourselves most mornings here at the Towers. Far easier that way." Then he crossed his arms and leaned against the wall as he waited for me to make my selections. "My aunt has tasked me with showing you around the house and grounds this morning. Did you know?"

A slice of bacon slid from the serving spoon onto my plate. "No. I-I didn't." I wondered when my employer had time to arrange the tour considering she'd been in my room till one o'clock in the morning. I glanced up. "Will Mrs. Chalcroft be joining us for breakfast?"

It was then that I caught Miss Cantrell's piercing glare from her perch across the room. Her tight face framed what I could only call wolf eyes, which by morning's light had taken on a kind of arrogant seriousness. Apparently, her sentiments from the previous day hadn't changed.

I took a deep breath, placed a muffin on

my plate, and found a seat as far away from her as possible. She must not approve of me eating with the family, and for once, I agreed with her. Abovestairs or not, at the first opportunity, I would speak to Mrs. Chalcroft about taking breakfast in my room or the kitchen.

The older, crow-headed man who'd been asleep the previous night sat to my right. He picked up the paper beside his plate. After a moment he said, "It seems our little band of ruffians has struck again."

"Again? So soon?" Miss Cantrell asked.

"You don't say." Mr. Cantrell wandered over, hovering just above my right shoulder and the paper in the man's hands. He paused to review the article, then looked down to catch my wandering eye. "Miss Delafield, I don't believe you've met my cousin, Mr. Roth."

I couldn't help but remember what Mrs. Chalcroft had said about switching the teacups the previous night. He looked to have had a nice sleep. "No, I —"

Mr. Roth gave a sort of snort as he dipped his chin. Apparently Miss Cantrell had already told him all about me. He pointed to the bottom of the *Morning Post* and spoke as if Mr. Cantrell had said nothing at all. "Seems it was a courier on the same road as the mail coach."

I stretched to see if I could read anything. "I wonder if the robbers found what they were looking for this time."

All eyes in the room shot my direction as if I harbored a secret I hadn't disclosed the previous day.

I added quickly, "I mean, they must have been looking for something."

Mr. Cantrell took the *Morning Post* and crossed the room only to toss it on a side table. "Well, it's none of our affair, thank goodness."

Mr. Roth wrinkled his nose but added nothing more.

Chastised, I turned back to my muffin, but what had once been warm and soft now felt dry in my mouth. It was interesting that Mr. Cantrell had all but interrogated me about the robbery the previous day, but now — now he thought it none of our affair. Quite a change of heart. Perhaps I was right to keep the highwayman's identity a secret. And where was the constable Mr. Cantrell said would come by light of day?

I could tell he was pondering something as he paused mid-stride, but whatever it was passed soon enough and he shot me a grin. "Would you like to see the gardens on our little tour?"

I mirrored his light tone. "Yes. As long as it doesn't take too long. Mrs. Chalcroft might need me for something. I-I wouldn't wish for her to be looking for me."

"Good morning. Has the mail come?" Miss Ellis's sweet voice rang out at my back. I hadn't heard her come in. She touched my arm like a fairy as she flitted across the room. "And don't worry, Miss Delafield. Aunt Chalcroft won't be up until later this afternoon. Plenty of time for a tour of the house. And who better to do it? Lucius knows all the best places. Don't you, Lucius?" She added a mischievous smile. "Do you think it proper to show her the east tower?"

The two cousins held a knowing look until Miss Ellis laughed. "I'll never forget that time you scared Elizabeth and I —"

Miss Cantrell shoved to her feet. "Evie! If you intend to be ridiculous so early in the morning, I shall bid you all good day."

Mr. Cantrell slid the chair out at my side, seemingly unaffected by his sister's outburst. "Really, Elizabeth, Evie's only having a bit of fun." He raised his eyebrows. "I think it quite likely Miss Delafield would enjoy a tour that includes the home of our resident ghost."

Nothing about Mr. Cantrell's demeanor

gave me cause for concern, but my muscles twitched. Perhaps it was the excitement of the tour or the way he looked at me as if I was the most interesting person in the room. I couldn't help but smile at him. "So you do have a ghost here? I wondered."

He cast one last glance at Miss Ellis. "Of course." Then he drummed his fingers on the table. "Finish that muffin you're eating like a bird, and we shall begin in the gardens."

"Not the tower?"

"Ahh." He winked. "We shall save the best for last."

The morning was crisp and cool, but the sun hovered on the horizon as bright as ever. A few distant birds cried out amid the tugging breeze. It seemed the closer England crept to winter, the quieter the country became.

"Are you warm enough, Miss Delafield?" If it was possible, the flush to Mr. Cantrell's cheeks made him look even younger and more alive. I tried not to stare. He probably knew his attraction well enough without the unwanted attention of his aunt's companion.

I wondered if my own nose had changed color too. It never did behave properly —

not in the cold. "Yes, I'm warm enough for a short stroll." I pulled the peach pelisse tighter around my shoulders. I'd found the coat with the other clothes in the wardrobe Mrs. Chalcroft had filled so kindly for me. It fit perfectly, and I would require something warm if she meant for me to take letters into town at this time of year.

Mr. Cantrell swung open an old iron gate nestled between a pair of stone pillars. Miss Ellis, though full of ideas for my little tour, had decided not to join us due to the cold weather, so it was only the two of us in the quiet morning.

He led me to the garden's center then stopped and waited for my reaction.

I looked around, not quite sure how to respond. The unbridled hands of nature had made over the small space, each wild plant interweaving into the next, the hardiest species fighting for control. Even the small pond felt crowded out by weeds.

"There's not much to it, as you can see. The gardener was turned off years ago for economy. My aunt didn't think to keep it up since she's no longer able to enjoy it, but it's somewhere to come if you need to be alone."

I walked from one corner to the next, breathing in the scent of grass and leaves. I could see them all now, each individual plant that had fought neglect to survive and flourish. The chaos was beautiful in a way, as if the plants had struggled against uniformity and won — as if this might be the way it was created to look before man bent it to his will.

I smiled, thinking of Hyde Park and my own little garden back at the school. Hopefully it too, if left unrestrained, would work to find its own balance. I doubted anyone would care for the plants as I had.

I turned around, suddenly conscious of Mr. Cantrell's eyes on me and the curious way they lightened my heart. I'd been silent for too long. "Mrs. Chalcroft doesn't come here at all?"

"No. My aunt rarely leaves her room most days, which is probably why she decided to employ a companion. Lonely, I expect."

Like a shield, the stone walls blocked the howling wind, and I was able to take a deep breath of the dampened air. Tendrils of ivy climbed the far walls, winding fingers in and out of chipped statues and a large vase. The tips of the vines reached up the house wall to a large window where a darkened figure stood facing out. Watching us?

Mr. Cantrell anticipated my next question. "Sinclair, I suppose. He just can't seem to mind his own business. I'm sure he's already been in to see Aunt Chalcroft this morning to discuss everything as if he has the charge of the whole estate."

The mention of the highwayman's name caused a flinch. Thank goodness I'd missed him in the breakfast room. I wasn't sure I was prepared to face him again yet, particularly after hearing he'd robbed another man on the road that same day. The shadowy figure disappeared from the window, and I cleared my throat, hoping Mr. Cantrell hadn't read my thoughts. "Does Mr. Sinclair come often to the Towers?"

"Too often if you ask me, but he is my aunt's godson, I suppose. Although I daresay he only pops in when he is coincidentally short on money."

"Ah." So he wasn't exactly related. "And are you well acquainted with him?"

Mr. Cantrell gave me a tight-lipped smile. "Yes. We were at university together, but I wouldn't exactly call him a friend."

I ran my fingers along the ivy leaves as I paced one of the walls, the soft rustle taking a ride on the breeze. "Oh. I only asked because he seemed a bit upset last evening."

Mr. Cantrell trailed behind me, his long legs narrowing the gap between us. "The gentleman is upset as a rule. I wouldn't regard it. My sister delights in his company, but I hope he won't be staying long."

I could imagine Miss Cantrell delighting in a highwayman's company. I almost laughed out loud at the thought. Of course, the two of them were alike in many ways, both unconcerned with anyone other than themselves. "I hope not either — for your sake."

"Thankfully, he usually keeps to himself." Something flashed in Mr. Cantrell's eyes, and he stepped closer. "But you will let me know if he bothers you."

I nodded easily enough, but I couldn't help but wonder what he meant.

The talk of Mr. Sinclair seemed to sour Mr. Cantrell's mood. I knew it had changed mine. He held out his arm. "Shall we head back into the house? I wouldn't wish you to get chilled. Not after your escapade yesterday."

"You're quite right." I turned to meet him near the corner of the garden where the towering stone walls met. But as I reached for his arm, my foot snagged on something beneath the layer of withered plants. I stumbled and was forced to catch my balance on the far wall.

Mr. Cantrell grasped my hand and met my curious glance with one of his own.

"What the devil?"

He kicked at the dried leaves for a moment until the toe of his boot found the culprit, and we were rewarded with a loud clank. It wasn't a rock I'd tripped over. I knelt, pulling the weeds aside as best I could.

There, hidden by years of neglect, was a square iron grate with a round handle. I pressed my finger into the space between the bars, expecting to feel the wet earth below, but there was only cold air.

Mr. Cantrell dropped to the ground beside me. He looked at me as if he'd meant to say something but stopped himself, turning his attention back to our little discovery. He too shoved his fingers through the grate into the darkness below.

Our breaths mingled in the cold air, both of us peering down . . . at what? My chest felt light. I'd read of secret passageways and hidden rooms. Could we have found something the family knew nothing about — in the garden? A friend at the school had told me stories of her ancestors who'd held Jacobite fugitives beneath the floor of their country estate. Could this iron door lead to something similar?

Surely not. I bit my lip and took a quick glance at my coconspirator. Of course, Mr.

Cantrell's silence did little to lessen my imagination. "Do you know what this is? Can it be possible there's a room below?"

I caught the hint of a grin before he reached for the handle. "I've never seen it before. The gardens have been covered in weeds for as long as I can remember. There's only one way to find out. Shall we open it?"

I nodded, slowly at first and then quickly as if the two of us had found some undiscovered treasure that might disappear the longer we delayed.

He wiped his forehead with the sleeve of his coat. "I'm sure it's nothing, but I'd like to be certain."

The metal door ground open with a terrible squeak, dirt sliding off the sides in all directions. For a breathless second neither of us moved as if the magic might float away and be lost forever. Then we leaned forward.

I blinked for a second, allowing the sunlight to seep into the dim space. I could see a small room, empty, carved out of the earth below us, probably only about ten feet across at its widest part. We'd need a ladder to inspect any further.

Mr. Cantrell surprised me as he guided my shoulders back and settled the iron door into its place with a loud clank. "Nothing

71

but a little room. I was hoping for more. Weren't you?"

I thought the room interesting enough, but I was far too ladylike to admit I wanted to go down into the darkness to see what we could find. "What do you think it was used for?"

"A priest hole possibly . . . or merely a storage space." He glanced up at the east tower. "You'll find this house holds a few secrets."

"Secrets?"

He lightly touched my shoulder, but he couldn't keep his eyes off the grate. "You know." He took a breath. "I am quite glad you've come to the Towers, Miss Delafield, if for no other reason than to share in this discovery."

Gently, he helped me to my feet and settled my hand on his arm. We both saw the grass stains across my skirt and laughed.

"You really are a unique woman, aren't you?" He patted my arm for a moment, then rested his hand. "Forgive me. That did not come out the way I intended. What I meant to say is I've never met a lady quite like you — you intrigue me." He leaned in and lowered his voice. "I cannot explain all at present, but I must beg your discretion about the grate. It's important. Can I trust you, Miss Delafield?"

I wasn't sure what he meant and I loathed secrets, but I nodded. I imagine I would have done a great deal for such a pair of kind eyes.

He held my gaze for a long moment then lifted my fingers to his lips. "Thank you, Miss Delafield. I feel quite safe in your hands. Now, let us finish the tour. I still must introduce you to Evie's ghost."

5

The access to the east tower rose from a turn in the hallway behind the servants' quarters. Mr. Cantrell explained that no one used the upper rooms anymore. By the look of the cobwebs and dry rot, I believed him. A few steps into the corridor and the heavy door Mr. Cantrell held open for me slammed shut, sealing off the kitchen's familiar clatter for abrupt silence.

Miss Ellis had seemed so keen on joining us in this adventure to the tower. It was her idea after all, but when the time came, she was nowhere to be found. Walking the gardens with Mr. Cantrell had been one thing, but the tower . . . I wished to goodness she hadn't abandoned me. I was forced to bring my maid in her stead, and Portia couldn't stop muttering that she might rather jump off a cliff than go up to the east tower. But she came nonetheless. Who wouldn't when Mr. Cantrell had asked so kindly?

I found myself climbing the tower stairs with Portia prattling in my ear and my thoughts still reeling from the discovery of the priest hole and my time alone with Mr. Cantrell. I knew a gentleman of his stature would no more look at me than a scullery maid, but I couldn't seem to completely put the idea out of my mind.

Without warning he grasped my hand. "Watch your step. The railing isn't secure here."

The narrow stairwell settled into a circular pattern, and the stone steps stretched farther apart. I followed behind him as closely as possible, conscious of the feel of his fingers, so strong and smooth, all the while smiling to myself. His hand looked quite nice wrapped around mine. It was then my voice left me for a whisper. "Thank you. I'll be careful."

The farther we climbed, the thicker the air seemed and the more the damp walls closed in around us. I cleared my throat. "I don't suppose anyone comes up here at night."

"It would be near impossible without a light. And then I daresay most haven't the stomach for it." He released my hand and set his candle in a small alcove. "Ah, here we are."

I heard the door creak open rather than saw it, the blackness was so thick ahead. Mr. Cantrell motioned with his chin. "After you?"

I gave him a questioning glance, hesitating where I stood, but I'd agreed to meet this ghost of Miss Ellis's. I crossed my arms. "Does the ghost stay in this room all the time?"

"It's the only place Evie and I have ever seen him."

I gave him a sideways look as I crept by, my arm brushing his jacket. Tingles crawled up my spine. I tried to keep my voice light. "So it is a he?"

Mr. Cantrell laughed. "As far as we can tell."

The wooden floor creaked as we crossed the tiny room, Portia sidling up against me. Dust hovered on the air. Shadows shifted around us. I started to duck then realized the roof only felt low. Giant beams crossed above my head. The candle's glow from the stairwell didn't penetrate far. What items weren't swathed in Holland covers wore a thick layer of filth. I chose the safest spot I could find to wait. "Well. Where is he then?"

Mr. Cantrell slid beside me, a slight smile curving his lips. "You must be quiet and still."

I knew I'd agreed to some such nonsense when I'd taken up the challenge of meeting Miss Ellis's ghost. Of course, I knew it was all a game, but climbing those gloomy stairs with the fingers of darkness pushing me on as if something waited at the top had put me on edge in a way I wasn't expecting. I'd just as soon get the whole thing over with.

Something made a popping noise behind me. The hairs on my arm stood on end. I rubbed the feeling away.

Portia, however, staggered to the left, crashing against the wall in her haste. The creak of the floorboards pierced the silence. "I'm so sorry, miss. I be too scared to stay." Her footsteps echoed as she quickly descended the stairs.

Mr. Cantrell moved to close the door, a laugh in his voice as he said, "As we were."

Darkness fell like a black curtain. I forced the muscles in my arms to relax and waited. Whatever Mr. Cantrell had planned would be over soon enough. I counted in my head to avoid panic . . . one . . . two . . . three.

"All right, Mr. Cantrell. You've had your fun. Let's get on with this ghost or I'd like to go back downstairs."

A shuffle sounded at my back. Then silence. I waited like a statue as my eyes adjusted to the dim light. Thank goodness we weren't in absolute darkness.

A slender shape took form almost as if it had appeared from somewhere in the wall. A grayish-white shape, like a person a few feet away. Coming toward me. My heart jolted to life. On instinct, I took a step backward, stumbling against a tall crate.

Laughter rang out on either side.

"I told you she wouldn't scream." Miss Ellis's voice echoed across the room before I heard the door open and she fetched the candle from the stairs. "What do you think of our little ghost?"

A painting. It was nothing but a horrid painting. "I —"

"I was only nine years old when Lucius played that trick on Elizabeth and me. I daresay it was far more believable then. He howled and moved it around and added a dreadful story I won't repeat. And at the time I didn't know Aunt Chalcroft had all this stuff up here." Her shoulders sagged. "I don't think we fooled you at all."

My heartbeat slowed to a more manageable rate, and the ringing in my ears faded away. I took a deep breath. "Anyone would be frightened in a room such as this. What on earth was it used for?"

Mr. Cantrell swept a clump of dust away from their "ghost." "Years ago, it was only an access room for the lookout on the tower." He pointed to a door. "Now it's been storage for as long as I can remember. My great-aunt keeps her late daughter's things here." He turned back to the painting. "And other odds and ends." He paused. "I hope you're not vexed at me, Miss Delafield. After our pleasant stroll in the garden, I wouldn't wish you to think ill of me." He poked Miss Ellis's arm. "It was Evie's childish idea."

I smoothed out my gown, hoping to give the impression of ease. "Oh no. All in good fun." I smiled but found my gaze drifting back to the painting. Whoever the man was, he sure fit the part of a ghost — there was something about his devilish eyes. "Who is he?"

Miss Ellis wrinkled her nose. "The Earl of Stanton. Isn't he deliciously stern?"

I froze. Stanton. The man who'd sent me the letter. The bracelet.

The way Miss Ellis's gaze fell longingly on his face seemed at odds with her declaration. She touched the edge. "He was married to my cousin Anne — Aunt Chalcroft's daughter. But that was a long time ago, and I was told they didn't suit."

I stepped forward with hesitation. So Lord Stanton was familiar with the Chalcroft

79

family as I'd suspected — by marriage. My fingers sought the bracelet on my arm. I had been right to come.

Squinting, I took a second assessment of the painting. Though apparently young at the time, *harsh* was the only word I could think to describe Lord Stanton. He exuded the idea of good breeding in the arrogant turn of his chin and a look that told you he knew his worth. His shoulders were broad, the cut to his clothes exceptional, but his eyes — so shallow and cold. Even the painter couldn't help but catch an essence of pure emptiness. Goodness, I wasn't sure I'd like to find myself alone with him. Yet, as I stepped closer, I wondered if I had seen him somewhere before. In London? "A perfect candidate to play your ghost. How long ago did he die?"

"Oh, Lord Stanton's alive and well. A friend of mine actually. He's been in the West Indies on business for the past few months." Mr. Cantrell settled the cover back over the painting then turned to face me, seemingly startled by the look on my face. "What's the matter? Are you acquainted with him?"

I shook my head, but was I?

Mr. Cantrell crossed his arms and tilted his chin. "You know, for some reason I get the feeling that you are."

I inhaled a quick breath. "No." And laughed. "We run in quite different circles, I'm sure." I added a head bob for emphasis and turned away. "Well," I huffed. "I really should return to Mrs. Chalcroft's room. She could be awake and expecting me."

Mr. Cantrell cocked an eyebrow then motioned to the door, the candor all but drained from his voice. "Then by all means. We don't mean to keep you."

"I really should go." I hurried past him to the door, ready to make my exit, but my hand lingered on the rusty handle, a slight chill skirting across my shoulders. Was Mr. Cantrell angry with me? I glanced behind me, certain I'd seen something in his eyes as I passed, but he stood there smiling as he had in the garden when we made our little discovery.

I cleared my throat. "Thank you both for the, um, lively tour of the house. I do appreciate it, but I must attend to Mrs. Chalcroft."

I didn't wait for an answer and followed the first curve of the stairs without looking back. The tower room had set me on edge. As it would anyone, I told myself. And the painting? My second clue. The second connection to my past.

I paused, glancing back up the corridor, my shoe resting on the bottom of the first flight of stairs. In the cloying stillness I could hear Miss Ellis and Mr. Cantrell murmuring in the upper room.

Mrs. Chalcroft's bedchamber was not as I'd expected — small and Spartan, not a painting or knickknack in sight. Just bare walls, a wardrobe, and chairs all standing like His Majesty's soldiers at attention. I found myself straightening my shoulders, unprepared for what I might encounter.

Dark curtains hid a solitary window, staving off any hint of daylight. The scent of rosewater hung heavy on the air. The mistress lay propped up on pillows, a mere wisp of a shadow, nestled beneath the covers of a massive bed. As I approached, I was shocked by what I hadn't seen the previous night — Mrs. Chalcroft on her throne, the true queen of the Towers.

Her hair was neat, her eyes serious. The wild look of the night had vanished from her face, replaced by a vestige of power one couldn't ignore. I followed Mrs. Chalcroft's lady's maid, Dawkins, to the bedside, trying to make sense of the two very different versions of my employer.

Mrs. Chalcroft met my arrival with a

crooked smile. "Still here, eh?"

I gave a little laugh. "Of course." I sidled over to the window to allow Dawkins a moment to finish clearing the breakfast tray and wiping her face. The look in Mrs. Chalcroft's eyes indicated I was not to watch.

I parted the curtains for a peek. Outside, the gray sky had starved the landscape of its summer hues. The morning sunshine Mr. Cantrell and I had enjoyed a few hours before had vanished into low-hanging clouds. I watched a bird swoop back and forth from treetop to sky before my gaze fell onto a tiny figure striding across the lawn. A woman, dressed in a thick brown cloak, darted between the misty corners of the far wall before pausing at the garden gate.

The woman first appeared to be a stranger, but intrigued by her impulsive movements, I leaned a bit closer to the glass for a better look. She rewarded me with a long view of her profile before slipping through the gate. Thompkins! The maid from the coach. My eyes widened. But why was she here — at the Towers?

I seized on the absurdity at once. Thompkins had never said a word of familiarity about the Chalcrofts. She'd had ample time to speak up on the coach. So why was she here? Scampering across the lawn to the garden like a mouse?

Mrs. Chalcroft cleared her throat and I turned back to face her. Dawkins eyed me for a moment then reached around Mrs. Chalcroft's frail body attempting to plump the pillow, but Mrs. Chalcroft popped her on the arm.

"Enough with all this ridiculousness. I'm not on my deathbed yet." Mrs. Chalcroft flicked her fingers in the air. "Now, get on with you. I will speak with Miss Delafield alone."

Dawkins cast me a sideways glance as she left the room. Was it curiosity or anger she attempted to hide behind those narrow eyelids?

Mrs. Chalcroft waited until the door closed before moving the bedside candle near her face. "So you see me now as I truly am, child. A pitiful, frail creature hidden away in this torturous room day after day, reduced to the sniveling attentions of servants."

I opened my mouth to deny it, but I would have no lies between us. "As you say."

She grunted, then laughed. "What does a young girl know of such things?"

I folded my hands at my waist. "Not much, I assure you."

"Humph. Never mind. I'll not bore you

with my troubles. They'll find you soon enough." She reached for a sewing bag lying beside her on the bed. "Have you settled in, had something to eat?"

"Yes. Thank you. And Mr. Cantrell gave me a tour of the house."

"Good, because a pressing matter has come to my attention." She wrinkled her nose as if she'd tasted something bitter. "I had hoped to give you a few days before I needed your assistance, but it seems you must deliver a letter for me tomorrow morning. There will be no delay. Do you understand?"

"A letter? Oh yes, but —"

"Don't gape at me like that, gel. Of course you'll have a horse to do as I bid you and a groom." She shot a quick glance upward. "My godson, Curtis Sinclair, has agreed to make the necessary arrangements — secure you the horse and groom for whenever you need them. Thank goodness he is here. I don't know what I would do if I was left to bungle my way through all this with those unnatural nieces and nephews of mine." Her hand shook as she retrieved a slender envelope from the bag. "Listen. This must go to the milliner in Reedwick. Mrs. Barineau is her name. It contains instructions about a hat trimming I ordered a few weeks ago. She won't question you when she sees what you've brought her."

If I could have sat down, I would have, but I was forced to conceal a reaction, pinned by Mrs. Chalcroft's thoughtful gaze. My feet itched, my palms felt wet. Even Mrs. Chalcroft seemed tense, her head stiff on her pillow, her gaze fixed to the underside of the poster bed, looking for all the world like a wooden doll.

Mr. Sinclair would secure me a mount? I wondered if I shouldn't disclose the terrible truth about him right then and there. Goodness knows I itched to expose him. But again, that feeling that I should remain quiet fought its way into my consciousness.

Mrs. Chalcroft's slender fingers clenched into a fist. "Do you understand what I'm telling you, gel? You've been staring at the fire now for nigh on two minutes." She leaned forward. "You're not the addled type, are you?"

I took a deep breath. "No. I am sorry. I-I was woolgathering. Do you have a message for the milliner, or do I simply hand her the note?"

"Pay attention. This is important. You must find a way to be secret. No words need to be exchanged, my dear, only . . . no one must see you give it to her." She held out the sealed letter between her thumb and forefinger; the Chalcroft crest was visible in dried wax.

I took it blindly, a million questions swimming through my head. "And the groom?"

She leaned forward, that look of wildness returning to her eyes. "I said no one, child."

"I-I understand." But I didn't.

"In the morning, find your way to the stables first thing. Curtis will await you there and see that everything is arranged properly." She squinted her eyes. "You did say you could ride?"

"Oh yes. It's not that. I . . ." It was my one chance to tell the truth, to reveal his secret, or I would be guarding it forever. Yet how could I finish such a bold statement? *Umm . . . I do believe your godson, the man you obviously care greatly about, is a notorious highwayman. In fact, he robbed the mail coach only yesterday.* I closed my mouth.

"Then what is it, child? I can't stand mindless babbling."

I nodded, a newfound resolution forming in my head. "I will do my best to deliver the letter and anything else you need me to do." Then I leaned forward, my arm resting on the coverlet, my jeweled bracelet glinting in the candlelight. "Mrs. Smith is like a mother to me, and I will do anything to help her dearest friend."

Something flashed in those dark-brown eyes. "Good girl. I'll expect you to report back when you return. Perhaps then you can begin to read to me in the afternoons." She patted my cheek. "I find I like the sound of your voice."

6

The following morning Mr. Sinclair stood at the door to the stable complex, a riding crop gripped in his gloved hand, his chin tilted in the way I imagine a rake would appear if I ever really saw one.

Avoiding his gaze, I followed the gravel path around the paddock, running my fingers along the wall's edge. He watched my approach with the same cynical look he'd worn the previous night. There was a hint of a smile, however, captured by the early-morning sun. I imagined it to be quite like the one he'd hidden beneath his mask on the day of the robbery.

The arrogant wretch.

I stopped a few feet from him and he paused before addressing me. "I don't believe we've been properly introduced."

Ha! I lifted my chin to meet his gaze. "No? Yet somehow I get the strangest feeling we already know one another." I waited for a reaction, but he didn't even blink. "I mean to say, Mrs. Chalcroft spent yesterday afternoon singing your praises."

"Ah." He gave a satisfied sigh. "My one admirer. Then again, she did take a vow at my birth to like me." He leaned against the stable wall, an air of distracted levity about him. "How long do you suppose it shall be before she discovers the truth?"

"I do wonder."

We stood there for a quiet moment, a nearby robin filling the space between us. The worthless impostor was appraising *me*. Strangely enough, I didn't mind his critical eye. Of course, I was annoyingly glad I'd not been forced to wear that hideous gray gown this morning. I glanced down at my fine new pale-blue riding habit of Georgian cloth, which matched perfectly the ribbons on my bonnet. Mrs. Chalcroft had chosen well.

A tangy scent filled the breeze, almost as if it might rain, but the sky was filled with puffy white clouds and blue sky beyond. Taking a long breath, I wondered if the worst was over. By the looks of things, we were to pretend our little encounter on the mail coach had never happened.

I motioned toward the stables. "Mrs. Chalcroft indicated there was a horse I might ride. I understand I'm to travel with a groom to Reedwick."

"Yes. I spoke with John moments ago, for I too have business in town. I thought it best that we should travel together. It would be absurd not to." He glanced over his shoulder. "I'm not certain what is taking him so long. If you would be so good as to wait here, I will go find him." He disappeared through the stable door as a cold wash of fear surged into my mind.

So my highwayman had wheedled a way to escort me to Reedwick. The image of Mr. Sinclair with a rag on his face flashed into my mind, followed by the image of his sharp blue eyes and the feel of his steel grip on my arm, my back pressed to his chest.

How could I allow myself to be at that man's mercy again? In truth, he hadn't harmed me the day of the robbery, not really. He had also been kind in an arrogant sort of way in the drawing room the night of my arrival, and the groom would be with us. But Mr. Sinclair was a liar and a thief, and a . . .

He reemerged from the stables with two horses in tow, the groom still fiddling with his saddle.

I recognized the black beast in his right hand from the day of the robbery. He snorted then tossed his head as if to say his own version of good morning. He looked even more imposing in the bright sun with his shiny coat and broad back. Beside him pranced a beautiful chestnut mare, light and fresh, with a look about her I couldn't resist.

"What a darling."

Mr. Sinclair rubbed the horse's nose. "Miss Cantrell told John she wouldn't mind if you exercised Aphrodite. Liz isn't one for riding much these days." He turned to observe his own mount.

Miss Cantrell? I swallowed my distaste. So I was to share her horse. I covered my disappointment in a smile and sauntered over to the mare's side.

I ran my hand along Aphrodite's neck before giving her nose a rub. It seemed unlikely Miss Cantrell had agreed to such an arrangement, but I tried not to hold my feelings against her beautiful horse. Aphrodite seemed a gentle soul and deserved exercise as much as Mr. Sinclair's beast.

I cocked an eyebrow at him. "I will have to thank Miss Cantrell when I see her next. It was kind of her to think of me."

Mr. Sinclair coughed. "Suit yourself, but I wouldn't bother if I were you. I daresay you're doing the poor horse a favor."

Turning back to Aphrodite, he checked

the saddle and bridle to make sure they were secure, then cupped his hand beside her flank. "Now, shall we get on with this?"

I walked right up and settled my boot in Mr. Sinclair's outstretched hands. Highwayman or not, I knew now the reason Mrs. Chalcroft longed for his presence at the Towers. Mr. Sinclair possessed an intensity one couldn't ignore and the authority of a man who got things done.

Honestly, if I hadn't seen the scar on his wrist, I would have been hard-pressed to identify him as the robber who held me at gunpoint that day in the rain. In all likelihood that was the gentleman's greatest asset — the ability to act convincingly in a role. I grasped the pommel. What role was Mr. Sinclair playing now?

He lifted me into the sidesaddle easily enough, and I settled my habit around my legs as he mounted beside me. I forced myself not to look to see if he'd brought a pistol for our little ride. I motioned to his horse. "What do you call him?"

"This brute here is Hercules. He's been with me the last few years." He settled the reins in his hand then tugged to the right. "I daresay there's not another horse like him."

Hercules edged forward, and Aphrodite

93

moved in alongside him with John following behind at a respectful distance. We crossed the paddock and passed through the gate onto the main drive. Freed from fence and stable, I could tell Hercules itched to run, but Mr. Sinclair held him back, motioning for me to ride up ahead of him.

Aphrodite trotted beautifully with a bit of encouragement, and Hercules matched her stride until the horses found a comfortable pace next to one another. Mr. Sinclair rode tall in the saddle, the reins taut in his hands, and made no move to engage me in conversation. I'd not forgotten what he looked like that day, galloping toward the mail coach, a pistol in his hand.

Today, however, he was all gentle ease. His lithe form joined with Hercules's smooth muscles, breaking the trot for a canter. I urged Aphrodite to match stride, and I felt the heaviness of my present situation lighten in a way only riding on the back of a horse can accomplish.

The icy wind met us head-on, chilling the tips of my ears beneath my bonnet. The horses' breaths came out in little puffs of air that floated for a moment then disappeared. Away from the house, woodsmoke hung on the breeze. The damp morning had left a light blanket of dew on the ground, which the horses trailed through as if they ran on water.

Every now and again, I'd hear a small animal scamper somewhere in the undergrowth along the road, or a bird swoop near. Mr. Sinclair didn't seem to take notice of much but the road ahead.

I pulled Aphrodite to a trot, hoping to elicit conversation. However, it seemed it would be up to me if anything was to be said. I licked my lips and called out, "Tell me, Mr. Sinclair. Do you ride much?" I immediately pressed my gloved hand to my mouth, but the question was out before I had a chance to stop it.

He shot me a probing glance before nodding. "I do, as a matter of fact."

He frowned at first, and I feared the daunting silence would return, but he angled in his saddle to look at me, assessing me with those eyes of his. "Miss Delafield?"

It felt as if my name lingered on his lips.

"I believe we would do each other a favor by dropping this ridiculous charade. I find I haven't the patience for it." He paused, but I couldn't manage a word, so he went on, "I, uh, hadn't planned to discuss that day any further, not with anyone. Certainly not with my godmother's companion." He cast me a wry glance. "But for reasons I can't explain, I've decided it imperative to take you into my confidence."

A gust of wind fought its way into my habit, chilling me to the core. Aphrodite slowed as if I'd pulled her reins. I glanced down at my clenched fingers. It seemed I had.

Mr. Sinclair leaned toward me. "We're both adults here, Miss Delafield. Surely we can discuss this situation rationally. Come to some sort of understanding, I hope." He took a long breath. "Considering Mrs. Chalcroft's present illness, I will be forced to remain at the Towers for some time to manage her care. We're likely to meet on several occasions, and I don't wish to continually wonder where I stand with you."

Mr. Sinclair slid his reins into one hand and reached out to grip Aphrodite's as well.

We came to a full stop and my eyes widened. Instinctively, I glanced behind me down the narrow lane. We were sheltered from the groom by a grove of oak trees and the road beyond by a small hill. He'd found the perfect spot for this tête-à-tête.

The cool air made his voice sound edgy. "Come now, we're both well aware it was me that day at the mail coach."

"Yes." I raised my chin. "You pointed your pistol at me."

He pressed his lips together. "You do understand that I had no idea you were in that coach." He released Aphrodite's reins as if he only now realized he'd been holding them. "Would it help if I told you I had no intention of firing the pistol?"

I let out a pinned breath. "No."

I wasn't sure if I imagined it or if he looked down at the place where he'd held my arm that day in the rain. "I am sorry. But you must admit, you didn't make things easy on me."

"Easy!" How dare he? "I was frightened to death."

"Sure you were. I saw you watching me through the window as I came up to the coach. You looked at me as if I were playing the part in some great adventure of yours."

My legs tightened around Aphrodite of their own accord. "I did not."

"Hmm. As you say." He waved me off. "It is fruitless to discuss what cannot be changed. What I'd like to know is the reason you've kept quiet. I expected you to expose me the instant you saw me in the drawing room. But you didn't. Why?"

"It seemed the best course of action at the time. I wasn't certain you were the same man until I saw your wrist."

"My wrist?"

I pointed to his right arm. "You have a scar there, just beneath your glove. I saw it when you were, um, holding me." Warmth rushed to my cheeks. I added quickly, "You've been in a fight before?"

His shoulders slumped and he looked off into the distance. "Well, at any rate, I stand in your debt." After a moment he added, "Tell me, what is it that brought you to the Towers, Miss Delafield?"

I paused to consider my answer. The letter from Lord Stanton was none of his concern or the fact that the anonymous patron who had been funding my living expenses at the school had suddenly ceased payments. "I had no other offers of employment."

"None? That seems unlikely. A girl your age with a fine education should find it simple enough to secure a position."

"Perhaps . . ." I didn't like his questioning. He was too close to the truth. "I needed something straightaway."

"And you came here?"

"One of the teachers at the school is an old friend of Mrs. Chalcroft's. It was she who arranged the position for me."

"I see." He tapped his finger on his horse's mane. "I must admit, I was a bit surprised to read your letter that day in the rain. You see, Mrs. Chalcroft never said a word to me about hiring a companion. We . . . She's quite important to me, and in general, she discusses everything with me first."

Discusses everything indeed. I thought of the letter in my reticule — the one I was to deliver without anyone's knowledge. I daresay I was privy to much that would surprise him about his godmother.

"Miss Delafield." His voice was lower now. "It is important that you should know something. The last time the doctor came to visit, he informed us — all of us — that Mrs. Chalcroft has but a few months left to live, and her mind is not what it once was."

"A few months." The words struck me with a force I'd not expected. "And Mrs. Chalcroft has been told this?"

"Yes." He sat back in his saddle. "I was concerned you were not aware. And finding out your situation is as it is . . ."

"I-I understand." I swallowed hard. "Thank you. I appreciate you giving me the time to make proper arrangements for my future, but you mustn't worry. When the time comes, I'll have somewhere to go." If only that were true.

"If you'd like me to put in a word for you, I can speak to a few families I know in the neighborhood who might be able to find you a governess position, if that is something you would be interested in."

I stiffened, my gaze never leaving his face. The man was serious. And I, caught up in the moment, found I couldn't help but laugh.

Mr. Sinclair seemed taken aback. As well he should. I was acting outrageously. But honestly, how could he expect me to discuss my future with him, a highwayman, the very one who only two days ago held me at gunpoint and forced me to empty my pockets?

"Put in a word for you" — he was lucky I hadn't turned him over to the authorities.

Recovering as quickly as possible, I made sure I phrased my next sentence carefully. "Thank you, Mr. Sinclair. I would appreciate any help you can offer. But if I may be so bold, I would like to ask you something first."

"Go ahead."

"Why did you do it?"

"It?"

I'm not sure he knew what to make of me, let alone whether to take my question seriously. Honestly, I didn't know what to make of myself. So I raised my voice. "Rob the mail coach, of course!"

"Of course." He rubbed his chin, his gaze

on the horizon. "A lark, I suppose. Boredom. I doubt you would understand."

I blinked, waiting for him to say more, but he merely sat there watching me with that piercing gaze of his, the kind I generally try to avoid but found impossible with him. Self-conscious, I crossed my arms. "You're right. I don't."

He shrugged then slapped Hercules's reins. And as irritating as it was, I was forced to follow him like a lost puppy.

He didn't look back when he spoke next. "I cannot discuss that day in any way where you might find me less reprehensible than you already do. The only thing I must plead for now is your discretion." Suddenly, he turned. "Can you do that, Miss Delafield? Keep what you know to yourself? I find it admirable of you to have done so thus far."

I didn't think it admirable — cowardly more like — but something about the tone of Mr. Sinclair's voice gave me reason to doubt that what he called a lark was not something far more grave. Perhaps it was my current situation or the many questions I had, but after a few seconds of uncomfortable silence, I consented.

He looked pleased. "Then I will consider myself in your debt. I expect you to let me know the first opportunity that I can repay your kindness."

"As you wish." I wasn't sure I could trust this wild person who paraded around as a gentleman one day and a ruffian the next, but what harm would it do if he was indebted to me?

I hated secrets with a passion, for they were usually kept from me. However, within two days of my arrival to the Towers, I had become the unlikely bearer of three. One for Mrs. Chalcroft, one for Mr. Cantrell, and one for the highwayman.

7

The town of Reedwick sat tucked between two gentle swells, a sort of handmade valley amid the rolling hills of the countryside. The horse cart track we'd been following opened to the town's center just past the blacksmith's shop and what turned out to be a circulating library.

We walked the horses down a line of two-story buildings, each stacked one against the other like dominoes. Mr. Sinclair reined Hercules in at the open corner and I followed his lead. A breeze whooshed through a wide gap between the buildings, and I was forced to better secure my bonnet.

Fresh bread scented the air, and I turned to find a group of peddlers gathered in the town's center selling their goods. A child's laughter rang out, followed by a bit of commotion as a woman with a basket chased a little boy around a display, stooping to scoop him into her arms. Every corner of the quaint village thrummed with movement, but not like the loud and crowded streets of London. This was more like a joyful restlessness.

Mr. Sinclair dismounted and assisted me to the ground. I stretched my legs as I took a few steps into the central square. Hercules and Aphrodite were handed over to the groom before Mr. Sinclair looked to me. "Mrs. Chalcroft indicated you'll be visiting Pasley and Co., which sells most items a lady might need." He paused as if waiting for me to add more. "Have you any other business in town?"

"Well, no." I smiled, hoping that was the end to his questioning.

"Pasley's is just ahead on the right." He held out his arm. "Shall we?"

I settled my hand on his coat sleeve and allowed him to skirt me around the busy market. Though the ground was quite dusty, the recent rains kept the dirt from climbing my pelisse.

A church bell resounded in the distance, sending a momentary hush over the town. At the same moment, my gaze fell onto a rough-looking man skulking in the shadows of a nearby shop. A chill tickled my shoulders as our eyes met. It was strange that he seemed the only person interested in our stroll across the square. Tracking us as we passed, he shoved a pipe into his mouth, which resided between two clumps of shaggy gray whiskers.

I tightened my hold on Mr. Sinclair's arm. In a strange way I was glad to know he could handle a pistol. Only, as I glanced up, my escort seemed miles away, his jaw clenched, his gaze fixed on the road ahead. It was then I remembered he had spoken of his own business in town. I wondered just what sort of business he meant.

At length he touched my hand. "I'll see you to Pasley's and then, if it meets with your approval, I must leave you in their capable hands." He gave a short laugh. "I'm sure you don't need me looking over your shoulder while you shop for the things you need."

So I would be left alone to deliver the letter. "You're quite right. I am more than able to take care of myself."

He stole a quick glance. "I'm sure you are."

I don't think he meant the words to be patronizing, but by the look in his eyes, we were both probably thinking the same thing. He thought me reckless and adventurous, but he was wrong. I took one more peek at the man in shadows, but he had disappeared.

Pasley's and Co. resided in an active, squarish building set apart from the other rows of shops. Mr. Sinclair led me up the stone steps to the door before giving me a gracious but disinterested nod. Whatever it was he meant to do in town, he was obviously anxious to get on with it.

"I'll find you at the market in the square in three quarters of an hour. Will that do?"

"Thank you. Yes, that will be fine." I tightened my bonnet ribbons and smoothed my skirt. It was time I met this Mrs. Barineau.

Shelves of folded fabrics and drapes lined the shop's wall as people milled about the many floor displays. Down the central aisle I passed tables of ladies' gloves, parasols, and handkerchiefs.

A young man at the reticule display directed me to the rear corner — the milliner's domain. I paused beside a few fetching chip bonnets and ribbons before finding a middle-aged woman hunched over a counter at the back, leafing through a large book.

She glanced up as I approached and adjusted her spectacles. "Good morning." Her voice was calm and cool with the delightful hint of a French accent. Yet I was surprised by her harrowing expression.

"Yes, um, good morning. I am in search of a Mrs. Barineau."

She lowered her chin. "I am Mrs. Barineau."

I'm not sure if I was glad or disappointed by the revelation. "I have come from Croft Towers on behalf of Mrs. Chalcroft."

Her nose twitched. "Am I to be put off again?" Then something flashed in her eyes, and I followed her glare to a few other shoppers who had entered the store, but no one was near the milliner's counter.

She lowered her voice. "He won't like it."

I blinked for a second, uncertain how to proceed, then retrieved the letter from my reticule and slid it across the counter. "Mrs. Chalcroft sent this."

The milliner stared at the folded paper a moment before snatching it up. "This better be what I hope it is."

I had no idea what she hoped for, so I cleared my throat. "Mrs. Chalcroft did not discuss any particulars with me, but I believe it to be the instructions for the hat she purchased." I gave her an encouraging smile. I'd learned long ago a touch of kindness went a long way.

"Hmm."

In the time it took for her to look over the

paper, a young woman had crossed to this part of the store, perusing the available ribbons no doubt. Mrs. Barineau glanced up, seemingly startled by the lady's presence. She thrust the note beneath the counter in one swoop, then affected a pensive smile. "Miss, if you will step with me into the back room, we can discuss the details in private."

Details? Mrs. Chalcroft had said nothing to me about the hat. What on earth would I have to say about it? I had little choice but to follow the woman wherever she wished to go, as I was determined to properly finish my first task in my new position.

Mrs. Barineau motioned me through a narrow door behind the counter. It led to a workroom of sorts, and she paced the space with a newfound frantic energy. She circled me then stopped, pulling the door closed before coming to rest on a stool behind a wide table. She thrust a basket of ribbons out of the way of her elbows, then turned to appraise me.

A single candle kept the room in a sort of dim haze, highlighting the woman's sharp features, angular shoulders, and drooping nose. With no windows I thought the room a poor working space, but reams of cloth, straw bonnets, and hats were strewn across a workbench on one side and rows of narrow shelving on the other.

A heavy dampness hovered on the air, reminding me more of a cave than I would have liked. "Perhaps it would be best for me to give Mrs. Chalcroft a message. I'm really not privy to her wishes regarding the bonnet."

Mrs. Barineau spread out her worn hands on the counter as if laying out a piece of cloth. "Sick or not, she put me in a bind, you see. It's not so simple this time." She squeezed the knuckle on her first finger, her skin blanching white. "He already came yesterday. And he was in a taking, I'll tell you." She held up the note. "But I'll get it to him somehow. I promise you that. You tell her not to be late again or we're done. She must be on time every time or . . . Well . . . you just tell her that."

"I-I will." I had no idea what she meant, but I supposed Mrs. Chalcroft would. All I could deduce was that another man was involved. With a hat trimming? I turned slowly, almost unwillingly. But I had nothing further to say to the woman, and really, the whole affair was none of my concern. The note had been delivered — my task was complete.

I exited the shop for the cold sunshine of the square, relieved to be away from the stifling room and out of the presence of the strange milliner. The town square was as busy as ever. A man on a horse trotted by, the sweet scent of hay trailing behind him. A bell echoed from somewhere around the corner.

"Miss Delafield!"

Startled, I looked up to see the woman from the mail coach lumbering across the street.

" 'Pon my soul," she called out. "It's the young lady from the carriage and looking quite smart today, you are."

I forced a smile. "Why, good day."

The woman plodded over with a bit more enthusiasm than I would have guessed, considering how we'd parted. "You remember me — Mrs. Plume — don't you? So you have recovered, I see."

I don't think the woman had ever bothered to tell me her name. "Yes. Very well. Thank you, Mrs. Plume."

"And settled in at the Towers . . . with Mrs. Chalcroft."

So it was gossip she wanted. Well, I'd none to spread — not to her at least. "Yes. Quite settled. The family has been very kind. I've only come into town to shop, so if you will —"

"Have you? Well, that is very good to hear.

Very good to hear." She narrowed the space between us. "We were worried sick about you. Thompkins and me."

Thompkins. I'd nearly forgotten all about seeing her at the house the previous day. I lifted an eyebrow. Could it have been Mrs. Plume's concern for me that brought her maid to the Towers? I doubted it.

"If I've said it once, I've said it a thousand times how concerned I was for your welfare since you left so suddenly that day — particularly after *the incident*." She touched her chest. "Oh. What a time I've had."

I kindly refrained from mentioning the fact that she had pawed her way from the mail coach to secure her own comforts without looking back for me. "Well, it has —"

"And the dragoons — crawling all over the town like ants. I never thought I'd live to see such a thing. It is as if they expect France to invade any day now." She dabbed her nose with her handkerchief, then paused. "Have you happened to run into any?"

"Well, yes. I did see a couple of officers that day at the Boar's Head Inn, but I didn't stay long enough to learn much."

"As well you did not, I'll tell you. The proprietor of the inn was beside himself.

111

Such talk of spies in the dining hall. If the inn had only had a private room, I could have escaped such vulgarity, but alas, Thompkins and I had to deal with the worst of it. 'Pon rep, I could barely eat my food."

Normally I would find such a thing amusing, but something Mrs. Plume had said caught my attention. I leaned forward. "Spies, you say?"

"Oh, my dear. So you haven't heard. Our little problem with the highwaymen is nothing compared to our Prince Regent. You see, he sent the dragoons down here personally to flush out the traitors. I've heard it was something of an assassination plot." Finishing her declaration with the flap of her fan, she moaned as if she might faint.

I paid no attention to the hartshorn she whiffed beneath her nose.

"Traitors? Here in Reedwick?"

"That, my dear, is the worst part. They say all signs point to one of our own. Of course, my estate is in Adisham, so I'll not be lumped in with such horrid people, but my brother, John —"

"And you heard this from the dragoons?"

"Of course not. Don't be ridiculous. I had the whole of it from the Blunt sisters and my dear Robert. He's a parson hereabouts. You remember? I spoke of him that day on the mail coach."

I nodded, glad I wouldn't have to listen to all that again.

"And then with Thompkins's sudden disappearance —"

My gaze shot to her face. "Thompkins?"

"Have you not heard? My faithful maid — missing. Vanished without a trace yesterday afternoon. Left all her belongings behind. What this world is coming to I cannot know. My Robert is certain she's run away. But I cannot credit such an assumption. How could she leave the hat I gave her last Christmas?"

"Gone," I whispered almost to myself, imagining her strained face in the garden. "But . . ."

Mrs. Plume narrowed her eyes. "Do you know something, child? If so, you must speak up at once. She left me in quite a fix, I'll tell you."

"I saw her at the Towers only yesterday." I touched my cheek. "At least, I think I did. There was a woman out the window, but I did not —"

"You must be mistaken. Thompkins knew no one at Croft Towers. She would never go there. And she would certainly not do so without her coat."

"Perhaps."

"Faith, but I am beside myself with worry. What if her sudden disappearance has something to do with the dreadful dragoons and the traitors? They say it could be anyone, you know, and I believe it is my duty as a British citizen to keep my eyes and ears open. 'Pon my word, if anyone can find a liar and a cheat, it's me."

"Good morning, ladies." I turned just as Mr. Sinclair removed his hat. "A pleasant day for a stroll."

Calm and cool, he took Mrs. Plume's hand into his, laying a kiss on her glove all the while slipping me a wink. So my highwayman turned gentleman recognized one of his other victims.

Mrs. Plume's bosom heaved with each breath. "So glad to see you again, kind sir. And how nice of you to stop."

"I would never miss an opportunity to do so, I assure you. I've just been to the post office and am happy to report the mail has arrived."

"Ah . . . thank you, Mr. Sinclair. You didn't forget the purpose of my daily walks. Such fine condescension." She tapped his arm with her fan. "But I had hoped to find word of my missing maid."

Mr. Sinclair's brows drew in. "Still no clue as to her disappearance?"

Mrs. Plume pursed her lips. "I suppose if Thompkins wished to run away with a blacksmith or some other preposterous young man, it's none of my affair. She can be replaced easily enough." She took a dramatic breath. "I, however, shall be forced to return to London soon to find a replacement if nothing turns up. But what of you, Mr. Sinclair? What brings you to town?" She held out her hand. "No, wait. Let me see if I can guess."

She took a quick glance at the clouds as if they might provide her with the necessary insight. "Ah, yes." Her fingers wiggled. "I remember now. You were waiting for a letter from Lord Stanton. Have you finally received it?"

Hearing that name, I stifled a gasp.

Mr. Sinclair returned Mrs. Plume's smile with a half-hearted one of his own. "Unfortunately, I continue to wait. Mail from the West Indies can be quite slow. I imagine I shall hear word from him soon."

"Quite right. I expect it won't be too long now."

I studied the two of them, but it seemed I would learn nothing new about the man in the painting. The flapping of Mrs. Plume's fan began again. "Perhaps Thompkins has taken up with the wretched highwaymen.

Can you believe they still have not been caught and made to see justice? It is as if we live in a den of thieves."

I couldn't help but glance at Mr. Sinclair then. Surely he'd have little desire to continue that topic.

But I was wrong. He tilted his chin. "Only a matter of time. The dragoons are closing in."

"Yes. That is true. And I am grateful to you for finding my necklace, but what a beastly business it was. Of course, I am no better off, for it was Thompkins who had my emerald ring and now that has vanished with her. Am I to be forever plagued by liars and thieves?" She waved her fan once more in front of her face, but this time it reminded me of a young lady in her first London season; her other hand circled the pendant on her necklace. "Imagine you seeing my necklace for sale the very day I had described it to you. Thank goodness there are some honest souls still left in this world."

It took all my willpower to keep my mouth from gaping open.

Mr. Sinclair avoided my gaze. "Quite right. Now, Mrs. Plume, if you would excuse us, Miss Delafield and I must be on our way."

I could feel her estimation of me rising

with such a distinguished gentleman offering me his arm. How quickly she would change her tune if she knew the truth.

We took our leave, and I allowed Mr. Sinclair to direct me down the street. An empty feeling settled in my chest. Thompkins was missing. No matter what Mrs. Plume implied, I'd seen her at the Towers yesterday. There was no mistaking that.

And Mr. Sinclair? I took a deep breath. What was his role in all this? The truth that I was aiding and abetting a fugitive didn't sit well.

8

Mr. Sinclair declared we must eat before he escorted me from town. I was quickly learning that whatever Mr. Sinclair wanted, Mr. Sinclair got. He didn't look famished, as he claimed, but I imagine he had my comfort in mind when he suggested it. Any other time I would have protested, but I had to admit, he was right — I was starving. Either way, he led me to the Rose Inn on the other side of the square, suggesting that John would be pleased enough to wait for us in the taproom.

The galleried inn had a smiling look to it, fronted by a red door and two shuttered windows with a stone walkway rounding the front. The wooden sign above the door tipped and squeaked in the breeze.

We paused a moment in the front room where a servant scattered to find us the best seat. I eyed Mr. Sinclair, whose very presence seemed to ensure us the finest of everything. How different from the last time I'd stopped at an inn.

This place was managed by a Mr. Cunning and his plump daughter, Rose, who had obviously inspired the name. She seemed a hardworking girl with a kind look about her, but I saw tiredness in her eyes. Words were nonexistent with her, which presented an uncomfortable void at the table, leaving Mr. Sinclair and me to an awkward pattern of glancing up at each other every now and then.

A bite to eat and a lemonade in the parlor of the inn — certainly — but when I'd agreed to come, I hadn't imagined myself alone in a large room with Mr. Sinclair's indeterminate gaze. A healthy fire snapped at my back as the little window by the table framed a chilly town square. All things considered, it was good of him to allow me to rest my legs and give my toes a chance to thaw. If only my mind weren't elsewhere.

The scent of onions followed Rose to the table, where she plopped down two plates and wiped her hands on her apron. "Will there be anything else you need, sir?"

Mr. Sinclair shook his head. "No. Thank you." He cast me a shrewd glance before forking into his plate of cold roast beef.

I took a quick sip of my soup, scalding my

tongue, then poked at a pile of hard potatoes.

Mr. Sinclair raised his eyebrows. "A ghastly dinner, is it not?"

I pressed my lips together and nodded. "You better not let Rose hear you."

"I wouldn't dream of it." He glanced at the door then smiled, leaning forward. "Though I'm afraid it shall take quite a bit of chewing to get this lump of meat down my throat."

"Such a thing to say in the presence of a lady."

I couldn't help but wince. Who was I to speak so to a gentleman? An orphan girl, hired as a companion under the strangest of circumstances. And Mr. Sinclair? I cast a glance at his face. What could his story be? The staff at the inn seemed to think him the king of England. And who wouldn't when he so often displayed such an arrogant countenance?

I swallowed another spoonful of thin soup. I had come here for answers, so I'd best get on with it. "What do you make of Mrs. Plume's maid's disappearance?"

He shrugged his shoulders. "Not much really. The poor thing probably did run away. Her situation could not have been pleasant." A slight smile creased the corners of his lips. "Although you would think Mrs. Plume would be a bit more accommodating, considering she was once a housekeeper. Or so I heard."

"Really? A housekeeper?"

"Apparently she met and married a wealthy cit a few years back and enjoys playing the grand lady a bit too much."

"Ah." I eased the spoon back into the bowl. "But do you not think it remarkable that her maid left her protection without even her coat or the rest of her belongings?"

"I suppose it does sound odd." He took a long drink before meeting my gaze. "Do you imagine something more sinister at play?"

My mouth felt dry. What was I suggesting? "I don't suppose so. It was just that I . . ." I'd meant to tell him about seeing Thompkins at the Towers, but my tongue fixed in place, the danger of my position creeping once again into my mind. Mr. Sinclair was one of the highwaymen after all. The very ones — I took a quick bite of my stiff roll — who might be relieved to learn Thompkins had gone missing. Particularly if she had recognized one of them. My stomach tensed.

He tilted his chin. "You were saying?" A light smile played on his lips, brightening his eyes.

"I . . ." I managed to shake my head. Goodness, I was allowing my imagination full rein. If I had been in Thompkins's situation, I might very well have run off too. Besides, I had more pressing concerns to discuss, considering I might not be alone with Mr. Sinclair again — and he could do little to me at a public inn. I decided to risk it. "I, um, heard Mrs. Plume mention Lord Stanton in our conversation in the square. Do you know him?"

Mr. Sinclair's fork froze in midair. "Do I know him?"

"Right. Obviously you do if you are waiting for his letter. Only, I saw a painting of him at the Towers, and it made me curious as to who he is and, I don't know . . . other things. Like how he is related to the family." I could hear myself rambling and it made me nervous, which in turn caused me to ramble all the more. "Mr. Cantrell said he'd been married to Mrs. Chalcroft's daughter, only I suppose since her death, well, Miss Ellis said he was quite the bachelor in London. She seemed to have a bit of a fancy for him, but that's not what I meant to ask, only, I . . ."

Mr. Sinclair waited for me to find some semblance of a stopping point. He kept his face impassive, but I noticed the merest bend to his right eyebrow. His voice took on the placating tone I'd heard him use with Miss Ellis. "Miss Delafield, you did say you lived in London, did you not? And your family? I only ask because I have a hard time believing you ignorant of my situation."

"Your situation?" I paused for a moment, wondering where this could possibly be leading. "I am sorry. I do suppose I spoke out of turn. I haven't any family; I . . ." I'd forgotten what I was saying. Heavens, I'd admitted to being an orphan of indeterminate birth numerous times before. Why did my stomach roll at the thought now?

He leaned back in his chair, that gaze of his never leaving my face. "Perhaps I am the one who spoke out of turn." He crossed his arms. "I was laboring under the impression you were an educated lady of good standing, possibly come down in the world as to need a position with my godmother."

No wonder he had been so kind as to escort me to town and to pledge to find me a position as a governess. How wrong he had been. I shrugged my shoulders. "I am none of those things. I have no standing in society, no parents. I was fortunate to receive a surprising charity from a stranger to attend a school in London usually reserved for the upper class. I am sorry that it gave you the wrong impression."

So there. I had shocked him. Of course, I'd left out the part of my wonderful teacher whom I loved like a mother and all my happy years with the other girls. My past was not something I was ashamed of. My future, well, that might be a different story.

Slowly, he leaned forward. "Miss Delafield, please accept my apology for my insensitive comments. It was never my intention to cause you discomfort, which I fear has happened on more than one occasion." A slight smile emerged. "I haven't forgotten what I owe you. Nor will I." He didn't move. "Perhaps it would help if I told you my own sad story."

I blinked and bit my lip. Naturally, that was just what I was eager to know, but I politely shook my head. "Please, Mr. Sinclair, don't feel the need —"

He held up his hand, halting my words. "If I may . . ." He took a large sip from his glass. "You sit across from the second child of eight of the late Charles and Mary Sinclair, the only son, and somehow, the heir apparent to my distant cousin, the infamous Lord Stanton. His title, estates, and living are entailed upon the male line — in effect, me."

I nearly spit out my lemonade. "So you're

to be the next earl. Dreadful indeed." No wonder Mrs. Plume had hung on his every word. She probably had a daughter or niece she hoped to pawn off on him at some local assembly.

"It is dreadful — to a man who doesn't wish for a meaningless title or encumbered estates."

"Pardon me if I find that hard to believe."

He ran his finger along the edge of his glass. "I suppose it is in a way. But let me assure you, my expectations are abysmal. I shall inherit nothing but debt. And as long as Lord Stanton lives, I am but a pawn for the devil to play with. Now, does that sound more appealing to you?"

"But with the title, surely you can marry well and remedy such a turn of luck."

"A happy union indeed." He held up his glass as if in a toast. "Call me a romantic, but I'd hoped for more."

I thought of the figure he posed galloping the countryside as a highwayman. Some hapless girl would be all atwitter at the thought of marrying such a man. But not me. I'd seen the other side of his pistol and his lies. Such a man would never be applauded by me.

It seemed he'd misinterpreted my silence, because he pinched the bridge of his nose like Mrs. Smith did when the young children had gotten out of hand. "My wretched cousin, if I dare call him that, usually corresponds quite regularly from wherever he is. But his letter, as well as my pittance of an allowance, is . . ." He paused. "Overdue. Mrs. Chalcroft has been kind to assist me with funds from time to time, as well as allowing me to stay when needed at Croft Towers to avoid rent on a room in London. She knows I have three sisters still at home and wholly dependent on me, but it cannot go on much longer."

I took a deep breath. Perhaps unknowingly Mr. Sinclair had revealed a possible motive for the robbery. And could I blame him? Many would do far more to feed their family.

The theory felt right as I considered him from across the table. He was not as I had first thought — a rogue or a cad. Granted, if it was money he needed, he wouldn't have returned the necklace, would he?

I cleared my throat. "And Lord Stanton has nothing to say to you accepting charity from Mrs. Chalcroft?"

He laughed. "I'm sure he would if he knew of it, but he'll not give me a farthing. Naturally, there's still time for him to father a child and relieve me of such a delightful title."

"And what then? You'd have no expectations. Believe me, being homeless in this world is not a thing to envy. Of course, it would be different for you. You're a man; you have options."

"I won't disagree that a woman's opportunities are limited. But mine at present are nonexistent."

"Yet you seem to ride the countryside at will."

He stiffened. "Only because I cannot serve my country abroad as I'd always intended to do. I'll have you know, I bought my colors to join the horse guards before Lord Stanton put a stop to it. As heir, I may do nothing of the sort. Lord Stanton would never approve. If my sisters have any chance of a suitable marriage, I must play by all his rules. Outrageous or not."

He seemed lost in thought before looking up. "You'll have to excuse my loose tongue, Miss Delafield. I had no intention of boring you with such details about my life — certainly not when we've only just met." He tapped his fingers on the table first one direction then the next. "In fact, I'm not sure why I said anything at all. Your time would be well spent to forget it."

He breathed out a quick laugh, a line forming across his forehead. Then he lowered his voice, a mischievous look settling across his face. "Perhaps over the course of the day, I've come to think of you as a partner, so to speak."

"A partner?"

"Or comrade, if you like." He shrugged his shoulders. "You do see that, now that you've agreed to keep my secret, you've thrown your lot in with us highwaymen." He grinned.

Loud voices sounded from somewhere beyond the parlor. Mr. Sinclair held my gaze as the door burst open and a group of soldiers plodded over to a nearby table. I hoped they couldn't hear the hammering in my chest or read the fright in my eyes.

Mr. Sinclair was right. I was one of them now — an accomplice. I'd traded my dignity for peace at the Towers. I bit the inside of my cheek. What else would I be forced to give up?

"Captain Rossiter." Mr. Sinclair's voice broke the muffled silence of my thoughts.

I looked up to see the officer I met the day I arrived in Plattsdale. He wore the same blue coat, but his expression was bleak. "Sinclair. So the Colonel was right. You've come back. I'd just informed him of

128

your return to London."

"I didn't know my whereabouts were a concern of the Colonel's. But it is no matter. Naturally, it was my intention to return to London as I told you that day on the road, but I received word Mrs. Chalcroft had taken a bad turn. I was forced to come back."

I watched Mr. Sinclair's lips move so easily, so smoothly, as he spoke to the officer. But could anything he say possibly be true? I looked for a telltale twitch of his right eyebrow, but Mr. Sinclair was far too well trained to betray even the hint of a lie.

The officer gave me a cursory glance before turning back to Mr. Sinclair. "Interesting. When did you arrive?"

"Two days ago. Miss Delafield here can attest to my whereabouts."

I felt a boot at my shin. "Yes." I nearly coughed out the word. "I-I met Mr. Sinclair in Mrs. Chalcroft's drawing room when I arrived."

The hooknose officer squinted then took a step back. "Very well, but you should know we'll be in the area for some time. It may become necessary to post patrols and search some of the houses."

Mr. Sinclair rose to his feet, dwarfing the officer. "I'm happy to hear we shall be so well protected at the Towers." He held out his hand to me. "But, if you will excuse us, Miss Delafield and I must be getting back."

Without thinking, I stood and allowed Mr. Sinclair to lead me from the room. Only I wished I hadn't glanced back — that I hadn't seen the look of suspicion on the captain's face.

When I returned to the Towers, I went at once to Mrs. Chalcroft's bedchamber. Surely getting the milliner's message off my mind would be the best medicine to calm my increasing anxiety.

The hall sat quiet for the early afternoon, none of the family or servants about. Just dark walls that seemed to breathe as I passed by. At Mrs. Chalcroft's door I paused for a moment to gather my thoughts. Dust covered my habit and a good portion of my hair had escaped down my neck. It was presumptuous of me not to change, but I knocked on her door nonetheless.

No answer.

I waited a moment then knocked a second time, a bit louder. The pounding echoed in my chest, and I shrank back. Had Mrs. Chalcroft fallen asleep early for her afternoon nap? I crept back a step, wishing I hadn't been so foolish, when I heard a sound from inside the room.

"Mrs. Chalcroft?"

Nothing but silence answered. I bit my lip. The bedchamber door looked to be made of mahogany, so I leaned forward to be sure there was no response. A faint, high-pitched squeal reached me, so soft I pressed my ear to the door to make it out.

An animal's cry? I knew at once I had to be mistaken, but a cry was the closest thing I could imagine the sound to be. Either way, I didn't like it. Not at all.

I tried the latch and the door clicked open, a puff of air wafting over me.

"Mrs. Chalcroft?"

Again, no answer, only the distant wail. Was something inside hurt? I had to be sure. I glanced behind me before pushing through the door, unconsciously closing it behind me. "Mrs. Chalcroft?"

A solitary ray of sunshine beamed through a small opening between the curtains and spread its long finger across the rug. I hunched my shoulders and tiptoed over to the bed, the quiet of the room pressing against my ears. The covers were strewn about but empty, though the room had a distinct feeling of movement. A faint breeze slid in through a crack in the window, joined by Mrs. Chalcroft's heavy rose scent.

I checked the dressing room and found it as tidy as I'd seen it before. Mrs. Chalcroft hadn't left her room since the first night I arrived. I wondered where she could have gone. All at once a strong gust of wind surged against the windowpane, and I heard the high-pitched howl, just like a cry. I'd discovered my hurt animal and took a breath of relief.

It had been the wind, nothing more. I turned to leave, eager to change out of my dirty riding habit, but paused. Was this not the perfect opportunity to look about the room? Mrs. Chalcroft might not leave her bedchamber again for some time.

I peeked into the wardrobe and through the odds and ends of her bedside table's drawers, unsure what it was I hunted. Someone in this house must know something of my past. Yet I found nothing remarkable. Not in her many drawers, nor on her escritoire.

Another loud burst of wind fought its way through the crack in the window, flinging a stack of papers from the fireplace mantel to the floor. Quickly, I tiptoed over the mess and closed the window before shuffling through the pages.

Above the fireplace hung two thick crimson drapes that came to rest on the mantel, a gold cord dangling at each side. Having found nothing of interest in the papers, I paused for a moment before I returned the stack to its resting place. This particular wall, beyond the drapes, was the same interior one that sided my room. So there could be no window . . .

I lifted the drape's corner with my index finger. Wood — a frame? The farther I drew back the curtain, the more a painting became visible until I could see the work of art in its entirety.

It was a woman, one I didn't know. She had golden hair and green eyes and was painted so well she appeared almost alive. I gasped. I'd seen many grim-faced paintings before, but this one was different. This one framed what no one wished to see — sadness and pain.

I took a step closer, rising up to my toes to get a better look in the dim light. The lady could be no more than five and twenty. She wore a beautiful gown of pink crape over satin, and a large gold ring graced her right hand. Could it be Mrs. Chalcroft as a young woman? Although I did see a resemblance, I was certain the lady in the picture was not my employer. She was exquisitely beautiful, and I found it hard to look away.

"I see you found Anne."

My breath caught and I spun to the door. Thank goodness it was only Miss Ellis, for I would have had a hard time explaining myself to anyone else.

She strolled over, stopping on the rug, and angled her chin. "Do you find Anne as lovely as everyone says she is?"

My voice escaped me, but I managed to whisper, "Yes."

"Yet Aunt Chalcroft keeps her hidden beneath those drapes."

I wondered why. "Can you tell me about her?"

"Anne was my late cousin — Lady Stanton. I didn't know her. She died several years before I was born. As a child I would sneak in here and stare at her likeness. What do you think of that horrid expression on her face? I always thought she wanted to tell me something, maybe about her death."

"She does look quite unpleasant. You would think Mrs. Chalcroft would have another painting of her daughter to remember her by."

"This is the only one I've ever seen. It matches the one of our ghost up in the tower room. You remember — her husband, Lord Stanton. I'm told they had them painted together a few months after they were married and sent the pair as a gift to

Mrs. Chalcroft for Christmas. I don't wonder at the earl being so uncomfortable in his painting with a wife like that."

I could only imagine what Mrs. Chalcroft must have thought when she received such a likeness of her daughter. I suppose the artist could have made a mistake. But something in Anne's eyes told me he knew what he was doing. I touched the corner of the frame. "Miss Ellis?"

Her answer came several seconds later. "Yes?" It seemed we were both entranced by what we saw before us.

"How did she die?"

"No one speaks of it. There are few servants still around from that time. All I know is that she ran off one night into a terrible storm. She later died of pneumonia. Mrs. Chalcroft had her buried alone on the eastern slope on the way to Reedwick."

Not at the church? "How sad . . ." I wanted to know more, to understand the feeling of gloom that permeated the walls of the Towers, but Miss Ellis had already lost interest, humming to herself as she straightened the coverlet on the bed.

I looked back at the painting. Lord Stanton again. His presence crawled all over the house, all over the town. Why would he write to me? I was sure Mrs. Chalcroft could apprise me of all the details of his marriage to her daughter, but I could never ask. I pulled the drapes back over Anne, hiding her sadness behind a soft sea of darkness. "Do you know where Mrs. Chalcroft is at present? She asked me to see her directly when I returned from town."

"The sun came out, so she's sitting by the large window in the chapel." Miss Ellis shrugged her shoulders, then flitted to the doorway, but paused. "You haven't noticed if Hodge brought the mail?"

I shook my head.

She frowned. "Oh, and I wouldn't mention anything about Anne to my aunt. It might, well . . . set her off."

9

I didn't find Mrs. Chalcroft in the chapel, as Miss Ellis had indicated, but in the sitting room on the first floor accompanied by the other members of the family. A lovely melody drifted from the room. I wasn't sure if she wished me to enter, so I lurked in the doorway like a mouse waiting for a bread crumb.

It was Mr. Cantrell who saw me first and motioned me inside. Miss Cantrell sat on the edge of the sofa opposite Mr. Roth, her gaze fixed on the pianoforte and Mr. Sinclair, who had his nose buried in some sheet music. He didn't look up as I crossed the room, nor did his composition falter.

I went straight to where Mrs. Chalcroft lay across the length of the settee near the fire, a heavy blanket hiding her thin frame. She smiled when she saw me and I thought I saw a bit of Anne in her eyes. She took my hand and pulled me down beside her. "Here you are, my dear girl. Was your trip to town prosperous?"

Though I doubted I could be heard over the pianoforte, I decided not to deliver the milliner's instructions in the crowded room. Instead, I let out a steady breath. "I gave her your letter; however, she did seem a bit put off. Of course, she assures me it will be completed as you wished."

The arthritic fingers once quiet on the blanket curled up into a stiff ball. "She said nothing else?"

I cast a quick glance around the room. Miss Cantrell must have grown tired of sitting and circled about us, seemingly lost in her own world. The music held Mr. Sinclair in a sort of trance, but Mr. Cantrell surprised me as he'd crossed the room to my side when I wasn't paying attention. I wasn't sure how much to say in company. "The milliner did have a message for you, but it's not important now. You seem tired. Is it not time for your afternoon nap?"

"Quite right, my gel. I'll have you read to me to put me to sleep. If Lucius would be so kind as to —"

Miss Ellis rushed into the room with a squeal, a paper flapping in her hand. "Elizabeth! It is just as we'd hoped. They're to have a country dance at the inn in Platts-dale."

In an instant, Miss Cantrell was at Miss Ellis's side and tore the paper from her hand. "In only a month." The closest thing to a smile I'd ever seen on Miss Cantrell's face rounded out her pale cheeks. "It is delightful. Surely most everyone in the area will be in attendance." She touched her forehead. "Lucius, I must have a gown made up at once."

Miss Ellis seconded the request and the room came alive. Mr. Cantrell denied the need for anyone to have a new gown, Mr. Roth asserted that a dance would be a welcome break from our tedious company, Miss Ellis declared herself ready to be the toast of the ball, and Miss Cantrell listed everyone present in the district who might be in attendance. They all seemed thrilled. All except me, of course, and curiously Mr. Sinclair, who looked at the display as if he thought it a bore.

Mr. Cantrell called out across the room. "We will need two carriages if we are all to go."

Mrs. Chalcroft leaned forward and patted my arm. "This will be just the thing for you, my dear."

I turned to face her. She couldn't be serious. I could feel the blood draining from my head. I blinked a few times then searched her face. Had she just said what I thought she had? The companion? To attend the family to an assembly?

Mrs. Chalcroft gave me a wry smile. "It will do you good to get out of the house."

Out of the house? I'd only just arrived. "Please, Mrs. Chalcroft. I would rather stay here with you — to keep you company and watch over you while the family is away."

"Fiddlesticks. I wish I could go myself, but I can't. You will be my eyes and ears, child. I will expect to know everything. It's part of your position, you see."

My voice faltered. "I-I beg of you not to ask me to do this. Certainly Miss Ellis could —"

Mrs. Chalcroft clicked her tongue against her teeth. "Don't be absurd. I understand your qualms, but I don't care a fig for such things." She motioned me closer. "I will have a small package that needs to be delivered to a gentleman I know will be there. I was at a loss as to how I should get it to him. This is the perfect opportunity."

My eyes grew wide. "But, Mrs. Chalcroft, I-I've never . . . danced."

She pulled back. "That's silly. Didn't they teach you anything in that school of yours?"

"Well, they did, only I haven't practiced in a long time and never in company."

"Curtis," Mrs. Chalcroft called out across the room. "Come here at once."

Only a woman of her age and status could get away with such behavior, and without fail, he plodded over to the settee, resting his arm on the fireplace mantel.

He too had changed clothes since our outing to town, and I had to admit, the sleek, dark-green coat became him. He grasped the iron poker from beside the fender and jabbed it into a log. Sparks burst like fireworks in the grate, then he turned to face the both of us. "I'm at your service, of course. What is it you would have me do now?"

He added a tight smile, but the barb hit home. We both knew he would be required to do Mrs. Chalcroft's bidding, whatever it was — for the money, for his sisters — for *me*. My stomach clenched.

"Miss Delafield tells me she hasn't danced in some time and may need a refresher course if she is not to embarrass us at the assembly."

Oh dear. I wanted to sink into the floor.

He coughed out a laugh. "Whatever made you think of me to play dancing master?"

She poked him with her cane. "You've two

strong arms, and I've yet to see you step on a girl's foot. Why not, pray tell?"

"Because you know very well how I detest it."

My head felt dizzy. Must I endure such embarrassment? He obviously loathed dancing, and helping me was likely second on the list. "Perhaps this is not such a good idea. I . . ."

Both Mr. Sinclair and Mrs. Chalcroft turned to face me as if they were surprised I had an opinion on the subject. Mrs. Chalcroft held up her hand to stave off any more from me. "You may be right, my dear. Perhaps I wasn't thinking clearly."

I breathed a sigh of relief, glad she could be made to see reason.

"Lucius will do much better."

I kept quiet all through supper, intending to return to my room when the gentlemen took their port. But Miss Ellis grasped my arm first thing, leading me back into that dreadful drawing room, chattering all the way.

"Well, you've been in here before, but you haven't told me what you think of the room. I call it *sale blanche,* the White Room. Isn't it awful? Not a stitch of color. If I were to own this house it would look quite different, I assure you." She pursed her lips. "It's horrid if you ask me."

Miss Cantrell clicked her tongue and pushed by me. "Hush. Mrs. Chalcroft isn't far behind us. You'll only make her cross."

Supported by Dawkins, my employer staggered into the drawing room, looking tired, but keen as ever.

Miss Cantrell motioned her forward. "Aunt, allow me to help you to a seat near the fire." She took Mrs. Chalcroft's free arm, casting an irritated glance at me. "And you. The screen now, if you please."

"Nonsense, girl. I can find my own way. Do not put yourself out." Mrs. Chalcroft freed herself of Miss Cantrell's grasp and edged down onto a nearby chair. "This will do well enough. All this fuss. 'Pon my word, I don't have the stomach for it tonight." She tapped her cane on the floor. "And as for you, Dawkins. That will be all for now. I have Miss Delafield here should I decide I need anything."

The room seemed to take in a collective breath, but I might have imagined such a thing.

Dawkins paused for a moment then retreated without a word, but I felt the chill of her gaze as she passed by me. Nervous, I slipped into a small chair at the back of the room. The perfect spot for a companion — out of the way and, most importantly, out of the conversation.

The other two ladies inched over to the brocade sofa at Mrs. Chalcroft's side, where Miss Ellis took no time before flicking open a magazine, her fingers shuffling through the pages as if she'd seen the pictures a hundred times, while Miss Cantrell stabbed at her needlepoint.

The draft from the nearby window fought its way into the room, and I pulled my shawl tight across my shoulders. Outside, a turbulent night wind tossed a tree branch against the windowpane. A plump orange cat tiptoed across the low interior sill and came to rest at my feet. I reached to pet his head just as Miss Cantrell broke the silence. "I do wish Mr. Sinclair would return. I —"

Mrs. Chalcroft glanced up. "Return?"

"He left quite mysteriously after supper and told us nothing of his plans. Didn't he, Miss Ellis?"

"Yes. It is as if he means to vex us on purpose. Here one minute, gone the next."

Mrs. Chalcroft laughed. "Serves you right. The both of you. Curtis's whereabouts are none of your concern."

I lifted an eyebrow, taking one more furtive glance at the empty lawn.

Miss Ellis pushed her magazine aside. "I suppose he went back into Reedwick. I heard Parson Blakely plans to do some work on the church. He spends a good deal of time with the man, doing all kinds of odd jobs, whatever is asked of him."

Mrs. Chalcroft wrinkled her nose. "Humph. Well, I hope you are wrong. He's done enough for that ungrateful man. It's been less than a fortnight since he started all those tongues wagging the last time. Probably another wretched wall. You remember the one he built when none of the village people showed up to help. Ridiculous to hear he'd been out there working with his jacket off, building what apparently none of them wanted or needed. Mark my words. They'll use him till he's spent."

Mr. Sinclair — helping the villagers? It didn't fit my ever-changing impression of the man, but perhaps there was more to Mr. Sinclair than I had thought.

Unfortunately, Miss Cantrell had been watching me and my face must have betrayed my surprise. "And what do you think of our Mr. Sinclair, Miss Delafield?"

"Well . . ." I paused. "Wherever he is, I hope he is inside, for it looks to be raining buckets again."

Miss Ellis stood and crossed the room,

flinging the drapes wide. "Oh dear, you are right." Water droplets littered the window. "And quite breezy. Do you think it a storm?"

Mrs. Chalcroft roused herself from the verge of sleep and called out across the room, "Quiet. Be still."

We all froze before slowly turning to face her.

"There . . . there it is again." Her eyes grew wide and her hand crept to her mouth. "A baby's cry."

Miss Cantrell rose to her feet, mumbling beneath her breath. "What did you say, Aunt?" She smiled but shot Miss Ellis a worried look.

Mrs. Chalcroft raised her voice. "A baby. Screaming. Get Dawkins at once to attend to the child."

A cold feeling crept across my shoulders, and I slid the book I'd been pretending to read onto a side table, speaking more to Miss Ellis than anyone else. "I don't hear anything."

Miss Ellis raised her voice. "It's the storm, Aunt Chalcroft. As we've told you time and again, there's not a baby at the Towers."

"Don't lie to me, you unnatural child." Mrs. Chalcroft's hands, now desperate, jerked frantically from her ears to her hair, gripping and pulling. "Dawkins. Dawkins. Where is the baby?" She tried to stand but couldn't, nearly falling off the chair.

Miss Ellis headed for the door. "I'll get Lucius. She must have her medicine at once."

Miss Cantrell bit her lip. "But Mr. Sinclair said —"

"He's not here. He's never here when this happens."

"Perhaps it won't be as bad as last time."

At those words, Mrs. Chalcroft began rocking and babbling, her words incoherent. Miss Ellis raced out the door.

I edged across the rug but stopped cold at Miss Cantrell's piercing glare. "Can you not do something? Is this not why you were employed here?"

I took a quick breath. "What do you mean?"

"What else did my aunt want a companion for than to calm her down before she gets hysterical?" Miss Cantrell shook her hands in the air, backing away from the sofa. "My nerves can't handle the screaming. Last time it went on for hours and hours."

I turned to the sofa, my stomach in knots. I hadn't the least idea what to do, what to say. How did one calm such a person? My voice came out in a whisper. "Smelling salts?"

"They only make her angry."

Mrs. Chalcroft took no notice of me as I knelt at her side. That is, until I spoke. "Mrs. Chalcroft?"

A light sparked in her eyes and she almost smiled, her finger tracing the edge of my bracelet. "Anne."

I took her hand. "No. It's me, Miss Delafield. Your new companion. I believe it is time for you to return to bed."

She took a long, hard look at my face and sucked in a deep breath, answering my kindness with a terrible scream.

I pulled back, my ears ringing, sure I'd made things far worse. I felt a hand on my shoulder.

"Miss Delafield. Allow me."

It was Mr. Cantrell. His calm strength was just what I needed, and I melted into his arm as he led me over to a chair.

The next few moments passed in a blur as I learned why Mr. Sinclair did not like Mrs. Chalcroft to be given laudanum.

Mr. Cantrell was forced to hold her down while Mr. Roth wrenched open her mouth and Hodge assisted, pouring the medicine in between choked screams and vicious biting. Then the waiting began. I wondered how long it would be before the medicine took effect.

Twenty minutes passed by the time the screaming subsided, and I was the only one left in the room besides Mr. Cantrell. He lifted Mrs. Chalcroft's frail body into his arms, then paused a moment before leaving the room. "I'm sorry you had to witness that, Miss Delafield, but I daresay it won't be the last time."

He crossed the hallway and mounted the stairs until he was lost to view. Like a curtain had fallen, drowning out my hopes for the future, the room suddenly felt cold and empty. Rain beat at the window. Silence thrummed in my ears. I lowered my face into my hands. Why had I come here? How could I possibly hope to help?

10

It was the following day before I was able to deliver the message I'd received from the milliner. I felt a bit foolish having allowed time to slip by, but what else could I have done? There had been all those people in the drawing room, then the storm and Mrs. Chalcroft's . . . episode. Surely she would understand my silence.

I stood before my formidable employer in the middle of her bedchamber rug, a cold feeling at my core. Staring into the dim poster bed, it didn't take long to realize Mrs. Chalcroft had not fared well over the night. The incident in the drawing room had chiseled grooves down her face and, if possible, racked her slender frame more than I'd expected. She lay buried under her covers like a fragile piece of china, gaunt and weak. Those green eyes, however, were as keen as ever. "Speak up, child, or allow an old woman her time to rest."

I wiggled my toes in my half boots. "Yes, ma'am. I came to tell you the milliner had a message for you, and I —"

She struggled to sit up, coughing out for Dawkins to leave the room.

I never meant to relay the milliner's words in company, but I was beginning to fear I wouldn't be allowed any time alone with Mrs. Chalcroft. Now I wondered if I had made the right decision to speak up. But surely her lady's maid knew of the arrangements with the milliner.

With a heavy tread and a swish of her skirt, Dawkins brushed my shoulder as she stole from the room, put out as far as I could tell.

Mrs. Chalcroft didn't seem to notice or care and waited for the sound of the door latch before motioning me to a slat-back chair beside the bed. "Sit. Now."

I did so, folding my hands on my lap like a child in school.

"So." She cocked an eyebrow. "Mrs. Barineau had something to say to you? Why on earth did you not tell me yesterday? Well, it is no matter. Do so now."

I took a deep breath. "She indicated the man had already come and that you must be on time for your next order."

"But she took the letter anyway? You saw

her put it away?"

I nodded quickly, hoping to reassure her.

Her voice shook. "I see." She took a sip of water from a glass at her bedside. "Mrs. Barineau acted the victim then, eh?"

"Yes. It seems the man wasn't pleased to be inconvenienced. I'm not sure she had all the particulars about the bonnet; however, she did say he would see to it as planned."

"Hmm." Mrs. Chalcroft shook her head as she spoke. "One cannot be too careful with Mrs. Barineau." She spit out the woman's name as if it burned her tongue. "I'm not sure how far the wretch can be trusted." She met my gaze. "Or depended upon."

Trusted? For a hat? Since that late-night visit the day I arrived, I'd felt uneasy about the letters, but the more Mrs. Chalcroft spoke, the more I wished I understood the secrecy.

"Perhaps I should —"

"Never mind that." Her fingers were in a flurry. "Get me a quill and some paper. I wish to write a letter at once."

I hurried to the escritoire, fumbling through several drawers to gather the needed items. Upon my return to the bedside, Mrs. Chalcroft snatched them from my fingers, her hand quivering as she plunged the quill into the ink. In a wavering script, she wrote:

Dear Mr. Aberdeen,

Slowly, her chin tilted up, her glare leveled at me. "That will be all for now, Miss Delafield."

The following week passed with little fanfare compared to my first few days at the Towers. My mornings were spent walking the estate; my afternoons reading at Mrs. Chalcroft's bedside. The gentlemen of the house had found more pressing matters to attend to, urgent business calling Mr. Cantrell and Mr. Roth to London, while Mr. Sinclair simply vanished for a time.

Which is why late one afternoon when I hastened into the drawing room to fetch Mrs. Chalcroft's shawl, I shuffled back a step at what I found — Mr. Sinclair seated at the writing desk and Mr. Cantrell plunking away at the pianoforte. I'd heard the music in the hallway, of course, but I'd assumed his sister to be the performer.

The music ceased, Mr. Cantrell meeting my eyes over the music rack. "Why, Miss Delafield, you have come at the most auspicious moment." The men stood, Mr. Cantrell flicking a piece of lint from his coat sleeve. "Come over here at once. You are just the person we need to settle a little argument between Sinclair and me."

I hesitated at the door before advancing into the room. "Please, as you were."

Mr. Sinclair glanced down at his letter before casting an indifferent look at Mr. Cantrell. "I doubt Miss Delafield has time to play your insidious little games, Lucius."

"I —"

Mr. Cantrell motioned me forward, patting the available space on the bench beside him, a smile gracing his lips. "Pay Sinclair no mind. He is simply writing his sisters, and whenever he does so, it seems to dump the man into the worst of moods."

The wooden slat-back chair creaked as Mr. Sinclair returned to his task. "Don't be ridiculous. I take a great deal of pleasure in my letters to my sisters; however, I had hoped to have better news regarding the possibility of an upcoming season." He tossed the quill back onto the desk. "Yet here I sit, forced to find the right words to quell any hopes and dreams that might have arisen."

I crossed the rug to his side. "Does that mean you've still no word from Lord Stanton?"

Seemingly startled by my sudden nearness, he tugged the paper out of my view. "None, I'm afraid."

Mr. Cantrell motioned me again to the pianoforte, eyeing Mr. Sinclair for a brief moment. "There is little we can do to help Sin's sisters at present, isn't there? However, I am in great need of your very feminine assistance."

I tapped my fingers against my gown, wavering in my answer. "I cannot stay long. Mrs. Chalcroft is awaiting her shawl."

Leaning to the side, he found my hand and guided me onto the bench. "Nonsense. My aunt can wait but a few more minutes. We won't keep you long." He took care to adjust his seat on the bench. "Besides, you must settle the argument. We were discussing the romantic nature of music and its effect on the fairer sex. Who better to advise us than you?"

I raised my eyebrows. "I was unaware that you played."

He rustled out a quick scale. "Sin and I both do, which brings us to our present difficulty. Do you find that such a talent gives a gentleman the advantage?" He winked. "Moreover, do you fancy Handel or Mozart?"

Warmth filled my cheeks. "I'm not certain."

He shuffled the music on the rack. "Then allow me to enlighten you. Perhaps then you will be able to settle our little disagreement."

Mr. Sinclair stood, shoving the chair beneath the desk. "There was no argument, simply Lucius rambling on about music while I chose to ignore him. I'm afraid I have far more pressing matters to attend to. Good day, Miss Delafield." Straightening his jacket, he nodded and paced from the room, leaving Mr. Cantrell and me staring at the open door.

Silence reigned until Mr. Cantrell's fingers found the keys and Mozart's Fantasia in D Minor materialized. "Bristly, isn't he?"

I shrugged. "I suppose he's distracted by concern for his family."

Mr. Cantrell nudged my arm, turning his attention to the pianoforte and the music. "Perhaps."

Captured by Mozart's tender melody, I listened motionless as the song swelled to a crescendo, the notes and rhythms winding their way through my veins. Mr. Cantrell was right. Music did invoke particular feelings, especially when played by a master. Involuntarily, my thoughts raced back to how Mr. Cantrell had looked at me that day in the garden and how close he sat beside me now, his very presence tickling my nerves.

He didn't glance up from the music as he spoke. "There is much I wish to know about you, Miss Delafield."

"Oh?"

"Don't sound so surprised or so insipid. You've not been missish with me before." He nudged my arm. "Tell me, have you family hereabouts?"

The warmth that had gathered in my chest turned cold. "Um, no." My shoulders sank. "I am but an orphan who is regrettably unaware of the identity of her parents."

His mouth slipped into a smile, and he edged a bit closer on the bench, feigning a hard-to-reach key. "Yet you are quite well-spoken and educated?"

"I was fortunate to attend a very fine school in London, but . . ." Twice I'd had to recount my embarrassing past. It wasn't getting any easier.

At the same moment, Mr. Cantrell's finger found a wrong key, and he drew his hands into his lap, letting out a breathy laugh. "I daresay I cannot play with perfect accuracy if you will not turn the pages, and then how will you be able to determine how enchanting each composer is? Or how alluring you find the performer?"

I rushed a breath, pushing to my feet. "I am sorry. I don't seem to be able to follow the notes at present." I touched my forehead, casting a quick glance at the door as I backed away. The last thing I wanted was for Mr. Cantrell to detect the feelings churning within my chest or further any ill-advised intimacy. "If you will excuse me, Mrs. Chalcroft is likely missing me by now." I grasped the shawl from the sofa and rushed from the room, unable to spare a look back.

Hurrying into Mrs. Chalcroft's bedchamber, I wrapped the shawl around her slim shoulders, my mind still arrested by the encounter in the drawing room. Surely Mr. Cantrell was simply having a bit of fun. I only hoped Mrs. Chalcroft would not regard my marked distraction.

"Thank you, my dear." She didn't look up. "I must finish with my knitting before I can let you read to me today. I trust you've a book or something to keep you entertained."

I grimaced as I scanned the room, brightening at a thought. "I do need to pen a letter to Mrs. Smith and a few others at the school. Would you mind if I sat at the escritoire and did so?"

"Not at all, child. That is just what I mean." She shook out her needles and yarn. "My hands ache so frequently I prefer to finish my knitting when I am able to do so."

I could feel her gaze on my back as I settled into the chair and procured a paper and quill. Her voice was a bit dry as she spoke, her tone on edge. "I suppose my friend must be vastly curious about your new life here." She mumbled something to herself. "And I find myself wondering just what is it you intend to tell her about all of us. Particularly about my younger sister's silly grandchildren."

I squeezed my eyes shut and took a calming breath. "That you have all been most accommodating and that I am quite pleased I applied for the position."

"What a silver tongue you have. I only wish I knew if you meant it."

"And why would I not?"

"Yes, why not?" She lowered her voice. "I wonder." I could hear the knitting needles clicking as she continued the work on her lap. "Pay me no heed. It is no matter, no matter at all if you are not happy here. I could just as easily find another companion if the situation presented itself."

"I suppose you could; however" — I scooted my chair about so I could see her face — "I've taken a fancy to this drafty old house, and do you know? I believe you like me."

"Stuff and nonsense." She hid a smile. "I daresay one young lady is as good as the next."

"Possibly, but only yesterday you asked me to stay while you had your dinner, and we had a good laugh then, did we not?"

Mrs. Chalcroft chuckled behind her hand, shaking her slender form. "My dear gel, when you compared Mr. Roth to a turkey, I could not help myself."

I returned a laugh. "It was a bit indelicate, I admit. However, he does allow one to lead him around so." I turned my attention to my letter. "Perhaps I shall tell Mrs. Smith about him."

The bed gave a loud creak. "Don't you dare expose me to gossip."

I shot her a smile. "As you wish."

Several minutes passed as I detailed my arrival and how pleased I was to have come to the Towers before my mind turned to my own difficulties. I laid the quill down for a moment, resting my arm over the back of the chair. I'd thought to remain silent, allowing Mrs. Chalcroft to direct any conversation, but I found myself speaking up instead. "If I may be so bold to ask, would you mind telling me how you met Mrs. Smith?"

Mrs. Chalcroft drew her knitting close to her chest. "We've known each other many years, child. I suppose we met while we were both still in the schoolroom. Her father was steward at the Towers, you see. But it was only later that we formed a lasting connection."

I bit my lip. "Did she — well, when she reached out to you about the position, did she happen to mention anything about my parentage?"

A sudden coughing fit drove Mrs. Chalcroft to reach for a sip of water, and I waited patiently while she regained control.

She set the cup back on the table, her movements indolent. "Pray, why do you ask, child?"

I shrugged my shoulders. "Curiosity, I suppose."

She rested her head back on the pillow, her lips pressed tight. "Deborah Smith merely relayed that you were respectable and what a good student you had proved to be. She felt it time for you to see more of the world."

"It is true. I have seen little beyond

London, and there is much I yearn to see and do . . . and learn."

Mrs. Chalcroft smoothed her hair off her forehead, then gathered the eiderdown beneath her chin. "So you wish to roam the world, do you? Well, such a thought makes my old bones a bit tired. In fact, I believe I've changed my mind and won't have you read to me today. I should rather take my nap."

I hesitated before responding. "Indeed. Till tomorrow then." Slowly, I grasped the letter I'd begun from the escritoire and paced to the door, turning back at the last second to take my leave, hopeful I might ask one more question. But Mrs. Chalcroft had already twisted down into the covers, her eyes hard on the shadows lingering in the corner of the room. Startled by her stark gaze, I pressed my lips together and slipped out the door in silence, swallowing my questions for another day.

11

I found Anne's grave on a blustery morning a week later, on a day I should have remained firmly within doors. Winter had rolled in from the north, and the temperature plummeted overnight, leaving the landscape a formidable companion for my walk. It was all I could do to keep my hands warm within my muff, but I needed to walk and think.

As I plodded across the lawns, the wretched dance entered my mind. Thankfully, I'd not been pressed about it again, even though I knew I would have little choice whether I was to go or not. I also recognized I might as well accept the lessons Mrs. Chalcroft thought necessary, but I hesitated to do so.

Lucius Cantrell had been kind — too kind really. I was so far beneath him in rank and fortune I found it hard to explain his partiality, which only seemed to grow the more I saw him. He was always the first to speak to me, the first to rush to my side after dinner, anticipating all I might need — quite frankly, the way a suitor might do.

I could tell it drove his sister mad. And could I blame her? What a horrid misalliance he would make if he were indeed serious, which I doubted very much. Yet part of me wondered what it would feel like to touch his hand again, to have him watch me turn the figures of the dance.

Near the back hedgerow, I angled east along the main road to Reedwick. A gaggle of houses was visible on the horizon and brought Thompkins's plight to mind. I hadn't seen her again or learned anything more about her disappearance, although questions about it never strayed far from my mind. Who had she been meeting out there in the garden? And where had she gone? With no one to trust, I had little hope of solving the mystery.

I crossed the east rise, turning my back to the Towers and plunging into the trees, as I did often on my walks of late, particularly when I needed to be alone. I wish I could say those times were few, but between Mr. Cantrell's attentions, Miss Ellis's gabbing, and Miss Cantrell's haughty looks, I spent more and more of my time out of doors, which is where I made the discovery.

Anne's grave lay just where Miss Ellis said it would be, beyond the swell of the rear hillside where two mounds met at a winding brook. Even battered by the icy wind, I realized I must be close and chose to press on.

The gurgling sound of the brook drew me to the base of the hill where I nearly stumbled over the grave. An earthy scent tinted the wind as if the ground had been wet for too long. Moss circled the overhanging tree branches, while creepers lay as carpet along the path. Exposed, the headstone had a worn look to it as if it had been there for centuries, but as the tombstone revealed, Anne had only been dead about two and twenty years.

Her name — Anne Chalcroft — had been hastily chiseled across the top in block letters. It was not as I thought it would read. She had been married to Lord Stanton at the time of her death. At least, that was what Miss Ellis said. If that were true, why had his family name been left off?

I thought of the earl's portrait covered in the east tower, the harsh look on his face. I was sure there was more to Anne's story than a simple case of illness and death. Something had to have driven her out into the storm that night, something that caused her death.

She was but a few years older than I on that fateful night, another resident of the Towers. My fingers found the bracelet on my wrist. I hadn't forgotten how Mrs. Chalcroft had stared at it in the drawing room the night of her episode. How she had called me Anne. Did I have a connection to her daughter?

Squatting down, I spread my hands across the damp earth and closed my eyes. Almost at once my back felt heavy, my arms weighed down with the immensity of Anne's untimely death. Though it had happened long ago, I sat there for a moment without moving, thinking of her life as if it had ended only yesterday.

A bird fluttered overhead. The bare trees creaked with each gust of wind as the rush of ivy leaves rolled like waves over the ground, moving in unison as if they were part of the sea. I folded my hands together, and for the first time in many months, I thought of heaven and peace and hope.

After several minutes I stood and gave the small marker one last look before turning away. More than ever I wanted to know Anne's story. I needed to know her story.

She was real to me now in a way I couldn't explain.

I followed the bend of the brook for several yards before realizing it was time to head back to the house. I had wandered too far and they would be missing me soon. My fingers ached from the biting cold. But all at once, my movements were arrested near the edge of the path.

Voices — just ahead.

Like lightning I slipped behind a nearby tree, pulling my skirt against my legs. I knew that deep timbre. My stomach clenched. I took a moment to catch my breath before peeking out from my hiding spot.

I swallowed hard. I had been right. It was Mr. Sinclair and the whiskered man from the town square, talking as if they were great friends. All kinds of terrible suppositions raced through my mind. Why hadn't Mr. Sinclair acknowledged the man that day as we passed? Was he the *business* Mr. Sinclair had referred to? And why were they meeting out here in the wilderness, so far from the house?

I squinted to get a better look, wondering if the rough-looking man could be another one of the highwaymen. I bit my lip and wiggled my fingers. Why couldn't I remember what the others had looked like?

Mr. Sinclair laughed then popped the man on the arm. "Let us hope it doesn't come to that."

The man nodded. "Don't you worry. That unfortunate incident is all taken care of. We'll give Captain Rossiter a merry chase. He'll not interfere. I promise you that."

"You've been a good friend. *Fait attention à toi!*"

I attempted a deep breath, but my chest felt tight. Mr. Sinclair not only knew French but spoke without a trace of an accent. The web of lies he'd spun for my amusement continued to grow.

That unfortunate incident? Why I thought of Thompkins at that moment, I don't know. But I could see her stern face as if she stood in the forest watching them with me.

Could Mr. Sinclair have had something to do with her disappearance? No. No. He'd been as surprised as I that day at the inn. Hadn't he?

I touched my forehead. Regardless, I had foolishly agreed to be his partner in crime. Without thinking, I took a careless step back and — *snap!* — a twig broke beneath my boot.

Both heads turned my direction. "What the devil?"

Mr. Sinclair motioned with his chin for

the whiskered man to head the other way, and the man took off at a run. For a breathless second I thought I'd been spared from discovery, but Mr. Sinclair flew across the path, his eyes bearing down on me.

I took another wild step, hoping he hadn't actually recognized me and that somehow I could disappear into the trees, but I was wrong — dead wrong. My foot slipped on a wet rock and I fell in that wretched way that shifts like a dream. My misstep, however, was all too real. The icy cold brook slapped against my backside with a vengeance, fighting my stays to steal what was left of my breath, but I managed a ridiculous scream.

Shocked, I tried to stand, but fell back as the frigid water soaked its way through every last layer of clothing. My skin stung as I soon realized I'd scraped my arm and my back. Though I attempted to move, my legs only kicked at the gravel. My hands shook as I felt for a rock to help me.

"A bit cold to be swimming, don't you think, Miss Delafield?" Mr. Sinclair laughed then slipped his arm around my back and lifted me from the icy clutches of the brook.

"I-I —" I couldn't speak as the blustery wind wrapped my body in a new wave of wintry cold.

Mr. Sinclair's voice grew serious as he met

169

my eyes. "Please tell me you have a horse."

I shook my head, my teeth chattering.

Setting me on my feet, he ripped off his jacket and wrapped it around my shoulders, buttoning it just below my chin. "I'm afraid we're in for it then. You'll be chilled through by the time I can get you back to the Towers." He glanced first to his left and then his right. "We haven't much time. You must rid yourself of these clothes and get in front of a fire as soon as possible."

Every muscle in my body shook, and he drew me against him, wrapping his arms around my back. Lowering his voice, he spoke at my ear. "Do you trust me, Miss Delafield?"

What a question. Not one I wanted to answer, of course. But I had little choice. I lied. "Y-yes." It would be the perfect opportunity for another disappearance — mine.

"Then I have a plan. Not a great one, but a plan nonetheless. There is a gamekeeper's cottage not far from here. I've used it from time to time. It stands empty as Mr. Davenport was turned off last year. It has firewood, however, and supplies to make some tea." He pressed his lips together. "I'm afraid we have no choice but to make use of it."

I nodded, taking a few wobbly steps in the

170

direction he'd indicated, but all my joints complained and my muscles rebelled. I'd only made it a few steps before I caught my toe on a tree root and pitched forward, slamming into the icy ground, bruising my already sore knees. Before I could regain my footing, Mr. Sinclair swung me into his arms as if I weighed nothing, my drenched frock probably dripping down his legs. "I believe you could stand for some assistance, Miss Delafield."

I didn't answer. Wet, cold, embarrassed, I closed my eyes and turned my head into his chest away from that knowing look. Yet there, all I could do was listen to the beat of his heart through his thin shirt.

Though I wasn't near as cold cradled in his arms, I couldn't stop shivering as he rushed down the uneven path. I told myself to stop being hysterical, but after what I'd overheard in the woods, the last thing I wanted to do was go to a cottage with Mr. Sinclair — alone.

12

"Your clothes will have to come off."

My gaze flashed up to Mr. Sinclair's shadowy figure as he ducked back into the front room and casually leaned against the cottage's corner beam, as if he'd suggested nothing out of the common way. I wondered if he'd even tried to hide that smile of his.

Of course not. And why should he? Regardless of what I overheard in the woods, I'd been the one to look the fool. Trembling down to my very core, I allowed him his moment of triumph, fighting instead to regain some semblance of control.

He thrust a folded blanket into my hands, motioning me to the open doorway at the side of the room. "You can change in there while I light the fire. I found some clothes I left here on my last visit and laid them out on the bed for you." He paused, waiting for me to do as he'd instructed.

The bed. His clothes. What folly had I gotten myself into? My eyes grew wide as I glanced through the doorway and back, unable to move one wretched step toward it with propriety screaming in my ears.

He took a deep breath. "You can wipe that look off your face. I have no intention of ravishing you. Not today or any day."

"No." I forced myself to take a breath. "I didn't think you would."

He gave me a wry smile. "Don't look so disappointed." He touched my wet shoulder. "You promised to trust me, remember? There is no other reasonable way to get you warm and fast. I, for one, have no intention of risking your health for some misguided sense of decorum. No one will know we were here." He motioned toward the silent room. "Who's to tell them? The rats? Now, get on with it. You've wasted enough precious time already. I'll not be responsible for the illness that incites your death."

He was right, of course. How could anyone possibly learn we'd been the inhabitants of the old gamekeeper's cottage for the afternoon? Two partners in crime — whether I wished such a thing or not. I met his penitent glare with one of my own as yet another freezing shiver wound its way down my spine. There was no choice but to get the wretched business over with.

I stumbled past him into the adjoining room, the worn floorboards creaking beneath my dripping feet, and closed the door behind me. The room seemed to tilt as I removed my bonnet, and I grasped the edge of a nearby wardrobe. An unexpected wave of nausea hit my stomach. I fought the pain to strip the icy pelisse from my shaking body, then fumbled with the frock. My muddled progress was reflected in the looking glass as my numb fingers tugged at the wet stockings.

I felt as if I watched a stranger, my skin was so pale, splotched with blue and purple. If I'd waited much longer, I'd have had to ask Mr. Sinclair for help. Thankfully, I was saved that embarrassment at least.

Sluggishly, I pulled on the large pair of pants and thin white shirt, then drew the wool blanket tightly around my shoulders, glad it was long enough to wrap my body. I glanced down and winced. Poking from beneath the long pant legs were my two bare feet.

All at once I imagined running from the cottage as far as I could get, escaping what could only be my ultimate humiliation. How could I bear his knowing look? But it was no use. The minute I decided to spy on a private conversation in the woods, I'd placed my safety and my integrity in the hands of a highwayman — a gentlemanly one, mind you, but a highwayman nonetheless.

I rested my hand on the door latch before finally releasing it. The popping sound of a rich fire met my ears, and I hurried into the front room, surprised to find Mr. Sinclair absent.

"Mr. Sinclair?" I whispered as I crossed the rug, taking note of the parts of the cottage I'd not noticed before. Cobwebs and mouse pellets crowded the corners and water stains painted the ceiling. A pervasive stale scent added its own delightful color to the room.

He had pulled a worn sofa near the edge of the fender, and I eased down onto it, dust settling around me. After a sneeze, I took a breath, forcing my shoulders to relax. My *partner* had thought of everything. He might very well turn out to be a traitor to England, but as my toes stretched near the warmth of the flames and the scent of his pomade drifted up from the collar of his shirt, I found I'd no choice but to trust him. At least for now.

The door slammed behind me and Mr. Sinclair appeared with an armful of firewood. He dropped the logs beside the sofa.

"Warmer, I hope?"

I snuggled into the blanket. "Quite. Thank you." I tried to reconcile the words I'd heard in the woods with the man who stood before me in his dirt-stained waistcoat and rumpled hair. But I found it nigh impossible. Curtis Sinclair was far too well rehearsed in whatever role he chose to play.

He gave me a heavy nod. "You had me a bit alarmed back there." He threw another log on the fire, his voice husky from the cold. "I won't ask what you were doing hiding behind that tree. Quite frankly, it's none of my concern. And I'll say no more of it, if you promise me this will be your last foray into winter swimming. I hear it's brutal on your health."

I smiled and pointed to the ball of wet clothes. "Your jacket, sir, and my . . . well, all my clothes."

"At your service, *madam.*" He bowed like a servant then gathered the pile into his arms. "Tea shall be ready in a moment."

"Tea as well. Goodness, you are quite thorough in your nursing duties."

A smile parted his lips. "Let's just say I've had cause to use this little cottage from time to time. It is not wholly bare."

I widened my eyes but did not respond. After the adventures of the day, I was too tired to pursue such a thought.

He laid out his jacket then every delicate piece of my clothing. I tried not to cringe as he stretched each one of my stockings across the fender's edge. Satisfied they would dry, he dragged a wooden chair near the sofa and took a seat, resting his elbows on his knees. He flicked open the top button on his collar and slid his cravat from his neck, carelessly tossing it on a side table.

Startled, I raised my eyebrows. It seemed my partner meant to be easy as well. And why not? Whatever ceremony was left between us, I'd put it to bed when I fell in the brook. Goodness, I was wearing the man's clothes.

I tried not to stare as he leaned back in his chair, swinging his boot across his opposing knee. Such missish airs would not be welcome, so I bit my lip and glanced away; however, I couldn't very well ignore my rescuer completely.

So . . . I took a quick peek.

Mr. Sinclair had placed his arm behind his head, giving me the impression of ease, but I didn't think him wholly unaffected. He'd learned something today in the woods from the whiskered man. And he didn't like it.

His arm sank down to his side as he

turned to face me. I caught a hint of his broad chest inside the open collar. All too easily I remembered being held in those arms as he conducted me through the woods.

Surely it was mere curiosity that urged me to look where a gently bred female should not. It wasn't as if I was attracted to Mr. Sinclair — the rogue, the traitor with his miserable, dreary expressions. I tried to imagine spending the afternoon in the cottage with the far more handsome Mr. Cantrell, but the thought fluttered away as quickly as it had come.

Though it was daytime outside the windows, clouds had moved in, shrouding the sun. It was strange how the gray haze made the flames brighter and Mr. Sinclair's dark hair and blue eyes that much more alive. He didn't look particularly evil. I wondered what he could be thinking, brooding as he was in his chair. I'd thought endless hours about him as a robber but no time of him as a man. Had he a lady that he loved? The thought caused my heart to tick a bit faster.

"Mr. Sinclair?"

He turned to meet my gaze. "Hmm?"

"How long do you think it will take the clothes to dry?"

He raked his fingers through his hair. "I'm

not certain, but a long while. They will be missing us at the house before too long. I could account for my absence, but you?"

A slight chill swept my frame. I leaned closer to the fire's warmth.

"Your hair is still wet. It cannot be comfortable as it is."

I shook my head, and the sopping lump sprinkled a few drops of water across my neck. "No, and I have little hope of it drying as it is. I'm not sure how I shall explain it."

"Why don't you let it down? It's absurd not to be comfortable now."

I reached up, but the blanket shifted and I gripped it fast. The white shirt was far too thin for my liking. "As you can see, I can hardly do so in my present state."

"Then by all means, allow your nurse to do it." He crossed over onto the sofa, a light smile reviving his face.

Suddenly he was close, too close. His presence was immense beside me. "My hair is fine." My words sounded hollow. We both knew it wasn't.

"Don't be ridiculous. You'll feel a great deal better without it pulling at you so." The sofa creaked as he leaned forward, the candle glinting with the rush of air. I blew out a long breath, but I couldn't help but grin. Gently, he slipped the first pin from my limp coiffeur, and my skin fluttered beneath his touch. *So this is what it feels like — the rush of the unknown.*

A few more pins and the tangle that had once been my chignon fell, allowing the bulk of hair down onto my shoulders. My hold on the blanket slackened and it tumbled to the sofa. I didn't move to retrieve it, for he was already running his fingers through my hair, fishing for more pins, the damp ends feathering against my neck.

Warmth flashed, then tingling cold. I opened my mouth to speak, but I could think of nothing to say. His finger grazed my shirt's edge. My eyes slipped closed, my heart whispering with each wild beat, Turn around. Turn around. But I was bound to the sofa by invisible cords.

His fingers stilled. Silence settled into the room like new-fallen snow, beautiful yet cold. I ran my hand down the blanket with unsteady fingers. "Thank you."

His hand lingered on my arm for the merest second before he slid back over to his chair. "Not at all." The veiled look he wore so well returned to his face, making me wonder if I had imagined the last few intimate moments.

I glanced down. "Mr. Sinclair?" All at

once I needed to shift the conversation, anything to stop the drumming in my chest. "Did you ever receive that letter you were waiting for from Lord Stanton?"

His eyes clouded. "No." And he turned his attention back to the fire. "I'm at a loss as to what I should do. It weighs heavily on my mind, I assure you." He picked a wood chip from his breeches, tossing it into the fire. "What about you? Have you thought any more about your future?"

I pinned one of my arms against my stomach and wrapped the blanket around me once more, then sighed. I wanted to lie. I wanted to say I had all kinds of plans for where to go when Mrs. Chalcroft died. I certainly didn't want Mr. Sinclair's pity, but I found the words strangely empty. When I left Winterridge I had never planned to return.

I shook my head, the warmth of his hands still fresh on my neck. If no one knew me this side of Reedwick, I supposed my wretched partner should.

I met his eyes. "I have no idea what is to become of me."

He lowered his gaze, and I wondered if he had been listening at all. But when he glanced back up, there was a seriousness about his look. "You have much to recommend you."

I drew my legs into the blanket, tucking in my feet. I hadn't been begging for a compliment.

"But I do not think you realize it."

I let out a quick huff. "Considering the circumstances of my birth, I do what I can."

He held still as if in expectation. "And yet . . ."

My stomach tightened. "What?"

"Passion, intellect, courage. All admirable traits, and wasted in your current position, unless . . ."

I waited for him to finish his sentence, but he chose to stand and stoke the fire. I tucked a wet curl behind my ear and squeezed my eyes shut. Allowing Mr. Sinclair to touch my hair did not give him the right to pry into my personal affairs.

Resting the poker on the fender, he turned. "I apologize if I spoke out of turn."

"No." I straightened my shoulders. "You've set me thinking is all, which I believe was your intention from the start." I tilted my chin. "Perhaps, since you possess such a clarity of mind, you could tell me what you plan to do about your own future."

"Touché. And a difficult question to answer."

I was glad the teasing quality had returned

to his voice. I offered a smile. "All right. Then what would you have liked to do — if you weren't Lord Stanton's heir?"

He sat in thoughtful silence for a moment, then lifted his gaze. "Run a horse and stud farm."

"A stud farm? Raise hunters, you mean, or something else?"

He rubbed his chin, a spark coming into his eyes. "I don't believe I've ever shared this idea with anyone before."

"Well, I've never shown a gentleman my bare feet, so I believe we are even."

He laughed. "And we're partners, don't forget." He crossed one leg over the other then uncrossed them, finally hopping to his feet. "You see, I have this idea . . . for His Majesty's cavalry. How to breed and train the horses, selecting for certain characteristics." Something distracted him and he glanced above my head. "Ah, your tea is ready." He crossed the room.

I called out over the back of the sofa, "Sounds like an interesting idea. The horses, I mean. Why won't Lord Stanton fund such a project now?"

"He's never been much of a military man, and even with a seat in the House of Lords, he cares little for England's affairs. More importantly, he won't have his heir dabbling in anything that even looks like trade. And with my sisters dependent on his good graces, you can imagine the difficulty there."

He rounded the end of the sofa and passed a teacup into my hand. "Careful. It's hot."

"But if he were to understand your interest, your ideas . . ."

He held up his hand. "My dubious cousin is not a man to listen to anyone, least of all me. And without any cavalry experience . . ."

The hot tea felt like satin sliding down my throat, warming me from the inside out. I peeked at him over the rim of my cup. "Thank you. This is wonderful."

He waved off the compliment. "Any gentleman would render aid to a lady in need."

I thought of my arrival at the Towers, how cold and awkward it had been. How little anyone did to help me. "No, I don't think they would."

He leaned forward. "Now that you know of my dreams of a stud farm, I think it fitting that I should know more about you. What hopes does Miss Delafield keep hidden in her heart?"

I stalled for a moment, taking a long sip of tea. My dream was a secret one — to know the identity of my parents. I would never toss such a thing out lightly. Particularly to a man I wasn't sure I could trust. But what dreams did I have beyond that? Had I allowed my search to consume me?

I stared into the dark corner of the room, the awful truth sinking in around me. "I'm not certain."

Mr. Sinclair's voice dropped to a whisper. "I find that difficult to believe. A woman of your ingenuity."

We sat in relative silence for a moment before he rose and felt my gown. "I'm afraid it will take several more hours for your clothes to dry completely. Considering you've had time to warm up, these will have to make do. We must head back to the house before you are missed too terribly much." He cast a quick glance over his shoulder. "If you roll up the pants, you can hide them beneath your skirt, and I'll lend you my coat till we are nearer the house. Do you think you can manage?"

I nodded, glad to make my escape. His words had hit a nerve. I helped him gather up my damp clothes and headed for the back room.

"Miss Delafield."

I hesitated before turning at the doorway.

"You have a great many talents, far more than you realize. You could do much good in a world sadly in need of it. And someday, I'd like to ask you the same question again." He twisted his cravat in his hands. "By then, I hope you'll have an answer."

13

Late the next day, Portia beckoned me to Mrs. Chalcroft's bedside, tight-lipped about what could be wrong. Fearing the worst, I dashed through the bedchamber door, where I found her alone in bed, worrying her fingers across the eiderdown's edge.

Her wide eyes shot to mine as I slowed my approach. "You must deliver another letter . . . today if at all possible." Then she flicked her fingers in the air. "Bring me my quill and ink, and there's paper in the escritoire there. I shall make do with this book to write on. Hurry. We shall have no time to read today. You must set out at once."

I gathered the items as instructed and then cautiously sat back down, waiting for her to finish writing, hoping I might get a glimpse at the text. Anything to put my mind at ease.

" 'Pon rep, Sybil . . ." She angled her chin.

187

"What are you waiting for? Change into your riding habit immediately."

I flew down the grand staircase, the letter Mrs. Chalcroft had penned clenched in my hand. I knew I'd have to be quick in order to make it to Reedwick and back before dark. The thought left me a bit breathless, but I forced myself not to think, only to move. Thank goodness I wouldn't need a guide, as I'd spent a great deal of last week familiarizing myself with the area.

A deep voice met my arrival on the ground floor, breaking the heavy stillness of the entryway. "Off somewhere in a hurry?"

Startled, I jerked my hand behind my back.

Mr. Sinclair frowned, his gaze tracking my arm to where it disappeared behind my skirt.

Drat. I couldn't have made a bigger mistake if I'd tried. Why hadn't I tucked the letter in my pelisse, or my reticule, for that matter?

He raised his eyebrows. "I see you've fully recovered from your little escapade in the brook."

I cast a quick glance around the empty room. "Yes. I'm feeling much better, thank you. But you led me to believe our adventure would not be drawing room conversation."

"Quite right." He smiled and leaned forward. "But we are not in the drawing room, are we?"

"I suppose not."

I glanced at the casement clock against the wall. I had no time to argue so I skirted around him for the door, the letter pressed to the folds of my habit.

"And Mrs. Chalcroft, is she well?" He matched my stride to the door, extending his arm at the last second.

I took a deep breath then ducked beneath the sleeve of his jacket. "Yes. Mrs. Chalcroft is recovering from her spell as well as can be expected." I grasped the door handle. "But I'll have to speak more with you later as I have a great deal to do this afternoon. Miss Ellis might be a better person to ask. Now, if you will excuse me."

Mr. Sinclair leaned his shoulder into the door with a thump, his face mere inches from mine. "Certainly, as soon as you show me whatever it is you're hiding, *partner.*"

He had seen it. I swiped a stray hair from my cheek. "It's nothing you would be interested in. Now let me pass. I'm in a hurry."

A smile crept across his face. "Nothing I

would be interested in, hmm? You've used those words before if I remember correctly, and that time I found myself vastly interested."

I allowed him a peek at the outside of the note before smashing it in my reticule. "It's a letter, a private letter. Hence, not for your eyes, sir. Now —"

"Why don't you just drop the letter in the platter with the other mail and allow me to accompany you into the drawing room?" He pointed to the rococo table against the wall. "I have something I wish to —"

"You think of everything, don't you?"

"Assuredly."

"Well, I do thank you for your insight, but I have been asked to deliver this particular letter myself."

He raised his eyebrows. "Ah, so it is a secret letter?"

"I said nothing of the kind." I pushed against his arm. "Listen. If I'm to reach Reedwick this afternoon, you better get out of my way. You've wasted nigh on ten minutes with this useless banter."

"To Reedwick? At this hour? You have me interested." He rubbed his chin. "Allow me to fetch my riding boots and crop, and I'll meet you in the stables in no less than five minutes."

Goodness, all I needed was Mr. Sinclair following me around like a puppy, taking note of all I did. Though a splash of warmth filled my cheeks, I hadn't forgotten what he'd said in the woods. I gripped my reticule, a darker thought dawning. Did Mr. Sinclair have another reason for wanting to accompany me?

I forced my voice to sound light. "You are kind, Mr. Sinclair. But I shall do well enough on my own this time. No escort required." I opened the door.

He caught hold of my arm, whispering this time. "If you think I would allow a lady to ride out alone with the possibility she could be benighted on the road after dark, you don't know me at all."

"You forget, Mr. Sinclair. I'm only the companion. I do as I'm told. And I don't care how you protest." I paused as the musty scent of the gamekeeper's cottage tinted the air between us. "Riding to Reedwick today alone is just what I'm going to do."

Footsteps echoed along the back hallway, growing louder as the person approached.

He released my arm in a flash, running his fingers through his hair as he backed away.

Within seconds, Miss Ellis burst into the

front room. "Mr. Sinclair, there you are. I have been waiting an age." She looked first at me then back at Mr. Sinclair. "And Miss Delafield. Are you going out?"

Miss Ellis stopped abruptly at the other end of the rug, slowly crossing her arms. "You promised, remember? I've got the chessboard all set up."

Mr. Sinclair moved to open the door wide, leaning down to my ear. "You win this time, partner, but if you're not back before dark, I ride out for Reedwick. Understand?"

I nodded then rushed through the door before he could think of another way to stop me.

Sunday evening brought a change to Reedwick I'd not expected. No happy sellers marking the square, no horses or drays busy with the work of the day. Other than the tavern, the sleepy town rested as I should have been.

A few candles flickered within the buildings, their soft light wavering against curtained windows. The setting sun had left a chill in its stead, and after dismounting Aphrodite, I pulled my pelisse tighter around my neck.

Mrs. Chalcroft had instructed me to take the letter to a side door of Pasley's that led to the family's room above the store. Fearing the waning light, I hurried across the square and down the row of shops, Aphrodite trotting in my wake. Gravel crunched beneath my half boots and the horse's hooves. My hasty breaths echoed the clip-clops of the horse until I stopped at the shop's corner, which rounded into a dim alleyway.

Lovely. Just lovely.

I bit the inside of my cheek. Aphrodite would have to wait here. In a hurry, I looped her reins around an iron post and plodded back.

The narrow corridor stretched into darkness as the stoic walls of the two-story buildings stood watch over the slender path. It took all my willpower not to picture the man from the woods with the bushy whiskers waiting for me at the other end, concealed somewhere in the blackness. Ridiculous, I knew. Still, I took a quick glance behind me, conscious now of an imaginary presence, as if someone watched me from afar. Why didn't I bring a groom?

Thompkins's strange disappearance was wearing on me. If only I hadn't seen her at the Towers, I could believe she had simply run off. But someone met her there. Someone I likely knew, and then she vanished without even her portmanteaux. One of only three passengers that day in the coach.

Standing still, I noticed the soft crunching of boots in the distance, the peal of laughter, the rattle of doors. There were others out and about. The hairs on my arms pricked to attention, the eerie scent of pipe smoke steady on the breeze. I scanned the shadows behind me one last time.

What I needed to do was put a stop to my vivid imagination. I'd been sent to deliver a message for Mrs. Chalcroft, nothing more. It had nothing to do with that day we were stopped in the coach or the scramble of dragoons in town.

I rolled the letter's wax seal, the Chalcroft crest, between my fingers. What if my instincts were right and there was more to this business than I'd been told? Perhaps a connection?

I held out the folded paper in front of me, then hesitated. There could be all kinds of innocent reasons for Mrs. Chalcroft's correspondence — an urgent request, a private relationship, something to do with her imminent death that she didn't wish the family to know about — all within the realm of possibility. She was private and eccentric and intense . . . and should be able to trust her hired companion. I let out a pinned breath. All good reasons to finish the request and get back to my warm bed at the Towers.

The shadows retreated as I walked, my steps a bit more determined, and soon enough, I was relieved to see a small brown door at the far end of the building.

Climbing the solitary step, I wiggled my gloved fingers before rapping my knuckles against the peeling paint. The hinges must have been loose, for the door shook in its frame. I heard shouts from within and then footsteps. Once more I questioned my sanity.

The door popped open a crack, and I let out a sigh of relief. It was Mrs. Barineau.

She scowled, the worn lines wrinkling on her face. "You. What do you want?"

"I have another letter from Mrs. Chalcroft." I held the note into the beam of light angling from the door.

She snatched it from my hand. "Good. He'll be glad to hear it."

The letter disappeared from my sight and my stomach lurched. I'd made no attempt to ascertain what Mrs. Chalcroft had scrolled across the thick paper, no thought to hold it to the light or peek in a corner, but all at once I was afraid of what might be inside.

I cleared my throat. "Any return message this time?"

"You just tell her to keep them coming or I'll not be responsible for the consequences." The door slammed shut.

The wind wandered like a hungry lion down the corridor. My body tingled. I stood frozen to Mrs. Barineau's step.

Who would send letters by darkness? To a milliner?

I stumbled back down the corridor gripped by questions, but just as I reached the edge of the building I heard voices.

Men.

They spoke far too loud for such a quiet street. My leg muscles tightened and I slipped into the shadows, hoping they'd pass without notice. I didn't wish to explain myself. Peeking around the corner, I strained to see what I could of the street. Had Aphrodite wandered off? A bead of sweat ran down my neck.

I forced myself not to think but to listen — I recognized one of the voices. A group of soldiers strolled into the dim square, their blue uniforms darkened by dusk. I was right. It was Captain Rossiter and some of his comrades.

I pressed myself tighter against the wall,

disappearing into the shadows as best I could.

Their voices were as clear as if they stood beside me. ". . . all signs point to Croft Towers. We must be vigilant."

The younger redheaded officer nearly tripped on the uneven road but caught himself. "What a feather that will be for your cap, *Cap.*" He laughed. "You'll flush out the traitors before long. They can't hide forever. Of course, there was that last report."

The captain paused. "What of it?"

"That it was a girl he'd seen running away. Not a —"

"I don't credit it. A drunk like Barrow. He couldn't see straight, I 'spect."

The other man spit on the ground. "Blasted French. You'll get 'em."

Captain Rossiter slapped the side of his leg. "You're right. Jove, you're right. I'm too close to finding the truth. We'll step up the watch. I know it's prudent to wait, to catch the wretch in the act. No one goes in or out of Reedwick without a thorough search. And the Towers? More guards. We'll surround the place if necessary. Napoleon can't succeed without money from his vile spies in England. Once they are gone, we'll bleed him dry . . ."

A door slammed in the distance. Leaves scattered in the wind. Then nothing. I inched forward, my fingers feeling their way along the stone wall to the open corner. I could hear no more of the conversation. The soldiers must have entered the Rose Inn.

Carefully, I slipped into the street, scanning the area for Aphrodite. One more foolish mistake on my part. Obviously, I hadn't secured her well enough, and now I had no idea where she'd gone.

A hand grasped my shoulder. Cold as ice.

My heartbeat thrashed in my ears, and I spun to find a figure looming over me in the darkness. "A pretty thing, you be." The filthy hand slipped down to clench my arm.

Terror shot through me and I blurted a few words. "Unhand me at once." I jerked back, but the bony hand turned to iron.

The man wore brown trousers and muddy boots, his shirt half-tucked, half-loose at his waist. He grinned, his bearded smile missing several teeth. "It be just a few steps down to the Crown. Might'n you wish to join me?"

"Certainly not. You've a pretty picture of my character if you think I would ever go there."

"Easy, easy. Perhaps I made a mistake." He squinted his eyes, his ruddy nose crinkling, but he didn't relax his fingers. "These old poppers don't work as they once did. Come with me into the light so we can get better acquainted."

"I'll do no such thing." The man had obviously mistaken my reason for being unaccompanied at night in town, but why did he persist?

Little by little he edged me back into the shadows of the buildings. His breath stank of ale and his clothes of sweat and animals. The thought of Thompkins's clothes waiting for her to return flashed into my mind. Was this my day to disappear? My arm throbbed beneath the man's grasp. Escape was my only option, but without Aphrodite I had little chance but to run.

A large shadow emerged from the gloom of the nearby wall, unnoticed by my captor as he dragged me from the square. Fright pulsed through my veins, and I pawed at the man's grubby fingers. He only laughed, a deep tone far too young for his appearance.

In a wink, the shadow tore from the wall. It was a tall man, broad shouldered and lightning fast. As startled as I, the filthy man released my arm, but it was too late. The butt of a riding crop slashed across his face and he fell to the ground.

"Are you hurt, Miss Delafield?"

My gaze flicked up into a pair of familiar blue eyes. "Mr. Sinclair. How did you . . ." Shaking, I fell into his solid arms as the man stumbled to his feet and slinked away. "How did you know?"

Mr. Sinclair drew me back a pace, searching first my face then my arms, his eyes part concern, part surprise. Again he asked, "Did he hurt you?"

I let out a sigh of relief before shaking my head. "Only frightened me."

"I told you to be back by dusk."

The sharp tone of Mr. Sinclair's voice brought the moment back in terrifying intensity. I turned away. "There wasn't time. I took a wrong turn on the way here and . . ."

He hesitated, his hand tightening against my shoulder before relaxing. "I found Aphrodite by the church and I, well, I thought . . ." He seemed to take a long time to catch his breath. "Let's just say you have a way of getting yourself into trouble."

"I'm not sure what I would have done if you hadn't come along when you did."

He glanced over his shoulder. "Were you able to deliver your, uh, letter?"

Right. The letter. I'd forgotten about it. But not Mr. Sinclair. My shoulders slumped. If the soldiers were to be believed, there was a spy at the Towers, a traitor to England. And that man who'd attacked me . . . Had he followed me to town? I had best figure out what was going on before I found myself the next victim, or worse, an unwitting accomplice to treason.

The Towers lurked black on the hillside as Mr. Sinclair and I finished our late-night journey home. He said little on the ride, but now he seemed nervous as if questions rankled in his mind and he could no longer put them off.

"Did you recognize that man in town?"

"No." I took a deep breath, guiding Aphrodite a bit closer. "I'd never seen him before, though I don't believe he was as old as he appeared."

Mr. Sinclair rubbed his chin. "Neither do I. Did he say anything to you? Ask you any questions?"

"Nothing of consequence."

"Nothing about that day in the coach?"

I tightened my fingers on the reins. "Why do you ask?"

"I —" Suddenly his hand shot up, his finger pointing toward the stables. "What the devil?" He narrowed his eyes. "Something's wrong at the Towers. Come on." He spurred his horse to a gallop, leaving me in his dust.

Lights bobbed on the horizon. Voices clipped through the night air. I kicked Aphrodite, urging her to match Hercules's brisk pace, but he was several strides ahead.

John met me at the edge of the paddock. "Oh, miss. You must go in at once. Something terrible has happened. Just terrible."

Panic gripped my heart. He was trembling as he helped me off the horse.

I grasped his shoulder. "Tell me. Tell me at once. Is it Mrs. Chalcroft?"

He brought his shaky hand to his forehead before accepting the reins. "Oh no, miss. Not that."

Mr. Sinclair hurried over from where he had been speaking with Mr. Cantrell and hastily offered me his arm. A nod at John and I took it, allowing Mr. Sinclair to lead me to the far side of the fence. Out of earshot, I pulled him to a stop. "What is it? Tell me."

Mr. Sinclair's face looked strange in the moonlight, his eyes an owlish gray. "There's been a discovery in the woods behind the stables."

"What do you mean, 'discovery'?"

He paused before whispering, "A body. Partially buried."

I flinched, the cold truth winding its way to my core. "Who?"

He gave me a pained stare. "You remember the maidservant from the mail coach?"

"Of course I do." My hand shot to my chest. "We spoke with Mrs. Plume about her disappearance that day we went to the Rose Inn."

"Right." He shook his head. "It looks as if there's more to her leaving than we thought. She's been murdered. Here at the Towers it seems."

My breath caught. Was this what I'd been fearing all along? Her face when I saw her that afternoon out of Mrs. Chalcroft's window had been not only withdrawn but afraid. My voice was scratchy. "How did she die?"

Mr. Sinclair touched my hand. "Must you know the particulars? Really, Miss Delafield, I think it best if you return to your room at once. You've had a trying evening."

"I said how did she die?"

Mr. Sinclair looked at his boots. "Strangled. Possibly with her necklace. There was an open wound on the back of her head as well."

I stumbled back a few paces toward the east fields. I had to get away. Any direction would do. My thoughts ran wild, my legs

203

were sluggish. Who could have done such a terrible thing? Here? My head swam.

"Miss Delafield, wait."

The stable door flew open and I caught a look inside. There lay Thompkins's body on the ground. Several men in uniform were staring down at her lifeless form. Her face was stone still and dusky gray. Weakness crawled up my legs. My ears rang.

I backed away as Mr. Sinclair's arm slipped around my back. "We should go. Mrs. Chalcroft will need you. There's nothing you can do here."

I nodded, dizziness claiming my body like a consuming sickness. I saw what Thompkins had been wearing — the same long brown cloak she wore as she scurried across the grass the day I watched her out Mrs. Chalcroft's window.

14

Miss Ellis caught me four days later and ushered me into the library to look over some fashion plates. Very little had been said about the terrible discovery. None of the women seemed a bit affected by the murder of a maid they didn't know. An investigation would begin and the truth sought. There was nothing to worry over.

She smoothed out her peach morning gown before perching on the settee by the window and flicking open *Ackermann's Repository* on her lap. "I want this one." She planted her finger on a pale round robe with white crape. "And Lucius will have none of it, as if it is not even *my* money."

I took a deep breath before settling down at her side. Though Miss Ellis, with her fairy innocence and childlike beauty, proved a shining light in the otherwise dreary house, she also possessed an unfortunate tendency toward selfishness. I gave her a wan smile.

"It is a lovely gown, but" — I slipped the magazine closed — "you have so many beautiful gowns already, and as Mr. Cantrell reminded you at the dinner table the other evening, no one around here has ever seen them."

"Yes, but soon enough I shall have to wear black and Lucius will probably demand I commit to three or even six months. Can you imagine? Me — wasted on half a year of mourning?" She tossed the magazine onto the side table and huffed. "It's my money after all. Why Papa thought Lucius a suitable guardian I will never know. I'm quite certain he never meant for every notion I have to be thwarted. I begin to wonder if Lucius is determined to spoil any opportunity I have. If I were given half a chance, I daresay I might be able to marry before Aunt Chalcroft, well, you know . . ."

"Miss Ellis, Mr. Cantrell is only doing what he feels is for the best. You cannot deny he treats you well, and after what has happened, I —"

"Well enough, I suppose. But he's far too busy trying to find a husband for Elizabeth when he should be focusing on me." She splayed her hand across her chest. "I haven't even had a season yet. Elizabeth has had two and not one offer. I know I could do better." She leaned over until our arms touched. "Before we left London I had a great deal of interest from a particularly fine gentleman, although I shan't say any names. What do you think of that?"

I hadn't the least clue who she meant and didn't care, but before I could answer, she flopped back against the sofa as if she'd been blown over by the wind. "And then — *poof!* — here I am waiting attendance on a great-aunt I'd never even met, miles from anyone I care about." She held up two fingers. "With any luck, I'll miss two seasons."

Considering she would be only nineteen in two years, I shook my head. "Miss Ellis, you're young and beautiful and full of possibilities." I tucked a stray hair behind her ear. "You still have plenty of time to realize your dreams. I think —"

She jerked away and gave me a scathing look, as if advice from a single woman of two and twenty, who had already failed in such an endeavor, must only give credence to her point.

She dabbed her nose with a handkerchief. "When I first learned I was to be trapped here, I thought to amuse myself with Mr. Sinclair, but I believe Elizabeth was already ahead of me there. I can't know why because she is grouchy and horrid. And as far as I know, Mr. Ashworth actually cut her at the last ball of the season." She arched her eyebrows, turning to meet my gaze. "And what about you, friend?" Her voice sounded pointed. "Have you also set your sights on my Mr. Sinclair? I daresay most would consider the two of you a terrible mésalliance, but after I saw you standing in the doorway the other day, I did wonder."

I swallowed hard, a bit off balance. "Goodness, no." I searched her eyes for what could have brought about such a question. "I would never have you think that. Mr. Sinclair enjoys teasing me, nothing more." Her back stiffened and my heart sank. I'd discovered the reason Miss Ellis asked me to the library in the first place. It had nothing to do with gowns.

I bit my lip. If Miss Ellis had detected a familiarity between Mr. Sinclair and me, who else might have come to the same conclusion? Mr. Sinclair, of course, meant nothing to me. A friend, yes. But certainly not a romantic interest. He was far from an amiable suitor like Mr. Cantrell. Of course, Mr. Sinclair would inherit a title one day, but I cared nothing for such things.

I thought of his dark countenance, surprisingly kind eyes, the feel of his fingers in my hair. "He was only following his godmother's instructions."

"I suppose. I've had a hard time understanding him at all. If I even mean to understand him. And I'm not sure I do. Men are usually so easy to read, but Mr. Sinclair keeps me guessing. In and out of the Towers at all times of day. I watch him from my window sometimes." She seemed to consider her words. "I suppose he would make a wretched husband — here one minute and gone the next, and he has little time for society and few friends. I daresay I would prefer someone more like Lucius. Always in the know, always trying to please in just the right way. *He* is received everywhere. In fact, there shall be quite a line of young ladies when we return to London, particularly if he has inherited all the money."

I wondered if she had brought Mr. Cantrell into the conversation for my benefit, or if she had softened toward him in only a few minutes.

She bobbed the edge of her skirt with her half boot then paused. "You do know that is why we came here. For the great Chalcroft fortune, or whatever it is Lucius likes to call it — who it shall go to, I mean. It is all a great mystery. One I don't believe my aunt will betray before the end. She enjoys having us fawn all over her far too much. It makes me fairly sick to watch Lucius at her beck and call. If only Anne's child hadn't died so long ago, everything would be different. *I* certainly wouldn't have left London for this desolate place. The money is nothing to me. Although that would mean other things, as well."

My body tensed. "What do you mean? Anne's child?"

"The heir, of course." She cast me a curious glance. "I guess you wouldn't know. Years ago my cousin Anne gave birth to a child a few days before her death. The child died in his infancy, poor soul. At least, that is what I heard. No one seems to want to speak of it. Elizabeth says it is all Aunt Chalcroft's fault, or at least she thinks it is. I don't know how my great-aunt could have been the cause of her own daughter's pneumonia or the child's death." Mindlessly, Miss Ellis rolled a stray ribbon from her gown through her fingers. "I suppose Dawkins was Lady Anne's abigail at the time. She could tell you more about it. I don't wish to drudge up the past, particularly about Anne."

Dawkins? Anne's tragic story had perked my interest since I'd learned of the connection to Lord Stanton. So much sadness in one house, and I was no closer to discovering my place in all of it. But the thought of asking Dawkins anything sent a flutter of apprehension to my stomach. "I don't suppose it is any of my business. And as to your future —"

"Don't scold me, Miss Delafield." Miss Ellis widened her eyes. "I know you are about to and I wish you wouldn't. Goodness, the look on your face has chastised me enough. It reminds me of a beastly governess I had a few years back." She pressed her lips together. "And I am determined that we will be friends."

Miss Ellis reminded me of a wild filly — flighty, beautiful, but unharnessed and certainly uncontrollable. I had to be careful or she would bolt. I didn't want to lose what little companionship I had at the Towers. "I'm sorry. Who am I to scold?" I touched her hand.

"Good. Then you will make it up to me by asking Lucius about the gown." She squeezed back. "You will, won't you?"

I couldn't help but smile. She'd managed to change from perfect seriousness to frivolous gaiety in one breath. I knew if I refused, our relationship would never be the same, so I reluctantly nodded.

Her eyes brightened as if she'd anticipated my acquiescence the minute she'd proposed it. "I knew you had a kind heart the first time I saw you and that we would get on so well together." She kissed my cheek. "I don't care what Elizabeth says. I'm glad you have come to the Towers." She rose from the sofa like a butterfly and waved her hands for me to follow. "Lucius should be in the drawing room. You know how my aunt joins us on the first floor after her nap, and he of all people wouldn't miss a chance to bestow his attentions on the old lady. Let us go before she arrives."

We found Mr. Cantrell in the drawing room as well as Miss Cantrell, who promptly vacated the gilded sofa for the window seat after heralding my arrival with a snide, "I thought you'd be with Mrs. Chalcroft. You were hired to entertain her after all."

Mr. Cantrell stood the moment he heard my name, running his finger down the lapel of his blue superfine coat. "Ah, Miss Delafield."

If I said my fingers didn't tingle, or that Mr. Cantrell looked anything other than perfectly handsome, I would be lying. His smile could win anyone's affections. I hated that he directed it at me so often, but at the same time I searched for it anytime he was near, as if his very presence proved a secret intoxication forbidden only to me — the companion.

He *was* forbidden to me and I knew it well enough, only I'd had a difficult time convincing my heart. Miss Ellis was right. He would make the ideal mate — for some other highborn, gently bred girl with money.

I averted my gaze from Miss Cantrell, for I knew his attentions would only make her sour attitude worse. Talk would consist of Miss Ellis's gown, nothing more, then somehow I'd find a way to make it clear to him he need not address the companion from now on.

The thought stung with a fresh barb, and I tried my best to appear unaffected. I took a deep breath. Hopes and dreams were reserved for the wealthy.

Mr. Cantrell found his way over to my side, ignoring everyone else in the room, and took my hand. "Have you come for your dance lesson?"

Shock surged through my body and for a moment I was speechless. I'd forgotten all about Mrs. Chalcroft mentioning such a thing. After the murder, I thought the family might not attend the assembly.

Miss Ellis squealed with delight. "Oh yes,

yes," she said, clapping her hands. "We must teach her at once so she shall have time to practice." She leaned to my ear as she floated into the room. "This is just the thing to put him in a proper mood before I ask to have the gown made." Then louder for everyone else to hear, "But who shall play? We must have music. Elizabeth?"

Miss Cantrell turned her cold glare on Miss Ellis. "I have no intention of —"

"Well, of course you do. Don't be a pea-goose, Elizabeth." Miss Ellis paused. "But I suppose you cannot play and make up a set of four at the same time. We need at least four dancers for proper instruction."

"Evie's right." Mr. Cantrell shot me a quick smile. "Elizabeth, we need you to dance opposite Evie in the set."

Men seemed to be the only creatures capable of bringing Miss Cantrell from the confines of her icy shell. She took a quick breath and rose gracefully to her feet. "I will help if it brings you joy, dear brother, but only for you."

I wondered what she meant, but before I could say a word, Mr. Cantrell was bowing before me with an alarming smile. "Would you do me the honor of accompanying me in the next dance?"

Miss Ellis giggled. "Yes, we must do this

quite proper." She bowed to Miss Cantrell and spoke as low as her little voice would allow. "Miss Cantrell, are you free for the next dance?"

Miss Cantrell let a slight laugh slip out. "I am not engaged." Then stepped over next to me as our partners took their places opposite us.

Miss Ellis spoke first. "Do you remember the quadrille, Miss Delafield?"

"A bit."

"I'll count it out as I show you the figures."

I watched then repeated, the familiar patterns still buried somewhere in my brain, just waiting to get out.

Mr. Cantrell smiled. "I believe you were fibbing to Mrs. Chalcroft when you told her you did not dance."

"No, it has been some time, and I have never had a chance to dance in company, let alone at an assembly."

He grasped my hand. "Then let us do so now."

"What's all this?" A man's voice sounded from the doorway and I thought I felt Mr. Cantrell's fingers stiffen.

Miss Ellis waved her arms. "Mr. Sinclair. You are just the person we need. Come in here at once."

Unconsciously, I slipped my hand from

Mr. Cantrell's grasp, realizing belatedly how it must have looked to Mr. Sinclair, who held a peculiar expression as he entered the room.

Miss Ellis grasped his elbow and led him to the pianoforte before he uttered another word. "You must play us a quadrille, Mr. Sinclair. We are reminding Miss Delafield of her steps."

He raised his eyebrows. "Are you?" He scanned the room for a moment before taking a seat on the bench.

Everything about his tone of voice, the way he spread out the sheets of music on the pianoforte, and how he nodded at his cousin, all seemed quite amiable, more so even than I had seen him before. But just before he began, he met my gaze across the room, and I couldn't help but sense irritation. At what? Dancing a few days after a murder? I had far more cause for discomfort than he did. The last thing I wanted was another spectator for my dance class.

The music started abruptly and I struggled to remember the steps I'd perfected just moments ago, turning first the wrong direction, then on the wrong count. "I'm sorry, Mr. Cantrell. Perhaps I'm not able to focus as well with the music."

"Nonsense. I'm here to help you in any

way I can. If you would but watch my face, I may be able to help you remember."

Slowly, I lifted my gaze and smiled, glad to realize the flutters I had before experienced in his presence had been subdued. He was handsome to be sure, but out of reach and, quite frankly, comfortably so.

"You are doing splendid," Miss Ellis said as we passed each other.

And I was. Perhaps it was possible to meet my obligations of companion and spare dancer tolerably well, even with the alluring Mr. Cantrell.

Miss Cantrell stopped and the set broke up. "I'm sorry, but I am unwell."

Mr. Sinclair sprang to his feet and helped her to the sofa. Watching his swift reaction, I wondered if what Miss Ellis had said about the two of them was true. He was so attentive, procuring her a glass of water. He spoke quietly. "You've overdone yourself today. A long walk and now dancing. You may not be quite recovered from your cold."

Mr. Cantrell sounded cross. "Nonsense. That was over two weeks ago. Don't tell me you've something else, for I swear you're sick every time we turn around. I should employ a full-time doctor."

Miss Cantrell waved off her brother, the color returning to her cheeks. "No, I've nothing new. I'm quite all right now. Please, continue your lessons without me."

Now it was Miss Ellis's turn to act vexed. Her voice came out in a whine. "But how can we do so with only three people?"

Mr. Sinclair flicked his gaze upward. "This dance lesson, or whatever it is you call it, can resume at a later time."

"No." Miss Cantrell touched Mr. Sinclair's arm, unable to take her eyes off her brother. "I will play and you can take my place in the dance."

Mr. Sinclair gave a slight head shake. "Are you sure you are feeling well enough to do so? I think it better if you were to lie down."

"I am not a child, and I shall be perfectly content to play if you would help me over to the bench."

"Excellent." Mr. Cantrell stepped back into his place in the set. "We shall all be happy now."

I wished I could have agreed with such a sentiment, but everything about the previous interchange had left me unsettled. What was wrong with Miss Cantrell? And did a familiarity exist between her and Mr. Sinclair? It was certainly none of my affair, but if he proved to be a danger to the house . . .

Miss Ellis shot me a wink. She had not forgotten her quest to ask about the gown.

"Lucius, my dear, would you partner with me this go-around?"

His smile retreated, but he nodded nonetheless. "Of course. I would be happy to."

Mr. Sinclair slowed his steps as he approached, meeting my eyes. "I suppose that leaves the two of us."

"Yes. I suppose it does."

He took his place next to Mr. Cantrell, standing several inches taller than his blond friend. Mr. Sinclair's dark jacket faded into his black hair, making his eyes that much more vivid. It had been four days since he'd saved my life in Reedwick and we'd learned of the murder. All of a sudden I realized I had been avoiding him. Why?

Mr. Sinclair and I had shared a sort of intimacy that day in the woods after I fell into the brook and then again in town. I wasn't sure I was ready to revisit the memory. Surely it clouded my emotions where he was concerned. For the man wasn't to be trusted — let alone thought of at all.

I forced myself to meet his gaze, but I couldn't read what I saw in his eyes — boldness, tension, or something else, something predatory?

The music began with a loud chord and I jumped. Mr. Sinclair motioned with his chin, indicating it was I who was to move to the left. Snapped back to the present, I set the first figures as well as I could remember. Round him I swayed, then paused to watch his turn.

For a man who despised the practice, he danced beautifully, closing to meet me as we passed down the line, only to start again. I noticed he held a smile I'd not seen before, one that transformed his features. It was interesting that dancing became him even more so than riding, or robbing for that matter.

He hid a subtle side to those dark features, the way his eyes lit when he talked, how uncommonly attractive he was in his own way. No wonder Miss Ellis considered him a catch, although I doubted many people saw this side of him, as guarded as he always was. But I had seen more of him — in Reedwick when he'd defended my honor and in the cottage when he'd been so kind and gentle.

All at once, I could think of nothing but the touch of his gloved fingers, the closeness of the dance, the warmth of my cheeks. My heart felt light, my legs unsteady until the pianoforte held the last note. There I was caught in Mr. Sinclair's gaze, unable to turn away.

Miss Ellis giggled and the spell was broken.

Mr. Sinclair bowed. "I don't believe you need any more lessons. You dance lovely, Miss Delafield." Then he turned and walked from the room.

I closed the collection of Byron's poetry as Mrs. Chalcroft's eyes fluttered shut. The bracelet Lord Stanton had sent me dangled around my wrist, now cold on my arm.

"You're troubled." Mrs. Chalcroft raised her chin. "What is it?"

I didn't know she was watching me. "Just puzzled, I suppose."

"Tell me, child."

"I find my thoughts a bit difficult to put into words at times. I wonder if it isn't the murder, as it seems to hang over the entire house." I met her gaze. "I'm afraid I cannot stop thinking of it. Poor Thompkins. Struck down before she had a chance to make something of her life."

She took my hand. "I daresay we all struggle with when and how the future will find us. The girl must have had a dismal life working for that woman. Her death may have had nothing to do with the Towers at all."

"True, but sudden death, in such a personal and horrid way. It makes one question one's own path — when it will end and what you are doing in the meantime."

She took a sip of water. "The more difficult the journey, the sweeter the reward."

I listened to the steady click of the mantel clock for a long moment, processing her words. "And life itself is so confusing at times. People are not always as they first appear. Moments of our own journeys seem meaningless at one point, then later of great consequence. It is difficult to know if you are making the right decisions, no matter how hard you work to do so."

"Yes, but we must live nonetheless." Mrs. Chalcroft tapped her coverlet. "Take the word of an old woman who has made a great many mistakes. No one promises us a perfect life, my dear. You must do the best you can with what you've been given."

A perfect life? Was that what I meant? I pressed my lips together. "I suppose Mr. Sinclair would say I should look beyond my own troubles and find a way to use my talents for the greater good."

"He said that to you, child?"

I nodded, suddenly wishing I hadn't brought up his name.

"He is a discerning man. And thoughtful. I daresay I wouldn't take anything he suggested lightly."

The clock pinged the hour, and I flew to my feet. "Goodness. It's far later than I thought, and I still need to dress for dinner."

"One moment, please, my dear." Mrs. Chalcroft reached into the bedside cabinet and pulled out a sealed envelope. "You must take this with you to the dance tomorrow and deliver it to a friend. His name is Mr. Aberdeen."

Another letter. My heart sank. Yet, I'd seen that name before.

She licked her lips. "This is personal and important. Can I trust you to deliver it in secrecy?"

So many questions filled my mind, but I could give voice to none. Who was I to question my employer? I hesitated to answer, caught in the pleading warmth of her gaze. Somehow, within the confines of the long afternoons, our reading sessions had taken on new meaning. My peculiar employer had slipped into the role of an elderly friend — like Mrs. Smith in a way, but different. I took the letter and nodded.

A wrinkled smile crept across her face. "I'm thankful every day you came to the Towers."

15

The night of the dance proved even colder than expected. The dark, evening wind whistled through the trees as the horses pulled off the road and into Plattsdale's main square. Streetlamps lit the coach for seconds at a time before fading from view. The chill silence gave way to laugher somewhere beyond as the horses approached the inn.

Smashed between Miss Ellis and Miss Cantrell, I couldn't help but envy Mr. Cantrell and Mr. Roth who looked far more comfortable in their heavy coats. Particularly Mr. Cantrell. I took a deep breath, trying in vain not to meet his eyes, but he'd chosen the seat across from me, making it all the more difficult. He stretched out his long legs a few inches from mine as we waited for the door to open.

I returned his quick smile all the while guarding my thoughts. What was it about

Lucius Cantrell that kept my heart in anticipation? His confidence? His marked attentions? I was in no way his equal, yet . . . time and again I'd found myself thrown into his intimate company, particularly when I'd set out to avoid him. Was there more to his attention than mere pretense? Was there more . . . to us?

Miss Ellis bumped the window as she fought for a view of the entryway. "Oh. There is but one coach ahead of us in line." She shot a quick glance back at Mr. Cantrell. "It is just as I feared. We are probably the last to arrive."

Miss Cantrell huffed. "Which is exactly why Lucius delayed us at the Towers. And I for one am glad of it. I deplore long waits."

I gripped my fingers inside my muff. The less of the evening I had to endure the better, but I had promised Mr. Cantrell the first two dances. I didn't want to disappoint him.

"And look. There is Mr. Sinclair," Miss Ellis said, a shrill of excitement in her voice. "So he had time to come from the Phillips's after all. And he would come alone in what looks to be a hired carriage. I'm surprised he's not on horseback."

Miss Cantrell's arm relaxed at my side, and strangely, mine did as well. Whatever tension I'd felt in the drawing room with Mr. Sinclair the other day must have been mere fancy. I knew now I was glad of his presence, even if it meant I would have to be discreet while delivering Mrs. Chalcroft's letter.

Mr. Roth tapped his cane on the floor of the coach. "What the deuce is taking so long? Cursed nuisance if you ask me . . . all this" — he flicked his fingers in the air — "dancing . . . and whatnot."

Mr. Cantrell laughed. "I wonder why you came at all, Henry."

Mr. Roth grunted. "Just so."

The carriage lurched forward and came to rest beneath the inn's slight portico. A man in dark-blue livery yanked open the door, and the scent of rain and woodsmoke greeted us.

Mr. Roth rolled his eyes. "That is all we need now. A downpour."

"Oh hush." Miss Ellis took the servant's outstretched hand, glancing up as she stepped from the coach. "There are plenty of stars about. It shall be a glorious night, free of doom and gloom if you'd only control your tongue."

Mr. Roth pulled his jacket tight about his neck and followed her descent, muttering to himself. Mr. Cantrell slipped out quickly behind him, turning at the last second to assist Miss Cantrell and me. Clear of the coach, he settled my hand on his arm before offering the other to his sister. "Shall we?"

A spark of nervousness mixed with genuine excitement as we made our way inside. I took care with my steps, cautious of the white crape evening gown and silver-lined shawl Portia found in the wardrobe with the other gowns. Mrs. Chalcroft had been more than generous. My fingers sought the pearl cross necklace she insisted I borrow for the dance. It lay perfectly situated above the celestial-blue bodice of the gown.

The front door whooshed closed behind us, my feet sliding across a well-tended wooden floor. The sudden warmth brought a smile to my lips. Beyond a grand fireplace, two wide doors parted into a galleried room. However, even rising to my tiptoes, I couldn't see beyond the droves of people. Miss Ellis had been right. Late arrivals indeed.

At first, people took little notice of us, still fawning as they were over the unexpected pleasure of Mr. Sinclair's arrival. Only the best greeting for the next Earl of Stanton. But within minutes, the roar lessened and people observed our group, Mr. Cantrell being a fine catch himself.

We made our way across the floor, where the blur of satin and lace focused into gentlemen and ladies. I recognized Mrs. Carrington and Mr. Radbourn from my trips to town, but there were so many people I didn't know. How would I ever find the mysterious Mr. Aberdeen?

Miss Cantrell deserted us as we neared Mr. Sinclair, grasping his arm and whispering into his ear. He looked a bit distressed at her hasty movements but paused to listen before grasping her hand and circling the room. Within seconds they escaped through a back door, which led onto a large terrace and gardens, as I later learned.

I remained perched at Mr. Cantrell's side watching them go, first with a mild curiosity then a modest interest. The gestures they had shared, the light touches, the whispers, all spoke of an intimacy I'd not witnessed before. One more secret to add to the ever-changing Mr. Sinclair.

Hmm. Quickly, I thought back through our conversations. Had there been something I missed? Was there more to his relationship with Miss Cantrell?

No. Mr. Sinclair had never mentioned her in any sort of way to make me believe him interested. But perhaps there was an attachment I was ignorant of. Had not Miss Ellis thought the same? And if so, was Miss Cantrell aware of the time Mr. Sinclair had spent with me? Of the things he had said and done? Of course, I could claim no romantic connection. But there was *something* between us — a sort of loyalty carved from that fateful night in the rain and the confidences I still bore.

"Are you nervous?" Mr. Cantrell asked, giving my hand a pat.

I hoped he hadn't seen me lost in thought, or worse, watching Mr. Sinclair and Miss Cantrell escape. I tried a smile. "A little I suppose, but I am pleased Mrs. Chalcroft insisted I come."

"Good." He winked. "Because I daresay it won't be long before every eye in the room will be on you."

"Me? But why?" I sought to hide the waver in my voice, but Mr. Cantrell had a look in his eyes that startled me.

"Surely you know, my dear."

"Know what?"

He laughed, but I hadn't meant to amuse him.

"That I have brought with me the most beautiful lady in the room. And, my darling Miss Delafield, all these people will want to know the person who has found a way to capture my attentions at last."

I took a quick breath, my eyes widening, the same moment the orchestra in the balcony struck a chord, signaling the start of the first dance.

Mr. Cantrell took my arm, a fastidiousness to his movements. "Come, let us enjoy the moment."

I'm not sure whether I walked or stumbled onto the dance floor. I couldn't have looked anything but shocked as I forced myself to turn the figures. Capture his attentions? The man couldn't be serious. Could he?

But he said no more about it nor acted the least bit partial through either of the dances, which unfortunately had come to be the way with us. One minute serious, the next humorous, all the while Mr. Cantrell horribly unreadable.

Almost at once I began to question whether I had even heard him correctly. He cast me a determined glance as I passed him on the floor, but I couldn't rest secure in his affections. Something didn't feel right.

As if he meant to confuse me further, he deposited me at Miss Ellis's side at the close of the second number and went to dance with the other beautiful ladies in attendance. Miss Ellis made some offhand remark about how it was Mr. Cantrell's role to humor the local residents, but I thought it far more likely that like all men, he could be turned by a pretty face.

I was glad of his distance, however, as it gave me precious time to gain my bearings and, more importantly, seek out Mr. Aberdeen and relieve myself of the letter burning in my reticule. Regardless of Mr. Cantrell's sudden declarations, I had no intention of shirking my duty to Mrs. Chalcroft. It was she who had arranged my being here in the first place.

Within minutes Miss Ellis had a partner for the next dance and I was free to roam without notice, though I found myself disappointed at every turn. Unsure who Mr. Aberdeen was or who I could deem safe enough to ask, my cautious searching turned up nothing. Apparently the man was not well-known in the district. I began to wonder if he was present at all.

I hovered in the corner where I could get the best look at the room. Mrs. Chalcroft had described him as an older gentleman, his hair thinning, his sideburns gray, his mouth unpleasant. Like a hawk, I studied each gentleman from the shadows of a pillar.

"Are you engaged for the next dance?"

My cheeks warmed, caught lurking as I was. Slowly, I glanced up to find Mr. Sinclair towering over me. My nerves were on edge, and I almost laughed. Of course I was free. After my dance with Mr. Cantrell, no one seemed the least interested in taking a turn with the local companion. But Mr. Sinclair wouldn't know that. He'd been missing since Miss Cantrell urged him away. The thought did little to recommend him.

I smiled. "I am not. And you? Have you had many partners this evening?"

He gave me a look as if he knew quite well I'd been keeping tabs on him, then offered his arm. "I don't mean to disappoint you if you had hopes of a quadrille. I'm not proposing a dance just now." He motioned with his head. "I need an excuse to step onto the terrace. Would you be so kind as to accompany me?"

I stared at him for a moment, then glanced back toward the French doors — the ones Miss Cantrell had pulled him through at the beginning of the evening. What did he want with me out there?

Mr. Sinclair let out a long breath. "I need your help, and at the moment, I fear you are the only one I can trust."

Cautiously, I answered, "All right, but I don't wish to cause a stir. For any reason."

"Don't be ridiculous. It will only further your intrigue to be seen taking a breath of fresh air with me. Lucius has spent the last hours singing your praises."

My back stiffened. "I don't know why. I've given him no cause to do so."

We reached the French doors and Mr. Sinclair pushed them open. "Haven't you?"

"No." My eyebrows drew together. "I have not."

He seemed to relax. "If that is the truth, then let me be honest." He took a deep breath. "I find his sudden attachment to you a bit hard to believe."

Though I had wondered the same thing, hearing the words from Mr. Sinclair shook me. I froze at the door before plodding through, my irritation growing with each step. The cool night air splashed my face and I swung around. "Hard to believe that Mr. Cantrell might wish to fix his attentions, or that he should choose *me*?"

"That he should choose to attach himself to a lady without any money. The man's been branded a fortune hunter for the past three years."

I touched my lips, searching for the proper response, but with my pride involved, I could think of nothing.

Mr. Sinclair softened his voice, his finger grazing the edge of my arm. "Forgive me, Miss Delafield. I should not have been so blunt, but I thought you should know. I would want to . . ."

"No. Thank you." I pulled away. "You have no need to be sorry. I-I never took him seriously, at any rate."

"As I thought. You are far too intelligent to fall for the wiles of Lucius Cantrell."

I wondered if he considered *Miss* Cantrell to share the wiles of her brother. He enjoyed her company often enough.

"Now, partner, to the business at hand. We've dallied long enough." He cast a quick glance behind him before meeting my eyes. "I need you to pretend you would enjoy a private walk with me in the garden."

Mouthing the word "private," I took a quick step back, but he grasped my arm. "Wait. Please. It's not what you think. Just a few loving looks to smooth our exit. Do you see Mr. Madden right over there? I don't wish to be asked any questions. This is important. It's time for answers." He lowered his chin. "Can you trust me again? You'll be safe enough in my care. Besides, we won't be gone long enough to cause comment."

"And is that what I am? Safe?"

Mr. Sinclair smiled as he bent to place a kiss on my hand, his gaze never leaving my face. "What do you imply?" He touched my cheek. "You know, that blush is quite becoming on you. You really should bring it out more often." He settled my hand on his arm. "By all means, keep it up as we pass by."

My pulse pounded in my ears and I squeezed his arm — hard.

Mr. Sinclair, however, didn't respond as he drew me into his side and urged me down the wide stone steps of the terrace. I hesitated to give him what he wanted. Privacy with Mr. Sinclair never went well, and he had a dangerous look in his eyes, one I had seen before. Of course, he had said it was important. Could it have to do with Thompkins's murder?

As we descended into the well-lit garden, I scoured the area, hoping I wasn't making the biggest mistake of my life, surrendering my reputation once again to this highwayman, but I was ready for answers — about Mr. Sinclair, about the murder, everything. I'd been hiding in the dark for far too long. Thompkins had been an easy target — an insignificant maid. The two of us had much in common. If Mr. Sinclair was on a hunt for answers, I'd be right there beside him.

Several couples perused the hedgerows, each far more interested in themselves than the people around them. We wouldn't be alone. We'd join their promenade, and I could stop the irritating quivers inside of me.

Mr. Madden tipped his hat. "Capital evening, is it not?"

Mr. Sinclair pressed my hand on his arm. "Yes, it is. Beautiful night for a stroll with such agreeable company." A wide smile crossed his face as Mr. Sinclair looked at me. For a split second I was transfixed, taken in by those piercing blue eyes. But as we rounded the corner of the hedgerow, he stepped away. "Thank you for that. You did well. I almost believed you to be attracted to me."

"A worthy challenge for the best stage actor." I ran my fingers along the hedge. "I don't wish to dethrone you, however. I, for one, prefer honesty."

"As do I."

"That is interesting to hear. Then you will kindly tell me what we are doing here, partner."

He took a deep breath. "There is a man at the party tonight whom I wish to observe unnoticed. Nothing more."

"A man? Does this have something to do with —"

He pressed his finger to my lips. "The man went into the library a few moments ago, and I'd like to know why. There is a large window that flanks the edge of the garden. I needed an excuse to wander out here at will. One that would not incite comment."

"I see."

He grasped my hand. "And we haven't much time, so come on." He took a step, then paused. "And don't bother asking. I have no intention of leaving you out here unattended. Lucius may wander up."

My mouth slipped open, but before I could say a thing, he pulled me along the east stone wall far quicker than I would have liked in a pair of slippers. We stole past a circular pool before entering a long bush-lined lane, peppered with the scent of verbena.

Around a sharp corner, Mr. Sinclair made an abrupt stop before skirting me beneath the hanging branches of a willow tree, slipping into the darkness behind me. "There." He parted the branches. "You can see the window plain as day."

Just above the garden's corner wall a rectangular light beamed from the house, permitting a wide view of the library. Whatever qualms I had before rushing down the terrace steps with Mr. Sinclair were forgotten as I watched the window in anticipation. I bounced onto my toes. "Are you sure he's still in there?"

"Shh. Yes. There he is."

A plump figure appeared pacing across the room with a watch fob in hand, moving in and out of our view until he stopped at the far-left corner of the window, jerking around as if startled. The garden fell quiet and still. Mr. Sinclair's breath tickled my ear. The crescent moon played tricks with the shadows around us, and for a brief moment I was brought back to that day in the rain when he'd held me against his chest, demanding to see what was in my pocket.

What a lifetime ago it seemed, but Mr. Sinclair — no less mysterious. My feet itched to move. Farther away or just a little step back?

But back where? Into his arms? Arms that had no interest in me being there? I focused again on the window. This business with Mr. Cantrell had gone to my head.

"Look," Mr. Sinclair whispered into my ear. Another dark figure joined the man's side. I didn't breathe. Could they see us watching them? I knew neither person, but my skin crawled.

The men talked, first with smiles and then angry expressions. We had no way of knowing what they said, but I could tell it wasn't pleasant as one man kept flinging his arms in the air. What if they came to blows? I jumped as Mr. Sinclair's hand came to rest on the small of my back.

He leaned down once more to my ear. "That is all I needed to know. Let us return to the dance before you are missed."

I spun around, surprised by the breathless quality to my voice. "All you needed? They did nothing but talk. Why on earth —"

He covered my mouth. "We can discuss more later."

He guided me back along the narrow pathway in silence before suddenly grabbing my arm. "Dash it all. Someone is coming."

We stopped cold, unsure which way to turn. Whoever it was, was approaching fast.

In a whirl, Mr. Sinclair swung me around, pinning me against the adjacent wall, his hand sliding behind my head. I held in a scream. He flicked open his jacket, drawing me into the warmth of his waistcoat. The footsteps grew louder, and I looked up just in time to hear Mr. Sinclair's whispered words.

"I'm sorry, Miss Delafield. Please forgive me." Then he pressed his lips to my forehead, trailing kisses down my cheek. "Put your arm around me. Now."

My mind fought to make sense of what

was happening as I tentatively touched his broad shoulders. We were acting. Nothing more, but my reputation . . .

The breeze ruffled the nearby willow leaves. The wall felt cool at my back. I thought I might faint as hordes of butterflies flitted inside my chest. But the pounding footsteps never slowed, fading away in due course as if Mr. Sinclair and I — two lovers — warranted no further investigation.

Then as quickly as I had been gathered into his arms, he released me, the scent of his pomade hanging in the air. We had trouble meeting each other's eyes, like two children caught doing something naughty. But had we? Two friends merely protecting one another?

Mr. Sinclair raked his hand through his hair. "I-I don't think they knew who you were, thank goodness. I tried to cover you as much as possible. They were moving quickly. They never gave us a second look."

"Could you see them? Who was it?"

"Miss Cantrell and a man you don't know."

Warmth flooded my face. "Miss Cantrell! But what if she did see me?"

"They didn't. So we needn't discuss it."

I wished I could believe him, but my emotions were wound up like a spring. I pressed my hand to my forehead. "Why didn't we run back to the tree?"

"It was too late. They had already seen me."

"But, I-I thought you said they didn't."

"I said they didn't see *you*. Either way, they didn't stop, which is why I had to put you through that. I'm sorry. I —"

I pressed my hand to my head. "Sorry indeed." I peeked out from between my fingers. "Just not sorry enough."

Mr. Sinclair kicked a leaf with the toe of his boot. "The degree of my *sorriness* has no bearing on the outcome."

"No bearing on you. But for me, my reputation is —"

"Currently intact." He smiled, making it difficult for me to remain cross. "Just think of it as one more thing I owe you." He raised an eyebrow. "At this rate I may never be able to repay my debt. Any ideas?"

I shook my head slowly.

"I'm sure you'll think of something, but right now we mustn't linger."

Could he be right? That my being there — alone with a man — would go unremarked? I hoped so. "Yes. Let us go at once."

We retraced our steps through the garden in silence as an invisible wall sprang up between us — one I didn't understand and loathed to find so awkwardly there.

And one more thing. Why was Miss Cantrell out in the garden — with a man?

At the terrace, we stopped cold, unprepared for what we stumbled upon. There in the shadows stood Miss Cantrell, pleading with a well-dressed gentleman, tears streaming down her face.

Like lightning, Mr. Sinclair guided me behind a large planter pot where I was hidden from view, but I watched through the branches, shocked by what I heard.

Miss Cantrell grasped the man's arm like a child begging to be held. "Please, please don't do this. If you'll just wait and see."

The man glared at Mr. Sinclair and then back at Miss Cantrell. "I have no intention of doing so, and I have nothing further to say to you, Elizabeth. This must stop. I expect not to be harassed in public again. You do yourself no favors to be seen like this."

Miss Cantrell sought Mr. Sinclair with her desperate gaze. The movement broke whatever imaginary strings held the man to her side. He stomped off, the tails of his dress jacket waving in the wind. Miss Cantrell covered her face with her hands.

Gently, Mr. Sinclair touched my elbow,

his voice all but gone. "If you would excuse me." He didn't even look back before hurrying to Miss Cantrell's side, where she melted into his arms.

All at once I felt like a stranger, watching them. A personal moment I had no right to see. Even after Mr. Sinclair and I . . . I turned away, stumbling into the shadows and then the ballroom, my thoughts a jumbled mess.

Shoulder to shoulder, people passed by as if in slow motion. Laughter. Whispers. Music floated down from the balcony above, but the tune had soured. Did the people look at me longer than before? Was there a tilt to their smiles?

Restless, I paced the available space for a time before retreating to a lone pillar outside the hall. Mr. Sinclair and Miss Cantrell? Surely I was wrong. And that man. He'd been so heartless and cold. Had they seen me — us — so intimately on display? I lowered my head into my hands.

Mr. Sinclair. He'd been so warm and desperate and gentle. My heart had broken out into a gallop as he held me, but it had only been an act — and I the fool.

Belatedly, I wondered where Miss Ellis was and Mr. Roth and Mr. Cantrell. Rallying at the thought of Mr. Cantrell's kind smile, I forced myself to recover and made my way back into the ballroom, where I collapsed onto a chair by the wall, the desire to dance long gone.

To my surprise, Mr. Sinclair arrived a few minutes later, a dark look across his face. "I have just come from speaking with Lucius. The plan is for me to take Miss Cantrell back to the Towers in my carriage. I don't like leaving you like this considering what has happened, but I haven't a choice."

I bit my lip, wishing I could run away. "How is Miss Cantrell?"

"She is unwell." He paused for a moment then continued. "Lucius will be happy to escort you home whenever you are ready."

I was ready, but I had to deliver the letter. I wanted to cry. Time was running out and I'd done nothing for my employer. The whole night had been a terrible waste. I took a steady breath, my options limited. "Mr. Sinclair?"

"Yes. What is it?"

"Do you know a man named Mr. Aberdeen? I mean, is he here tonight?"

Mr. Sinclair's gaze shot to mine and he held it there for a long moment before tilting his chin. "Interesting that you should ask. He was the plump man in the library . . . the one we watched from the garden."

16

Before he left the dance, Mr. Sinclair pressed me to find Mr. Cantrell, but I knew I couldn't do so, not yet at least, regardless of that look in his eye or his half-hearted shrug. *"Don't do anything stupid,"* he'd said.

Well, I didn't plan to.

I slid my hand over my reticule and the hidden envelope and turned around yet another lonely corner of the inn, each one dimmer than the last. Mr. Aberdeen had probably left long ago, but I had to at least try to find the library.

A musty scent hovered in the darkness. My foot snagged a loose board, and I tumbled against the wall, the scuffle echoing down the passageway, breaking the eerie silence in a way nothing else could. I eased into the shadows against the dingy wallpaper and listened for the slightest movement somewhere beyond.

Music and the taps of dancing shoes

murmured from the distant ballroom, nothing more. I breathed a sigh of relief then continued my search, a bit more careful than before.

The slam of a door ahead caused my nerves to tighten. I knew I had no business wandering this way unescorted. A light emerged at the far end of the hallway, wavering as the glow loomed larger. I closed my eyes for a brief second, searching for a suitable response should I be questioned about my presence here.

An empty feeling hit my stomach as I pictured the plump man's angry face. Was I in some sort of danger? Mr. Sinclair hadn't cautioned me about the man, but should I have decided to meet him alone, considering all that had happened?

I spun to leave but turned back only to pause. Goodness, what an indecisive mouse I was proving to be. Such warring thoughts came only from my imagination. Mrs. Chalcroft surely wouldn't have asked me to do something unsafe. The man in the library was her friend, and I'd been tasked with delivering a letter to him. I couldn't let what had happened in town sway my judgment. I squinted into the light, waiting to see if it was he who held the candle.

A large figure took shape beyond the glow,

raising the solitary flame to his face as if he too wanted to see who was lurking in the dark passageway. "Pardon me?"

I exhaled a quick breath. It was him, the man from the library — Mr. Aberdeen. I smoothed out my skirt. "Why, good evening. I am sorry to disturb you, but I believe I have gone and gotten myself lost. I was on my way to the ballroom and must have taken a wrong turn somewhere."

He narrowed his eyes at first then relaxed. "Yes, there are quite a few hallways in this old building. Allow me to show you the way back."

I smiled and took his outstretched arm. "Thank you, Mr. . . . ?"

"Aberdeen."

I licked my lips. "Ah, Mr. Aberdeen. I believe I have heard your name before." I forced myself to keep my voice light. "You must be acquainted with my employer, Mrs. Chalcroft of Croft Towers."

He stopped midstride, casting a probing glance at me, the earlier kindness fading from his face. "Why do you ask, my dear?"

"Well, she sent me here tonight to give you something."

"Something?" His jaw clenched and his voice grew cold. "Then get on with it while we are alone. This is not an evening to be found stalking in the shadows."

My hand shook as I removed the envelope from my reticule and held it into the candlelight.

Quickly, he grasped it with his sweaty hand and shoved it into his jacket. "This is most unusual. Generally I don't conduct business in dark hallways." He pinched the bridge of his nose. "Most unusual indeed. But you may tell Mrs. Chalcroft I will see it is handled — personally if it comes to that. Now, my dear, you must return to the dance. It is not the thing for a young lady to be off wandering alone."

He gave me a genuine smile, and I thought him a decent sort of man, fatherly, not scary as I'd previously supposed. Possibly the perfect person to shed a bit of light on this strange letter business. I paused. The chance to gain some information might not present itself again. "I don't wish to keep you, but I would ask you a quick question, if I may?"

"A question?" His sideburns did a little jump as wrinkles spread across his forehead.

Now or never. "I —"

Footsteps pounded behind me. "Miss Delafield," a man huffed, clearly out of breath.

I knew the voice before turning — the last person I wished to find me speaking alone with a man so far from the ballroom.

Slowly, I turned. "Thank goodness you are here, Mr. Cantrell. I have been searching all over for you."

I thought I saw a pointed glance between the two men, but I couldn't be sure. I released Mr. Aberdeen's arm. "This kind gentleman was showing me the way back to the ballroom. Would you believe I got myself lost?"

"Ah, lost." Mr. Cantrell scratched his eyebrow. "And probably my fault. I have sorely neglected you this evening." He gave a slight nod to Mr. Aberdeen. "Thank you, sir. I'll escort Miss Delafield from here." He took my hand and placed it on his arm, forcing me to turn without another word.

We neared the ballroom before Mr. Cantrell spoke into my ear. "Surely you know this isn't proper, Miss Delafield. You can't simply wander off at will. Particularly when you are in my care." He softened his voice. "I was concerned when I couldn't find you."

"I promise I would never leave the inn. I am not so wholly lacking in conduct." I steadied my tone. "Do forgive me. I didn't mean —"

"Yes, but I've heard differing accounts of your whereabouts this evening."

"Wh-what do you mean? Accounts?"

"Only that when I went looking, several people informed me they'd seen you take a walk in the garden — with Mr. Sinclair."

"Oh, is that all?"

"What do you mean, 'Is that all?' " He narrowed his eyes. "After what I said to you before our dance, I'd hoped . . ." He took a deep breath. "Come with me. I've already called the coach. The horses have been left standing far too long as it is."

We made our way back to the front door of the inn where I accepted my pelisse from a waiting servant. Mr. Cantrell donned his own coat in silence, a look of bitterness across his face. I'd hurt him somehow. I knew that now, but I'd not thought Mr. Cantrell's declaration serious, especially after what Mr. Sinclair said earlier. I pressed my lips together. How could I believe either one of them?

The same liveried servant pushed open the inn door, and I was ushered into the dreary night. Gas lamps hissed and the horses stamped in place. Mr. Cantrell stood aloof, allowing the man to open the carriage door, but he stepped up and took my hand to help me inside at the last moment. I slipped my fingers around his York tan gloves, forcing myself to meet his eyes. "I —"

"Not now." He tipped his head. "Inside."

I ducked into the coach but then turned back. "Where is Miss Ellis?"

"She left with Elizabeth and Curtis."

"And Mr. Roth?"

A slight smile stole across his face. "I arranged for him to find another way home."

"Oh." I slid across the bench. So we were to be alone.

The seat was cold, the window foggy with mist. I should have been glad to clear the air between us, but the hairs on my neck stood at attention. I crossed my feet at the floor, wiggling my toes within my slippers. There hadn't been enough time to untangle my feelings, let alone form an apology for what must have looked like strange behavior on my part.

Mr. Cantrell settled in across from me, tapping the roof to signal the driver. With a jolt, the horses tugged forward, the coach rocking in their wake. The inn drifted from view and the lights faded to a moonlit darkness around us. Mr. Cantrell must have decided to ignore me, for he barely looked my direction. I, however, found myself unable to bear the stark silence. "Mr. Cantrell, I —"

Somewhere in the shadows his hand found mine, and he brought it to his lips.

I gasped, the sudden movement inciting a flinch.

"No. Don't pull away."

My voice came out shaky. "I-I believe I owe you an apology, Mr. Cantrell."

"Miss Delafield, please." He squeezed my hand. "I don't want an apology. I fear I'm as much to blame for what happened tonight as you, allowing you to leave my side as I did. And I don't wish to fight. What I want is . . ." A smile took shape in the darkness. "Surely you cannot be ignorant of my feelings."

"But —" My mouth felt dry. "This feels quite sudden — you and I . . . Quite frankly, it doesn't make any sense."

There was a rustle as he crossed the coach to the bench beside me, the scent of brandy heavy on his breath. I wondered how much he'd had to drink.

His shoulder pressed hard against mine, and he leaned against me. "What do you mean? A beautiful lady . . . and a gentleman hopelessly in love. Please say I have a chance."

I yanked my hand from his grasp, shrinking into the only available space left, focusing my attention out the window. He'd see how confused I was and put an end to such declarations — my one chance at romance dashed.

But he didn't. Instead, he relaxed against the seat back. His fingers found the nape of my neck in what should have been a heartfelt caress, but it felt foreign and uncomfortable. I could imagine him sitting there, watching me in the darkness — a natural at intimacy, and me, no more than an innocent girl. What a fool I was. How I had dreamt of such a moment, a handsome gentleman in love with *me.* So why did my heart beat a rhythm of retreat? What was wrong with me?

"Mr. Cantrell?"

"Hmm." He shrugged.

"You do me a great honor, but you and I . . . We are too far apart." I took a deep breath. "It would be remarked everywhere."

"As if I cared for that. My parents have been gone these many years. I assure you, there is no family to disappoint. And I must marry you."

So he did mean marriage. "But what of money? What should we live on? I have nothing."

His fingers stilled around a curl that had wandered from my coiffeur. "I'll give it to you there, my darling. The crux of our difficulties." His lips touched my shoulder.

254

"You're far more rational than me. Presently, I can't see much past the moment." Another kiss, on my cheek this time. "Join me. Love is a delightful thing to fall into."

I pulled away as much as the coach would allow.

I thought I heard a laugh under his breath. "My little innocent, I won't press you now for an answer, but Mrs. Chalcroft is family, and, well, I do have some hopes there."

I froze for a long moment, digesting his words as a prickle ran up my spine. Did I care for this man at all? This handsome gentleman who saw Mrs. Chalcroft's death as a possible chance for our future?

Once I had been attracted to him. The day he'd taken my hand on the way to the east tower stood out in my mind. He was the first man who paid the least bit of attention to me. I'd been lost to him then, but now, now everything felt different.

I couldn't help but think of Mr. Sinclair. How safe I felt with him earlier in the evening, even in the garden. What would he say about Mrs. Chalcroft's imminent death? He needed the money more than anyone. I shook my head. I couldn't imagine him being so cold and thoughtless.

"Miss Delafield, I see your mind working." Mr. Cantrell's hand slipped down my arm. "There's been something between us since we met. I've felt such a connection."

I couldn't disagree. Mr. Cantrell had been a good friend, but I pushed him away. "I-I need a moment to think. I don't —"

"Shh." He touched my lips. "Don't answer now. Let us see how we get on together over the next few weeks. Give me a chance to prove myself."

Allotted the space to breathe, I eventually nodded, easing back against the seat. Mr. Cantrell had offered me everything — his heart, his life. I would be a fool not to consider the proposal. There were hardly any other options. No other suitors. And within a few months, no position at the Towers. And more than anything else, there were no answers.

I dragged myself up to Mrs. Chalcroft's bedroom with a heavy heart. Surely she'd be asleep and I could go to my room to work through the events of the night.

Moonlight crept through a slit in her curtains. The slight figure on the bed didn't move.

"Mrs. Chalcroft," I whispered, tiptoeing across the Aubusson rug. The small fire in the grate had died away, leaving a smoky scent in the room and a lingering chill. I rubbed my arms as I approached the bed.

Mrs. Chalcroft's eyes were shut, her thin face tucked against her pillow. She looked peaceful, lying there in the shadows. I was about to turn to go when her eyelids flicked open.

She licked her lips. "I wasn't asleep."

I smiled and took her hand in mine. "Well, you should have been. It is late." I noticed a book slanted on the bedside table. "Did Dawkins read to you before she left?"

Mrs. Chalcroft nodded. "I needed a bit of comfort, but I would have preferred you."

"After the evening I've had, I would rather it had been me too."

She stiffened. "What do you mean? Did you deliver the letter?"

"Yes, yes, of course. I didn't mean to startle you. That is all taken care of." I paused for a response, for the merest clue as to what I had carried with me to the dance, but she gave none. "Mr. Aberdeen said he would personally see it taken care of."

"Good." She turned her gaze to the space above the fireplace mantel. "Then it is done for now."

It was then I noticed the thick curtains had been pulled back and Anne's painting was exposed, her haunting eyes presiding over our conversation. A slight chill pricked my shoulders.

Mrs. Chalcroft lifted her gaze. "Thank you for helping me tonight, but why do you say you wish you hadn't gone?"

I bit my lip. I couldn't speak of Mr. Cantrell or Mr. Sinclair. She wouldn't understand. "There was an incident with Miss Cantrell."

She wrinkled her nose. "Ah. That. Yes, Curtis has already been to see me."

I pulled back. "He has?"

"And I suppose you agree with him. That I should leave a portion of my money to the minx."

What? Mrs. Chalcroft breathed in and out slowly as my head pounded. Mr. Sinclair had made an appeal to Mrs. Chalcroft — for Miss Cantrell? "I don't know what you mean —"

"Anne's money." Her eyes narrowed as she once again sought the painting. "If only she hadn't run out that night, so reckless, and the heir . . . I wouldn't be here alone with my guilt, left to grieve in the darkness." A tear slipped down her cheek. "Pay me no mind tonight, child. My demons are out in full force."

My voice faltered. "Miss Ellis told me Anne's baby died. I'm so sorry."

258

Her hand moved to her throat. "Do not pity me, child. I do not deserve it."

A bead of sweat gathered on her brow and I wiped it off. "It is late. We can talk more tomorrow." I tugged at the covers. "You need your rest."

"I get little sleep most nights, Sybil. I . . ." She pulled me closer, her hand quivering. "I need to tell someone . . . I must tell someone." She pounded her fist against her chest. "It has burned inside me these many years until there is nothing left."

Fearful of another episode, I acted quickly. "Speak if you must, but . . ." I covered her hand. "You know you are safe here with me."

"I know, child. I know." She swallowed hard as if a bitter taste had entered her mouth. "I-I thought I knew him, but he was nothing more than a devil in gentleman's clothes. Abuser, manipulator, and I, her own mother, was the one who forced her to marry him."

"Lord Stanton." I froze.

"Yes. She came to me one night alone, very near her confinement, swearing she wouldn't return to the fiend. But what did I know of such things? I thought her young and foolish. And scandal — I thought to guard against it at all costs. Her father's legacy, you see. It would have been ruined. I told her she would find no shelter at the Towers. That she must return to her husband. She ran off that very night — straight into a winter storm. She died of pneumonia shortly after childbirth."

I allowed a silence to settle between us. "I will not speak to something I know so little about. But no one can know the future. It was a mistake. What I hear is that you made a mistake. It does no good to dwell on the past, to keep it close and punish yourself day after day. Somehow, you must find a way to forgive yourself."

Her lips pressed into a thin line. "Yet doing so will not change the past."

"No, only your heart, I suppose."

She opened her mouth as if to say more, but changed her mind, patting my hand instead. "How did one so young get to be so wise?"

"I had a good teacher."

Her wan smile faded. "I am glad you understand. It gives me more comfort than you know. For there are days when I find my own guilt unbearable."

I rubbed my brow, trying to read her expression in the dim light.

She pulled the covers beneath her chin. "Good night, Sybil. Your eyes look tired."

I leaned over and kissed her forehead. "Sleep well, Mrs. Chalcroft."

17

Since I'd spoken with Mrs. Chalcroft about her daughter's death, I couldn't get the desperate look on her face out of my mind. It was tragic what had happened between them. I thought of Anne's lonely grave buried deep in the woods, isolated and all but forgotten.

But not by Mrs. Chalcroft. No, she felt her daughter's passing as keenly as if it had happened yesterday. What mother wouldn't? However, there was more to Mrs. Chalcroft's memory, more to her strange behavior. She'd said it was guilt.

And the letter Lord Stanton sent me never strayed far from my mind. Mrs. Chalcroft called him a fiend. How could I, an orphan from London, be involved in all this? Why would he write to me? I turned the bracelet around my wrist, the way I did when I was nervous. Whether I wanted to admit it or not, I felt something that day by Anne's grave. Some kind of connection. I needed to know more.

I pulled my pelisse tighter around my neck. The blustery winter afternoon brought a chill from the north. The trees stood bare, their naked branches groaning in the wind and dried leaves crunching beneath my feet.

Freshly fallen acorns dotted the walk, but I paid little attention to them. The sunlight was waning and with it my comfort. I must hurry if I was to return from the churchyard before dark. Miss Ellis said Anne's child had died as a baby. Considering the child had not been buried by Anne, there would be no better place for the grave.

I followed the stone wall that separated the church from the east wilds until I came to the stile. Gathering my skirt, I hopped up and over with little difficulty. Pink-and-orange begonias littered the path that wound between the graves.

Slowly, I walked along the headstones, passing name after name I didn't recognize. There were several Chalcrofts and a Sinclair or two, but no infants in the first row. A feeling of sadness permeated each weathered stone until I too felt the melancholy of loss and death. I had no family, but many had filled the holes in their absence — Mrs. Smith, the girls at the school, Mrs. Chalcroft. I wondered where Thompkins had been buried, where her family lived. If she had any.

So little had been said or done about the murder at the Towers, except by Miss Ellis, who seemed to find the investigation entertaining. Part of me wondered if she meant to solve the case herself. I, however, who knew the sullen maid, however briefly, found her sudden death tragic. If the truth never came to light, Thompkins's plight would remain a meaningless wisp on the wind. And that would be unbearable.

A rustle broke the somber silence and I watched as a starling took flight over the top of a beech tree. It was then I noticed a small, square stone nestled by the base of the tree. I took a deep breath. Could this be the marker for Anne's child?

I rushed over to the stone and dropped to my knees. There, framed by snowdrop bulbs, an inscription was buried beneath a layer of golden leaves. I brushed them off and leaned down to read the words chiseled into the stone:

IN MEMORY OF ANNE CHALCROFT

So it wasn't a grave exactly . . . or was it? I touched the cold earth, wondering what lay beneath. A spider skittered across my hand and escaped into the web it had built in the dew of the nearby hedgerow. I stood, shaking off a chill. The memorial wasn't clear. I glanced around again, searching without results. There were no answers — not in the church's graveyard at least. I took one last look at the stone before backing away.

Methodically, I checked the last of the gravestones before returning over the stile and heading home. I had discovered nothing. Nothing that would quench my new-found curiosity. It was time to start asking the difficult questions.

Dusk fell before I stumbled onto Mrs. Chalcroft's eastern rise and made my way through the thin layer of woods that separated the fields. The moon had already set up guard for the night, but a remnant of the sun's light remained.

All at once, like an arrow shot through the twilight, shouts rang out ahead, followed by the pounding of horses' hooves. Then a gunshot resonated off a nearby hill. I clapped my hands over my ears, my pulse throbbing. Earlier, I hadn't wanted to explain my destination to a groom so I hadn't taken a horse. But as the wind carried new, angry cries, my heartbeat doubled, and I wished I hadn't been so hasty.

Another shout pierced the air, closer this time. I bolted straight for home, my bonnet ribbons flapping in the breeze, my feet frantically crushing the earth beneath my boots, past trees and shrubs into the heart of the small forest, unwilling to stop until I felt sure of being a safe distance away from the sounds.

Eventually I slowed to a jog, my skirt clenched in my fingers. I couldn't maintain such a desperate pace, and my arms dropped to my sides, my lungs gasping for air.

I looked around, relieved to find I'd covered significant ground. As far as I could tell, the noises had faded off over the horizon. Whoever it had been, they were gone now. Recognizing the familiar Chalcroft land, I knew it wouldn't be long before I was safe within the walls of the Towers.

My walk turned languid, but I couldn't shake the nervousness that had crept over me, and my steps became stilted. I watched the breeze stir the leaves on the path in front of me, swirling them around. The rustle of the flurry, however, couldn't hide the cock of a pistol.

Cold rushed across my skin. Inwardly I

panicked, but my legs kept moving forward as if I were caught in a dream — or a nightmare.

Surely an animal had simply snapped a twig as it walked. But as I scanned the area ahead, somehow I knew I was not alone.

"Stop right there."

I nearly screamed as I turned to see the toe of a boot slide out from the far side of a tree.

"Wh-What do you want?"

The man coughed and I saw a flash of moonlight as he lowered the pistol. "Is that you, Miss Delafield? Thank God!"

It took me a moment before I could place the muffled voice, but as the man slid down the length of the tree and plopped on the ground, I recognized the rag on his face easily enough. "Mr. Sinclair! You frightened me. What on earth are you doing out here?"

"Oh, just a lazy evening stroll." He shrugged, and then I noticed his blood-soaked shoulder.

I gasped. He wore no jacket, and as I rushed to his side, I realized his pants were torn and his hat missing. I jerked the rag down. "Tell me what happened."

He shook his head. "I wish I knew. I've been betrayed. Ow —" He winced as he tried to adjust his position. "I believe you'd call it a setup."

"What do you mean? The men — I heard shouting. Were they chasing you?"

"Yes. Apparently the dragoons didn't approve of me searching the mail." He gave a wry chuckle. "I suppose I had a bit of luck because my head found a tree branch that unseated me, but my noble mount kept going. They are chasing the blasted horse now."

"Hercules?"

"No. I didn't risk him today as the dragoons have been getting closer. It was a borrowed hack. And probably for the best because the devil didn't even look back for me."

"This isn't a joke. As soon as they find that horse, they'll be back to get the rider."

His smile faded. "I'm well aware of that. I was in a fix until you showed up."

"Me?"

"Yes, you, partner. Do you think you can help me back to the Towers?"

Frowning, I glanced down at his legs. "Possibly. Can you stand?"

"Yes, but you better tie this up if I'm not to swoon on the way." He motioned to his shoulder where the bloodstain had nearly doubled in size.

"Oh, Mr. Sinclair." I tentatively touched

the sleeve of his shirt. "Did this happen in the fall?"

He shook his head, and I remembered the sound of a pistol echoing in the distance.

"I'm hoping it was a clean shot. Do you think you can tie it up?"

I took a deep breath. "How?"

With his healthy arm, he ripped the bloody sleeve from his shirt. "With this."

The bullet wound oozed with its new-found freedom and I pressed the torn cloth against his shoulder, my hand shaking. "I'm not certain I can do this."

"Sure you can. Just take a few deep breaths, then do me a favor and look for the exit wound."

"The exit wound?"

"On my back. I'm hoping the bullet went clean through."

I had to lift his shirt to get a good look, but as soon as I did I looped the cloth around his arm. "Congratulations. You have two very respectable wounds."

"Good." He bowed his head. "Now tie it tight. I'm already a bit light-headed."

I coiled the end of the fabric, then paused. "This may hurt."

He coughed out another laugh. "May? I'm quite certain it will. Now get on with it."

"Should I count to three?"

"Whatever, I don't care."

"On three or right after, like it would be four?"

He threw back his head. "Do it right now or I may put a bullet in — Ow!"

"All right. It's done."

"You little minx. You were trying to distract me."

I held out my hand. "Come on. I don't wish to meet a pack of angry dragoons."

His arm slid over my shoulder. "Neither do I."

The trip through the cold woods and up the east field was difficult. Mr. Sinclair said little, and I believe it was due to significant pain. He seemed quite easy to move at the beginning, but by the time we reached the side servant's door, I was pretty sure he weighed a thousand pounds.

"What shall we do if we run into someone?"

Mr. Sinclair's voice was barely audible. "Let us hope we don't." He motioned to the left. "If we take the first hallway . . . and go up those stairs, I doubt we'll see anyone . . . They're preparing for dinner."

"But do you think you can make it up the stairs?"

"Yes . . . I have to."

270

I wished I had his confidence. The hinges squeaked as I thrust open the door, and I didn't breathe until I was sure the interior corridor was empty. We had no additional light as the sun had set, so I carefully dragged Mr. Sinclair around the first corner in near darkness. At the dreaded stairs, I propped him up in an alcove. "Let me check that our way is clear."

He nodded, no longer trying to hide his grimace from me.

I flew up the stairs to an empty hallway. "Thank goodness." I returned only to find Mr. Sinclair on the floor. "Mr. Sinclair," I whispered, but he didn't answer. All was lost if he'd fainted.

I grasped his good shoulder and his eyes flicked open. A tear found its way down my cheek. "Not much farther, but I can't do this alone."

"Go find my valet. His name is Booth."

My voice was choked with emotion. "But you can't stay here."

"Why not? I'm mostly hidden in the shadows. If you're quick, no one will know I took a rest here."

"And if I'm not?"

"I shall take the consequences." He pulled his feet into the dark corner. "There. No one will see me."

271

I tilted my chin. "Unless they do." I squeezed his good arm and fled up the stairs, unable to look back for fear he was not as well hidden as he hoped.

Booth would be awaiting Mr. Sinclair in his room as it was almost time to dress for dinner. I erupted onto the first-floor landing, nearly crashing into Dawkins in my haste.

"What a hurry we are in, Miss Delafield."

I smoothed back a bit of my hair, startled she'd deigned to speak to me at all. "I am late for dressing for dinner. If you would excuse me."

She narrowed her eyes. "Certainly."

I waited as she walked by, but it wasn't until she reached the side stairs that my stomach lurched. "Dawkins!"

She turned slowly. "Yes?"

"I-I believe Mrs. Chalcroft mentioned something about coming to dinner this evening. Have you been by her room?"

"I have just come from there. She has instructions for Cook that cannot be delayed."

I rushed to the small entryway of the stairwell, barring her way. "I see, but would you mind coming with me just now? I'd like to have a word with you, um, in my room."

"I am not your servant, Miss Delafield."

"No, I didn't mean that. I would like to speak with you as a friend."

"I have no time for friends. Now get out of my way." Her shoulder brushed mine as she pushed past me.

Dear, maddening Mr. Sinclair. Dawkins would alert the dragoons as soon as she saw him. "Wait," I called, following her.

"What instructions does Mrs. Chalcroft have for the cook? I-I could deliver them myself and save you a trip."

She paused. "Don't be ridiculous."

Within seconds she was eye level with Mr. Sinclair, but she turned back to face me. "I believe you mean to curry affection with Mrs. Chalcroft, but I won't allow it. I have been her confidant for the past twenty years. No unnatural upstart like you shall take my place."

"You misunderstand me. I only meant to —"

"Don't you dare importune me any further. I have nothing to say to you." She plodded down the remaining steps in a flurry of black lace, so intent on leaving me, she didn't spare a glance toward the alcove. I pressed my hand to my chest, closing my eyes for a split second. Mr. Sinclair was safe. For now.

I found Booth as I'd expected, awaiting

Mr. Sinclair in his room. I had no more interferences as I ushered the valet down the stairs like a long-lost friend.

Booth looked to be in his thirties with dirty-blond hair and kind eyes. Thankfully he was a large man, towering over me and Mr. Sinclair's injured form. "Well, you've done it now, sir."

Mr. Sinclair smiled. "As you see."

I sidled over to the entryway. "Hurry," I whispered.

Booth reached down. "Up you go."

He brought Mr. Sinclair to his feet as if he were nothing but a sack of feed and planted his arm firmly across his master's back.

"Must you be so rough?" I rushed up the stairs ahead of them, cringing with each one of Mr. Sinclair's sharp breaths.

The hallway was empty as well as the landing, but as we neared the corridor that led to Mr. Sinclair's bedroom, we heard voices.

Mr. Sinclair rolled his eyes. "What is everyone doing . . . out and about before dinner?"

I pointed to the hallway to the right. "My room . . . quickly."

The men shared a pointed look until

Booth spoke. "Figure 'tis our only option, sir."

Mr. Sinclair turned his attention to me. "Booth can help me to my room after everyone is abed."

I nodded. "This way."

Booth pounded down the hall and pushed through the door I indicated, flopping Mr. Sinclair onto my bed.

"Wait, my coverlet." I grabbed a towel from my dressing area and slid it under Mr. Sinclair's shoulder.

Booth wasted no time in unbuttoning Mr. Sinclair's shirt and removing what was left of it. I handed him my water pitcher and stopped midstride, unprepared for what I saw. "Perhaps it would be best if I fetched more towels."

Booth glanced up. "No. I'll clean the wound thoroughly with the water, but I also need some alcohol, ointment, and bandages. I'll get it all in a moment while you stay with Mr. Sinclair." He meticulously poured what was left in the pitcher onto the wound, then brushed past me in his haste to leave, stopping at the door. "Keep it locked. I'll knock three times when I return."

I didn't speak or move. Mr. Sinclair seemed to be in and out of consciousness. He lay so still on the coverlet. A chill slid across my shoulders, causing the hairs on my arms to rise. I crossed the rug to the window, keeping my back to the bed. What was I thinking bringing Mr. Sinclair in here? To my bedchamber?

He cleared his throat. "You know . . . you don't have to be afraid of me."

My hand flopped to my side. "I'm not afraid." But I didn't turn.

"Then come over here and keep me company. I am in a great deal of pain."

I gripped the chair from beneath my escritoire and dragged it to the side of the bed. "You're hardly decent."

"Oh . . ." He glanced down. "I'd forgotten." He pulled a towel over his chest with his good arm. "Better?"

I laughed. "A little."

He took my hand. "I owe you so much more than I can repay at present." He kissed my fingers. "You were wonderful. Thank you for everything."

My face felt hot and I was sure I was blushing. "Shh. You should be resting."

A slow smile spread across his face as he glanced down at my hand. "My arm doesn't hurt so bad right now."

"Nonetheless." I smiled, meeting his firm gaze.

Two knocks sounded at the door.

My pulse vanished for a moment and I was unable to speak. I cleared my throat. "Who is it?"

The doorknob rattled. "It's me, Miss Ellis."

I cast a quick look at Mr. Sinclair, but he'd closed his eyes. "I-I'm indisposed at present. What is it?"

"Miss Delafield, you'll never believe it. The house is in an uproar. Soldiers are here at the Towers, waiting downstairs, and all the men are away. Mr. Cantrell, Mr. Roth, and Mr. Sinclair — not a one to be found in our time of need. Mrs. Chalcroft wants you to accompany her to meet the officers."

I shook my head as if in denial.

Mr. Sinclair must have heard, because he pulled me close and whispered, "You better go down."

"But what shall I say?"

"Whatever comes to mind. You've a great deal of sense. You'll think of something. I trust you . . . with my very life." He tilted his head to the door. "Go."

I stood on shaky legs, smoothing my skirt as if I'd been invited to meet the king. "I'll be right there."

18

My heart pounded as I waited on the landing. The dragoons were here. In the Towers. And Mr. Sinclair appeared lifeless. Was it possible they already suspected him somehow? Of what? Treason? Murder?

Hodge joined me from the hall with Mrs. Chalcroft on his arm. She looked older in the candlelight, her back crippled, her gait slow and unsteady. I moved to her other arm, and she seemed pleased to greet me.

I kissed her cheek, breathing in her stoic strength. I would need it if I was to fool the soldiers. My hands were clammy with sweat and I ran them down my skirt. "Do you know why they are here?" I tried to sound flippant, but her eyes sought mine with a pointed glare, sobering me in an instant.

"Not the least idea, child; however, we must be careful." She drew out the last word as if she too feared the dragoons' presence in the house.

She couldn't know about Mr. Sinclair. Could she? Thoughts raced through my mind. The letters. Mr. Aberdeen. Was I right in my earlier suppositions about her? Or was there something Mrs. Chalcroft might not want the soldiers to know? Nausea settled in my stomach as we reached the banister.

It must have looked like a great production, the three of us descending the main staircase — Mrs. Chalcroft in her elderly dignity; Hodge with his arrogant, butler airs; and me scared out of my wits.

One foot in front of the other. Help Mrs. Chalcroft balance. I'd done it often enough. Of course, this time I had to contend with my nerves.

Finally, we reached the white drawing room — the very room that had determined my fate the night of my arrival. Before Hodge could open the door, Mrs. Chalcroft's hand shot out. "What is that?" She pointed to a long brown stain slashed down the right side of my frock.

My breath caught, and the dizziness I'd held off until now threatened to overtake me. How had I not seen the blood on my gown? It was so obvious — so incriminating.

Like lightning, I folded the fabric closed

around the stain and held it in place. "It is . . . well . . . just a bit of mud. I walked to the churchyard today."

Mrs. Chalcroft narrowed her eyes, searching for far more than I cared to reveal. "Unfortunate indeed. Keep it covered. I don't want any unwelcome questions concerning my companion. I would have preferred for you to change, but it can't be helped now."

"I'm sorry. There wasn't time."

She cocked an eyebrow. "No. I suppose there wasn't. But I thank you for making haste to join me. I need your youth and strength right now." She motioned to the door. "Let's get this ridiculous intrusion over and done with. We hide no ghosts in our closets, and I'm famished. I don't want to hold dinner."

Hodge thrust the door wide and the tiny flames of a nearby candelabra winked back at us as we passed over the threshold. Mrs. Chalcroft seemed to straighten, affirming her position as mistress of the house, as she walked inside and I followed her lead.

Three dragoons lingered by the fireplace as if they felt right at home in the lush room. They watched us, waiting for Mrs. Chalcroft to take a seat. I cringed when I recognized one of them. Captain Rossiter.

He smiled as he bowed, but his whiskers barely moved above his tight lips. It was a formality, which he clearly took no pleasure in performing.

"Mrs. Chalcroft, it is good as always to see you." He raised his chin. "However, I have not come tonight on a mere social call." He glanced at the casement clock. "You know I wouldn't dream of disturbing you at such an hour, but it cannot be helped."

I held my breath as I took a seat on the sofa, wondering if Booth had returned to my room with the bandages, if Mr. Sinclair was being cared for in my absence. I could still picture the gunshot wound oozing on his shoulder, him trying his best to walk back to the house as I supported him. He looked so weak lying there on my bed.

The captain waited for the door to close behind Hodge before continuing. "I don't wish to alarm you ladies, but we have cause to believe a fugitive has taken refuge within the Towers. A dangerous man, armed, a traitor to the Crown." He paced the long carpet that stretched across the room, his fingers forming a triangle in front of him, his polished boots reflecting the firelight.

Then he stopped cold, turning his piercing gaze on Mrs. Chalcroft. "I am sure you would wish to be a help to your country. The premises must be searched at once."

A sudden cold hit my core. Mrs. Chalcroft gasped, her hand flying to her chest. "Heavens, you shock me, Captain. This has always been a quiet community — loyal, hardworking, honest. You must have patience, as I find your story a bit hard to believe. This man you say, this traitor, why would he be inside my house?"

"A good question." Unhurried, the captain drew his shoulders back. "Why indeed. After a murder was discovered on the estate. Will you also be surprised to learn, madam, that it has been many months now since we began following a spy route through this 'loyal' town? A trail of blood this very evening has led us to your doorstep. As you can see, my patience runs thin."

Breathless, I clenched my skirt. Mr. Sinclair was trapped.

Mrs. Chalcroft leaned forward. "Do you accuse us of helping this man?"

A smile played at the corner of Rossiter's mouth. "Not at all. I spoke merely as a courtesy to you, to explain the search of your house, though I need not have done so."

Mrs. Chalcroft gripped the arm of the sofa. "Of course the man should be looked for, the house searched. I assure you my servants are quite thorough. We'll find this traitor of yours if he's here." She turned to Hodge. "Gather the staff and begin the search. We don't wish to keep the good captain waiting."

Captain Rossiter picked a piece of lint from his sleeve. "My dear Mrs. Chalcroft, willfully or not, I see you misunderstand me. Such help will not be necessary. My men stand ready to search at my command."

She lowered her chin. "But at such a time? You ask too much, Captain. The household is preparing for dinner. You may return and search in the morning with my goodwill."

He tugged on his jacket. "I'm sorry, but my orders are clear." He nodded to the other officers and the three left the room in a rush, their swords banging against their legs.

When we were alone, Mrs. Chalcroft grasped my hand. "Go to your room to change at once. I need you to do something for me." Her eyes grew wide as a far-off look settled into those dark-brown pools. "Right and wrong are not always easy to define in the world we live in, my dear. I'm sorry to ask this of you, but there is a letter hidden beneath the edge of my bed. I cannot risk its discovery. Throw it in the fire, then go and change. I'll wait for you here."

I nodded, relief washing over me. She'd given me the excuse I needed to warn Mr. Sinclair and Booth. Somehow we would find a way out of this horrible mess. As I stood to leave, I found I was not completely numb to the implications of such a hidden letter.

Mrs. Chalcroft squeezed my hand again. "I must be able to trust you in this."

Forcing myself to focus on the present, I met her eyes. "I won't let you down."

"Good girl." She motioned to the door. "Now hurry. It will take a moment for the officers to organize the rest of the men outside and begin the search."

I flew up the stairs faster than I'd ever run before, my heart pounding with the need to protect Mr. Sinclair, to protect Mrs. Chalcroft, and what? Do the right thing for my country? I couldn't think of that now. Now, I could only respond to what was right in front of me. Regardless of any connections to France, my two dearest friends did not deserve death at the hands of an overzealous captain, who apparently took delight in other people's ruin.

I crested the first-floor landing, gasping for air. Mr. Sinclair. Mrs. Chalcroft. If either was discovered, my innocence could not be maintained. Whether I liked it or not, I was a part of this too. I wouldn't doubt my actions now. There had to be more to this business than I was aware of.

I raced silently down the hallway, passing my room for Mrs. Chalcroft's, and slipped inside. Even with a fire in the grate, the bedchamber stood cold and dark. Mrs. Chalcroft's rose scent enveloped the room, but I felt the lack of her presence as keenly as ever.

Quickly, I slid my fingers along the wooden bedrail, down one side and up the other. My hand shook as I frantically swiped farther and farther between the bed and the slats, pawing desperately for some kind of a paper. Where was it? I was wasting time.

Finally, my fingertips brushed the sharp edge of something. I released a long breath and held it between two fingers, carefully, bringing the letter into the moonlight. The corners were worn, the heavy paper wrinkled, and the seal barely affixed. Whatever was written inside had been penned a long time ago. Curious, I lifted the edge with my little finger.

Lord Stanton and *agreement* were the only words I could make out without affecting the delicate seal.

Footsteps pounded down the hallway. For a quiet moment I glared at the note in my hand. Did it concern Anne . . . or me? My breaths came short and fast as I cast a glance toward the fireplace then back to the letter. Mrs. Chalcroft would never know if I read it before disposing of it. My hands shook.

Voices echoed off the walls. A heavy crash followed by a bang resonated from the lower floors. The dragoons had begun searching the grounds and the lower part of the house. My chest hurt. All at once I crushed the note and threw it into the fire, jabbing it with the poker until a flame burst forth from the center.

I turned away, tears stinging my eyes. I stumbled back to the door and tiptoed to my room, back to Mr. Sinclair. I would never know what the paper said.

In my haste to enter the room, I nearly knocked Booth straight to the ground. "Steady there, Miss Delafield. What's all this?"

"Dragoons," I panted. "Here. In the house."

Booth's gaze turned cold as he slowly looked back at the bed. "We can't move him now, miss. He's lost far too much blood."

More footsteps hammered down the distant hallways. Each set sounded louder than the last.

Booth swiped his arm across his forehead. "How much time do we have?"

"I don't know. Not long."

"Then we're done for." He covered his face with his hands.

I paused as a thought took shape in my mind. "Quickly, help me clean up the blood from the floor, and get Mr. Sinclair under the coverlet and flip it over. I hope the blood has not soaked all the way through."

Booth shook his head. "As you say, miss, but it's no use. I can't carry him out of here with the dragoons crawling all over. And they'll find him just as easy in his bedroom."

"Once the blood is gone, you must leave at once. I've got to change into my night-gown and robe." A rush of heat filled my cheeks as I glanced once more at Mr. Sinclair's still form. "He is asleep, right?"

"Ah, yes, miss. Out cold, but I don't follow you."

"Never mind that. Do as I say."

He wiped up the last of the blood by the door and walked over to the bed. "Can you hold him while I pull the coverlet from beneath him?"

Mr. Sinclair moaned as Booth rolled him onto his side, but he didn't wake up. I gingerly held his arm before being forced to support his bare back. I bit my lip. What had I gotten myself into? This plan of mine was ridiculous. So ridiculous it might just work. But if we were discovered? I couldn't think of that.

"All right, miss. A couple more spots on the floor and I'll be out of your way."

I nodded then held my breath as I flipped the coverlet over. Thankfully, only a tiny bit of blood had soaked through to the other side. I would have to rumple the sheets to cover it, but it would be possible.

"Leave the door unlocked," I called over my shoulder.

Booth paused on the threshold. "What is it you plan to do? I can't let you —"

"There isn't time to explain. He'll be safe enough in my care."

He shook his head. "You've the courage of a badger, miss." He smiled. "There's nothing I wouldn't do for Mr. Sinclair. There's nobody like him in this world." He winked. "I think you understand that."

I shooed him out the door and ran for the wardrobe, slipping out of my muslin frock with each step. Mr. Sinclair moaned but I didn't look back. I couldn't. He was asleep — unconscious really. I repeated the words as I wiggled out of my chemise and threw my heaviest gown over my head, following it up with a thick robe. I was hardly less dressed than before, but I hoped it would do the trick.

I checked over the room. Other than the large man in my bed, it looked just as it had before. A knock sounded and I jumped beneath the covers, my arms tingling with nerves. "Yes?"

Quickly, I adjusted the pillows and bedcovers until I was satisfied. I whispered into the bedsheets, "Please forgive me, Mr. Sinclair." Then I sat on him.

He didn't move.

The soldier's voice boomed through the closed door. "Pardon me, miss, but I am one of His Majesty's soldiers. You must step out into the hallway, as we've been tasked with searching every room."

I folded the coverlet down to expose just enough of my present state of dress. "I'm sorry, but I am indisposed and confined to my bed. Could you wait there while I call my maid?"

A pause at the door, and then, "I, uh, suppose so, but the room must be searched."

I reached up and yanked the embroidered bell pull for Portia. I hoped she'd come quickly.

Several minutes passed as I waited, but I

289

didn't dare get off Mr. Sinclair. Was I crushing him? I peeked under the blankets to be sure. I'd found a way to avoid his shoulder and put most of my weight on the bed, but it couldn't be comfortable the way I'd smothered him in the pillows. His breathing sounded unlabored, and his chest was warm. A slight quiver ran through my body as I looked at his hands, his fingers, resting so lightly beneath the sheets.

I forced myself to look away, but my heartbeat didn't slow. In fact, I began to sense that I heard his too.

But I was wrong. It was the door again. "Come in."

Portia rushed inside, concern written across her face. "Miss Delafield, I had no idea you were ill, and these horrid soldiers turning us out of our rooms." She crossed her arms. "Don't you worry, I won't let them come in here."

I didn't move an inch as she circled the bed. I yawned for emphasis. "Yes. The dragoons have come at an awful time. I don't think I'm well enough to stand. Perhaps if they force the issue, they can take a quick look inside while I rest here. You can stay and guard me."

"Be sure I won't leave your side, miss." She pulled up a chair. "I've heard of what these soldiers do to unprotected females. It's a disgrace. My cousin Mary had one kiss her full on the mouth."

Mr. Sinclair moved a leg and I cringed.

Portia flew to her feet. "Here they are now. Keep yourself covered."

The latch clicked and the door slid open a few inches. A soldier's timid voice came through the opening. "Are you ready to leave the room?"

Portia held up her fist. "She won't be going anywhere. How dare you suggest a lady leave her sickbed. You would have her contract pneumonia to fulfill some silly order."

He took a deep breath. "I suggest no such thing, but I do have orders to search every room in this hallway. I cannot leave without —"

"You unnatural, horrid wretch of a man! How would you feel if this was your sister in this bed?"

A chuckle came from the other side of the door. "I only have five brothers."

Portia pounded the bed. "Oh . . . your mother then."

Mr. Sinclair must have felt her fist, because again he shifted. The thought of him waking with me pressed to his side had never crossed my mind. I'd never be able to look him in the eye again. This little scene had better end — and quick.

I pretended to cough. "Allow me a suggestion."

The young soldier poked his head in. "Yes?"

He was just what I'd hoped for, young, inexperienced, still scared of women. "Could you search the room quickly, but allow me to stay here in my bed?"

Portia cast me a look as if I'd forfeited the battle without even trying.

The boy hesitated. "I-I believe that would complete my order."

I laid my head to the side as if I was too weak to argue. "Then get it done."

Portia held my hand as the soldier scoured the room, opening every drawer, shifting through my things. No wonder Portia was angry. I felt the intrusion too, but I said nothing as he tossed my private things about. He looked behind the curtains and beneath the escritoire, then approached the bed, rubbing the back of his neck.

"I need to search around here." He circled his finger in the air.

Portia stepped between him and the bed. "Don't you dare touch her."

He halted, his voice shaky. "Touch her? I-I would never. What do you think me, a libertine?" He leaned down to the floor, probably hiding from his own embarrassment. "I only meant to check underneath."

"Then hurry it up. Miss Delafield needs her rest."

He remained on the floor for a minute or two, then rose to his feet, staring at me in the bed before backing away. "I'm sorry to have bothered you."

Portia followed him to the door, slamming it inches from his heel. "Now" — she turned back to face me — "I will sit with you till you fall asleep. What book would you have me read?"

The bed shook slightly and I thought I heard a muffled laugh buried under the pillows. I hoped Portia hadn't heard it too.

19

It took several minutes to convince Portia to leave me. When she finally did, she seemed hurt by my sudden change of heart. But I had no time to soothe her feelings. I waited only for the door to click shut before jumping from the bed and tossing pillows and covers aside as if I'd found a spider within the blankets.

I paused, my legs leaning against the mattress, my hand pressed to my chest. Of course I knew what I'd find under all that bedding, but seeing Mr. Sinclair again — hurt yet sleeping peacefully — brought the whole experience rushing back. He lay at an angle, his eyes closed, arms still tucked against his body. The bloodstain on his bandage had darkened to a reddish brown. I touched my brow. We had escaped.

"Mr. Sinclair," I said aloud, still concerned I'd heard him laugh earlier, but he didn't move an inch. Perhaps I had been mistaken.

I hurried to lock the door, then scooted the chair Portia had used closer to the bed, my gaze falling to the empty room, my hands working to recover Mr. Sinclair with the linen sheets. How long would it be before Booth felt safe enough to return? I glanced at the small casement clock on the escritoire. He wouldn't dare chance it before everyone retired for the night. It could be hours.

I closed my eyes for a brief second, Mrs. Chalcroft popping into my mind and giving me a start. Oh dear. My harrowing night was far from over. Mr. Sinclair would have to be left alone so I could make the trip down to Mrs. Chalcroft to assure her I'd destroyed the letter. But what of Portia and the dragoon I'd fooled? I was supposed to be too ill to rise. And what of my present state of dress? Did I dare appear before the captain in my robe?

I glanced down once more at Mr. Sinclair's sleeping form. I had no choice. If I didn't go to Mrs. Chalcroft, she would assuredly come to me. I gave his arm a reassuring touch before pulling the coverlet over his head. "We've almost made it though. Be good while I'm gone." I left the room, locking the door behind me.

I found Mrs. Chalcroft taking her leave of

the captain at the bottom of the grand staircase. "Ah, Miss Delafield." Her eyes took in my change of clothing. "Have the dragoons gone from the first floor?"

I nodded, all too aware of how I must look.

The captain spared me a cursory glance before turning back to Mrs. Chalcroft. "I already assured you, madam, my men have cleared the house."

"Humph." Mrs. Chalcroft's bony fingers wiggled their way around my arm. "Then I shall bid you good night, Captain. Hodge will show you out."

Captain Rossiter bowed. "Thank you for your cooperation, though I am sorry our search was not as fruitful as I had anticipated." He crossed his arms before turning back. "Oh yes . . . One more thing. Guards will be posted across your property for the remainder of the night — for your protection of course. We don't want another *incident* happening on the estate."

She straightened her back as best she could. "You forget nothing, do you, Captain? I thank you for your concern, even though such a thing is not necessary. Come, Miss Delafield, I am more than ready to retire. You will tell Dawkins I wish to have my dinner brought to my chamber."

Though she led me slowly up the stairs,

we made no real progress until I heard the door close behind me. I leaned down to her ear. "Do not be anxious. The letter was destroyed before anyone searched the rooms."

She squeezed my arm and let out a slow breath. "Thank you, child." She stared at me as if something had changed between us. "You have been my sole comfort since your arrival."

After returning to Mrs. Chalcroft's room, it took me far longer to leave her for the night than I would have wished, as her nerves were raw. She ate anxiously as I read to her from the novel *Waverley,* trusting that Mr. Sinclair still slept in the adjoining room. I'd heard no movements through the wall.

Gently, I closed the book, thinking of the letter I'd burned, of Mr. Sinclair and the dragoons, of Thompkins's death, even of Mr. Cantrell's offer of marriage. What did it all mean? I felt so much uneasiness; there was so much to doubt. As I crossed the thick rug to leave the room, I nodded to Dawkins, who I believe had long been anticipating my departure.

Silently, I slipped back into my bed-chamber, locking the door behind me, and made my way to the side of the bed. Moonlight had crept upon the room in my absence, bathing everything in shadows. I rubbed a chill from my arms before sliding back the covers.

The small movement must have disturbed Mr. Sinclair because he rolled toward me, tossing his head back and forth against the pillow. His eyes blinked open, but they didn't seem to focus. I reached out and felt his forehead — hot. He thrust my hand away.

"Shh . . . Mr. Sinclair, it's me. Miss Delafield."

His panicked movements calmed almost at once, his eyes clearing before his gaze found mine. He licked his lips. "Oh . . . yes . . . I believe I was dreaming." He rubbed his eyes. "Though it felt so real." A slight smile brightened his face as he took a moment to look about. "I am still in your room. Where is Booth?"

"He's staying away until the household has all retired for the night."

"Right." He nodded, but winced at the movement. "I fear I've been a terrible trouble to you."

"No more than usual, but let us not talk of that now. Are you thirsty?"

"Yes, very."

I poured him a glass of water from the fresh pitcher Booth brought up earlier. "It's been sitting out a while, but it's better than nothing. I don't suppose I can call for a tray. The both of us shall go hungry tonight."

He met my gaze. "I am sorry — for everything."

"Forget it. I was only teasing, and I should know better than to do so with a man who was shot just a few hours ago." I held out the glass then paused. "You do look a little better, but you will have to sit up a bit to drink this. Do you think you can? I mean, does your shoulder pain you terribly?"

He glanced down at the bandage. "It does hurt, but I find I can bear it well enough. Booth forced me to take a dose of laudanum earlier." He pressed his lips together as he pushed against his good arm.

I tried to help but found myself watching the struggle as nothing but a useless bystander.

One last push and he collapsed against the headboard, gasping. "There. That will have to do for now."

I waited until he extended a shaky arm before passing him the glass, and he managed well enough on his own. It was only after he'd had a long drink that he squinted at me. "What on earth are you wearing?"

I hoped he couldn't see the blush I felt splashing across my cheeks. "My night robe, of course."

His eyebrows pulled together. "How long have I been asleep?"

"A while . . ."

"And you?" He tilted his chin. "What have you been about?"

I smiled. "Nothing I wish to discuss at present. Perhaps later. When you are feeling better." I moved the candle onto the bedside table, hoping the continued light wouldn't be remarked by anyone else in the house. I couldn't let it burn for long, but I wanted to see Mr. Sinclair, every strand of his dark-brown hair, wild from today's adventures, the rise and fall of his chest as he breathed, the way his lips curved slightly at the corners. I needed to know he was safe.

I leaned my elbow down on the bedside table. "The dragoons have set up watch outside the house, but we're out of immediate danger."

"Good." And just like that he slipped his fingers around my hand as if he'd done it a thousand times. "I was worried I'd involved you irrevocably in this mess."

His grip was warm and strong like his arms had been the day of the dance. I didn't breathe. He didn't let go. My fingers tingled. "I knew the risks. I wanted to help."

"But I never should have involved you."

He stared down at our hands, a strange stillness taking over his face as his thumb traced the lines on my wrist. "What you must think of me, I have no idea. I won't put you in danger again. You have my word on that. Your life is too precious." He breathed a sigh before focusing back on my face, his piercing gaze uttering something his lips wouldn't.

The candle flickered. The room fell quiet around us like it too felt the stirring tension between us. My pulse raced, and all at once I knew the truth. The very thing I had been fighting for weeks, the reason Mr. Cantrell no longer interested me — I was in love with Curtis Sinclair, the next Earl of Stanton.

And he must never know. My fingers fell out of his grasp.

A pain swept my frame and we both awkwardly turned away. I was all wrong for him — penniless, common. And he, just as wrong for me. I never should have trusted a man with so many secrets. I stood, forcing my mind to come out of the muddle I'd allowed it to slip into with a simple touch of his hand.

Mr. Sinclair rubbed his eyes. "I need you to do something for me."

I leaned forward. "Yes?"

"No more letters to town. No more rides to Reedwick alone."

The muscles in my shoulders tightened. Mr. Sinclair was worried — for me? My gaze traveled to the dark window. He told me in the woods he'd been betrayed. By the same person who had killed Thompkins? Possibly. But she had been on the estate, in the garden at one point, meeting someone. Who?

My voice came out in a whisper. "I understand, but —" I cleared my throat, daring to venture where I never had before. "Why are the dragoons chasing *you*? What have you done?"

My question was met with Booth's quiet knock on the door.

The light of morning brought with it more questions than I cared to think of, and certainly no answers. Pacing the confines of the small garden behind the house was doing little to ease my mind.

Booth had come to my room the previous night with two men I'd not seen before, and Mr. Sinclair was whisked away without more than a quick "Thank you" in passing.

I glanced up at the first-floor windows standing in a line, dark and foreboding. He was behind one of them, and I longed more than anything to know how he fared. There was no question of me inquiring, of course. I would have to bide my time until he was up and about. All I could do was wait and worry.

I'd already heard the rumors at breakfast that he'd taken ill. Booth would see to all his needs now. And a good thing too. I couldn't risk another encounter. The time apart would do me good. Time to think. Time to plan.

Though I hated to face the truth, Mrs. Chalcroft would pass on soon, and I would be dismissed with nowhere to go. The thought frightened me more than I cared to admit, but I had to be honest with myself. Thompkins's murder and the dragoons had become a distraction. I'd come to the Towers to discover the truth of my past. I'd found out little from Lord Stanton's cryptic letter, and grave or no, Anne gave birth to a boy that tragic night — the heir. Mrs. Chalcroft had told me so. Yet I had to fit in somewhere. Lord Stanton would not have sent me the bracelet otherwise.

I thought of the painting that had startled me that first day in the tower. Though I'd been flustered at the time, I had felt a hint of familiarity, like I had seen the earl before. Perhaps I had not given the thought due course. What was it about his hard face that I remembered? That possibly held a clue?

My shoulders grew tight and I took a deep breath. Could I find my way back up to that tower alone? A shifting breeze played with what was left of the dried leaves, scattering them across the path. I clasped my hands in front of me, hesitating. I had come for answers, hadn't I? Perhaps I'd best get on with it. I pushed my shoulders back, turned, and walked back toward the house.

The morning sun aided my ascent up the musty tower stairs. Soon enough, the darkness fought for control, and I was forced to be guided by candlelight. My hand shook as I held the solitary flame into the air, a thin line of smoke disappearing above my head. I compelled my feet to move. Higher and higher I climbed into the wretched blackness. A prickling chill met my advance. One more turn and the small brown door appeared beyond the last step.

My fingers fumbled with the rusty latch, and for a terrifying moment I thought it might be locked. At last the door creaked open with the gentle nudge of my shoulder, depositing me within the confines of the ghostly room. I shuffled forward, the white Holland covers leering at me as I passed to where I remembered the painting residing.

It was no longer there. I peeked beneath various covers, certain Lord Stanton's likeness had been somewhere in the far corner.

Nothing. I spun around, catching sight of the large gilded frame against the opposing wall. A chair had been perched beside it as if someone had spent time admiring the artist's work. Odd. Slowly, I strode forward, holding out the candle, watching the colors of the canvas spring to life as the glow of the unsteady flame reached it.

The earl's cruel expression struck me as it had before, but I settled into the chair, caught by the devilish gleam of his green eyes. After a quick look, I shook my head. I did not know the man, but a chill wriggled up my neck just the same. Seconds passed as I studied the picture before my mouth slackened and I leaned forward. Could it be?

The first time I'd seen the painting, it had been so difficult to look beyond those insensitive eyes, but I saw it all now in its entirety, the truth laid bare for anyone to see who endeavored to do so.

Lord Stanton had a long straight nose and a pair of thin eyebrows that peaked in the middle — just as mine did. And his lips . . . I had spent a great deal of time looking at my own. They were a perfect match. No one could deny the resemblance between us. All at once I was restless, standing, sitting, pacing the small space, the candle quivering in my fingers.

The shadows pressed in around me and I needed to get outside, into the sunlight and the cool breeze. Down the stairs and out the servants' entrance, I raced across the east lawn, stopping only when I reached the back wall of the garden, collapsing against the cold stones.

Breathing in the crisp air, I gave voice to the thoughts lashing through my mind. I was somehow related to Lord Stanton. Could there be any other conclusion? But how? Could I be his illegitimate child? The daughter of a servant or nursemaid? Someone had paid for my schooling. Someone with money who demanded Mrs. Smith keep my identity a secret. Stanton fit the description. I glanced back at the house.

It was the only thing that made sense. And if I was correct, it meant I had no real tie to the Towers. These people were Anne's family, and I would be leaving upon Mrs. Chalcroft's death.

Mr. Cantrell's kind offer came to mind. He loved me in some sort of way. Me. The orphaned girl from London with no money, no status. Not some adventurous version of myself I'd fabricated to gather information. He'd been honest at every step, and we had a connection — one I'd at least felt at the start. I could find my way back to loving him, if I ever really had. Either way, I couldn't dismiss his proposal so quickly.

I heard a voice from somewhere in the yard. Was it Mr. Cantrell, here this very moment? Boots crunched into the gravel of the path on the other side of the garden wall. Whoever it was, they were moving quickly. By daylight the garden didn't frighten me as it did when caught up in the power of night, but I took a jerky step back.

The footsteps stopped and the voice I'd heard sliced through the old stones as if he stood next to me. "It will be the end of us."

It was Mr. Cantrell all right, and he was angry.

"Please, don't say that. Please, stop saying that." Another voice. Miss Cantrell was with him. "I-I'm sorry. I should have told you sooner, but I was afraid."

"Afraid of your own brother?" There was a shuffle and I heard a bump against the wall. "Well, you should be. You've likely ruined everything. You do realize my other . . . enterprises only keep us afloat."

"Please let go. You're hurting me."

"Did you think I wouldn't find out? Surely

there is something that can be done."

"No. It's too late. I wouldn't anyway. Ow. Lucius, I'm sorry. I made a mistake. One I will have to live with for the rest of my life. There's nothing you can do to me now that will make me feel any worse than I already do."

His voice betrayed an anger I'd not heard from him before. "This is how you repay me after all I've done for you! You worthless wretch . . . worthless."

"You're right about everything. I am the worst sort of person. But what will I do?"

There was a silence before another bump sounded through the wall. "You can blasted well figure it out yourself this time. I'm done with you. I was so close to getting everything, *everything* I wanted . . . so close, and you've thrown it all away."

"No, please. Don't say that. I-I couldn't bear it if you cut me off too." She was pleading now.

The scene on the terrace at the dance came to mind.

Mr. Cantrell's voice sounded strained as it took on a leaden tone. "I need time to think, but I make no promises."

"I understand. Please, just don't do anything rash."

"You don't get to say what I will or won't

do. Not anymore. You're nothing but a liability to me now. A duty I have no wish to fulfill."

I heard first one leave, then the other, but I didn't emerge from my hiding spot. Instead, I collapsed against the stone wall. What had I overheard? How did Miss Cantrell play into all this?

Everyone at the Towers had a secret. Every. Single. Person. And I could do nothing but claw my way through their web of lies.

20

A week later I left the house for a long walk. I couldn't stand to be inside or look at the drab walls anymore. Mr. Sinclair finally made a brief appearance in the breakfast room before he escaped back to his room. I wish I could say I was glad he left. Goodness knows he needed time to recover. But when he chose to ignore my presence as he'd done a thousand times before, my heart ached in a way I'd not expected. I'm sure he meant to protect me, but after our night of camaraderie, I found it difficult to resume my position as Mrs. Chalcroft's companion, who had no business setting my cap at a future earl.

I spent the whole of the morning reading and tending to Mrs. Chalcroft, fearing all the while she suspected my growing duplicity. Occasionally I noticed a keen look in her eyes that made me wonder if she knew more than she chose to let on. Before I left her, out of the blue, she reached for her head and declared she would retire to her room, insinuating I might wish to take a midday walk.

Of course, that was exactly what I longed to do, so I said nothing, retrieved my bonnet, and dashed from the Towers like a prisoner escaped from her bonds. Clouds threatened the sunny day, but it looked as if I'd have plenty of time for a walk before the weather changed. A quick burst down the front path and I found myself rushing across the east lawn with the express intention of losing myself somewhere in the woods.

The manicured hedgerow led me around the garden and through the rusty gate that separated the cultivated lawns from the rest of the estate. I'd walked that way often enough, enjoying every scent of nature and the quiet calm of the fields, but today — today I found the place sadly dreary. I saw nothing but bare shades of brown and gray — nothing to turn my mind from a certain gentleman and what I'd discovered about myself.

On the far side of the first field, the land took a gentle dip to the left, and long, flat rocks crested the soil. A small stream parted there from the line of the field and wound its way like a ribbon through bushes and gullies on its way to a thicket of trees that separated Mrs. Chalcroft's land from her neighbor's.

I followed the brook for a little way until the ground softened and the trees lengthened, making it difficult to go on. Most days, I would turn back at this spot for I was far too afraid to leave the estate. But for some reason, the tree branches pointed onward, cracking and moaning in the wind, whispering of adventure. Dried leaves flurried around me, tumbling down the shadowed path. There had been no news of the murder investigation or the dragoons for a full week.

My feet itched to move. My toes curled in my boots. I could feel the steady beat of my heart all the way from my chest to the tips of my fingers. Without thinking, I grasped my bonnet ribbons in one hand and my skirt in the other and ran — not the pitter-patter of a lady conscious that someone might be watching, but as a young girl, running only for the pure enjoyment of doing so.

The wind's gusts tickled the trees over my head as the brook sloshed at my side. I flew down the trail as if I were nothing but a bird, darting in and out of the shadows. What a glorious moment to be alone and free. To forget the sight of Thompkins's body and Mr. Sinclair's bloody shoulder. To forget to be afraid.

After a time, the muscles in my legs burned and I was forced to slow to a walk. Panting, I propped my hands on my hips and turned into the wind to cool my face.

It was then I heard an agonizing cry. Not a child's voice but a woman's.

Breathless, I stared down the path, pressing my hand to my chest. More concerned than frightened, I inched forward, following the sobs into a dark section of trees, where the branches blocked the sun and the bushes grew like curtains around me.

I stopped.

There, collapsed on a log, was a woman with her face buried in her hands, gasping for air.

"Miss Cantrell!" I called out but didn't move, still shocked by my discovery.

She glanced up at me through red-rimmed eyes but said nothing.

I lowered my voice to a whisper as I made my way to her side. "Whatever is the matter? Do you need help?" I looked her over from head to toe, trying to understand what had caused her to cry out as she had.

She lifted her head like a scared animal, her golden hair a ragged mess about her face. But she seemed to compose herself and stared me down for a moment before raising her chin. Her voice held her usual hint of irritation. "Why, Miss Delafield, I see you too took advantage of such a lovely day for a walk." She wiped her eyes. "As you can see, I am a bit indisposed. I-I suppose I got a little winded while walking. I'd only meant to rest a few moments. But I'm fine now. Please, go on your way and leave me be."

Beads of sweat dripped down the side of her face as her chest rose and fell with each shallow breath. I didn't move. It was obvious that something else was causing her distress.

I took a tentative step forward. "You're not fine. I don't believe that for a moment." I reached out for her hand, which felt icy cold and looked far paler than ever before. "You're chilled. How long have you been out here?"

She looked away as if lost in thought.

"I daresay you need some help. I cannot leave you to walk back to the house alone." I bit my lip and cast a quick glance at the trail behind me. "Perhaps it would be easiest if I were to run back to the house and bring someone to assist you. The groom can bring a horse."

A strange look crossed Miss Cantrell's face, so I prattled on, "I would only be gone a short time, of course, and then John can be sent straightaway from the house for the doctor." I raised my eyebrows. "Surely everyone is worried that you are gone. I'll hurry. This log seems a comfortable enough place for you to wait. Do you think you shall be well enough till I return?"

Her hand shot out like a claw, her fingers wrapping around my arm. "Please . . . don't." My mouth fell open, and she relaxed her grip. "Don't be ridiculous, Miss Delafield. All I need is a few minutes to . . . to catch my breath. I . . . ."

She was winded but also unnaturally quiet, barely making sideways glances at me as she crossed and uncrossed her feet.

"Miss Cantrell, surely you realize I must bring someone to come assist you. You look pale. I cannot allow you to walk back in such a state. Or perhaps we could walk back together — slowly?"

She shook her head. "Please, I beg of you to go and think no more about me. I am quite well. I'll return to the house" — she took a quick breath — "when I'm ready."

Should I believe her? Should I stay or go? The memory of my arrival at the Towers came to mind. When I'd been so cold and tired, Miss Cantrell had done nothing to help me and certainly didn't deserve my pity now. But no matter the memories circling in my head, I wasn't heartless.

Miss Cantrell closed her eyes as if she could read my thoughts, then opened them with that waspish look I knew so well. "I wish to be alone. Surely even a lowly orphan such as yourself can understand this request. You do realize you're not *my* companion. If I have to, I will be forced to order you to forget you saw me, and go on about whatever business it is you do around here."

I hid my hands behind my back so she wouldn't see my fingers clenched into fists. I learned a long time ago not to allow people to see when they hurt me. I took a step back. Nothing would be gained by staying any longer. Drawing in slow and steady breaths, I mouthed, "I tried."

Turning back the way I came, I walked away and decided from that point on I would avoid Miss Cantrell at all costs. It would take me a good half hour to reach the house, even if I ran as much as I could. Regardless of what she said, I intended to send someone back to help her. But who? Of course, my first thought was Mr. Cantrell, but after the way he'd railed at her last week, I wasn't sure.

Mr. Sinclair? If he wasn't lying injured on his bed, he would know what to do. He did seem to care for her in some way. Perhaps I could speak with him. At the edge of the trees, I took a fleeting look back and was surprised to see Miss Cantrell bending forward, holding her stomach.

I saw her painful cry before I heard it. She glanced up at me, the haughtiness stripped from her ashen face. "Miss Delafield. Please. I'm so sorry. Please, don't go."

Within a moment I was back at her side, using my sleeve to wipe the sweat from her forehead. She shrank at my touch, the effort to maintain her position failing. I brushed a lock of hair behind her ear and looked into her eyes — a beautiful emerald green like her brother's. It was strange that I had not noticed them before now.

I lowered my voice. "Miss Cantrell, we both know you merely tolerate me. I've come to live with that fact, however arrogant and ridiculous I think it is. But something is seriously wrong with you, and I'm the only one here who can help. Please, won't you come down from your pretentious pedestal and find a way to trust me — even if it's only for this afternoon?"

She didn't speak, but I caught the hint of a smile. Then she looked at me in a way she never had before, as if the stone wall be-tween us had crumbled at our feet. For the first time she felt like a real person to me, someone not unlike myself — alone in the world, harboring some unknown burden.

I felt her hand slide beneath my arm, and she hesitantly pulled me next to her. Her cheek felt wet against my shoulder, and her breaths slowed. In that silent moment as I cradled her in my arms like a small child, I forgave her again for whatever existed between us. She cried — not quiet tears, but those of a deep emotional release I soon learned she'd needed for some time.

We clung to each other for different reasons, bound by a new unspoken friend-ship. Hidden in the trees, we stayed like that for several minutes until the tears abated and Miss Cantrell was able to lift her head. "Oh, Miss Delafield."

I offered a smile. "You don't need to say anything to me if you don't want to."

"I'm afraid I must tell you the truth if you are to help me back to the house." She blushed. "I should never have walked so far. I-I had a fight with Lucius again. And I don't know . . . I suppose I was out of my mind. I barely remember running and fall-ing, but" — she touched her stomach — "I think the pains have stopped now. I was so worried. I thought perhaps I had done it on purpose and all was lost. But you see, I realize now, for the first time since this whole thing started, that I may be ashamed of what I did, but I don't want to lose the baby."

Baby? My gaze drifted to her rounded waistline, but I forced myself to look up, hoping I'd not revealed the shock coursing through my body. Elizabeth Cantrell was pregnant — all this time. Why had I not guessed it? Her moody outbursts, her nausea and sleepiness. I tried to keep my voice steady. "Does anyone else know?"

Her hands shook as she folded them and laid them on her lap. "Not many. Mr. Sinclair has known for some time."

Mr. Sinclair. Of course. My heart froze like a flower caught in the dead of winter, then pounded like it never had before.

She shrugged. "I-I'm glad he knows in a way. He's been so kind through the whole ordeal."

I didn't speak or move, so she continued. "You see, Mr. Sinclair was once good friends with the father, who you probably saw at the dance."

I nodded and relief washed across my tightened muscles.

"Mr. Sinclair tried to help in the beginning, but it seems the man I thought I loved doesn't want me."

I let out a slow breath. "I'm so sorry. And your brother?"

A spot of color reentered her cheeks. "He's having a hard time with the news." She picked at her skirt. "That's the whole problem. I'm afraid I've made him desperate."

"What do you mean?"

"You see, growing up, Lucius and I only ever had each other, sheltered away at our estate in New Castle. Our parents cared little for us, but we knew someday we would go to London. I would have a season and Lucius would be allowed to join the fun. That's all they ever spoke to us about — fun.

"You can imagine our shock when we learned from our solicitor ten years ago that they passed away in a carriage accident. We were further shocked when we learned the true state of the affairs we had been left with.

"Lucius came to my room one evening, looking so mature and smiling as I'd never seen before. I was only thirteen, but he was entrancing. He'd cut his hair and bought a new tailored suit. You can image what a figure he made, suddenly with the world before him. More importantly, he had a plan.

"First, he would take what was left and gamble wildly, hoping for some kind of payout to live on the next few years. When I was old enough, he meant for me to have a season where I was to make a brilliant match. And last, we would come to Croft Towers to find some way into Mrs. Chalcroft's will."

She shook her head. "He was so sure of himself then. I wanted to believe him. He looked so young and handsome, and he paid such attention to me. He swore that even if only one part of his plan worked, we would be fine. But it hasn't. None of it has. His gambling drove us further into debt. Aunt Chalcroft seems to care nothing for me or him. And then the baby. There will be no marriage for me — not ever.

"I will have nowhere to go soon. I cannot conceal my situation for long. I told him about it only last week. He wasn't pleased." She held up her hand. "Don't judge him. He's been under quite a bit of duress. If Mrs. Chalcroft forgets us in her will, as I believe she plans to do, particularly after she finds out about the baby, Lucius will be forced to make a new plan. And I shudder to think what it will be this time."

21

It took several long, arduous hours to assist Miss Cantrell back to the house, stopping as we did often to rest. Considering her surprising condition, I believed we couldn't be too careful. The return of her pains would have spelled disaster for her and the baby.

By the time I relinquished her care to her maid, we were both tired and, though we nursed a budding friendship, a little cross. I promised to check on her later that evening and hurried down the hall to Mrs. Chalcroft's room where I had been absent for far too long.

As I caught my breath, I began to wonder whether she might be irritated with me. I had never missed afternoon tea without telling her in advance. A retreating sun cast long rays on the carpet through the hall window, stretching past my toes to the end of the corridor. Resting my hand on the latch, I planned my words, then inched open the door and tiptoed inside.

Late-afternoon darkness had overtaken the room and a chill hovered on the floor. Any second I expected to hear Mrs. Chalcroft's brittle voice as she called to me from somewhere within the bedsheets. However, only silence greeted my arrival. The hairs on the back of my neck rose as I glanced around the room, which seemed far more foreboding than usual in twilight's silver light.

I took a step toward the bed and the shadowy figure lying there. I'd worked out a speech that highlighted Miss Cantrell's fall to the difficult journey back. Surely Mrs. Chalcroft wouldn't be angry if I woke her and explained. Besides, it wouldn't be long before she must dress for dinner.

Like a mother would wake a child, I reached out and touched what I thought was her sleeping form, only to realize such an explanation might not be necessary, for I was alone with nothing but pillows. Relief washed over me. I might have a few minutes to rest before dinner. But as I fluffed the pillows and laid them in their proper place, uneasiness crept into my mind.

Why were Mrs. Chalcroft's bedsheets tossed about, her fire left to smolder in the grate? Where could she have gone? And with whom? I stood there completely still for several seconds, listening to the wind rattle the windowpanes, before all at once I got the uncomfortable feeling I was not alone.

Slowly, I shifted to the right and forced myself to look. Above the fireplace, on top of the mantel.

Anne. The curtains had been flung back and her painting exposed. I backed away, a fluttery feeling taking over my stomach. Oh no.

I darted out of Mrs. Chalcroft's room, conscious only of my desire to find her. Of course, my hasty retreat propelled me straight into Dawkins's path on her way down the corridor.

I stopped short, my thoughts racing. "Pardon me. I apologize for . . . well . . ." I glanced back at the open door behind me, guarding my words. "Do you know if Mrs. Chalcroft decided to leave her bedchamber? I thought she said this morning she planned to spend the day in her room."

Dawkins narrowed her eyes. "Aren't *you* responsible for the mistress in the after-noons?"

I nodded, adding a bit of a smile for good measure. "Yes, generally she likes me to read to her, but today she decided to take her nap early. She suggested I go for a walk, and since the weather was fine, I agreed at once to do so."

The muscles in Dawkins's jaw twisted within her thin face.

I had made an error. "What is it, Dawkins?"

Her fingers tightened around the small jewelry bag she held in her hand. "You mean to tell me you went for a walk and left her all alone?"

"Why, yes. It was her idea. I meant to be gone less than an hour, but I was late returning because Miss Cantrell —"

Her voice turned to ice. "And did you tell a maid of your plans before you left?"

A slight shiver ran across my shoulders. "No, I didn't think it necessary. Why? Should I have?"

Dawkins sucked in a deep breath through her nose, the kind that lasts far too long, and left me wondering if the air in the room had thinned somehow. She tipped her chin. "I knew this wouldn't work. A lady's companion barely out of the schoolroom. Ridiculous. I've never seen the likes of it before." Her gaze met mine. "You better be careful not to take too many liberties and forget your place. You may sleep abovestairs, but you are not one of them. You are not family." Then she flicked her fingers down the hall. "Well, Miss Delafield."

She lingered on my name and I felt like I was shrinking under her glare.

"I suggest you find her."

Find her? "What do you mean? She couldn't have gone far. If she felt well enough to take a brief walk, I don't understand what business it is of either of us."

Something changed in her eyes. "Surely you are aware of her spells, Miss Delafield."

My stomach lurched. I had only seen the one spell shortly after my arrival. No one had even mentioned them since that day. In a way, I'd forgotten all about them.

Dawkins leaned forward as if she'd read my thoughts. "One time we found her down in the cellar — incoherent for hours afterward."

I thought I saw the slightest look of satisfaction cross her face. She planted her hands on her hips. "I certainly hope that's not the case this time, as Mr. Cantrell and Mr. Sinclair are in residence . . ."

And the dragoons. I finished the sentence in my head, unwilling to consider what Dawkins might know, and more importantly whether she could be trusted. "Would you help me?"

She stared then slowly nodded, and I

wondered if I might not want her help. But I had no time to lose. "Thank you. I suppose we should split up to cover more ground. I'll start here on the upper floors and then head to the gardens. If you —"

"I'll take the kitchens and servants' quarters as I have business there." She lunged forward, then halted as if someone had pulled her back by the shoulders, meeting my gaze with a callous smile. Her voice sounded strange. "Be careful who you tell the mistress is missing. That she's had another of her spells . . ."

Leaving the statement there in the hall, she turned to the landing, where she descended the central staircase without looking back.

My palms were wet, and I paused to wipe them on my skirt before launching into my search. The hallway felt empty, and I looked first one way and then the next. Either way I chose to go, I knew now I had to find her before anyone else.

I started like a mouse, tearing down the hallway, popping my head into each room, calling out her name at every turn, but nearing the end of the family wing, I'd already turned a few servants' heads. If I continued in such a manner, I would do nothing but alert everyone in the house of Mrs. Chalcroft's disappearance.

I crossed the landing to one of the large rear windows, hoping I might see her in the gardens below, her cane gripped in her fingers. But as I neared the corner, I caught sight of Miss Ellis in the sitting room, flipping through a magazine. I opened my mouth to call out when Dawkins's words came to mind — *"Be careful"* — and I slipped away, or at least I tried to.

"Good afternoon, Miss Delafield," Miss Ellis called.

For a split second I teetered on pretending I hadn't heard her, but something made me reapproach the threshold. "Good afternoon." My voice sounded hollow.

Quickly, she folded a slip of paper and tucked it into her reticule. "I suppose everyone is too busy these days to spare a second for me."

"I'm sorry, Miss Ellis, truly I am. But at the moment, I'm working and haven't much time for pleasantries."

Miss Ellis picked at the overlay on her white skirt. "I understand, really I do. But after Mr. Sinclair refused to go riding with me and Mr. Cantrell left for town, I'd hoped to spend a bit of time with my aunt. But do you know, when I asked her to join me for tea, she didn't even bother to respond. It was as if she'd not even heard me. Of course, I knew she had because she looked at me in that blank way she does sometimes when she says she's 'forming a plan.' I can only hope this time it includes me."

A spark of hope lit inside my heart. Perhaps my search had a direction after all. "Oh, Miss Ellis. I am so sorry you've been neglected." I motioned to the hallway. "But you said your aunt passed by this way?"

"Yes. A good half hour ago, I suppose. Looking stronger than I've seen her in some time. Can you believe she edged down the stairs on her own power? I watched her the whole way. It made me wonder if the doctor might not be wrong about her." She bit her lip. "We can hope, can we not? I —"

I crossed the room to grasp her hands and sat beside her on the sofa. "Never stop hoping." Attempting nonchalance, I tried to make my voice light. "Did you perhaps see her leave the house?"

"Goodness, no. At least, I don't think so. I gave up watching her after she turned the corner at the bottom of the stairs, heading into the servants' wing. I figured it was none of my business what she was about."

"No, I suppose not, but thank you. I-I need to speak with her at present." I flew to my feet. "You've been incredibly helpful. I do have to go straightaway, but I promise as soon as I get a spare second, I shall spend some time with you. We could go riding or shopping in town. Maybe John Coachman could take us to Reedwick."

Her face brightened. "I'd like that very much. Perhaps they'll have word of the murder investigation."

It took all my patience to walk away, hide my pounding concern, and descend the stairs like a lady of fashion, but the minute I was out of sight, I hoisted up my skirt and rushed into the kitchens. I nodded at Cook but didn't slow until I reached the door at the end of the servants' hallway. Somewhere in the middle of Miss Ellis's speech the thought had come to me where Mrs. Chalcroft might be.

The tower room. The chair by the painting.

I had no desire to see Lord Stanton's disagreeable face again, or to feel what I'd felt the day of my discovery, but I swung open the narrow door without another thought. A gust of stale air wafted into my face, and I peered up the rounding stairs. Could it be possible that the passageway was darker than before?

I secured a candle from the kitchen. With a quick glance back at the empty corridor, I took a deep breath and slipped through the door, inching it closed behind me.

Silence pressed against my ears, and I lifted the candle. One . . . two . . . three. The flame flickered, but the light held. The dust covering the walls and stairs lay so thick I could taste it. As if waiting for the faint light of sunrise, I watched as the dark stone stairs took shape before me, conscious only now of how alone I felt.

I climbed quickly, driven by a primal instinct to reach the top. But the farther I went, the more the damp smell of mold fought me back. A muffled crack of thunder found a way through the thick stone. I tried not to listen, but I remembered the storm that had threatened Miss Cantrell and me on our walk back, so I picked up my pace. What little time I had to find Mrs. Chalcroft was fading away. Round and round, the stairs narrowed and darkened until I was forced to slow my steps.

But I didn't have much farther to go. All at once, I was at the door.

I pushed it open and raised the candle to eye level, the Holland covers and piles of rubbish taking shape in the shadows of the room.

Nothing. The room was empty. I'd climbed the wretched stairs for my own exercise. I took one step forward to be sure, eyeing the horrid painting in the corner where Lord Stanton waited to stare at me with those cold eyes.

I had just turned to leave when I heard a creak.

My body went motionless.

It sounded again. Not an echo from far away like the thunder that followed me up the stairs, but an eerie crunch that reverberated down from above my head. Without thinking I ducked as if the wooden beams stood poised to fail at any moment.

That's when I saw the small door in the corner swinging open. The one Mr. Cantrell had indicated led to the battlements on the roof.

I hadn't heard thunder or wind. It was footsteps. Someone was up there — on top of the tower.

I set down the candle, realizing my light would be useless in the rain, then held my breath, hoping for a way to see. Amid the dreary clouds, a gray light persisted and illuminated a path beyond the door. I'd need the candle to get back down the stairs, so I left it on a small side table and made my way onto the roof.

The opening tunneled for a moment and cut off the majority of the wind and rain.

But once exposed, I spilled out into the full onslaught of the rain. A small stone ladder came into view to my left and appeared to lead to the overlook at the top of the tower. My hands felt cold and shaky, but I climbed one rung at a time, making sure I had a firm grasp with each step.

A thread of lightning streaked across the dark sky as I crested the top, illuminating the world in white light for a breathless second. There she stood, her pale nightgown flowing in the wind like an angel watching over the estate.

"Mrs. Chalcroft," I yelled as I made my way over the stone ledge, but she didn't turn, and the last thing I wanted to do was frighten her. I wasn't sure if she could hear me over the pouring rain, but I didn't want to take any chances. She was near the edge and the stone she leaned against for support looked far too unstable. The dark rocks of the old battlement were chipped and cracked, the floor littered with the fragments of years of disuse. I doubted anyone had come up here in some time.

Careful with my movements, I inched my way around the curve to Mrs. Chalcroft's far side, the howling gusts fighting me at every step. I never took my eyes from her feeble form. I couldn't imagine how she made the journey, let alone stood there as she was, staring out over the estate.

The clouds pulsed with electricity, and I blinked away the assault of raindrops, utilizing the uneven stones to guide me. My wet frock clung to my legs. What was left of my chignon slipped loose and a splash of icy water ran down my back.

The quivers began, first in my hands, then my legs. I was never very good with the cold, but I pressed on, finally nearing her side. "Mrs. Chalcroft." I reached out and touched her arm. It was ice beneath my fingers, but she wasn't shivering. All at once, she turned her head, her blue eyes gray in the darkness.

She took an uneasy step back, her foot slamming against the low wall. "Anne? You're here. You made it home. I-I thought I'd lost you forever. I was looking for you." She pointed over the stones and into the wild shadows. "They told me you ran away. I thought somehow to see you from up here, to stop you from leaving, but . . ." She squinted. "I was wrong. Here you are. Safe and sound."

I grasped her hand. "It's me, Mrs. Chalcroft. Miss Delafield, your companion."

She jerked back, covering her ears, her leg pressing against the edge. "Stop it, stop it now, Anne. I told you already. There is nothing to be done. You're married now. You best start acting like it."

The rush of rain stole my breath, but what could I say? Mrs. Chalcroft was not herself; she was lost somewhere in her mind. I touched her hunched shoulder, hoping to find a way to guide her back to the ladder. I hadn't the least idea how I planned to help her traverse the steps, but there was no way we could stay up here. "Won't you come with me?"

"Don't be ridiculous." Her voice deepened in a way I'd not heard her use before. "Mark my words. You will go back to him. You know what's due your family name even if you always were a spoiled child. Father's little angel. I'll hear no more of your fanciful notions."

I stood there still as a statue. How could I find a way to bring Mrs. Chalcroft back to the present and away from the horror of the moment she was reliving in her mind? "I'll do as you say. Please, come back into the house with me."

Something changed in her face. She pressed her lips together as the silvery light and the dark shadows fought to claim her. "A baby, you say." She looked about her as if she'd lost something over the stone's edge. "We must protect him at all costs. Lord Stanton. It's his fault, all his fault. How wrong I've been." She covered her face with her hand, then met my eyes. "Will you not come home with me now, my dearest Anne?"

"I'll stay with you, Mrs. Chalcroft. As long as you need me to. But please. You must come with me inside — now." I held my hand out into the rain, willing her to take it.

"No." Her voice turned dark, pulsing with a frantic energy. "First the letters. It's more important than anything else. We must send them to the Frenchman in town. He'll take care of everything. He'll save us all. I know I've more money just over here . . ."

For a moment I thought she meant to come with me, but all too soon I realized I was wrong.

She spun to the ledge like a wild animal, emboldened by a world that existed only in her memories. The pouring rain slowed before my eyes as if it too had been caught up in a dream. I screamed, but the thunder hid my voice as soon as it left my throat.

I lunged forward, but I was too late. In my panic to grasp her, I saw the broken stone behind her. I screamed again, but Mrs. Chalcroft slipped on the loose rocks at her feet, careening toward the shattered ledge, when two strong arms appeared and pulled her back, one harrowing step at a time, farther and farther away from certain death.

"Mr. Sinclair!" Tears fell from my eyes and mixed with the rain. My legs shook as I knelt at his side.

He too seemed unable to speak, his eyes a mix of fear and compassion, but his hand found mine in the darkness as he cradled Mrs. Chalcroft in his arms.

22

"The Frenchman. The letters!" Mrs. Chalcroft yelled, her gnarled fingers wrapping around my wrist, pulling me against the ledge. *"Go, now!"*

My knees scraped the jagged stones and I awoke with a start, surprised to find my clothes dry, Mrs. Chalcroft sleeping at my side, and Mr. Sinclair — watching me from the doorway.

A dream.

Breathless, I glanced around the room, all signs of the previous night's turmoil washed away, all except Mrs. Chalcroft's withered form.

I rubbed my eyes, wishing that too had been a dream. But it hadn't. Mrs. Chalcroft had taken ill within hours of her flight to the tower. Fever racked her body with violent sweats and bouts of confusion. We all feared the worst. She'd been too long in the cold and rain. I hovered over her bedside deep into the night, bathing her forehead in rosewater until sometime in the early-morning hours when I'd drifted into a fitful sleep, dreaming of those frightful moments on the tower over and over again.

Still a bit confused from my lack of sleep, I leaned back against the chair slats, slow to meet Mr. Sinclair's gaze as he approached. He didn't speak at first, only poured a cup of water and set it on the bedside table.

As I'd come to recognize all too well, I could feel his presence behind me, the tingling of my skin, the subtle change to the beat of my heart, the scent of his pomade. I didn't need to look to know he was near. Not anymore.

His whisper broke the silence. "I'll sit with her now. You need to get some rest."

I glanced over my shoulder. "What time is it?"

"About five o'clock. The maids should be in soon to light the fires."

"Oh," I yawned. "I-I must have let it go out sometime in the night."

"Don't be concerned. The room is warm enough." He brushed my arm as he leaned down beside the bed to swipe a clump of hair from Mrs. Chalcroft's forehead. "Her fever is down some."

"Oh?" I took in a long breath. "I don't

know what I would do if . . . if she'd left us like that."

I was tired and hadn't chosen my words well, but by the look on Mr. Sinclair's face, he knew what I meant. My gaze dropped to the bedsheets. "You're the hero in all this, you know."

He pressed his lips together. "Don't."

"Well, it's true. How did you know we were up there on the tower?" I rubbed my arms. "And how desperately I needed help?"

"I have a pretty good view of the eastern tower from my bedroom window. You can only imagine my shock when I saw the two of you up there in the rain."

"And you came and saved her."

"I did no more than anyone else would do." He shrugged his shoulders. "Did she say anything? Up there, last night?"

I hesitated then nodded. Most of what Mrs. Chalcroft had said didn't make any sense, but two words still haunted my mind — *the Frenchman.* Regardless of my hope against it, the letters I'd been carrying all over town had to have something to do with the dragoons. And the murder? I wasn't sure.

I felt Mr. Sinclair's eyes on me, so I assumed a light tone I didn't feel. "She called me Anne. You know — her daughter, Lady

340

Stanton. I believe she was remembering a time long ago. She mentioned the child that died. The heir." I watched for a response, but Mr. Sinclair only turned away.

"I shouldn't be questioning you at such an hour. We can talk more later. What you need now is sleep. I won't keep you any longer from your bed." He squeezed my hand. "You've been wonderful through all this. And even if Mrs. Chalcroft won't remember what you did last night, I will. She's lucky to have you."

I thought I saw his arm move as if he meant to touch my face or my hair, and oh how I wanted him to, but he settled it neatly on the coverlet at Mrs. Chalcroft's side.

I rose from the chair. "And your shoulder? Is it healed?"

He twisted his arm in the candlelight. "It's much better. I don't think I did too much damage. Besides, I can't stay hidden for much longer." He grinned, then rubbed his chin. "Now go on to bed, Miss Delafield. I'll keep Mrs. Chalcroft company."

I took one final peek through the open door before leaving the room, knowing full well how much my heart wanted to stay.

I didn't think it possible to achieve any semblance of sleep with my anxiety as fresh as it was. But with Mrs. Chalcroft's initial crisis over, I fell into bed and slept soundly until evening when the onslaught of hunger pains chose to awaken me. Sluggish, I dressed and journeyed down to supper, only to find the house had gone into something of an uproar in my absence.

The doctor had been out twice to see Mrs. Chalcroft, ordering several draughts and worrying Miss Cantrell with his grave prognosis, but Mr. Cantrell assured me he'd seen no evidence of a full inflammation of the lung. All I could do was hope he was right. I wasn't ready to lose her.

Though Miss Cantrell didn't seem to take Mr. Cantrell's cheery diagnosis as her own, I was pleased to meet her smile across the room. In the course of a day it seemed her small stomach had rounded and the house had been made aware of her joy. The burden of guilt and secrecy had vanished from her face, leaving behind a lady of distinction. I gave her a quick wink. It appeared our new friendship had every chance of success.

She motioned to the seat next to her. "I'm glad you had time to rest, Miss Delafield; however, your company has been sorely missed." She cast a quick glance at Mr. Cantrell, who couldn't take his eyes off his port.

I took a sip of water. "Any news from town?"

Miss Ellis sparked to life. "Is there! You'll never believe it, Miss Delafield. Another woman has been found dead."

Miss Cantrell widened her eyes. "Goodness, Evie, death is hardly a topic for dinner conversation. You've soured my stomach completely."

"Elizabeth's right." Mr. Cantrell's voice sounded hoarse. "She was no friend of ours at any rate." He ran his finger along the stem of his glass. "Of course, I suppose there is a possibility that you knew her, Miss Delafield, since you said you met her maid."

"Me?" I swallowed hard.

"I believe her name was Plume, was it not?"

I sat up straight. "Mrs. Plume? From Adisham?"

Miss Ellis chimed in again, undeterred. "And after her maid went missing and died and everything. It is interesting, is it not? What a mess the authorities have made of the whole affair." She smiled. "I begin to wonder just what it is they think they are supposed to do."

My plate blurred. Another passenger from the mail coach was dead. I cleared my throat. "What happened?"

Mr. Cantrell spoke slowly as if recounting a play. "Her carriage was found abandoned on the road this morning . . . her body still inside." He raised his eyebrows. "Shot in the head."

I closed my eyes for a long second before casting a glance at the ceiling, wishing I could see through the wood and plaster and into Mrs. Chalcroft's room, where Mr. Sinclair likely hovered over her bed. Another murder. What would he make of this terrible news? Did he already know?

I could see his dark eyes twinkling in the candlelight as they'd done earlier when he asked me so innocently about what Mrs. Chalcroft had said to me on the tower. How I wished I could believe his question nothing but idle curiosity, but deep down I knew better. But murder? I couldn't believe it. I wouldn't believe it.

Yet there was much I didn't know. Somehow, some way, my aging employer had gotten herself involved with French spies. The very traitors to England the dragoons were looking for. And Mr. Sinclair played into it all too somehow.

A part of me wanted to dismiss my warring thoughts, forget what all I'd learned. But there was one thing I couldn't overlook — I was the only passenger left alive from that infamous day on the road, and there were far too many secrets within the Towers — secrets I couldn't ignore.

Three arduous days passed before Mrs. Chalcroft's fever broke at last and she became responsive. Three days that I could barely think, let alone process the newest murder. So much horrible death and no answers. The local investigation had turned up nothing.

Though the doctor spoke of improvement, one look at Mrs. Chalcroft and I knew she wasn't long for this world. Her slight frame had aged over the past few days, and the spark to her personality, the one thing that set her apart, had dulled with her illness.

With what little strength she had, she asked me to read to her, which seemed to comfort her for a time. But she didn't stay awake for long; her sunken eyes slipped closed behind droopy eyelids after only a few sentences. I slid the book back onto the bedside table, gave her a kiss on her forehead, and left her in Dawkins's care as I headed back to my room to think, to make plans for my own future. Soon there would be nothing left for me in this place.

I sat on the edge of my bed to remove my slippers, and a knock sounded at the door.

"Yes?"

"May I come in, Miss Delafield?" It was Dawkins's voice.

Curious, I crossed the room and unlatched the door, where I found her on the threshold, hands folded at her waist, wearing her usual stormy expression.

"Is something wrong? Is it Mrs. Chalcroft?"

"No. But I would have a word with you in private."

I stepped back. "Then by all means, please, come in."

Leading with her shoulder, she trudged through the door and made her way over to sit in a chair by the fireplace, where she fidgeted with the lace on her sleeve. Portia had drawn up a small blaze for the evening in my absence, and I joined Dawkins there in an adjoining chair.

Lost as to why she had come to my room, I smoothed my skirt. "Would you care for some tea? I'm sure I could ask Portia to fetch a pot. She's rarely in bed at this hour."

Dawkins cast a sharp glance up. "No tea. What I have to say won't take long."

So the conversation wouldn't be pleasant. I lowered my chin, waiting for the attack to begin.

But she softened her voice. "I doubt Mrs.

Chalcroft has ever told you why I came here."

My mouth slipped open. "No, no, she hasn't."

"I was a child of seven. A village girl. My parents died of the fever and Mrs. Chalcroft brought me here."

"Oh?" I pressed my hand to my chest. "I'm so sorry . . . about your parents. I-I didn't know you'd been here so long."

"I have no need for your sympathy, Miss Delafield. I don't really remember them." She raised her eyebrows. "I only remember Mrs. Chalcroft. You see, she brought me here as a playmate for Anne, who was an only child — lonely, willful, forgotten. I was to become the sister she'd never had.

"But I was older than Anne by two years, and though we got on together, we were never that close. Because . . ." A slight smile crossed her lips. "Mrs. Chalcroft liked me better. Better than her own daughter, you see. Better than her own flesh and blood. She educated me, depended on me, loved me like no one else ever has."

I leaned back in my chair, my voice nearly deserting me. "Why are you telling me this?"

"You really don't know, do you?"

"Know what?"

She flicked a speck of lint from her frock.

"Listen, *Sybil.* If she cared for me more than her own daughter, you have no reason to try anything now. I will not be replaced in her affections. Not by you or anyone else. What she needs through to the end is me. Am I clear?"

"I have no intention of taking anyone's place." I shook my head, finding it difficult to choose the right words. "Why would you think I wield such power?"

Dawkins huffed. "She's grown frail, her spirit broken by years of guilt. She may not know what she's doing." Her piercing gaze shifted from the fire to me. "I'm afraid Mrs. Chalcroft brought you here for a reason, and it's no good. It won't appease her conscience. I suppose she thought no one would figure it out. But I did. You look too much like him."

A bolt struck my chest like lightning on a summer day, making it nearly impossible for me to breathe. "What do you mean? I look like who?"

She laughed. "Lord Stanton, of course. The devil himself." She lifted her chin, her words dripping out with precision. Clearly, she'd waited weeks to say them. "Who do you think took you to that school in London so many years ago?"

My mouth felt dry. "What are you say-ing?"

"It was me." She gave her shoulders a piti-ful shrug. "I did. Mrs. Chalcroft didn't want you then, and she doesn't need you now."

The words of Lord Stanton's letter came ripping into my mind along with the brace-let, the connection I felt to this place.

"That's right. I see you working it all out. I suppose you have a right to the truth. I'm sorry, but Lord Stanton is your father."

My hands shook. I'd known it since I returned to look at the picture in the tower, but the truth felt icily real coming from Dawkins's stern lips. But I had been right. I was Lord Stanton's illegitimate child, sent away to grow up in anonymity. I let out a long, low sigh, digesting it all, but then I sat up. If Dawkins took me to the school, could she answer the one question I'd longed to know since that day I'd seen my father's painting?

Who was my mother? My mind fretted through everything I'd seen and heard as a dark cold seeped into my core. I thought I might be sick. It was all too clear, the truth laid out before me like a puzzle with a solitary missing piece.

I pressed my arms against my stomach and tried to keep my voice steady. "You.

Are you my mother?"

A breathless silence swept over the room until a deep laugh erupted from Dawkins's wiry frame. "Of course not, you fool. You could be no one else but Anne's ridiculous daughter."

It was night when Portia knocked on my door, summoning me to Mrs. Chalcroft's room, but I hadn't slept a wink. Troubled by the late hour, I hurried into a robe and tiptoed my way next door.

Mrs. Chalcroft, my own grandmother, looked tiny, all but swallowed up by the large bed. I found it difficult to look at her now that I knew the truth — that she had tossed me away all those years ago. My initial shock at Dawkins's disclosure had turned to anger, then disbelief. My world had shifted. Nothing felt real anymore. Not the murders, not the truth. Was I living a dream?

Dawkins had tucked the eiderdown just beneath Mrs. Chalcroft's chin, making her appear like a small child.

I forced myself to the side of the bed where I found the usual chair waiting for my arrival — cold and empty. Before leaving my room, I made the decision to conceal what I'd learned. My complicated grandmother, with all her failings and secrets, could pass in peace. I wanted nothing from her.

I tucked my hands behind my elbows. "Is everything all right? Are you worse?"

"I don't know, my dear." It was a struggle, but she took a couple of breaths and then continued. "I don't believe I shall be here much longer."

Repressed tears gathered in my eyes, my chest choking as if beneath the pull of a tight blanket. My resolutions were already shattering. I opened my mouth then closed it. What could I say?

"Don't say anything trite." She met my eyes. "I know it all."

"Would you like me to send for Mr. Cantrell or Miss Ellis?"

Her eyes widened and she coughed. "Absolutely not. There is no one I wish to be with tonight but you."

"I-I don't understand."

A slight smile lifted her mouth. "I believe you do." She reached for the glass of water at her bedside and took a long sip. "I have one last package for you to deliver to Mrs. Barineau. It's for her husband actually, Mr. Barineau."

I'm not sure what I was expecting her to declare, but it wasn't that. "A package?"

My voice halted.

"Yes. It is of the utmost urgency and must go tonight."

"Tonight?" I glared at her curtained window, allowing her a chance to listen to the rattling shutters and the howl of the wind. Another storm was brewing out there in the darkness. Like my turbulent emotions, it had been growing all evening.

Mrs. Chalcroft attempted to sit up but fell back onto her pillow, pain etched across her face. "I wouldn't ask it of you if it wasn't a matter of life or death."

Life or death? She spoke madness, of course. Was she having another one of her spells? She was the only one in danger of dying. I met her gaze and the keen look in her eye. She seemed sane enough, but unreasonable. I took a deep breath. Even if I braved the cold and wind, the dragoons would be there to stop me before I left the estate — and what then? I would be found carrying a package filled with evidence of high treason. And the murderer still on the loose? No person in her right mind would do such a thing for a mere employer. But this wasn't just a position, was it?

I touched my forehead. "Surely there's another way." My initial shock seemed to be subsiding into rational thought. "You ask me to risk my life."

"I know what I ask of you, but you must believe me when I tell you it has got to be done." She took a sip of water. "And there is no one else I can ask to do it." She pressed her lips together. "You once told me you would do anything for me."

Every nerve in my body screamed. How dare she ask this of me after abandoning me so many years ago? My muscles itched to walk from her room and never look back. What did I owe her? Nothing.

But my throat grew thick. No matter what I believed about the past or what I thought I should feel now, whether right or not, I had come to love Mrs. Chalcroft. She wasn't easy to love, but she had been growing on me since our first encounter.

She was my grandmother, my only living relative. I had come to the Towers for one solitary reason — to uncover the truth of my past. And I'd found it, oh I'd found it.

It was then I noticed something I'd not seen before. My grandmother's hand was balled into a fist, quivering in the candle-light. The grand Mrs. Chalcroft of Croft Towers was afraid, deeply afraid. I sat there a moment without moving, suddenly aware of my strength and my own moral compass. If there was anything I could do for my grandmother before the end of her life, regardless of what had happened to me, I should do it.

She patted my hand. "You do understand, don't you?"

"I understand that you need me, and that is enough."

The hard lines on her face relaxed. "You are too good to me. It is difficult to find loyalty in such a world as this. You will carry in your hand something of great importance. Will you take it to Reedwick and find some way of avoiding the blasted dragoons? It must get safely to Mr. Barineau tonight."

"I don't know how, but I'll try. For you."

"That's my girl." She motioned behind me. "You must go at once. There is a pair of trousers and a dark frieze coat in the chest beside the wardrobe. Take them, put them on, and stay off the main road. His Majesty's cavalry is not your friend on this night."

I nodded, moving to the trunk to gather up the clothes.

"Come back to my room when you have finished this wretched work. There will be no sleep for me tonight." She slipped her hand beneath the edge of the mattress and pulled out a dark-brown satchel.

I took a moment before accepting it, for

what she held was more than just a letter. Then all at once, I grasped it, flipping the strap over my head, trying not to listen to the sound of coins rustling around inside the bag.

"Mrs. Chalcroft —"

"Ask no questions, my dear. I shan't be able to answer them, not yet at least. But soon, hopefully soon."

I chose not to state the obvious. That she may not live long enough to tell me. "But if I don't return?"

"I shall be forced to take Dawkins into my confidence."

I hesitated, nearly dropping the bag.

Mrs. Chalcroft coughed then lowered her voice, motioning me a bit closer. "I know what you are thinking." She held up her hand. "Don't. My relationship with Dawkins is complicated at best. Though I trust her explicitly, she has changed a great deal over the years. You may have noticed that she rarely leaves the house and never to go into town. I could not ask her to deliver this, nor would such a thing go unremarked."

I nodded then turned to leave as a thought came to me. "What about Mr. Sinclair? Can I not ask him to accompany me?"

Her eyes widened. "No. He of all people must be as far away from this business as he can get. Now, you're wasting time. The night grows cold around us."

"Right." I would be alone in this. Numb, I ambled toward the door, the clothes pressed to my chest, the heavy bag looped over my shoulder.

I heard her frail voice on the air before I shut the door. "May God go with you."

23

I raced from Mrs. Chalcroft's room into my own, shedding my robe and nightgown in one fell swoop. I could picture the perilous journey ahead of me. Darkness, rain, dragoons. Had I any hope of success?

I pulled up the trousers and fastened them around my waist, my fingers shaking as I belatedly wondered where Mrs. Chalcroft had procured the clothes. The bag she'd given me slipped from the bed onto the floor, landing with a metallic thump. I cringed as I fumbled with the shirt's front tie, my heartbeat sluggish in my chest. Doubts fought their way back into my mind. Was I a traitor to England? And to all I'd sworn to love? Or worse, abetting a murderer? I shrugged off the thought and focused on the task at hand. All that mattered now was to deliver the package as I had promised to do. It was a promise I might very well come to regret, but I had to try.

Slowly, I reached out to pick up the bag's handle, but my hand stilled of its own accord, hovering over it like a snake waiting to strike. Could I do it? Could I really deliver such a thing without knowing what my grandmother had placed inside?

As my indecision fought to claim me, a deeper voice spoke within. I had come to the Towers for my own selfish reasons. This delivery was a chance to prove my worth, to make a difference. I thought of Mr. Sinclair injured in the woods, Miss Cantrell overcome by her walk. I couldn't turn away. Not when my family needed me.

I stood before the full-length looking glass, the bag draped over my shoulder. It was the same oval looking glass I'd gazed into so many times before. Though I saw dark-brown hair and the plain features I'd always had, something was different — I was different. I smoothed the shirt and straightened my back, turning to the side before resting my hand on my stomach. Somehow, some way, the timid orphan girl who arrived cold and scared at the Towers had become a Chalcroft, wild and impetuous, but more than anything else, a lady with a mission.

I settled the heavy frieze coat over my

shoulders and pulled my hair into a tight twist at the back of my head and stopped for a breath. I, Sybil Delafield, would find my way through the dragoons and the rain and deliver a dangerous package because I must.

And just like that I crept from my room and down the long corridor to the grand staircase. Shadows lay in wait for me, filled with the thick silence and the lingering scent of the day's fires. The Towers had always slept with a nervous energy, and tonight was no different.

I rose onto the balls of my feet, taking the curve of the staircase one step at a time, my weight supported by the banister. I was glad I knew which boards creaked and which did not. Thunder greeted my descent to the first floor, marking its own rumbling warning to the already turbulent night.

I decided to escape through the eastern side door, which was the farthest away from any of the staff bedrooms. Carefully, I passed the kitchen with its lonely corners and yeast-scented air, then went down the moonlit servants' corridor to the side door, which I slipped through like a fox, quietly securing the old latch back into place behind me.

Wind gusts swirled my hair, and I turned

to find the night alive. Lightning flashed. Tree branches cracked and bent toward the house, scraping the stone exterior like a wiry comb. The muggy air swelled with imminent moisture. I had no time to think or plan. Crossing the yard, I kept to the darkest shadows, aware of the clouds amassing across the sky with menacing thickness, like a dense porridge, choking out any light from the stars.

The wind was at my back, pushing me on in icy waves as I followed the fence line. I made my way past the head groom's cottage to the stable complex just as another roll of thunder clambered across the horizon, splaying me against the wall. I panted, and sweat gathered at my neck.

I could hear the horses shuffling beyond the wooden door. I wasn't the only one affected by the growing storm. I thrust open the latch and pulled, but the heavy wood only shuddered.

I tried a second time, but the door held fast. The first drops of rain joined the tears on my cheek and I cried out in anger, "Open up, you — you old wretch of a door! I haven't time for such stubbornness."

As if it understood, the door flung open with such force I almost forget to let go. But the wind took care of that, ripping the heavy latch out of my hands and pinning it against the side of the stable. I reached out to nudge it back the way it had come but decided to leave it as I passed through. I'd only have to open it again on my way out.

The stables lurked dark and still until a crack of lightning lit the horses' black eyes and pointed ears; then the room once again plunged into shadows. Wind gusts whipped through the open door, catching the sweet-scented hay and swirling it about like a straw blizzard.

Cautiously, I made my way down the center aisle and stopped at the second crib on the right. Aphrodite's. She looked concerned but not afraid. A good sign, but she was prancing in place.

I retrieved her bridle, girth, and stirrups from the harness room. The metal jingled in the cold air as I returned to her partition. "Good evening, girl. What a night to come, but I need your help." After a trip to the saddle room, it took me a moment to quiet the horse enough to put the tack on her, but she soon warmed to my touch.

"What on earth are you doing?" A voice broke the silence.

I jerked around, my fingers clenched. I assumed it was one of the grooms, awakened from his bed above, then I let out a quick breath.

It was Mr. Sinclair. I hadn't heard him come in.

A thick layer of mud lined his boots. His hair had been tossed wild by the wind, but his clothes looked dry. Hercules snorted behind him, tossing his head.

I attempted a light response. "Really, I could ask you the same question, sir. Returning so late on such a night."

He smiled. "You're right, of course. And what a night. There will be repairs all over town tomorrow." He motioned toward Reedwick. "The miserable storm chased me all the way home. I was lucky to get here when I did. How is my godmother? She doesn't fare well on such nights." He led Hercules by his leather headstall to his crib while I continued saddling Aphrodite. "Speaking of which, why are you out here in all this? I hope you've not been sent on a fool's errand."

Of all the people to find me in the stables. I thought to mislead him but knew lying would be useless. He knew me too well. "I've something to do for Mrs. Chalcroft is all."

He stepped backward into the aisle to get a better look at me — all of me — confusion lining his face. He watched in silence as I tightened Aphrodite's girth, the truth finally dawning that I was preparing her, not putting her away. His eyebrows narrowed as he motioned to my attire. "What's all this?"

I shrugged off his bewilderment. "I'm afraid I'm not at liberty to discuss my plans at present."

He leaned against the wooden partition. "Don't tell me you mean to ride out in that getup alone, into this storm."

"I promise you, I would not travel on such a night without good reason to do so." I reached back for Aphrodite's reins. "Mrs. Chalcroft specifically asked me to go to Reedwick tonight and to trust her. I must ask you to trust me as well."

His gaze settled on the bag across my shoulder. I couldn't read the look in his eyes. "I do trust you — with my life, as you well know." He raked his free hand through his hair. "Faith, but that doesn't mean I can allow you to ride in this weather — dressed for mischief no doubt. 'Tis madness out there. And I don't know if you've heard, but Mrs. Plume" — he swallowed hard — "has been killed."

"I did know, but you won't stop me from going, not tonight."

His eyes widened. "You're serious, aren't you?" He touched his forehead. "Of all the stupid —"

"Please, step aside."

"No."

"It's no matter."

"Well, I daresay you haven't mounted your horse yet, and I have no intention of allowing you to do so."

"But I plan to leave nonetheless."

He tilted his chin. "Can you mount without help?"

"I guess we'll find out, won't we?" I pulled Aphrodite from her crib then shoved his arm. "Your chivalry is duly noted, but now you must get out of my way. There's a block right over there."

"Miss Delafield." He softened his voice as he motioned to the trousers. "Tell me what this is all about. You're being unreasonable."

Unwittingly, I turned back to face him. "I cannot say. Mrs. Chalcroft has ordered me to town. That's all I know. She said it is a matter of life or death. And do you know? I believe her."

"If you speak the truth, then by all means, tell me what you carry into this abominable night." He pointed to the bag.

My heart sank. "I-I have not been informed, but you have to let me go."

A crash of thunder clambered in the distance. He grasped my hand, forcing me to meet his sharp gaze. His voice changed, pleading almost. "Don't do this. I . . ."

I paused, arrested by his words, by the connection between us. Did he care so much about my safety? As a friend? Or was it something else?

As if in answer to my shifting thoughts, his gloved fingers intertwined with mine, sending my pulse racing. My breath caught. Heavens, he felt so good. I had to leave at once or my confidence would fail.

Scavenging gusts of wind beat against the stable walls as rain tiptoed on the roof. The storm raged with its metallic scent and fury.

"Sybil."

My gaze shot to his at the sound of my Christian name on his lips.

"What are you hiding?" Hesitation laced his voice, his fingers drawing me to him. "Tell me the truth. Is Mrs. Chalcroft a French spy?"

I jerked my hand from his grasp, my muscles twitching with indecision. "Your own godmother? What a notion . . ."

"Sybil."

My name had turned into a demand.

"What do you carry in that bag?" He crossed his arms. "I'll not be put off — even by you. No more games. This is important. Your life may very well depend on it."

I fastened the bag onto the saddle, a wave of cold splashing through my chest. "I'm told letters is all. She corresponds with a few different people here and there. I've never been informed why, but it's not my place to question her. She asked me to bring this to Mr. Barineau tonight. It is of great importance. Now, if you would help me mount. I've got to hurry."

Mr. Sinclair raised his eyebrows. "If you think I have any intention of allowing you to leave, you're dead wrong."

He cared for me. I could see it in his face, and I recoiled at the thought I would have to put that devotion to the test. "Let me pass."

He pressed his hand to his forehead. "You can't do this. You can't risk your life for an employer. A woman you knew nothing about only a few weeks ago."

A puff of breath left my lungs. There was a way to get Mr. Sinclair out of my way. But was I ready for my whole world to change? I met his gaze, my words spilling out in a whisper. "I have to go." I paused. "Because she is my grandmother."

Mr. Sinclair stood for a great many seconds without saying a word, his mind obviously working to understand what I'd said. When he looked up again, I saw something I hadn't expected to see in his eyes — pain.

"I didn't know everything until tonight. A few months ago, Lord Stanton wrote to me, revealing a connection between me and the Towers. I told no one." I tuned back to Aphrodite, unable to maintain Mr. Sinclair's weary gaze. "I've been uncovering the pieces to my past. Dawkins admitted the truth in my room only a few hours ago. I'm Anne's child. Somehow, they were all wrong. I didn't die that fateful day."

"How can that be?"

"Mrs. Chalcroft sent me away to a school in London. My father, Lord Stanton, must have also known of it."

Mr. Sinclair shook his head. "Mrs. Chalcroft did? How could she —"

"I was angry at first. As you can imagine."

"And now?"

My throat felt thick. "Now I don't know what I feel. I want to hate her, but for some reason I find I cannot. I don't think her decision to abandon me was as simple as that."

"But" — he began to pace — "why on earth did she introduce you to us as her companion?"

"I don't know, and I do not plan to ask

her. All I know is that she desperately needs me to deliver this package — tonight. And I plan to do it."

His gaze slid to the bag once again. "Do you understand the enormity of what you take on? If you are caught, I cannot help you. No one can. You'll be tried as a traitor to your country. And you will be one. You risk everything by riding through that door."

"Possibly. But I don't believe my grandmother would have asked me to do such a thing if it didn't have to be done. I trust her."

He lowered his arm and the howl of the storm filled the space between us. "Then I'm coming with you."

"What? No. Absolutely not. She specifically said you were not to be involved."

He laughed. "What the devil does she think I do around here? I'm already involved. Come on."

He pulled Hercules out of his stall and slipped the reins over the horse's ears, motioning me to follow him to the door.

"Listen." He pulled a dark-blue rag from his pocket. "Tie this around your face. You're already dressed the part. Tonight we're a pair of highwaymen, nothing more." He smiled. "You'll like that, won't you?"

I nodded, attempting a knot at the back

of my head.

"Here, let me help you. I've had a bit of practice at this myself."

He stood close, reaching around to the back of my head. I don't know why, but I felt shy at his touch, for I was no longer Sybil Delafield, the companion. I was Mrs. Chalcroft's granddaughter. I found I couldn't meet his eyes.

"There." He tied on his own mask. "If the dragoons come upon us and overtake us, I'll find some way to make a distraction. You gallop away as fast as possible and don't look back. Do you understand?"

"But what about you?"

"I have connections at Whitehall. It won't be easy, but I believe I can find a way out of it, if it comes to that, but you're no one, not yet at least. You must flee."

I wanted to believe the gallant words he spoke as if he were somehow connected within the government, but I knew very well Mr. Sinclair would be hanged as a traitor if we were found. He was only doing this for me.

"I've asked you this before; however, this time you must promise me something before we leave."

"What?"

"This package is the last one. No more.

Tomorrow morning you will reveal your true identity to everyone in the house." His tone changed. "Lucius will be quite pleased." Then he took a quick breath. "At any rate, there will be no more letters for you."

"All right." Part of me felt relief. "This shall be my final ride."

"Good." He reached out to touch my shoulder but apparently thought better of it and lowered his hands to Aphrodite's side. "Are you ready?"

24

The night wind hit my face with an icy welcome as the stars and moon lay veiled behind the clouds, but Mr. Sinclair set the pace as if he could see through the rain and darkness easily enough. I chose to focus on Hercules's retreating form, illuminated by the repetitive lightning strikes, and worked to keep my horse on track behind him.

We made our way across the estate without incident, like two ghosts moving through a black landscape. As we neared the edge of the property, I caught sight of our first group of soldiers. They stood like sentinels on the hill, their navy pelisses mere shadows to the long carbines at their sides. A thick mist hovered on the ground around them. They faced away from us toward the main road, probably watching for someone trying to enter Chalcroft land, not leave it.

I lay my hand on Aphrodite's neck to steady her as I reined her in. A simple sound by one of our horses and all would be lost.

Mr. Sinclair moved us into a clump of trees and dismounted, keeping his voice low as he circled Aphrodite. "I'll need to check the crossroads on foot. We'll have to find another way around." He helped me down from Aphrodite's back. Though he shot me a quick smile, it didn't mask his concern.

I caught his arm before he left. "Please, be careful."

He nodded then dashed away, keeping to the back side of a slight hill until the darkness swallowed him up.

The drops of sleet felt bigger and louder beneath the trees and wound their way down my shoulders. I struggled to find a dry spot. The grove was small but thick with undergrowth and a hovering musty scent. I glanced around, ensuring I couldn't be seen, before turning my attention to the horses, who'd seemed restless since Mr. Sinclair's departure. I bit my lip. Who could blame them?

"Shh." I patted Hercules's nose more to reassure myself than him as we waited for Mr. Sinclair's return.

The minutes ticked by in a kind of frigid agony. The reins in my hand became harder and harder to grip as the wet night air creeped into my bones. I shuffled my feet, first one then the other, hoping to regain the feeling in my toes, but I knew I was fighting a losing battle. The rush of adrenaline that had kept me warm as we rode over the past few miles had faded. Now, standing still with the wind whipping against the frieze coat, my feet planted on hard ground, I began to shake.

Within the next half hour I had convinced myself that something must be terribly wrong until Mr. Sinclair finally appeared from the opposite direction from which he had left. He didn't speak until he was at my ear. "I found a path around them. It will take us a bit out of the way, but we should be able to make it into Reedwick unobserved." He meant to say more but stopped, reaching out for my hand instead. "You're cold."

I nodded, no longer able to stop my teeth from chattering.

His voice sounded irritated as he shot a quick glance up at the clouds. "You picked quite the night to do this, you know. There's already a dusting of snow on the road ahead, and I" — he let out a quick breath — "I'm afraid we're in for a cold one. I'm concerned about you staying so long out of doors."

I couldn't argue. I'd been cold before, but

not like this.

His fingers tightened around mine and he whispered, "Come here." He pulled me against him, his hands moving up and down my arms, sparking a warmth that traveled much farther than the reach of his strong fingers and left me all too aware of my own heartbeat.

We stood there in the shadow of the soldiers with treason hanging over our heads, and me unable to speak or move. I relished his touch until I forced out a reckless, "Thank you," and stepped away, rubbing my own forearms in his stead.

Scared he might sense the feelings I fought to control, I moved to a safe distance and shook my boots. "If only my feet weren't frozen."

His voice came in an uncertain tone. "Perhaps we should walk the horses for a bit." He grasped the reins from my hands. "It's not much farther. Thankfully, we'll be able to take the main roads on our way back. If everything goes well, we should be home no later than two or three in the morning."

"I hope you're right. What time is it? It feels so late."

"The storm is deceiving, I know, but it is only half past eleven. Which is good for us because it will only get colder as the night wages on."

We traversed several yards on foot until the dragoons with their menacing uniforms had disappeared into the distance behind us.

I felt Mr. Sinclair's hand at my back.

"Do you think you can ride?"

"Yes. Please, I want nothing more than to get this business over and done with as soon as possible."

He lifted me onto my horse and gave me a steady look before mounting himself and setting off into what felt like the opposite direction of Reedwick, across the open countryside.

Thankfully, Mr. Sinclair's return had afforded me a second wind, for he drove the horses hard down the gradual slope of the land. We remained unprotected until we reached the northern cut, where we curved our way back to Reedwick hidden by the crook of an exposed rock.

There the path widened and a gaggle of rooftops appeared like triangles on the horizon. Mr. Sinclair pressed his finger to his lips and slowed the horses to a walk. Like a pair of silent travelers we passed through the outskirts of town, heading toward the post office and the Rose Inn.

The buildings crowded together the farther we went until Mr. Sinclair pulled Hercules to a stop. "We'll have to leave the horses here." He slipped from the horse's back and coiled the reins around a small tree. He tied off Aphrodite as well before reaching for me, his hands circling my waist as he lowered me to the ground.

I jerked the rag from my face to my neck and followed him beneath the back overhang of the inn into a narrow side street. We had nearly reached the town's center when the breeze brought a laugh to our ears.

Like lightning, Mr. Sinclair pushed me flat against the wall, his voice a sharp whisper. "Dragoons near the door, drunk I'd say."

"Oh dear. What shall we —"

He held up his hand to silence me, then motioned with his chin across the square. Four rough-looking men in uniform sauntered down the far street, laughing and talking, obviously off duty, but heading our way.

Pins and needles made their way down my spine, and I pressed my tongue between my teeth to keep them from chattering out loud. So many officers. How would we ever deliver the package without notice? Concern marred Mr. Sinclair's face, but the press of his hand on mine was steady, his breaths coming out like small puffs in the frigid air. Neither of us moved as the men came nearer.

For a moment I thought one of the soldiers had seen us as his attention lingered on our side of the street, but he continued with his comrades without looking back. I let out a sigh of relief but didn't relax until Mr. Sinclair crept to the corner once again.

He took a long look at the square, then signaled for me. "It appears we are alone at the moment. Let us get on with this. I've not had my dinner yet and I'm starving."

I pinched his arm. "How you can think of hunger at such a time, I don't know. *I* may not eat again for days."

He shrugged. "Suit yourself, but that smell coming from the inn might change your mind."

"Not likely. We've eaten there, remember?"

A smile crossed his face. "Right. Come on."

We skirted around the open courtyard to Pasley's, where we slipped into a narrow passageway between the two older buildings. We stopped at the small side door.

Mr. Sinclair lifted his eyebrow. "Now or never, I suppose." He knocked lightly on the door.

The corridor fell silent but for the rush of

wind between the buildings and the sudden flapping of a bird as he made his ruffled departure from a nearby tree.

I found it hard to keep my attention away from the end of the street, but it didn't take me long to realize the door hadn't been answered. "Knock again."

He pressed his lips together and knocked louder this time, both of us all too aware the dragoons could appear around the corner at any minute and there was no place to hide.

A loud crack and the door creaked open an inch. Mr. Sinclair met my eyes as a sliver of light passed through the opening. An elderly woman appeared, her shrewd eyes narrow, her forehead wrinkled with distaste. "What do ya want?"

It was Mrs. Barineau, so I stepped forward, regardless of my present state of dress, hoping to appear less imposing than Mr. Sinclair on such a night. "I'm sorry for the intrusion, but it is imperative that we speak to Mr. Barineau. We have urgent business with him."

Her gaze bounced back and forth between Mr. Sinclair and me, an owlish look taking over her face. "He's already left. And won't be back for some time, so you best be on your way."

My breath caught in my throat. "What do you mean . . . some time?"

"Just what I said."

I couldn't help the frantic whisper of my voice. "But we've ridden all this way in the storm to see him — tonight. Can you tell us where he has gone?"

Once again, distrust took over her features before she swung the door close to the latch. "None of your business where he's at. And it wouldn't do you no good if you knew. He'll be on the first packet tomorrow morning."

My arms fell heavily to my sides. "But I have a package —"

Mr. Sinclair rested his hand on my shoulder, effectively silencing me. "Thank you for your time, ma'am. We'll bother you no longer."

I thought I heard a grunt as the door slammed shut, and Mr. Sinclair tensed. I let out a long breath, wondering if we'd been sent on a wild-goose chase. Tears threatened and my throat grew thick. Had I fooled myself into thinking there was a purpose for putting our lives in danger? I'd been so certain that I had to face the terrible night, that I alone could help my grandmother when she needed me the most.

Mr. Sinclair tugged me along and didn't

stop until we were around the far corner behind the shop. "Listen. I know you have a multitude of questions. As do I, but we're not safe here. Dragoons are crawling all over." He dusted off the snowflakes from my hair and pulled the rag back over my face. "We must leave at once. We'll find another way to help Mrs. Chalcroft."

I nodded, but I couldn't see any other option. If I didn't deliver the package tonight, where did I stand on my promise? Broken. And then what would my grandmother think of me?

Numb, I trudged behind him back down the narrow side streets and through the trees to our horses, the wretched bag banging against my leg with every step, my limp hair dripping onto my shoulders. There Mr. Sinclair forced me to face him. "We'll go back to the Towers and speak with Mrs. Chalcroft. If I know her as well as I think I do, she'll have other ideas."

"I-I don't know. She said it had to be tonight. That it would mean life or death." I'd lost all faith in a matter of seconds.

He raked his hand through his hair. "I understand your disappointment, but I'm beginning to wonder if it is not best that this package remain with us. That perhaps we should see what it is we carry so blindly."

I glared down at the bag around my neck, the metallic thump I'd heard in my room echoing in my mind.

Mr. Sinclair slipped the strap over my head. "We're not breaking her confidence. We've come this far, have we not? We both know what to expect. Let us be sure."

I licked my lips then nodded, my chest tightening.

Slowly, as if the bag held fine china, Mr. Sinclair lifted the flap and pulled out a large envelope. I closed my eyes, unsure whether I could face what lay within.

"What in the world?" Mr. Sinclair nudged my arm. "Sybil, I think you should take a look at this."

I blinked open my eyes, focusing on the package in his hand. Bank notes emerged from the opening, then more and more pounds, piling up into his hands. "There's nearly twenty ponies here and a pile of crowns in the bottom."

My hand flew to my mouth. "Such a large sum?" Thoughts raced through my mind. "To finance Napoleon's army?"

"I don't know." He shook his head. "Whitehall is looking for gold guineas being shipped to the continent, not bank notes." He stuffed the papers back inside. "This little treasure trove doesn't make any sense."

My arms felt heavy. "No. No, it doesn't. So much money . . . and bank notes? If it's not guineas, then why . . ."

"Let us save our questions for Mrs. Chalcroft. It does us no good to interrogate her in her absence."

I stared down the road in front of us. "We still have to find our way home carrying such a fortune. Do you think the dragoons would suspect us if we were detained — with this?"

"Perhaps not, but we cannot test such a theory, now can we? And with you dressed as you are —"

"I know. I'm regretting that decision already. If we are stopped, they shall certainly search us." I pulled the coat tighter around my neck. "Mrs. Chalcroft told me to wear them. I was hoping they would help me ride unnoticed after nightfall. Besides, I needed to ride astride. I'm much faster that way."

He took a deep breath. "Regardless, taking the main road back is out of the question."

A winding shiver ran across my shoulders. In my distress I'd forgotten how chilled my body had become, and now more than ever I wanted to cry. "I'm not sure I can make it all the way back. Could we not get two rooms at the inn and return in the morning early?"

Mr. Sinclair gave me a hard look before taking a step back. "If only it were that easy. I'm afraid you're not considering everything. First, you are dressed as a man, but not a very convincing one. And you know as well as I if the two of us stayed at the inn . . ." He paused. "You'd be ruined. How could you account for your absence at the Towers?"

"I'm only a lady's companion. I doubt anyone would give me a second thought. Or perhaps we could —"

"What?" A winding smile curved his lips. "Do not tell me you mean to hide me in your bed again. I could not bear to have you sit on me all night."

My eyes grew wide, my fingers flying to my lips. "You *were* awake!" Warmth filled my cheeks.

He blinked. "Delightfully so. Nevertheless, I would not let you stay at the Rose Inn without a chaperone for all the world." He rubbed his forehead then jerked down his mask. "You know as well as I it is essential to return tonight. Portia must find you in your room in the morning. No one must know we've been alone together. I see no other options."

Properly put in my place, we left the town on horseback without another word, the rain chilling the space between us and allowing me an uncomfortable string of time to think back through all that had happened and what had been said.

"Not for all the world," Mr. Sinclair had declared as if the two of us were in solemn agreement. But we weren't — not a bit. I wanted to believe something had changed between us; however, Mr. Sinclair's words had been clear enough. If I were to be ruined on our adventure, as a gentleman he would be honor bound to marry me — and from what he'd said, he found the notion unbearable. We would return home tonight, whatever the cost.

The next few miles seemed interminable as if the Towers had disappeared into a winter's dream. No dragoons barred our way. I figured Mr. Sinclair had been taking steps to avoid them all along as we continually changed direction. The snowflakes had ceased, but the horses left a trail of disturbed snow that disappeared into the darkness behind us.

I had no idea where we were; I'd not paid attention. Not that it would have helped. Everything appeared the same in the dark and the snow, and he'd made me promise to remain silent, so silent I rode, frozen to my horse, feeling sorry for myself until a small barn appeared beyond a broken fence.

There was no farmhouse to accompany the failing structure. Mr. Sinclair, it seemed, meant to ride on past, but I decided to take a look, steering Aphrodite to the open door and peeking inside. The shack was abandoned. Paint peeled from the boards, and the roof was rotting at the edges. But it was quiet and it gave me a moment's rest from the frigid wind, so I headed inside.

"What are you doing?" Mr. Sinclair trotted Hercules in behind me.

"I need a minute. I'm sorry. I know how much you want to get back, but I can't feel my feet. They only hurt at first, but then numbness took over. I was becoming scared I might fall from Aphrodite."

I blinked and Mr. Sinclair was at my side, pulling me from my horse. "Why didn't you tell me?"

I tried to take a step but tipped right into his arms. "You said I should be quiet."

He gave me an angry look, but his voice came out kind. "Why don't you sit here?" He wriggled from his coat, tossing it onto the ground. "It's the best I can do with this cold ground."

"I most certainly will not. You'll freeze."

"As you can see I'm fine." He lifted me up as if I weighed nothing and set me on the coat before turning away.

I watched him pace the room, apparently unable to stay still. He was striking in his white shirt and brocade waistcoat. I adjusted the borrowed trousers around my legs before running my finger along the edge of the coat Mr. Sinclair had laid on the ground, wishing it was around my shoulders. "You're angry, and I'm sorry. I promise it will only take a minute to warm my feet and —"

He stopped midstride and crossed his arms. "I'm not angry, Sybil. I'm furious. Furious that Mrs. Chalcroft would send you out on such a night. This whole delivery business must end. She's been using you. To what purpose, I'm not certain."

The flame to his tone startled me and I remembered the terror I'd felt when a young man wearing a mask forced me from the mail coach. "What do you plan to do?"

He kicked one of the wall posts as he passed. "I haven't decided yet, but I have no intention of standing idly by while secrets are traded at the Towers."

"Are you not . . ." How to say it? He was involved somehow. We both knew it.

"What you must think of me, I can't image — highwayman, gentleman, French spy?

Goodness knows I've been nothing but trouble for you from the start."

A quick smile pricked my lips. "Yes, a great deal of trouble. But, Mr. Sinclair . . ." Serious now, I met his eyes. "You know I trust you. I always have, but there is something I must understand before we return to the Towers." I searched his face for how to proceed. "What part do you play in all this?"

He gave me a small nod. "More than anyone, *you* have a right to know." He tossed a small stone he'd acquired across the barn and watched it settle into the corner. "I should have told you everything long before this, but I've found I haven't the knack for trusting others. Very few people in my life have turned out to possess any strength of character." Glancing up, he added, "That is, until I met you."

I held my breath as the shifting moonlight poured through a side window, making the tiny barn feel that much smaller. Part of me wished I could hide from his words, but at the same time, my heart lightened. "Thank you. Your good opinion means a great deal to me."

"As does yours." Mr. Sinclair gave me a wan smile, but he was unable to meet my eyes as he continued. "If I may, I'd like to clear the air." He paused as if he searched for the right words, then gave a half-hearted chuckle. "Can you imagine me of all people — speechless?"

I gave my head a little shake. "Not at all."

"Well, I am." He rubbed his forehead. "What I have to tell you should come natural enough — goodness knows I'm proud of it — yet I find it hard to begin."

"Please. I'd like to know."

He drew his shoulders up and took a deep breath. "For the past few years I've been involved in the intelligence service — it being my only recourse to serve England since Lord Stanton won't allow me to join the cavalry."

My hand moved to my lips, and I was unable to respond for a few seconds. "*You* work for the Crown?" Instinctively I clutched the bag to my side. "Why on earth are we hiding from the dragoons then?"

"It's complicated. I have no official position per se. I'm an informant really. There's a small group of us who work in the dark, gathering what information we can, stopping the mail coaches to search."

"Then you weren't robbing us."

"No. Looking for communication rather — information on its way to France."

I felt disoriented as everything I thought I

knew about Mr. Sinclair dissolved into pieces. He was a spy — for England. It all made sense. His interest in my letters, his returning Mrs. Plume's necklace, his nightly rides.

"What about my grandmother — does she know?"

"I've an inkling she knows I am up to something, but we have never spoken of it. To this day, thankfully, she remains in the dark."

"Is there anyone else involved?"

"Actually, you have encountered another one of our little band of misfits."

I narrowed my eyes.

"The man you saw in the woods the day you fell in the brook. You may know of him. Mr. Lewis Browning. He was also one of the highwaymen who robbed the mail coach. Unfortunately, the other was a hired thug."

"Browning? He doesn't at all look like a gentleman. Of course, I've never met the man, but —"

"He stays well disguised and his identity must not be exposed as his estate is not far from here, and his role is too important to the cause." He rubbed his chin. "He and I have traced a treasonous spying network through Reedwick."

"The same one the dragoons are looking for?"

"I'm afraid so." His gaze drifted to the bag at my side. "However, you and I have something in common. I came to the Towers because I too wish to protect Mrs. Chalcroft."

I gasped, and I thought I saw his hand twitch.

"Quite right. A worse situation I cannot image. I've had to work both sides, hoping I can find a way to stop the flow of information and shield my godmother in the process. I've been riding as a highwayman all over these parts trying to come to the root of who is involved."

I felt drained as I digested his words. "But" — I drummed my fingers on the ground — "if my grandmother is what you fear, you place yourself in a dangerous position. You could be implicated as well. You helped me to Reedwick after all — twice."

"I'm still not certain of her guilt, which is why I've continued searching for the others concerned. And the murders — they just don't make sense. Even now, that parcel there isn't right. Yet if Mrs. Chalcroft is indeed involved, you, Miss Postal Carrier, are just as culpable." He shook his head. "What a bramble this has turned into.

Everyone who resides within the Towers could be questioned, charged. I dare not give the dragoons anything to work with. Captain Rossiter only means to make a name for himself, whatever the cost."

He knelt at my side, his voice soft in the chill air. "You are no more a traitor to England than I am. Neither of us wanted to deliver a package bound for France, not if it had any chance of furthering the war."

I shook my head, trying to make sense of what he said.

Mr. Sinclair slid closer to me on the coat, his voice at my ear. "Whatever happens, there can be no more secrets between us. We walk a difficult road, you and I, and we need to be able to rely on each other." He took my hand, and my thoughts scattered.

"Sybil, I've loved Mrs. Chalcroft since I was a small boy. I promised long ago that I would do everything in my power to keep the people I care about safe, and nothing will change that." A far-off look came into his eyes before he dropped his gaze to the floor. "There's something more . . ."

"More?"

"Yes, it's not easy for me to say, but it will be harder for you to hear it."

I stiffened. "Go on."

"Who told you that you're the heir to the

Chalcroft fortune?"

My pulse raced. "Dawkins." I swallowed hard. "She said she took me as a baby to London after my mother died."

"Has no one else confirmed your claim?"

I shook my head, my scalp prickling.

"I'm sorry I have to be the one to tell you. Anne gave birth that tragic night to a boy, not a girl."

"What?" I felt dizzy. "How could you know that?"

His hand found his forehead. "Mrs. Chalcroft and I have had a special bond since my birth. As her godson, I believe she took an added interest in me as I was the only one she could openly care for. Several years ago, when she had a bad illness, she decided that it was time I was made aware of my position in the world, that I could not go on thinking I was the heir to Stanton's vast holdings. She knew the truth would affect not only me but also my sisters, and she wanted to give me time to make arrangements, for she knew quite well all the facts would eventually come out.

"I know it was difficult for her, but she decided to trust me to keep her secret, which I have done these many years." Thunder cracked across the sky. "I've met him, Sybil. Mrs. Chalcroft told me his name, and he looks just like her."

25

The last stage of the journey home seemed endless. We were forced to change route twice to avoid the patrols. And worse, Mr. Sinclair had said nothing following his revelation in the barn. The bag I'd been sent to deliver to the Frenchman hung heavy around my neck.

I finally understood his decision to return to the Towers tonight and avoid a scandal. I was not Mrs. Chalcroft's granddaughter. I was nobody once again — penniless and desperate. A fine catch for any man. Mr. Sinclair's sisters would starve. My fingers tightened around Aphrodite's reins.

The clouds had broken into stringy clumps above our heads, and the full moon, which had been hiding all night, peeked through the mist from time to time, a steady eye watching our progress. We neared the brook's bank, and Mr. Sinclair yanked Hercules to a stop.

I pulled up beside him. "What is it?"

"Tracks." He motioned to the soft ground at our feet. "A great many."

Snowy hoofprints littered the path. Several horses had indeed taken the narrow crossing before us. The question was, why?

A cold fear settled into my chest. "Do you think they've discovered our absence? Could the dragoons be at the Towers already?"

Mr. Sinclair patted his horse then slipped from Hercules's back in one graceful movement. "I don't know, but either way it doesn't bode well for a quiet entrance."

He raised his arms to lift me down, but I held up my hand, holding him off for a second. "I have a suggestion if you will hear me out."

"I'm listening."

"Would it not be best if you were to go on ahead? You could take the horses back to the stables, possibly draw a bit of attention to your arrival. In the meantime, I can find my own way back with this wretched bag."

Mr. Sinclair gave me a knowing look, then slapped Hercules on the rump. "Get on, old boy." Then he turned back to face me. "Not a bad plan, but I'll not let you go it alone, no matter how well you present it to me. We agreed to do this together, remember?"

I remembered, but I'd made that deal as

Mrs. Chalcroft's granddaughter. Now . . . everything was different.

The conversation vanished as we listened to Hercules's retreating gallop intermixed with the trickle of the creek. Mr. Sinclair's voice came out in a whisper. "Don't ask me to leave you again, because I never will. Hop down so Aphrodite can find her own way back to the stables. The horses' arrival alone may give us the distraction we need to find our way in unobserved."

Mr. Sinclair helped me from Aphrodite and supported me as I worked the numbness from my legs once again. His touch was bittersweet — a glimpse of a dream I should never have indulged in.

When he was sure I could hold my own, he sent my horse scampering off in the same way as Hercules, snow flinging into the air from her hooves.

He rested his hand on my shoulder, misreading my emotions. "Don't worry. The horses know well enough where they are and only wish for their beds. Once I have you settled, I'll return to check on them. In all likelihood they'll wake old John and he'll do the work for me."

I wasn't sure he really believed what he'd said, but I allowed him to paint a pleasant picture. In all likeliness someone would be there to take care of the horses — the dragoons. I shrugged my shoulders, my voice a bit more despondent than I intended. "Then lead on, Captain."

He offered me a weak smile before turning down a thin line of trees, our sheltered path to the east garden's far wall. It was slow going through the icy undergrowth, but soon there was a break in the trees and I caught sight of the Towers. Light burst from every window on the ground floor. Wind ruffled the nearby trees. A battalion of dragoons swarmed the lawns, torches in their hands, straight sabers at their sides. I could hear Mr. Cantrell's dogs barking and growling from the rear of the house as if they too wanted to join the hunt — for us?

Mr. Sinclair grasped my hand. "This doesn't look good, but if we can duck into the hedgerow and take it around to the far side of the garden, we might stand a chance going in through the east servants' entrance."

"Yes. It's possible. I left that door unlocked." I squinted into the pale night. "But we can't be sure our way is clear to the door. Suppose they found it open and a soldier is in hiding. Would it not be safer to wait them out?"

Mr. Sinclair pressed his lips together. "I'm

afraid we haven't a choice. We'll start that way, hoping they've yet to discover the door, and change course if need be."

He sounded confident, and I followed his steps, keeping to the shadows as best I could until we reached the hedgerow. There we were forced to crawl in the snow-covered dirt, escaping into the small space at the base of the plants between the wall and the thick greenery. The ground was like ice against my elbows and knees, and it felt as if it might swallow me whole and bury me deep within the earth. I was glad for the trousers, but soon they became so wet and caked in mud, they too took on the frigid night air.

Mr. Sinclair stopped suddenly in front of me and I careened into his leg. Carefully, he maneuvered around just enough to reach my ear. "You were right. Soldiers on watch at this door as well. I can see one crouching in the bushes and a plume just passed through the dormer window, which means they lay in wait on the inside. It's as if someone alerted them of our plans."

As the words left his lips, the image of Mrs. Chalcroft came to mind. Grandmother or not, I still cared for her. Would she do such a thing to us? Every sensible notion in my brain fought to deny the thought, but I couldn't completely will it away. Trust was as difficult as Mr. Sinclair had said, and as far as I was concerned, I felt it slipping away.

He touched my shoulder. "I see your mind working, but I don't think it was Mrs. Chalcroft who sounded the alarm. Someone knows something in that house." He met my eyes. "We need to speak with my godmother as soon as possible."

"She told me she planned to wait up for my return. That is, if we aren't forced to hide in the bushes all night."

Like a flash, Mr. Sinclair's hand slammed against my mouth and he pulled my feet as far into the plants as possible, chills following the movement of his fingers.

Within seconds, four black boots trudged by a few feet from the hedgerow. Two men's voices cut through the breezy night air, the first a baritone. "I'm beginning to think this whole night was a farce."

A softer male voice answered. "The captain said they was to return tonight. So stop your complaining and get back to watching. I don't want to see this post empty again. Cor, then the captain will have both our heads. He'll be here soon enough with the dogs."

"As you say." His carbine swung down beneath the hedgerow. "Then you get on with it too."

A pair of boots crunched their way around the corner, leaving the baritone behind, mumbling to himself. "Blast you, Jenkins. Always acting as if you've a higher rank than me. Well, it won't be long, will it, old man, before you've to get out of the service? Best hope you're not cashiered for all your meddling."

A string of silence ensued before the remaining pair of boots began pacing again, down the length of the hedgerow, then back. I thought I heard Mr. Sinclair swear beneath his breath. As bad as our situation had been before, we were far worse off now — trapped like rats and the dogs due at any moment to search.

Sweat dripped down the side of my face and turned to ice in the wind. Mr. Sinclair looked almost primeval in the moonlight, the branching shadows of the bush playing tricks with my mind. He sat there as if readied to attack, his eyelids narrow, his jaw clenched.

The minutes ticked past and my initial fright turned to anger. How close we'd come to safety. How close I'd been to a family of my own. My thoughts blurred as tears threatened. Of course, I doubted very much the soldiers had even searched the house.

Mrs. Chalcroft would never permit it, not after last time. If we could only get to our rooms, this part of the nightmare would be over. But if we were caught in the bushes . . .

A loud clank resounded from far away as if one of the soldiers' boots had hit an iron fence. It was probably one of the many men searching the premises, but it brought back a memory, one I'd nearly forgotten.

My heart jolted to life, beating hard and fast in my chest. I reached out silently and gave Mr. Sinclair's arm a squeeze, then motioned to the garden gate a few feet away.

He nodded, but not as quickly as I would have hoped. He was in ignorance of the priest hole, for I'd not told anyone. Mr. Cantrell's secret had been faithfully kept.

Still crouching, I placed one foot at a time down the hedgerow, hoping the icy leaves beneath my boots wouldn't give me away. Within a few steps, my hand caught the edge of the gate, and I waited there until I heard the soldier's boots stomp to the far end of the wall.

When he was but a pace from the corner, I sprang from the bushes and slipped through the gate, collapsing against the wall on the other side. My hands shook. I gasped for breath. It would be only seconds before Mr. Sinclair was at my side, so I used the time to locate the grate above the priest hole buried in the snowy brambles.

There, I was surprised to see several branches broken at the opening and the overgrowth smashed down as if several people had trod about the area. The soldiers? I pulled on the handle. It was locked.

Odd. It hadn't been before.

I bit my lip and jerked on the small door again, but it didn't move. Dusting off the snow, my frantic fingers found the lock and my shoulders slumped. I cast a quick glance behind me in time to see the glow of torches bobbing over the stone wall. Dogs howled in the distance as footsteps grew louder along the path. I pressed my palm against my forehead. With limited hiding spots in the tiny garden, I'd found a way to make our pitiable situation even worse.

A round of voices met my ears and I fought my way into a scraggly bush, out of the shifting light. There would be no room for Mr. Sinclair. I only hoped he'd stay where he was.

But I was thwarted again as a silver flash of moonlight reflected off the gate and Mr. Sinclair slipped inside, closing the door without a sound behind him. Frantic, I waved him to the bush.

"It's locked."

"What do you mean? What's locked?"

"The priest hole."

A furrow spread across his forehead, and I grasped his hand, pressing his fingers down into the thick weeds at our feet. "Here."

He gave me an incredulous look. "You're saying there's a priest hole here? In the garden?" His fingers slid around the cold iron latch and he tried the square door.

Nothing.

He bent his neck forward. "How long have you known about this?"

"Since the day after I arrived. Mr. Cantrell and I found it quite by accident. We were —"

"Lucius, huh?"

"Yes, but it wasn't locked then. I had hoped . . ."

Mr. Sinclair fingered the lock, then looked up. "Lucky for us, it appears to be rusted through. See? All we need is a suitable distraction." He glanced around. "Do you think you can climb that far wall, the one with all the ivy?"

"I think so."

"Good. Take this rock." He pressed something cold into my hand. "Once you reach the top, throw it as far as you can. Understand?"

"Yes. But what do you plan to do?"

"If we're lucky, our friend out there will go and investigate. Once he's far enough away, give me a signal. I'll break the lock with the stone." I saw the flash of a smile for a moment. "Nothing to it."

"I hope you're right."

He touched my cheek. "Have I ever failed you before? Better yet, don't answer that."

I scrambled to my feet and made my way over to the wall, keeping a watch all the time for the soldier to cross the space on the other side of the gate. I didn't have to wait long, for he sauntered by as if he hadn't a care in the world, ignoring the shadowy garden.

I tested the icy wet branches one step at a time, but my climb proved easy enough, and in a few steps I could see from the top. I shot one quick glance back at Mr. Sinclair before flinging the rock as hard as I could into the night. I didn't hear the stone land, but it must have served its purpose because the guard shuffled around the corner in a hurry.

I waved my hand to Mr. Sinclair and cringed as I saw him lift a huge rock. It came down with sufficient force, the crash echoing off the stone walls. I jerked my attention back to the lawn and my lips parted. I could count them like ants scrambling toward us at full speed. One . . . two . . . three uniformed men trudging through the drifts on the horizon.

I flew down the ivy without bothering where I placed my feet and clambered back to the priest hole. "We have only a moment before the men arrive."

Mr. Sinclair met my gaze with one of his own. "Then we better hope this room is a well-kept secret."

I wondered if the soldiers had found it on the night of the search, but I kept the thought to myself.

Mr. Sinclair grasped my wrists. "Jump and I'll lower you down."

I didn't hesitate, not even for the black abyss below me. I fell for a heart-stopping moment until Mr. Sinclair pulled against me and strong-armed me to the floor of the room. The darkness felt absolute, but I knew I must move out of the way for him to follow. Moonlight highlighted his form as he lowered himself into the hole, hanging on to the rim of the opening. He let go and fell into a heap at the bottom.

I dropped to my knees. "Are you all right? Nothing injured, I hope."

He sat up. "Not graceful enough for you?"

I rolled my eyes.

Within seconds he was back on his feet,

his hands about my waist. "I'm going to lift you onto my shoulders. Do you think you can close the grate?"

"I hope so. I'll try."

"You better do more than try, my dear. Our lives depend on it."

He boosted me above his head as if I weighed no more than a small child. I found the flat part of his shoulders with my boots and released the grip on his arms. Gradually, I rose to my feet, his hands slipping to grip my legs.

"Hurry."

"Right." I was pleased to find the door but a few inches over my head. "Can you take a step forward?"

We toddled a pace and I slammed the door closed before he lifted me down.

I felt rather than heard Mr. Sinclair laugh. "I thought you might do it a bit more quietly."

"I-I'm sorry. I didn't think."

"No matter. They'd already heard us. We can only hope they aren't certain where the sound came from." He turned to the moonlit room. "I suppose we should hide. What's all this stuff anyway?"

It was only then I noticed dark shadows surrounding us, crates stacked clear to the earthen roof. "I don't know." A rank smell hovered on the air, laced with a sweet tinge. Perfume and . . . what? I wrinkled my nose.

I froze at the sound of a soldier's voice and dogs barking above us.

Mr. Sinclair reached for my hand and whispered in my ear. "Follow me." He led me to the far side of the small room, feeling his way along the wall until he pulled me down in a gap behind the crates where the stench was less noticeable. The space was narrow, but I was able to sandwich myself between Mr. Sinclair and a hard wooden box.

"Not ideal, but it'll do," he whispered. "Are you still cold?"

"A bit, but there's no wind in here."

"Good. We may be trapped for a while."

I released a long breath, trying to tune out the muffled voices above. But it was no use. There in the dreaded darkness the minutes felt like hours as we listened to the search — shouts, bangs, footsteps. Finally, a quiet wind gusted over the iron grate as a light rain added texture to the eerie melody. The search of the garden had faded away.

Mr. Sinclair squeezed my hand. "I believe the soldiers have moved on, but I doubt they will leave the estate until morning."

"Morning?" The word came out a bit louder than I'd meant it too.

He pressed my fingers to his lips. "I'm so sorry, Sybil. Why didn't I listen to you in town? We might as well have stayed at the inn for all the good the harried journey back did us. We were so close." He glanced up at the grate. "But don't worry. If we have to overnight in a hole, I have every intention of facing the consequences of my foolish decisions." He lowered my hand to rest between us but did not let go. "You may be stuck with me after all."

So he meant to joke his way through our situation. Well, I couldn't. The thought of his sisters brought pain to my chest. If we were forced into what he suggested, we'd ruin both of our lives.

"I wish you'd never come with me," I said aloud, and I meant it.

I felt Mr. Sinclair stiffen and he opened his mouth to respond. But at the same time, the squeak of the garden gate resounded above our heads. Then a loud clang as the iron hit hard against the stone wall. Someone walked along the garden path.

We both froze, not a breath between us. One of the soldiers had come back. Had he seen or heard something? Surely the priest hole would remain hidden beneath the brambles. The alternative was unconscionable. We would be hanged as traitors. Every hair on my arms stood on end.

Boots crunched the gravel over our heads. Branches snapped and brush swished about like the man cared nothing for the wild little garden. I imagined him beating against it with his saber, stomping the plants under his boots. He was so close I could smell the tobacco lingering on his breath. My palms began to sweat.

Then a voice rang out, causing me to jump.

It was the baritone calling to the others. "Thought I heard something, but I guess I was wrong. Back to your post."

The soldier's heavy tread passed out of the garden and my shoulders sank. I closed my eyes, glad I could hear once again over the pulse pounding in my ears. It was then I realized what I'd done in the darkness, clouded by nerves wound a bit too tight. Like a child, I'd crept into Mr. Sinclair's arms — where it felt so natural to be. Embarrassed, I attempted to slip away, but he held me fast.

"Sybil." His voice sounded like a thought on the wind.

He was warm. Secure. Goodness, what did it matter now? I leaned into his quiet strength, fixed by the steady beat of his heart. If only I could stay there forever tucked in his arms. It was such a blessed release to know if the worst happened, we would face it together.

Gently, his chin pressed against my wet hair and he took in a deep breath, his arms tightening around my waist. What was happening between us? I wished I could read his mind, know what he felt, this man who'd risked his life for my sake, who'd stayed by my side nearly the whole night through. Could it be possible that he too wanted more, even with all the obstacles between us?

My heart leapt wildly for answers, my muscles losing tension. Then, as if pulled by an unseen force, I glanced up, peering into the furtive darkness. I needed to know the truth. Did he care for me? But Mr. Sinclair's face remained a silhouette. My lips quivered. He didn't move. It was as if he could see me and was determined to learn every curve, every inch of my face, every subtle movement of my eyes. Could he read the thoughts that battled inside me?

Like a crack of lightning, the silent wall we'd erected between us that day in the gamekeeper's cottage crumbled to the floor. His hands found their way up my neck and into my hair, pulling me against him, his breath on my cheeks. His lips found mine in the darkness, and he kissed me, not as I'd imagined so many times as a young girl, but driven by a passion he'd kept at bay for far too long.

A few short seconds and I'd finally glimpsed into his heart. How could I help but respond with a piece of my own? My pulse raced as my hands slid up his broad back, pulling him tighter against me. Goodness, I couldn't get close enough. It was as if I'd discovered the depths of the ocean after merely sitting on the shore observing the waves, and how good it felt. How good he felt. I was lost to the mounting intensity between us.

At length, he drew away, his hands steady at my chin. "Forgive me. I never should have done that. Heaven knows, I'd not meant to. Everything I've done tonight was to give you a choice."

"Mmm." I found it hard to concentrate. A choice? "What do you mean?"

"Lucius." He pulled back. "He's in the house, waiting . . . for you. You cannot tell me you are indifferent to him."

My head swam. Mr. Cantrell? "He has been kind, but . . ."

"But what?"

"Well, he isn't you."

He grasped my shoulders and I thought

he meant to kiss me again. Instead, he met my gaze. "Sybil, my darling, maddening *partner,* can you mean what you say? Even with all the trouble I've caused you? Heaven knows, I've loved you from the moment I saw you dripping beneath the tree in that ridiculous gown of yours." His smile faded. "But have I cause to hope? A man without money or a proper future — I'm little better off than a real highwayman." His face looked pained. "I don't deserve you. As soon as Mrs. Chalcroft's grandson is revealed, I won't even be the heir to the Earl of Stanton."

Caught off guard, I fell silent for a moment. "You know none of that matters to me."

"You'd be a fool not to see that Lucius could provide you the life I never could."

All at once the grate above our heads flew open with a terrible squeak. I pushed Mr. Sinclair away. Candlelight poured into the hole, and just like that, the perfect bliss I'd reveled in faded to dread.

We'd been found.

26

A ladder plunged through the candle-lit opening of the priest hole, crashing down onto the earthen floor. Mr. Sinclair guided me behind him as we stood to face what could only be a soldier bent on our immediate capture. I was surprised to see a pair of tasseled boots make their way down the rungs, followed by a green superfine jacket and a blond head.

"Mr. Cantrell," I cried.

He spun around at the bottom, nearly dropping the light as he found his footing. His stark surprise faded to a hint of amusement. "Why, Miss Delafield . . . and Sinclair. What the devil are you doing down here?" His piercing gaze focused in on me. "At this hour?"

Mr. Sinclair spoke calmly, but there was a question in his tone. "We could ask you the same, *friend.*"

My momentary relief turned to concern

as I heard other voices at the opening. "Are the dragoons with you?"

"Certainly not. I have no use for an execution party." He glanced at the crate beside him and gave a little laugh.

Two additional men scampered down the ladder, joining us in the little room, dressed in trousers and coats, dirty from head to toe, the scent of salt and rum heavy on their breath. Mr. Cantrell directed them to some of the crates. "These two here, my good men, and that long one." Then to me. "Don't look so stricken, my dear. I promise you the dragoons are gone. I've paid the worthless creatures to turn a blind eye. As you can see, I've a few crates to unload." He yelled over his shoulder, "Be quick about your business, lads."

"Smuggling." A smile creased Mr. Sinclair's lips, but I thought it a threatening one. "Why am I not surprised?"

"Ah, Sinclair. I should have known you'd disapprove. Must you always be the hero of everything? Don't get me wrong. My aunt would be proud; however, tonight I'll have none of your sermons on duty and honor. I haven't the stomach for it. As you can see, this is merely a business venture that many men in my shoes have stooped to participate in." He flicked a piece of lint from his jacket sleeve. "Since I'm presently short of cash, this room provided the perfect hideaway spot for a lucrative venture . . . among other things."

So this was Mr. Cantrell's newest plan. Miss Cantrell had mentioned his next move might prove desperate.

Mr. Cantrell raised his chin. "Do not fear, friend. I'll not dirty my hands any further. I merely offered storage for a few days, nothing all that sinister." He lifted his eyebrows, his gaze dipping to my trousers. "Of course, we have yet to hear what you two have been about this evening."

I reached for Mr. Cantrell's arm. "Are *all* the soldiers gone?"

"For the time being." His indeterminate glare bounced back and forth from me to Mr. Sinclair. "Have you need of their services, my dear?"

"No." I cast a quick glance at Mr. Sinclair. "We're more than pleased that you sent them away."

Mr. Cantrell's companions forced a crate up the ladder, then another, sweating and cursing their way through the tight opening.

"What's in them?" Mr. Sinclair asked, crossing his arms.

"Goods, alcohol. You name it. I don't ask questions."

Mr. Sinclair shook his head. "Pity. For you put your aunt in a dangerous position."

"One too late to be avoided at present." The candlelight flickered as he motioned to the ladder. "May I escort you both above-ground where we can be a bit more comfortable? Miss Delafield looks about ready to drop."

Mr. Cantrell's business arrangement must have rankled Mr. Sinclair to no end, but we'd little choice but to follow his instructions considering what I carried around my neck.

Mr. Sinclair touched my back. "You do look tired. You should retire immediately to your room." He motioned to the ladder. "After you."

The merest jingle from the coins in my bag accompanied the climb back into the garden with Mr. Cantrell a step behind me and Mr. Sinclair bringing up the rear. When everyone was clear of the hole, Mr. Cantrell closed the grate, turning to face us in the moonlight. "I won't ask the obvious questions concerning the two of you; however, I shudder to think what such a discovery might do to Miss Delafield's reputation."

An alarming look skirted across Mr. Sinclair's face.

I slipped my hand through the crook of

Mr. Cantrell's arm. "And I know you won't speak of it, will you?"

He patted my hand. "Of course not, my dear. Not for all the world."

I flinched beneath the gaze of his kind green eyes — the same eyes that had cared for me since the moment of my arrival, with or without a family to speak of. His lips softened into a smile. Mr. Sinclair was right. Mr. Cantrell did plan to renew his offer. I took a deep breath. There was much to clear up between us. "Mr. Cantrell, would you be so kind as to help me back to my room? Mr. Sinclair must see to his horse."

Mr. Sinclair shot me a hard glare as he turned and walked toward the garden's gate, his arms stiff at his sides.

I'd shocked him, but I couldn't bear Mr. Cantrell to go on thinking for one more moment that I accepted his affections. Regardless of what happened between Mr. Sinclair and me, after tonight, Mr. Cantrell would no longer be an option.

His hand grazed my back. "It would be my pleasure." He offered me his arm. "This way. I, um, hardly think the front door appropriate for your attire. Don't you, my dear?"

Why did he keep calling me that? He rarely had before. Mr. Sinclair looked ready to call him out every time Mr. Cantrell repeated it, but he'd said nothing yet and neither did I. Our situation was far too tenuous. Like a servant, Mr. Sinclair held the garden gate and averted his eyes as I brushed by him. My hand wandered to my neck. Surely he knew what I intended to speak with Mr. Cantrell about.

Mr. Cantrell led me around the back of the garden wall to access the east servants' entrance, and Mr. Sinclair headed around the front of the house — to speak with Mrs. Chalcroft if I had to guess. He had no reason to hide. He was not an unchaperoned young lady caught returning home in the wee hours of the morning.

Fog had rolled in across the fields, gathering like an ominous cloud around the house, snuffing out my view of the trees and the ground floor. At least Mr. Cantrell and I would be concealed. That is, if Mr. Cantrell had spoken the truth about the dragoons.

I slowed my steps as we approached a narrow walkway. "You do understand my need for secrecy?"

Mr. Cantrell stopped. "Part of it." He grasped my hand, tugging me into the shadows of a nearby tree. He must have known there was a bench there, for he spun me around, guiding me to sit beside him. "But not all."

I landed a bit harder than I would have wished. "Oh my."

He brushed a bit of soggy hair from my shoulder, leaning into my ear. "My darling. Tell me you'll marry me this instant, and I'll never ask you the rest of what happened tonight."

My head pounded and I licked my dry lips. "That is what I wish to speak with you about."

His hand slipped to my waist, drawing me closer. "Everything changes today. I will make a great deal of money, and we'll have a nice start of it." He kissed my cheek. "You must know, the terrible risk, I did it for you."

I pushed against his chest, but he had no intention of letting me go. "Mr. Cantrell, I need to breathe. Please. I have something to tell you —"

His hands stilled. "Tell me what?"

"Mr. Cantrell." I wriggled away from him a bit. "You have been nothing but kind, and you do me a great honor by offering me something so precious, but I must tell you that . . . I have already given my heart to someone else."

His hand slipped down my arm, his eyelids narrowing. Even his voice turned cold. "I had hoped for much more from you."

The wind shifted. My skin tingled beneath his fingers.

"Then tell me, what is it you were doing out all night . . . with Sinclair?"

"I . . ." I bit my lip.

"If you intend to utilize my protection, you will answer me."

My chest ached. The Mr. Cantrell I knew had vanished. In his place was the one I'd overheard questioning Miss Cantrell. He grasped my shoulder. "Now."

My feet itched to retreat, but I willed the feeling away. He was merely angry that I'd not agreed to his plans. This emotional display would pass as it had before. I drew back as far as his hold would allow. "I had a letter to deliver for Mrs. Chalcroft."

"To Mr. Barineau, perhaps?"

My heart stopped. "You knew."

"Of course I knew. My aunt is not so foolish as to keep me in the dark."

I couldn't imagine Mrs. Chalcroft sharing such a secret with him. She had been so adamant about telling no one. "But I-I was unsuccessful in my quest. I plan to go to her as soon as possible, if you would excuse me."

"You were unable to find Mr. Barineau

because even now, he waits for me in the woods."

My eyes grew wide. "Waits . . . for *you*?"

He motioned to the stables with his chin, his hand relaxing on my arm. "He's the man I'm to bring the crates to."

The hair lifted on the back of my neck. I still had a way to deliver the package, risky as it was. Yet could I trust Mr. Cantrell, whose passions rose and fell like the wind?

I cast a quick glance at the Towers where I imagined Mrs. Chalcroft waiting in her room for word of my success. It didn't matter if I was her granddaughter or not. Somewhere along the way, I'd moved beyond that. I cared for her and she was counting on me. Life or death was what she'd called it. I touched the bag. Mr. Sinclair would definitely tell me not to go, but I couldn't involve him. Mr. Cantrell had seen too much between us in that little room and likely knew exactly where my heart lay. No, it was up to me.

Finding my voice, I met Mr. Cantrell's shifting gaze. "Will you take me with you?"

His fingers formed a steeple under his chin. "Now, in the coach?"

"Yes, to see Mr. Barineau."

A slow smile spread across his face. "If that is what you want."

My stomach quivered, but I fought it, remembering instead how fondly Miss Cantrell spoke of her brother, how he'd helped her all these years. Mr. Cantrell would help me too. "I do. Please, just an escort to see him briefly and a ride back home as soon as possible."

"As you wish, my dear."

I had no time to question my hasty decision as he sprang to his feet. "We leave at once. Our ride is behind the stables. My good men must have loaded the crates by now."

Like two children escaped from school, we flew across the milky ground, my feet aching to keep up, down the fence line and around the corner of the barn. The frigid temperature continued to nip at my fingers, but the wind had calmed and my core was dry. I'd have to worry about all that later. I had a promise to keep.

We rounded the stables and at first I thought the small grove empty, but Mr. Cantrell gave a little whistle into the trees and one of the rowdy-looking men emerged from the fog. "This way."

We followed his bulky form about ten yards, then the cart took shape, crates strapped to the back, a chestnut horse hooked to the front. Within a few steps we were upon it and Mr. Cantrell's hands circled my waist. A lift and a shove deposited me onto a wooden seat. No question came for my comfort, but a blanket was thrust over my legs.

"Thank you," I said coldly.

Another horse trotted beside the equipage, and I recognized the rider as the other man from the priest hole. Mr. Cantrell swung up next to me, claiming much of the bench, his caped riding coat blowing in the breeze. He slapped the ribbons and we were off. A fluttery feeling filled my chest, but I didn't move. I'd made my choice.

The cart was heavy and the going slow through the fog. Mr. Cantrell remained quiet at first, but I had questions. "How long till we arrive?"

"Patience, my dear." He touched my knee. "We'll be there soon enough."

But it wasn't soon enough. Reedwick faded to a memory behind us and still we didn't arrive. Worry took hold as I feared I'd not make it back before morning. Of course, had I really expected to? Either way, Mrs. Chalcroft would give me a reference. I'd be able to find another position — far away from Mr. Cantrell and the Towers.

We turned off the narrow road we'd taken for several miles and into a dense forest, the cart tossing about the rutted road, if you could even call it that. Mr. Cantrell grasped my arm. "You keep your mouth shut until I call for you. Understand?"

"Yes, but —"

"Shh."

A light appeared in the distance and a horse and rider took shape in the glow. Mr. Cantrell reined his horse to a stop, and the mare snorted and pawed the ground. I pulled the blanket closer to my chest as icy drops of rain dripped from the branches high above our heads, pinging the ground in hushed beats all around us. A smoke scent met my nose and I wondered if there might be a cottage close by.

Mr. Cantrell raised his hand in greeting. "Tom —"

The man waved back. "You're late."

"We had a bit of a situation." Mr. Cantrell jumped down from the cart. "But it's been handled."

Mr. Barineau raised the lamp, shining it on the cart. "Is that a girl you have with you?"

"Of course, as well as the crates you requested. I won't ask for my payment . . . yet." Mr. Cantrell gave him a wide smile.

"The devil you won't." Mr. Barineau laughed.

I carefully slipped the bag from my shoulder as the two men rounded the cart. Mr. Barineau cracked open one of the crates at the back, then whistled. "Oh, he'll be pleased with this, quite pleased."

"Then let us be off. We've to reach the coast by tomorrow."

We? A heavy feeling hit my stomach. "Mr. Cantrell," I whispered. Had he forgotten all about me?

He stopped. "Right, Tom. My fair lady has a package for you."

Mr. Barineau tipped his hat. "You don't say?"

They approached the side of the cart, and I extended a shaky hand. "Mrs. Chalcroft asked me to bring this to you."

He snatched the bag. "Much good it did me. She was supposed to have it to Pasley's by six o'clock yesterday."

"I'm sorry. It was my fault. There were patrols and a storm. I must have missed you."

"It better be all in here." He cast a quick glance at Mr. Cantrell. "Or you'll get yours, I 'spect."

Mr. Cantrell held out his hand. "No need to be crass in front of the lady."

"It's awfully hard dressed as she is." Mr. Barineau chuckled then plopped the bag into Mr. Cantrell's open palm. "Your last and final payment, my lord. It better be the lofty one you demanded this time."

"Don't worry, my aunt will not disappoint us. I daresay when I included my newfound information, I struck fear into the old lady's heart."

My gaze shot to Mr. Cantrell. "What?"

He took a quick breath, a look of satisfaction crossing his face. "It's mine, of course. My money. It shall set us up quite well for our first few months of marriage."

A cold feeling washed over me. Surely I had misheard him. "M-Mr. Cantrell," I stammered. "What do you mean?"

It was then I noticed the bend to his eyebrow, the hard lines etched across his forehead. His eyes looked ashen in the waning light, so completely unlike his usual handsome countenance. He tapped his watch fob before casting me a shrewd smile. "Darling, I'm afraid you have few options now, and we have no time to discuss them here. However, there shall be hours enough on our little trip across the channel."

Pain spread through my chest like a crawling spider, the truth of my situation sinking in. He meant for me to go with them. To France. I had made a terrible mistake.

"Oh, come now, love, marriage to me

won't be all that bad." His gaze slid down the length of my body. "I believe you thought quite differently at one time."

I swung to slap him, but his hand caught my arm and jerked it back against the side of the cart. I raised my chin. "I told you there is no future for us. It doesn't matter what happens tonight. Ruined or not, I'll never go with you." My gaze fell on the bag I'd carried through the rain, and I saw now what I'd been too blind to see before. "Mrs. Chalcroft would never send you money unless —"

"Unless what? She's been doing so for the past four years or more."

"Unless she didn't know it would eventually reach your hands." I turned away. "Take me home at once. You promised me a safe return."

Forcing my attention, he pressed his body against the side of the cart, his voice low. "I've promised a lot of things in my life, but I only keep the ones truly necessary for my own happiness."

"What of Miss Cantrell? She needs you now more than ever."

"She should have thought of that before getting herself with child. Besides, we'll be back within the year. Mrs. Chalcroft can't possibly live that long."

I recoiled. "And then what? You'll not inherit a farthing."

"No, my dear, but you will."

So that was his plan from the start. What a fool I'd been, basking in his attentions. He'd never loved me. I jumped down from the cart. "You are gravely mistaken."

His dark eyes flashed in the lamplight. How had I ever thought them kind?

"Mr. Cantrell, you must listen to me. I don't know how you came by the information, but I'm not Mrs. Chalcroft's granddaughter. Anne's child was a boy. Do you hear me? A boy. Mr. Sinclair knows; he'll tell you. You mean to ruin both our lives for nothing."

A flick of the fingers and Mr. Cantrell's two thugs drew up behind me, as if I could possibly escape. Four against one, in the middle of nowhere — flight would be impossible.

Mr. Cantrell touched my cheek. "My dear Sybil, do you think I would be so careless as not to be sure of my plans? You're right, Anne did have a son that night twenty-two years ago, but she also had a daughter — twins, my dear, are not so uncommon."

I gasped. *Twins.*

"That's right. We're cousins, you and I." He laughed. "Oh, I first learned Stanton had a child quite by accident years ago. The earl's been a good friend of mine for some time, and as you know, Mrs. Plume can hardly keep her mouth shut. Lucky for me she was Lord Stanton's housekeeper before her advantageous marriage, and she divulged the interesting information to me one day without even realizing she'd done so.

"Shocked to learn that not only had Aunt Chalcroft been part of such a devious endeavor but that she'd kept the secret all those years, I knew she would never stand for a family scandal, and I simply put that knowledge to my own use." He gave a little shrug. "In exchange for secrecy about the hidden child, I only asked for a bit of extra money here and there, nothing to cause too much of a fuss . . . until now."

Blackmail — so that was how he supported Miss Cantrell's failed London seasons. I swallowed hard, scrambling to put it all together. But what of the letters I'd delivered, the ones I'd risked my life for? My jaw clenched shut. I suppose they'd all eventually made their way to Mr. Cantrell's greedy hands.

He stepped closer. "But all those years I never knew who the mystery child was exactly, not until I saw your resemblance to

Lord Stanton's painting in the tower. A few pounds to the earl's solicitor, and I learned that Stanton's been funding your education all these years. It wasn't hard to put two and two together."

"Yes, but that doesn't prove Anne was my mother." I twisted the bracelet on my arm, the jeweled band raking against my skin. "I too noticed my resemblance to Lord Stanton."

He laughed. "Don't worry, my aunt filled in the missing details the night of the storm when she was conveniently out of her mind. She likes to talk when she's been given laudanum." A look of satisfaction settled across his face. "Twins, she said. You, my dear, taken to a school in London and the other child to the Aberdeens in Reedwick. Only, Lord Stanton knew of none but you. My great-aunt was more devious than I thought. She was so desperate to hide your brother, the heir, you see, she'd have done anything." He patted the bag. "And still is. Pity she's not aware Stanton died in the West Indies a month ago and she no longer needs to pay her blackmailer."

Mr. Barineau stepped forward. "Enough. We're losing darkness."

Mr. Cantrell grasped my wrist. "Quite right. We'll have plenty of time to talk on the boat."

I jerked away. "I'm not going anywhere with you."

"I was afraid you'd say that. Tom, bring me the flask." Then to me: "You can make this easy or hard, but either way, I have something for you to drink."

27

A flask was thrust into Mr. Cantrell's hand and he met my gaze. "Can't have you alerting the authorities till we're safely on board the ship, now can we?"

"Please. Don't do this." I splayed my hands in front of me. How it rankled to beg, but I'd do anything to keep that foul-smelling liquid away. "Can we not discuss this?"

Mr. Cantrell laughed. "I believe that is what we have been doing, my dear, and if my memory serves me correctly, you said no."

Tremors scaled my back and down my arms. *Run,* whispered a voice from the recesses of my mind. But to where? The dark depths of the forest circled me, choking out the stars.

Suddenly, I wrenched back, ducking around the cart's front before scampering to the far side. Desperate, I clawed at the blanket I'd used on the ride, fumbling with it as I ran. Mr. Cantrell merely walked into the open, amused by my actions.

"Tom," he called, motioning for him to come up on my other side. Then back to me: "I suppose this means you choose the hard way. Lucky for me." A pistol emerged from his jacket, and he leveled it at my chest. "Come here, my pet . . . now."

I inched forward, my legs weak. If I was forced to drink that foul liquid, Mr. Cantrell would take a limp puppet to France, likely never to return. I stared down, grappling for an answer, but I'd left the Towers willingly with him. There would be no clues to follow, no hope of rescue.

I had no one but myself. Me. Just Sybil.

A sense of purpose settled the quivers coursing through my limbs. Mr. Cantrell must have sensed the change in my attitude, as his smile slid away and he advanced in stride. The pounding hooves of a horse at full gallop met our ears. He jerked his attention to the opening in the trees.

One of Mr. Cantrell's thugs reined in his hack, panting as he spoke. "Highwaymen . . . coming down the road. Be here in seconds."

Mr. Cantrell seized my arm. "My overzealous friend must have missed you already."

Mr. Sinclair. My heart leapt.

My fingers tingled beneath a surge of energy as I jerked my arm free and thrust the blanket over Mr. Cantrell's head, then bolted for the trees. I heard a crash behind me and subsequent swearing, but I didn't stop running till I'd broken the tree line.

Darkness met me in the thick growth like smoke from a fire. I reached out, feeling for the damp bark and sticky brush, hiding somewhere in the black abyss. I wouldn't get far at this rate.

Leaves crunched at my back, branches snapped. I held my breath, my pulse pounding in my ears as I strained to be as quiet as possible. Someone had followed me into the copse of trees. My leg muscles tightened, and cautiously I maneuvered through the darkness to get a view of the far side of the cart, using the looming trees as an invisible veil and the shadows as my friend. I crouched in the snowy brush and waited, straining to hear anything amid the unnatural silence of the woods. There were no more footsteps, but I couldn't be sure I was alone.

At the cart, Mr. Cantrell stormed back and forth, passing in and out of the lamplight, his pistol ready in his hand. One of his hirelings came out of the trees where I'd been only a moment before and shrugged his shoulders. Mr. Cantrell thrust his stubby finger my direction to further the search, but called the man back as we all heard horses approaching. The highwaymen were here.

A shot rang out. Two riders broke into the clearing, and a large black horse reared up and tossed his head. Mr. Sinclair brought Hercules under control before aiming and firing his pistol.

The shot zinged straight toward Mr. Cantrell's clenched hand and sent his pistol flying into the underbrush. He cried out in pain.

Mr. Sinclair dismounted in a flurry, wrestling a small sword from his saddle. Advancing on Mr. Cantrell, he pointed the tip at Mr. Cantrell's chest then ripped the rag from his own face. "Where is she?"

Mr. Cantrell shrugged and cradled his injured hand. "She? What on earth do you mean, Sin? I was just about to conclude my business with these gentleman and head back to the Towers."

Like a predator, Mr. Sinclair circled Mr. Cantrell, his gaze fixed on his prey. "Don't trifle with me. I saw Sybil ride out in your carriage from the Towers. Have you lost her somewhere on the road?"

"Interesting choice of words." Mr. Cantrell inspected his fingers, then looked up. "You must offer us your felicitations. Only moments ago she agreed to be my wife."

"I find that hard to believe."

"Hard to believe? Doing it a bit too brown now, aren't you, Sin? Think back, my dear friend. Even you cannot deny that I've fascinated Sybil since the day she arrived. She could hardly take her eyes off me, and now —"

"You're a liar and a cad. I no more believe that than I believe this little business of yours is mere smuggling."

Mr. Cantrell moved to rise, but Mr. Sinclair's sword didn't waver.

Mr. Cantrell smiled. "What exactly do you plan to do with that thing?"

"Whatever is necessary."

"That's not like you, Sin." Mr. Cantrell shook his head. "I thought you were a gentleman who honored a fair fight."

The other highwayman, whom I recognized as Mr. Browning, stepped forward. " 'Spect we better check the crates."

Mr. Sinclair nodded. "Quickly."

Mr. Cantrell seemed to acquiesce for a moment before he motioned to one of his men with his chin. Silence reigned while Mr. Browning approached the cart. Then one of the men leaped forward and took a swing at the back of Mr. Sinclair's head just as Mr. Cantrell shoved to his feet. The sudden punch was a glancing blow that thankfully missed its mark. The scuffle drew Mr. Browning from the crates and he heaved to engage Mr. Cantrell's other man with his own fists.

Mr. Sinclair, though, was momentarily thrown off balance. Mr. Cantrell utilized the reprieve to spring to the side of the cart and pull out his own sword, passing it into his uninjured hand. "I'm afraid I cannot allow a search. We haven't the time."

"No?" Mr. Sinclair pressed his palm to the back of his head, then redirected his blade to meet Mr. Cantrell's. "Something tells me you're the filthy traitor we've been looking for."

Mr. Cantrell spit on the ground, enjoying a bit of a laugh. "Oh-ho. How you've got it wrong, Sin. Pity I won't be around to see you embarrassed." He attempted a step forward, but Mr. Sinclair held fast.

I looked around where I hid and noticed a large tree branch, ragged and broken at my feet. I curled my fingers around one end and stood. It was three against two out there and I had every intention of evening the odds at the right moment.

Mr. Cantrell bounded forward, his blade nothing but a blur as he thrashed into the void between the two highwaymen. Lightning quick, Mr. Sinclair leaped out of the way, deflecting the attack with a downward swing. The blades caught the moonlight in flaring streaks, illuminating the woods for seconds at a time.

It was clear everyone on the field knew what they were about — the flurry of swords, thrusting and parrying, the swinging of fists. One of Mr. Cantrell's men shouted in rage as he attempted first one blow then another. Mr. Browning was everywhere, taking on both assailants at once, leaving Mr. Sinclair free to focus on Mr. Cantrell, who thrust time and again, but Mr. Sinclair shuffled around the far side of the cart to maintain his edge. For a moment I thought him trapped, yet he broke free at the last second as Mr. Cantrell lowered his point.

Mr. Sinclair pinked his shoulder, and Mr. Cantrell fought back in anger, almost arrogant with his blade, slashing forward with a riposte, but Mr. Sinclair was quick and knocked it away. Their thrusts came away cleaner and quicker, like moves in a well-rehearsed play.

I held back a scream as Mr. Cantrell

lunged forward and missed Mr. Sinclair by mere inches. This was no Covent Garden.

Mr. Browning looked to be tiring between the two thugs' swinging fists, barely missing what could have been a fatal blow, but he threw himself to the ground and rolled out of the way. Crimson spread down his chin in a line, but there was no time to wipe it away as he hopped back to his feet. The other attacker pushed in from the side, edging the fight closer and closer to Mr. Sinclair.

I gripped the piece of wood as hard as I could and took one wild step forward, but my hair was yanked back.

"Where are you going, my pretty?"

Pain circled my scalp as I fell onto my back. Mr. Barineau's sweaty face came into view, and he smiled. "I figure we stay right here till they fight it out."

Tears welled. My gallant heroes would tire, and what then? Death? France? The branch. My fingers tightened. Mr. Barineau would never see it coming. I closed my eyes and swung up with a force I'd not known I possessed, crashing the branch into the side of his head. The man dropped like a sack of flour, motionless at my side.

I sprang to my feet and ran straight into the midst of the battle, swinging my club with all the passion and intensity I could manage. One of the two younger men fell first, reeling back against a nearby tree. It gave Mr. Browning the time he needed to strike the other attacker in one fell swoop.

Spinning around, I realized my surprise arrival had prompted a split-second halt to Mr. Sinclair's battle as well, but Mr. Cantrell was quickly recovering. He raised his sword, intent on death, and I screamed. With a streak of silver, Mr. Sinclair beat the blade aside, sending Mr. Cantrell's sword flying across the ground. Mr. Cantrell dropped to his knees.

Mr. Sinclair redirected his sword tip inches from Mr. Cantrell's neck. "Now." Mr. Sinclair wiped the sweat from his forehead. "I'd like to have a look in those crates."

Mr. Cantrell's hands were bound before Mr. Sinclair rounded the cart, using his sword to pop open the nearest crate. His friend and I ran up behind him, glancing around his broad shoulders, as he peered inside.

Cloth. Reams of thick furnishing covers and other textiles.

Mr. Sinclair fell back a pace before busting through another wooden lid, only to find more of the same. "What the devil?"

Mr. Browning helped him dismantle the rest of the crates before holding up his hands. "They're nothing but blasted smugglers."

I touched Mr. Sinclair's arm. "What is it?"

A pensive look settled across his features. "I was certain I'd found the traitors we've been searching for, but there is nothing here but goods for the continent." He shoved the lid back, sending it crashing to the ground. "No newspaper clippings, dispatches, or even gold coins."

The muscles in my body grew taut.

He ran his hand down his face. "I suppose the authorities will sort out the rest in the morning." He took a deep breath, his voice weary. "Right now, I need to get you home."

Mr. Barineau was collected from the forest and the four men tied and deposited in the cart like a pile of old clothes. Mr. Browning said he would drop them all off with the nearest dragoon, and he prompted the horse to a walk.

Mr. Cantrell glared at me as he rolled past, his eyes doing all the talking needed between us. Strangely, I found myself fighting a twinge of pity for him. People are curious creatures indeed, a unique mixture of good intentions, scarred nature, and bad decisions. I do believe at one time Mr. Cantrell had cared a little for me, before he learned my true identity, before his debts overcame him and greed entered his soul. Yet all along he'd been blackmailing his own aunt. And tonight he had intended something barbarous, but as Miss Cantrell had said, he was desperate.

Mr. Sinclair must have sensed my mixed feelings for he folded me into his arms. "Lucius fooled us all."

A waft of cold air christened the cart's exit, and we watched the carriage vanish from sight until the quiet hush of the forest leaked back into our consciousness. Mr. Sinclair held tight for a moment before gently turning me to face him. "Sybil," he said, his voice marred with strain. "What the deuce were you thinking, coming out here alone . . . with Lucius?"

My shoulders sagged. "He told me he meant to meet Mr. Barineau. I thought I could deliver the package. I had no idea . . ."

Mr. Sinclair pressed his lips together, his eyes closing. "If I hadn't looked out that window when I did . . ."

"I know." I took a long breath. "I know."

Gradually, a smile crept across his face. "You were fantastic, by the way, routing them all in one fell swoop."

"Was I?"

He cocked an eyebrow. "I couldn't believe my eyes. There I was in the heart of battle when you appeared, wielding that club like a dragon. I'll never see the like again. At least, I intend not to see such a thing again." He lowered his chin. "We've something to settle between us, you and I."

The serious tone of his voice made me look up, where I expected to see tiredness etched across his face. I was startled, however, not only by the soft intensity of his gaze, but by the irrepressible pull between us. Heavens, how I longed to fall into his arms.

His fingers feathered their way down my arms until they covered my hands. "You've a free spirit not daunted by this world, a beautiful soul, and a heart I love." His blue eyes seemed to glisten in the moonlight. "I dare not wait a moment longer to speak my mind, for you're likely to fall into some sort of trouble the minute I turn my back." He placed a kiss on my forehead. "Although, considering you're a veritable lioness, I'm not sure you need my humble associations."

I laughed. "I'm not sure I do."

"Little wretch. I should walk away with words such as those, but I find my heart would not allow it."

"Nor mine."

He tucked a stray hair behind my ear. "Our road will not be an easy one. I have nothing to my name at present to pay my sisters' board, but I'm determined to find a way. So, what do you say, partner? Shall we make this thing between us legal? Will you become my wife?"

Warmth filled my chest and I wanted to scream it to the hills. Curtis Sinclair loved me, no matter who I was or what I would become. A tear slipped down my cheek, and for the first time, dreams took shape in my mind, not only of the wonderful days I'd have as Mrs. Sinclair but also how I stood in the unique position to make a difference in the world. So many orphans, so many people like me who needed hope. Somehow I would find a way to help them.

Mr. Sinclair cleared his throat. "Am I to wait for your answer forever?"

"Oh, my darling Curtis. How can you doubt what I will say?"

His finger found a curl at my neck. "I'd still like to hear it."

I reached around his shoulders. "Very well, partner. I happily accept such a fine proposal."

My lips tingled with frost but warmed against his as I reveled in the promise we'd made. The first ray of sunlight broke the horizon and the earth bathed itself in an orange glow.

Curtis kissed my cheek. "Morning is upon us. I'm afraid there'll be no hope of a quiet return now."

I smiled. "Does it matter?"

"I suppose not, Miss Delafield."

I popped his arm. "That is Lady Sybil to you, at least until you may call me Mrs. Sinclair. Goodness, I'll lose the title just weeks after I knew it was mine."

Curtis drew back. "What do you mean — title?"

"Apparently you've captured an heiress after all. Of course half of the money will likely go to my brother, but I can't imagine my grandmother leaving me nothing."

"What do you mean?"

"Only that I'm half of a set of twins, born two and twenty years ago to Mrs. Chalcroft's daughter, Anne."

"You cannot be serious."

I nodded like a little bird eager for the first time to take flight. "Perfectly serious. However, I'd like to speak with my grandmother as soon as she's awake to be sure."

Curtis grasped the horses' reins. "As would I."

■ ■ ■ ■

Mrs. Chalcroft sat waiting for us in the drawing room with dark half circles under her eyes and her hair a mess of tangles. I wondered just how long she'd been there.

A shield separated her from a snapping fire, and the scent of smoke and roses circled the room. My steps were tentative until I met her troubled gaze. How we must have worried her. Like a child, I flew into her arms, careful not to crush her in my embrace. Her bony fingers clung to my back as they never had before.

When at last she spoke, her voice sounded weak. "I feared you'd never come back, and then . . ." She took my face into her hands. "Then I'd never forgive myself."

"I'm here. A bit cold, but nothing too dreadful."

She waved for Curtis to join us. "Bring chairs to sit by the fire. I won't keep you long."

I bit my lip. "I'm sorry I had to involve your godson."

"Never mind about all that. I'm well aware of your adventure to Reedwick even though Curtis dashed off before he could tell me the whole."

I gladly took the chair Curtis brought, leaning as close to the fire as possible. "Then you know we were unable to deliver your package."

"Yes." She took a long pause, heavy with emotion. "My greatest fear has finally happened, and the cursed letter had specifics this time. The payment the man demanded was exorbitant. Whoever he is, he knows it all, and I fear he means to do real harm." She turned to the fire. "I will have to send someone to Cambridge at once. I only pray we may still get out of this somehow."

"Cambridge?" I shook my head. "Why there?"

"Harland, your brother, must be told the truth at last. He is no longer safe in his ignorance. It is imperative we get to him before Lord Stanton does. The boy must not trust that devil. Oh, how Stanton hated Anne, and revenge can be far too enticing for a man like him. Harland is in great danger."

Curtis, who'd been standing beside my chair, touched my shoulder. "I'll change at once."

"Wait." I cleared my throat. "First of all, you've been up all night. I don't think it advisable to be dashing off once again without any sleep."

"Goodness knows I've done it before."

"Let me finish. Second, if it is because of the blackmailer, you mustn't bother."

Mrs. Chalcroft's hand crept to her mouth. "What do you mean, child? Speak at once."

The smuggling was enough to tarnish Mr. Cantrell's name, but the information I was about to disclose would end his relationship with my grandmother forever. I glanced first to Curtis then back, delaying the difficult revelation as long as possible. "It was Mr. Cantrell. He's the one who's been pocketing your money."

She gasped. "But the Barineaus."

I finished her thought. "Were merely working for him."

She went stone cold as Curtis paced the room behind me. A heavy curtain had fallen and I wished there was some way to smooth it away. But there wasn't. Nephew, friend, brother — soon enough, they would all know of Mr. Cantrell's duplicity.

Curtis grasped the poker and stoked the fire, hot embers bursting from the grate. "And Miss Cantrell?"

I touched his elbow. "As far as I know, she is innocent in all this."

My grandmother lifted her hand. "Secrets have surrounded these Towers for far too long, trapping me in a bed of loneliness and bitter despair." Her fingers curled into a ball. "And it's my fault. All of it."

"No."

She grasped my hand, but her voice faltered. "Allow me this moment to tell you the whole, and then we shall not speak of it again. Please, don't interrupt." She took a deep breath, her eyes glazing over. "You see, Anne and I had an argument that terrible night, the worst we'd ever had. She stormed into the drawing room, telling me wild stories of her husband, Lord Stanton — accusations I couldn't believe. She claimed she had discovered he was a French spy, that she had proof she meant to take to a man who worked for the Secretary of State in a secret position in the post office. The two of them planned to expose Stanton for what he was — a vicious spy.

"I didn't believe a moment what she was saying. How could I? I knew him to be a cold, callous sort of man who had likely lost her interest, but a French spy? Unbelievable. Then the far more daring accusations started, how he'd abused her, neglected her, used her for his own pleasure. She described a terror-filled life sheltered away with a master manipulator. In my shock and disbelief, I couldn't believe what she said. I threatened to lock her in her room. Surely it was madness, something brought on by the late state of her pregnancy. I knew their marriage had turned icy, but she'd never made such wild accusations before, not like that."

Mrs. Chalcroft took a sip of tea to steady her voice. "I thought at the time I was doing the right thing, saving her from herself, but at the first opportunity she tore free from the house on horseback like a prisoner escaping her chains. She chose to risk death or estrangement from her family than stay at the Towers, have her baby, and the two of them be sent home to *him.* She wanted a life for them both — one without fear. I remember desperately climbing the Tower, calling for her to return, but the rain and wind would have none of that. She galloped away and didn't even look back at me — her own mother.

"Hodge found her by the creek hours later, deep in labor, and brought her home to deliver the child. It was then we found the proof of Lord Stanton's treachery tucked away in her pocket. All the things Anne had said in anger about the spying were true. I can only assume the other accusations were as well. The man was a monster, and I hadn't believed her. There was no time for a doctor. Dawkins and I brought you and your brother into this world with tears on our cheeks. Anne never regained consciousness. She died but a week later from complications and an inflammation of the lungs."

She squeezed my hand. "You don't seem surprised by my story. Lucius must have told you the whole."

I nodded. "I knew much of it."

"If my nephew was the blackmailer, then you know all."

A chill wound its way across my shoulders. "Not all. May I ask why I was sent away?"

"Ah. A valid question, though it pains me to speak the truth. It was a decision I've wished a thousand times I could make again. Almost immediately after the birth, we knew something had to be done and much concealed. We had no wet nurse in the house, so you were both taken to the village to a girl who could care for you there, Mr. Aberdeen's niece."

Mr. Sinclair sat up. "Ah . . . I've been wondering for months how Aberdeen fit into all this. I knew the two of you kept regular correspondence, but at the dance I decided he was not the spy I was looking for — that is, until Sybil asked to see him." He narrowed his eyes. "She gave him something that night, didn't she?"

"Yes, I have sent regular payments to the Aberdeens for Harland's board and upkeep over the years. Mr. and Mrs. Aberdeen were not able to have children, so they stood in for Harland's family and raised him as one of their own. I am greatly indebted to Mr. Aberdeen."

I touched her hand. "But if we were brought to the Aberdeens that night, how did I end up in London?"

She licked her lips. "You see, when Dawkins and I returned to the Towers, Lord Stanton had arrived in our absence. He'd learned from the staff that his child had been born and demanded to see him. I was frightened and grieving, and most of all I was concerned what Stanton would do with the boy — his heir. A misogynist at heart, I knew he'd care nothing for a girl.

"I told him the only thing that came to mind, that he'd had a girl and she was being cared for in the village. At first he instructed me to leave you there, but then he seemed to change his mind. I'd gambled wrong. Fear racked my body for your safety, though an idea came to me through my haze of grief. Lord Stanton was a French spy and I could prove it. I wouldn't allow a family scandal, but I knew I could blackmail him.

"A lengthy discussion ensued, I intending

to fulfill Anne's wishes and keep the two of you apart, and he unable to bear the thought of me winning. In the end we agreed to a school in London at his expense, and I would never reveal the proof I had of his infamy. Your identity would remain anonymous and neither of us would contact you in the future.

"Over the years, I kept correspondence with Mrs. Smith and heard of all your accomplishments. Anne would have been so proud. I told myself it was best that you were away, that I couldn't care for you with my mind the way it was. Only, when I learned I was dying, I had to send for you, even if I had to conceal your true identity for a few months. I needed to see you, to know you. I've been able to watch your brother from afar as he was in Plattsdale, but not you. My daughter's daughter.

"Harland has much to learn of his true identity, only I dare not reveal anything until Lord Stanton can be located in the West Indies."

"Grandmama."

She smiled. "Yes, child?"

"Mr. Cantrell revealed to me tonight that my father is dead, and that he has been for a month or more."

Mr. Sinclair met my eyes. "Are you sure?"

"He had no reason to lie."

Mrs. Chalcroft's shoulders relaxed. "Then we are free at last, and your brother is the new Earl of Stanton."

Mr. Sinclair laughed. "Thank goodness."

"That would also explain why Mr. Sinclair has received no letters from him."

"Yes." Mr. Sinclair grasped my hand and the movement tumbled my bracelet down around my wrist, the cool metal stinging my skin. I stared at it a moment, mesmerized by the firelight's dancing reflection and the hundreds of little metallic lights pulsing in and out of the garnets, before averting my gaze to my grandmother.

She was looking at the bracelet too. "I see you haven't taken it off."

"It was my mother's, wasn't it?"

"A favorite of hers and mine." She took my hand, running her fingers along the circular pattern. "My husband, your grandfather, the captain, gave it to me soon after we wed so long ago. He'd bought it with his first round of prize money in the navy." She paused, slipping into her thoughts once again.

"When Anne was a baby she couldn't keep her hands off it, and then when she was a child I allowed her to wear it for short periods of time. I decided to give it to her as a gift on the eve of her marriage. She wore it every day from then on. Stanton teased her about it in the first year of their marriage, tempting her with far more spectacular jewels, but she would have none of that. I believe it reminded her of her father and the simple joy of childhood." Her smile faded. "She wasn't wearing it when she arrived at Croft Towers that awful day. I always wondered what became of it."

Mr. Sinclair leaned forward. "So Stanton had it all this time. Why did he keep it? And what caused him to send it to Sybil now?"

She raised her chin. "I imagine he wanted to make mischief, to send Sybil here to cut up my peace, to force me to confront my past." She turned to me, a brightness filling her eyes. "Only, he had no idea I wanted you here desperately."

"I suppose we shall never know his motives." I glanced once more at the delicate band. "I do wonder though. I suppose it is equally possible that he wished to do right in the end. That he sent it to me because he truly thought I should have it."

My grandmother grunted. "I doubt it, but you can think so if it gives you comfort."

"He did keep it all those years."

Mrs. Chalcroft tugged the embroidered bell rope, her tired eyes meeting mine. "I daresay what you say is possible, but you shall find me hard-pressed to believe it. At this moment, however, I'm afraid I am unable to stay awake any longer now that I know the two of you are safe. We can talk of everything else in the afternoon, my dear, sweet granddaughter." She touched my hair. "You don't look like Anne, you know, but you have her courage and her spirit."

I wondered if Mr. Cantrell's betrayal hung heavy on her heart as she stood, but she said nothing more. Hodge answered the call and escorted her from the room, leaving Curtis and me alone.

He knelt at my side. "No doubt the authorities will question Lucius, and I'm sure everything will come out eventually."

I knew he meant the murders and my shoulders relaxed. "Yes, Mrs. Plume was the person who told Mr. Cantrell about Stanton's child. I suppose he found the need to silence her at last as well as her maid."

"Let us think no more on it tonight." He kissed my hand. "Get some sleep, my love. The worst is behind us."

28

I reached the hallway to my room in an almost trancelike state. So much of my life had been altered by the choices of others, but for the first time I knew who I was. I had plans for the future and much to look forward to.

My hand rested on the latch to my bed-chamber, but I paused at what sounded like a flurry of movement behind me. Miss Ellis's door stood wide open. It was strange that I'd not seen her downstairs. My shoulders relaxed. We must have woken her.

All at once, I wanted to share my news about Curtis and me. There was no denying Miss Ellis's feelings were complicated regarding him, but I hoped in the end she would be pleased. "Miss Ellis," I called out quietly, making my way to her room and pushing the door inward. "I'm so sorry if we woke you. I —"

Her pink room lay empty in the early-morning light. Her bed was made and the long curtains were pulled back to reveal a balcony beyond a pair of closed French doors. I cast a quick glance behind me down the hall. Miss Ellis had said nothing about any plans for the night, let alone the early hours of the morning. I thrust a candle inside to be sure and followed its glow to the center of the rug. The room felt warm but ruffled with papers on the floor and a few books tossed about.

Goodness, what a messy girl she was. Curious by the state of the room, I entered and gathered the loose papers into a small pile, kneeling to retrieve the whole. However, at the edge of the great poster bed, I noticed a box tipped on its side, jewelry scattered across the floor. I shook my head. Poor, neglected Miss Ellis. She'd been sifting through her necklaces again, probably selecting one for the next dance. She didn't have many friends and no romance sequestered here all alone at the Towers, and more than anyone, she reveled in such games.

I stopped to right the box, placing the spilled pieces back inside one by one. A pearl necklace — quite right for a girl of seventeen. It would look lovely with her white gown. A diamond brooch — it must have been her mother's. An emerald ring.

My hand froze, seized by a memory. An emerald ring? Could it be? *The* emerald ring — the one Thompkins had hidden for Mrs. Plume the day of the robbery. I hadn't thought of it since that infamous day, but I remembered it well. I held the band into the light, my hand shaking.

The gold filigree, the large center stone. There was no mistaking such an intricate piece. But how on earth did Miss Ellis come to have it in her possession?

Moments with Miss Ellis flashed through my mind, but nothing made sense, not about France, not about the murders. And the ring . . . Here it was in Miss Ellis's room. Had I missed something? Something vitally important?

I rolled the ring over and over again in my fingers, the cold metal weighing down my hand, the emerald winking at me in turn. The dragoons had been looking for a girl the day I traveled alone to Reedwick, not a man, and I hadn't even bothered to take their comments into consideration. And the day of the murder, when I saw Thompkins in the garden — Mr. Cantrell hadn't even been home. If he could be believed, he had been miles away.

I stared off into the dim corners of the room, at nothing and everything. My fingers curled around the ring. Mr. Cantrell couldn't have killed Thompkins or Mrs. Plume . . . but Miss Ellis?

I shook my head, the image of her sweet face coming to mind. There was no way she would do such a thing. She had no reason. I stared at the loose papers in my hands for a moment in disbelief, hiding my pounding thoughts as best I could. And for a few seconds I was able to do so, resting back against the wall.

But then I saw something, and everything shifted.

My darling,

Two simple words scrolled across the top of one of the papers in Miss Ellis's handwriting, nothing more.

A heaviness rolled into my stomach, and I laid the candle on the floor. Then the questions came. The memories. Miss Ellis's trill laugh from the drawing room. She'd been the only one interested in news of the murder investigations, asking daily if we'd learned anything new. I remembered the look of longing on her face when she looked at Lord Stanton's painting in the tower. Did she know him? Did she know he was a spy so many years ago?

If she did, she would have been an easy target for a man like my father and, worse, would have been heading to the perfect location to do real damage to England, situated for the time being at Croft Towers, so close to the coast. My tangled thoughts took further root as more memories emerged. She was the only one who waited for the mail every day, was always the first to handle it, and was desperate to find one addressed to her. I flicked through the pile of papers before me with unsteady fingers, holding one in her handwriting into the wavering light.

My dearest love,

I'll go mad if you do not write to me. I cannot think but of you and our love. It's like a fire meant to consume me. I'm frightened without you, of what I have done. For what I might have to do so that we can be together. But do not worry, my darling. I remain as steadfast as I was in London. My heart aches. I will do anything to see you safely return to England. All is well at present. But oh, my dear, come back to me as soon as you can or I may die for waiting.

I turned the note over. There was nothing more.

I looked at another letter folded beneath the stack and shook my head as I picked it up. It was worn at the corners and heavily creased. Clearly it had been handled a great many times. Carefully, I opened it, my nerves clamped tight as I awaited what I might find inside.

My love,

I write this note in haste, and it shall be the last for a great many months. I'm to set sail at once for my plantation in the Caribbean under the guise of business to avoid something far worse at home. Guard my troubles with your life. You have my heart, and I can trust no one but you. I do not deserve your loyalty, yet I must ask once more of your service. Will you stand my friend and lover? I know your answer as I know every piece of you. Deliver these missives from my operatives as planned and when I return, I shall carry you off. Then we will be together as I dreamed and promised. I am a lucky man indeed and more so if you present me with the heir I've always wanted and needed. We shall not be so long away. Napoleon shall be triumphant soon and the world our plaything.

I fear I will not be able to write from the West Indies as I have come to learn our postal service is not safe and Whitehall is closing in on my connection with France, but my heart will remain constant until I hold you in my arms once more. Be extremely careful, for if anything should happen and my identity as a spy exposed, I fear I won't be able to return to England. I am counting on you to fulfill my work. There will be more important missives you will need to pass on if I am unable to return for some time. That military information both now and in the future could turn the tide of this war.

I was forced to make a hasty decision and send this letter and the missives by the hands of your old maid, Thompkins, hopeful she will incite the least attention as she attempts to visit you, but I trust no one and neither should you. If I was wrong to allow her into my confidence, please take whatever steps you feel are right. I trust you with my very life.

Your devoted servant,
Stanton

The letter slipped from my fingers and fell to the floor. Miss Ellis. Naïve, young, heedless girl. What had she done?

The bedchamber door slammed shut and I shot to my feet, my pulse snapping to life.

Miss Ellis tilted her chin, her voice a dull monotone. "Why, Miss Delafield. Whatever are you doing in my room?"

My mouth went dry. The expression on her face was so completely unlike her. I answered as quickly as I could, as convincingly as possible. "I was looking for you, of course. I have news."

Her gaze drifted from the letters on the floor to my face, but her mind seemed elsewhere. "News?"

"Yes . . . about . . . several things." What was it I had come to tell her?

"Hmm . . . You've been a bit busy tonight." She ran her finger along the mantel as if checking for dust.

I took a few steps back. "What do you mean?"

"I know you were supposed to leave for France with Lucius. Yet here you stand, rifling through my private things. What were you looking for exactly?" Her eyes were wide now, assessing my every move.

"Looking for?" My voice sounded far away. "Don't be ridiculous. I merely cleaned up the jewelry you spilled. Now, if you'll excuse me, I'm exhausted. We can talk more about Mr. Cantrell later today. We decided we wouldn't suit."

"Wouldn't suit?" She smiled. "He offered you an escape, but I suppose you were too stupid to see it." She reached up slowly, pushing the corner vase forward, and drew an object into the light. Her fingers curled around a silver pistol, and she leveled it at me. "You've done nothing but sneak around the Towers since you arrived. You and Curtis. Lud, you even intercepted the man I was to meet in Reedwick. Do you have any idea what a great deal of effort it took to reorganize all our plans?"

So that was the man who attacked me that day in town. He had seemed quite surprised by my appearance, ogling my face and dress. He had probably been waiting for Miss Ellis all along and was thrown off balance by the appearance of another unescorted young lady after dark.

Sweat gathered on Miss Ellis's forehead. "I didn't want it to come to this. I had planned to be your friend, but I cannot risk anything. Not now."

The dark corners of the room grew thick around me, the seconds stretching out like a black dream. After all I'd been through

465

tonight, everything had come down to this awful moment. "Wait." I held up my hands. "There is something you should know."

She shrugged. "If you mean Mr. Sinclair, he has his own troubles. If the dragoons weren't so inept, the information I keep giving them would have finished him by now, but it won't be long."

So it had been Miss Ellis who tipped off the soldiers, Miss Ellis who'd been the spy, Miss Ellis who'd killed her old maid. My head ached. "No. Not Mr. Sinclair." I met her shifting gaze. "It's about Lord Stanton."

Her face went ghostly still. I'd got her attention. Then she narrowed her eyes. "Stanton? What about him?"

I swallowed hard. "He's dead, Miss Ellis. I don't know the particulars, but he died in the West Indies."

A slight quiver shook her hand, but she forced it under control. "I don't believe you. You're a liar. You'd say anything to save your own life." Like claws, her fingers wound around a clump of her hair, her gaze flicking to the letters once again. "He's coming for me, you know. He loves me, more than anyone ever has."

"He can't come for you, Miss Ellis. He's dead." I lowered my chin. "Think about it. Why has Mr. Sinclair received no word for weeks, no money?" The more I spoke, the greater was my sense of Miss Ellis's emotional desperation — how alone she'd been at the Towers, how unhinged. I shook my head. "Please, don't say anything more. Just put the pistol down. Let us talk and find a way out of this mess."

She glared up at me with red-rimmed eyes, examining what I'd said with piercing concentration. Then a change took over her face, altering the darkness to a gray haze. It seemed the truth about Stanton's death was sinking in.

A breathy laugh slipped from her mouth. "A way out? There's no way out. Not without him." Her chest heaved. "Not for me."

I took a step forward. "Lord Stanton was a traitor to England, to Anne, and to many others —"

"Shut your mouth. I don't care about Anne."

I was muddling this. *Keep your wits about you, Sybil.* My thoughts tangled into a ball in my mind. I had no experience with a person so unstable as to pull a trigger.

A tear slipped down her cheek. "He never cared for Anne. Never! Not like me. We were beautiful together. He's not . . . gone. I can't believe it. I won't believe it." Her voice cracked.

"You're right. I don't think he ever did care for Anne." Recklessly, I thought of disclosing everything, who these people were to me, but I had no way of knowing her reaction. I remained silent, allowing the truth of Stanton's death to sink in on its own. Surely in the depths of Miss Ellis's soul, she had to have already thought as much.

Silence crept between us until she redirected the barrel of the pistol. "I was far more to Stanton than that insipid Anne. He loves me . . . my spirit, my courage. He trusts me with the very future of France. We're two of the same."

So she hadn't lost complete control.

For a split second, I considered lunging for her arm, but her nerves might prove flighty, and she had killed twice before. I held my breath. If I could get closer to the door, perhaps I could open it and signal for help. I had to try something.

With hesitation, I edged my way around her, all the time keeping the pistol in my sight, talking rapidly as I went. "No one knows who killed Thompkins or Mrs. Plume. You've been terribly clever and gotten away with so much. Perhaps Mrs. Chalcroft could help arrange something to avoid a scandal. You do have options. Would you like to go to America?" I released the door latch.

She mirrored my movements, the puff of cold air whipping against her auburn hair. I shrank into the corner, grasping the edge of the door frame. It was no use. The lawn stretched empty before me, dissolving into painful obscurity.

"I wish you were right, but Elizabeth knows that Thompkins was my maid. She knows I turned her off without reason or reference. She quibbled with me about it at the time, but I wouldn't be swayed because Thompkins was far too nosy about my relationship with Stanton."

Her free hand made its way to her hip. "And she told Mrs. Plume at some point. Can you believe it? How dare she! And that woman, shocked to find me in town after what Thompkins had told the old gossip, she confronted me, telling me the whole. She seemed to think she should report my connection with Thompkins and Stanton to the dragoons.

"I daresay she hadn't made the connection that he and I were the spies they were looking for, but I couldn't wait for them to come around and question me, could I?" Miss Ellis's gaze rose to the colorless tower looming to our right. "I did it all so he could return to me. So we could be together." Her voice grew breathless; her eyes clouded over. "You know, I always thought I'd watch him from up there, riding his horse down the main road, coming for me."

My voice came out unsteady. "I'm sorry."

Her eyes shot to mine. "Don't you dare say that. You don't care a fig for me."

"You're wrong, Miss Ellis. I know what it feels like to love and to long for it."

She leveled the pistol once again at my chest. "No, you don't." She fired.

I screamed as a puff of black erupted into the room and the pistol fell to the floor. My hands hysterically swam across my chest, hunting for the bullet wound. The floor tilted and I propped my arm against the wall, gasping for air.

Miss Ellis shook her hands, crying out as if in pain.

A misfire. I'd been spared.

A loud knock resounded at Miss Ellis's door. She shot a terrified glance into the room before stumbling backward onto the open balcony. "No. I won't be taken in." Her voice held a deathly chill, her eyes like those of a lost child. "It was for him. All of it. He loved me. But now —" A terrible wail spewed from her lips like that of an injured animal.

"Oh, Miss Ellis." Desolation swarmed my already trembling frame. There would be no hope for her now.

She shook her head, tears wetting her cheeks. "It was the only way to secure his freedom. Surely you see that."

I reached out for her, but she pushed my hand away. "Tell Aunt Chalcroft that I'm sorry. I'm so sorry." Fear choked her voice. "But I won't be tried as a traitor." She scrambled up and backed onto the stone ledge, crouching at the top like a vulture. She paused there for a breathless moment to glance one last time at the looming tower above her before tipping backward and plunging silently to her death.

I screamed at the same moment the door crashed open behind me. I rushed to the balcony's edge. Curtis appeared at my side, urging me back into the room.

I realized I was shivering as he wrapped his jacket around my shoulders.

My voice came out in a whisper. "It was her . . . all along. The spy, the murders. Stanton, my father, was her lover. She did it all for him. So he could return to England and marry her."

Mr. Sinclair said nothing, only drew me against his chest, resting his chin on my head. My hands crept around his warm

471

back, pulling him closer — so much closer. Cradled there on the floor below the eastern tower, I let the tears fall — for my mother, for my father, for Miss Ellis. It was finally over. My questions answered. My fear gone.

Epilogue

My grandmother lived for a full six months following the morning of Miss Ellis's death. She attended my wedding and witnessed my brother take his place as the Earl of Stanton. Though we grieved all that happened at the Towers to so many of our loved ones, we had many happy times before the end.

Harland has my eyebrows and my quick wit, as well as a propensity for getting himself into trouble. He plans to finish Cambridge but is uncertain what he will do next.

Grandmama left the Towers to me as well as money to fund Mr. Sinclair's pet projects. Mr. Roth has returned to London, but I asked Miss Cantrell to stay on with us here. She gave birth to a beautiful baby boy we all adore. They will both have a home with us as long as necessary. Motherhood has changed her in so many ways, and she has become my dearest friend.

Mr. Sinclair's three sisters have moved to the Towers as well, ushering in youth and vitality to the old structure. Miss Cantrell and I look forward to bringing out each locally, followed by a season in London. We have so much to look forward to.

As for my dearest husband, he is loath to leave the estate, but there is much to do these days. He pours his heart and soul into his dream, and I can't help but admire him for it. Although sometimes if he's late for the evening meal, I imagine him galloping across the countryside with a rag over his face. Such an idea exists only in my memories, but it's pleasant to think of from time to time.

In my heart I know he is happy. He's made plans to move forward with his horse breeding program, but he will never join the cavalry as he once dreamed of. He has found the one thing in the world he loves more than his duty to England — me.

ACKNOWLEDGMENTS

There have been so many who have been a part of my journey to publication. I could not have walked this road alone.

Megan Besing, my fabulous critique partner, encourager, and friend, there is not one step in the process of creating this book that you have not been a part of. Thank you for your enthusiasm, your spirit, your wisdom, your support, and your humor. I thank God every day that he brought you into my life. #iheartyou

Mom, you are not only an awesome librarian but my first and best teacher, and lifelong friend. Thank you for instilling in me the love of stories and the unending support to follow my dreams. Angi, can you believe it all started with Gonderay Ooflay and the creation of our fantasy stories as children? Thank you for always understanding me. Bess, thank you for rooting for me to succeed and supporting me along the way. Audrey and Luke, I could not have asked for two more wonderful children. You've been my biggest cheerleaders and greatest joy. Thank you for allowing me the time to write and encouraging me at every step. I love you all.

Mrs. Roberta Brooks, thank you for your excellence in teaching. Your love of British literature was contagious. I'll never forget the Scottish tea party you shared with our senior class.

And to my wonderful friends and family who have supported me over the past few years. Allison Moore, Karla McGinnis, Jerry and Wanda Lewis, and Tony and Ronda Smith, thank you for being excited for me over and over again during the long process of learning the craft of writing.

Mary Sue Seymour, thank you for taking me on and giving me my first glimmer of hope of publication. You encouraged me to write this very story. Nicole Resciniti, my agent extraordinaire, your knowledge, support, and passion inspires me every time we talk. Thank you for holding my hand and guiding me through every aspect of launching my first book.

Becky Monds, my amazing editor, words cannot express how thankful I am that I get to work with you and learn from you. Your insight was instrumental in shaping this book. And to the entire team at Thomas Nelson, thank you for your guidance and support. At every step, you all have been phenomenal.

And to my Lord and Savior, Jesus Christ, to You alone be the glory.

DISCUSSION QUESTIONS

1. There were several mysteries presented throughout the novel: the secret letters, Sybil's parentage, Mr. Sinclair's strange behavior, the murders. Did you figure out any before they were revealed? Which ones eluded you till the end?
2. Sybil finds it difficult figuring out who to trust at the house. Would you trust any of the characters at the beginning? In what ways do strangers earn your trust?
3. Sybil was forced to step out of her comfort zone at the school to investigate her connection to Chalcroft Towers. Would you make the same decision with so little to go on?
4. In what ways did Sybil change over the book?
5. Sybil ultimately decided to carry the final letter for her grandmother because she felt it was the right choice. Have you ever made a similar difficult decision? Even

against another person's advice?

6. Sybil did not open the letters throughout the book because such an act would be an invasion of privacy and a direct violation of her employer. Would you open the letters? Even after you became concerned about what might be inside?

7. Sybil and Miss Cantrell have a strained relationship throughout the book until Miss Cantrell's secret is revealed and everything changes between them. Have you ever misjudged someone who later became a friend?

8. Mrs. Chalcroft carried overwhelming guilt for her role in her daughter's death. Do you think her emotional turmoil played a part in her choosing to send both of the grandchildren away? How could she have handled the situation differently with her volatile son-in-law, Lord Stanton?

9. Curtis is "robbing" the mail coaches, Sybil using her position in the house to investigate her past. Neither of these things was wrong in and of itself, but both led to lies. When is it okay to use a white lie or hold on to a secret?

10. Did you find yourself having any sympathy for Mr. Cantrell? What about Miss Ellis?

11. Do you agree with this line: "People are

curious creatures indeed, a unique mixture of good intentions, scarred nature, and bad decisions"?

12. What do you think Sybil did with the Chalcroft fortune? Did she fulfill her desire to help other orphans?

ABOUT THE AUTHOR

Abigail Wilson combines her passion for Regency England with intrigue and adventure to pen historical mysteries with a heart. A registered nurse, chai tea addict, and mother of two crazy kids, Abigail fills her spare time hiking the national parks, attending her daughter's gymnastic meets, and curling up with a great book. In 2017, Abigail won WisRWA's Fab Five contest and ACFW's First Impressions contest as well as placing as a finalist in the Daphne du Maurier Award for Excellence in Mystery/Suspense. She is a cum laude graduate of the University of Texas at Austin and currently lives in Dripping Springs, Texas, with her husband and children.

Connect with Abigail at
www.acwilsonbooks.com
Instagram: acwilsonbooks

Facebook: ACWilsonbooks
Twitter: @acwilsonbooks